AN HONORED VOW

MELISSA BLAIR

UNION SQUARE & CO.
NEW YORK

UNION
SQUARE
& CO.
NEW YORK

UNION SQUARE & CO. and the distinctive Union Square & Co.
logo are trademarks of Hachette Book Group, Inc.

ISBN 978-1-4549-5494-1 (paperback)
ISBN 978-1-4549-5495-8 (ebook)
ISBN 978-1-4549-5845-1 (BN edition)
ISBN 978-1-4549-5846-8 (BN ebook edition)
ISBN 978-1-4549-6083-6 (signed edition)

Library of Congress Cataloging-in-Publication Data is available upon request.

Union Square & Co. books may be purchased in bulk for business, educational, or promotional use. For more information, please contact your local bookseller or the Hachette Book Group's Special Markets department at special.markets@hbgusa.com.

Printed in China

2 4 6 8 10 9 7 5 3

unionsquareandco.com

Cover design by Igor Satanovsky
Interior design by Colleen Sheehan and Jordan Wannemacher
Map art by Karin Wittig

To those who were forced to battle
but chose to learn how to lay their
weapons down when the battle was done.

There's honor in such grace.

Content Warning

This book is a fantasy romance that explores themes of alcoholism, addiction, colonialism, depression, and systemic violence. While it is not the focus of this book or depicted graphically on the page, some content may be triggering for readers who have experienced self-harm, assault, domestic violence, depression, war, or suicidal ideation. It also contains on-page sexual content.

Elverath

The Treaty of the Faeland
Aralinth
Caerth
The Dark Wood
The Burning Mountains
The Poison Fields
The Pool of Elvera
Myrelinth
Silstra
The Cliffs of Elandorr
Wolford
Belmoor
The Singing Wood
Volcar
The Barren Lands
The Frostlands

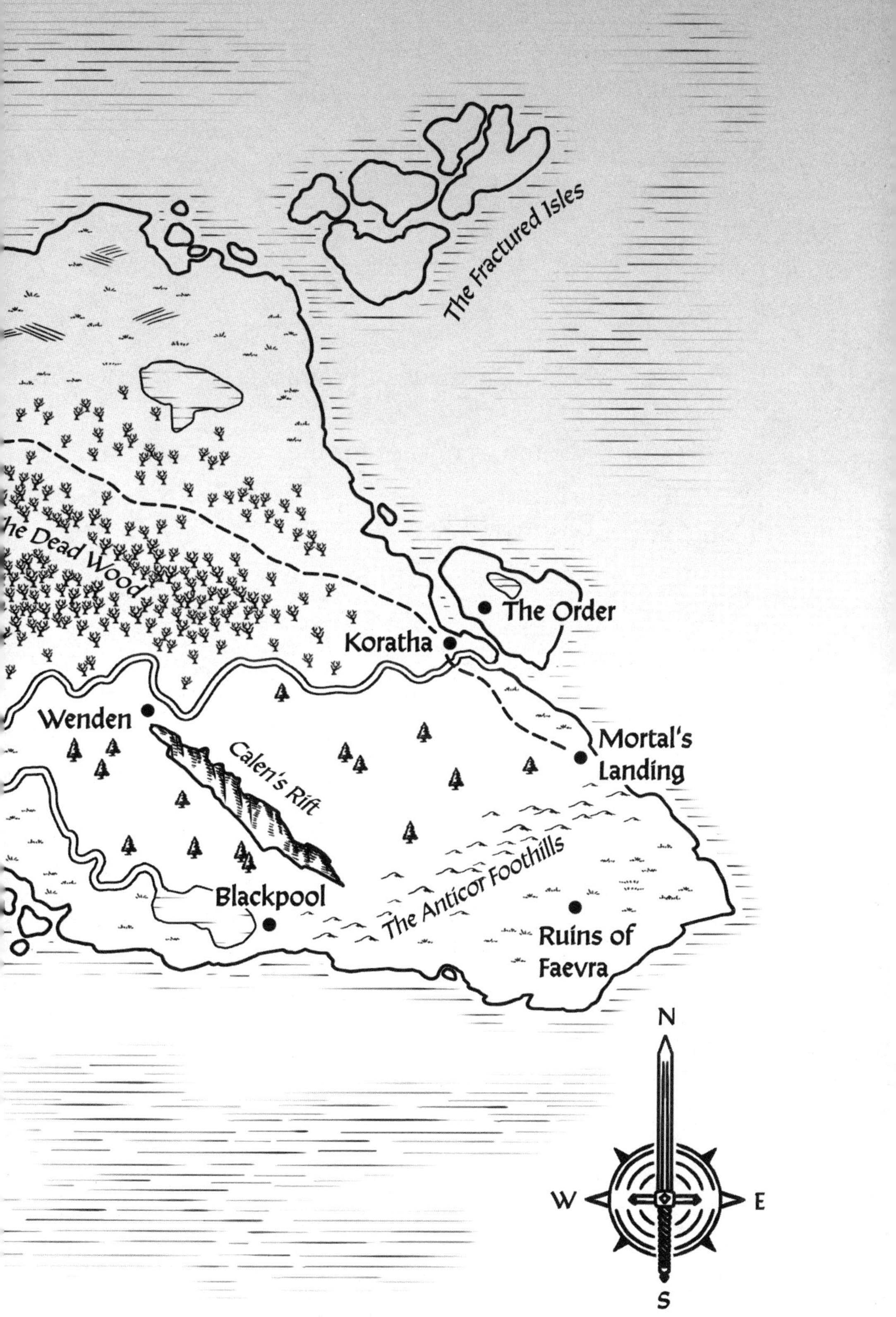

The Fractured Isles
he Dead Wood
The Order
Koratha
Wenden
Calen's Rift
Mortal's
Landing
The Anticor Foothills
Blackpool
Ruins of
Faevra
N
W
E
S

My body is made of promises,

Some were kept for me,

But most I kept for myself.

CHAPTER ONE

I PREPARED MYSELF FOR DEATH. Not mine but the soldiers' who were foolish enough to stand in our way. The heat of my magic pulsed under my skin in the same steady beat it had from the moment I'd broken the last seal. The new gifts bubbled in my veins, still untested in the three weeks since they were unleashed, but I would need to test them tonight.

I sheathed my bloodstone dagger. It felt wrong to leave it behind, even if the mission would be a short one. After all, it was the blade that had restored Elverath's magic; the blade that had turned my eyes gold. A small weapon, but hardy enough, though my dual blades were stowed between my shoulders for good measure.

The city of Myrelinth boomed with celebrations underneath my feet. I peered down at the Elverin from the treetops as they delighted in the revived magic. Children's laughter echoed off the spiraling branches of the giant Myram tree. My chest loosened. I was grateful they could indulge in celebration, even if the levity wouldn't last.

Magic had returned, but the war was not over.

I leaped from my burl. With a flash of light against the tangled vines, I took flight. It was easier to leave the city in my eagle form than walk through the crowds.

I scanned the skies as I flew, searching for signs of mercenaries or spies in the thick wood. Before the seals had broken, the wood was dark enough that any signs of fire were easy to spot. But now the Burning Mountains were aflame with their own inner light.

Leaves of every color glowed beneath my wings, swaying in the wind like luminescent algae caught along the surf. It was breathtaking. I couldn't blame the Elverin for celebrating the return of magic.

The land was completely new. Just as the rivers of snowmelt washed away the frost each spring, the sealed magic had flooded across Elverath, transforming it almost beyond the point of recognition. I had been too dazed to notice the extent of the changes when we journeyed back to Aralinth the day the last seal broke.

My mind was on everyone we had lost.

Lash.

Maerhal.

Nikolai.

I refused to believe that Damien had killed him. That would be too merciful. All I could picture were the different ways Damien had been torturing my friend. Some things were worse than death.

Dead or not, Nikolai's absence had fractured us completely. While the rest of the Elverin danced until dawn each night and spent their days rediscovering plants and life they thought had gone extinct, the heart of the rebellion no longer had a pulse.

Syrra refused to speak. She haunted the crypts as if waiting for her sister's ghost to come and find her there.

Vrail hadn't left the library. She was determined to find some kind of ancient magic to locate Nikolai, or to at least find out if he was dead or alive.

Their duties plus Nikolai's had fallen to me. And Killian's, it seemed.

I kicked the ground as I landed, shoving thoughts of Riven and his deception from my mind. My anger had had three weeks to roast, but it would do no good for me tonight. Riven had fled as he always did. And, as always, it was left to me to make the hard choices.

I took a deep breath, and the scent of honey filled my nostrils. I needed to focus on this mission. Nothing else existed. I looked down. Tiny yellow bells had sprouted from where I disturbed the soil with my boot.

Three weeks had not been enough to calm my newfound magic. My body was electrified, pulsing with life, and I could feel that same pulse everywhere I walked. Magic. That's what Feron had told me when I came to him with my concerns. I was overflowing with it.

He had told me that my powers would only grow stronger now that I was a *niinokwenar*. A Faemother. I pulled my hood over my head, covering my golden eyes. I didn't want more magic. Especially when the Elverin looked at me like a reincarnation of their sacred Faelin.

I would not bring them peace like she and her daughters had.

I had brought a war to their feet, and even with our magic stores returned, I knew that the death toll would spill over with blood soon enough.

Most of it amber.

My magic pulsed as I flattened my palm against the stony peak of the Burning Mountains. I could make out the trail through the thick foliage, but it was best to check for rogue Shades and soldiers before the others arrived. The pulse of life overwhelmed my senses. I winced as I focused my gift to just the trail below. It was clear. I took flight and dove through the glimmering leaves. A flock of faeflies scattered as my arms replaced my wings in a flash of light.

I gawked at the path. It was like walking a winding trail through the stars instead of a woodland. Every place I stepped was an eerie dream, equal parts familiar and new. I had traveled the paths along the western side of the Burning Mountains countless times; I'd patrolled it for half a year after I gained my hood. I would go to sleep with every turn drawn behind my eyelids like a map.

But even the woods in the kingdom were different now. The Elder birch had turned gold just like those in the *Faelinth*. They shimmered as the first signs of light broke along the horizon.

The others would arrive any minute.

I leaned against one of the massive trees. New plants and shrubs I had never seen sprouted between the white trunks. Tiny berries hung from purple leaves and spouted a tiny tendril of flame each time a faefly buzzed past. At night, the flames flashed so often they looked like stars had fallen from the sky and settled along the tree line.

I pulled the stalk of a thin weed the color of seafoam. The earth swelled around its roots as I lifted the hidden fruit from the dirt. The thrashing power of my magic swelled forward, and water pooled from the air to wash the dirt away. Underneath was a thick, round ball the size of my fist.

I hit the hard skin against the trunk of the birch tree. The sound echoed, and something in the darkness snarled.

I ignored it. I was still the scariest thing in this wood.

The tough, green skin of the fruit gave way to bright pink flesh. My stomach rumbled at the sweet aroma. The flight had exhausted me more than I thought, and I hadn't packed any sustenance. Nikolai was the one who always made sure to pack extra food.

I set one half of the fruit on the ground and bit into the other. It was one of the plants that had gone temporarily extinct without magic. I knew it was edible because I had watched Darythir pluck one from the ground to feast on, but I had no idea what it was called.

I groaned as I took the first bite. It was deliciously fresh. So much so that I barely looked up when the watery veil between the two Elder birches swirled with auric light.

"You make more mess than a horse." Gerarda's lip curled above her teeth in feigned disgust. She looked shorter than normal standing between two tall horses. The top of her short hair was pulled back into a small bun, not long enough for a braid. Her eyes darted in every direction as she scanned the trail.

Gerarda didn't have it in her to trust my magic to defend us.

She let go of my horse's reins as it gracefully licked at the fruit before swallowing it whole.

Gerarda might have had a point.

Fyrel and Gwyn slipped through the portal side by side, their horses trailing after them. Fyrel was mid-whisper when her gaze landed on me. "Morning, Keera." My name came slow and rough on Fyrel's tongue, like it still caused her pain to call me anything other than "Mistress."

Gwyn smiled and tossed me a small bag of cured meats.

I launched a piece into my mouth. "I knew there was a reason I let you come on this mission."

Gwyn's crimson curls fanned out as her head snapped back to me. "*Let* me?" She turned to Gerarda. "You said I earned this."

Gerarda planted herself right next to the portal. "You have."

I stuck another piece of meat in my mouth so I didn't say something foolish. Gerarda and I had been arguing about letting Gwyn accompany us for two days. She was certain that Gwyn's sword work and combat skills were well past an initiate. I couldn't deny

Gwyn's skill with a blade, but there was something familiar about her unearned confidence. She was impatient and overzealous just like I had been. Just like Brenna had been.

And that had gotten her killed.

A small smile played at Gerarda's lips as the veil of water shimmered once more. I didn't need to see Elaran step through the portal to know it was her. There was only one person on the entire continent who could make Gerarda focus on anything other than a mission.

Elaran slipped off her horse, her big curls loose but pushed back with a golden headband.

I stared at the portal. "Syrra? Vrail?"

Gerarda laced her hand through Elaran's and shook her head. "Syrra refuses to leave the crypt, and Vrail locked us out of the library before we could ask her."

"And you didn't break down the door?"

Gerarda looked at the ground with a guilty expression on her face.

"Feron fixed it," Elaran said through her laugh. She rested her arm on Gerarda's shoulder. "Though he insisted Gerrie leave Vrail to her books."

"And *you* didn't try?"

Elaran's face softened with pity. It made my back tense. "She's not coming, Keera. We'll try again next time."

Next time. What if Vrail never went on another mission? What if losing Nikolai changed her forever and she never held a sword again? I thumbed the scar along my forearm through my tunic. Losing Brenna had changed me. In so many ways—some I was only beginning to understand.

"Did you find Riven at least?" There was a desperate breathiness in my voice that only made me angrier. Riven had left Aralinth hours after we returned from breaking the last seal. All I had gotten was a notebook with a *I'm searching for Nikolai* scribbled onto the first page.

I hadn't written him back.

Elaran shook her head. "The four of us are more than capable of handling an extraction."

"There's five of us." Fyrel pointed to each of us, tallying it up on her fingers.

Elaran smirked. She looked as alluring as a fire lion, and just as dangerous. "I'm counting you and your sweetness"—she eyed Gwyn—"as only one. Untested halves, if you will."

Fyrel's cheeks flushed red and she had the sudden urge to reorganize her saddlebags. Her braid swayed behind her back as her leg bounced underneath her.

Gwyn's blue eyes narrowed. "Haven't we trained enough to be seen as individuals?"

"If that were true then you wouldn't be serving the same role on this mission." Elaran's horse bucked, his ears flicking to something in the forest. She patted its jaw, and it nipped at the grassy trail.

"Keera, what does she mean?" Gwyn crossed her arms, her red strands almost setting themselves aflame with the rage behind her eyes. "Gerarda said that I would play a crucial role."

Of course Gerarda had said that. I snapped a look at her, but Gerarda just shrugged, leaving me to answer Gwyn's questions.

"And so you shall." I lobbed another piece of meat into my mouth. "As lookouts."

Gwyn groaned. "So you don't mean for me to do anything at all."

I stood up from the base of the tree. "This is not some training drill, Gwyn." My magic flared behind me, and I could sense plant life sprouting from where I had been sitting. I didn't turn to look; I needed Gwyn to understand this. "These are real people. Real

Halflings we are going to save. I would never put their lives in the hands of someone I couldn't *completely* trust to do their job."

I stepped close enough to Gwyn that I could feel her swallow.

"Are you telling me that I shouldn't trust you with this?" I tucked my hands behind my back and stared down at her just as Hildegard had done to me countless times as an initiate. "If you are not ready for a real mission, say so now."

Gwyn straightened to her full height. "I am ready." Her nostrils flared as she spoke.

"Good."

Gwyn didn't relax her stance. "Am I meant to be a sentry forever then?"

Elaran stepped around Gwyn and placed her hands on her shoulders. "Patience is the sharpest weapon a warrior can have."

"And the largest shield one can carry," I added.

Gwyn turned to Gerarda, as if she couldn't trust what Elaran and I had said without her approval. I gritted my teeth. Gerarda was an excellent warrior, one of the greatest I had ever seen, but only one of us had been named Blade.

Gerarda nodded. "If we save Victoria and her Halflings, it will be in no small part because you and Fyrel were keeping the path clear."

"Who is Victoria anyway?" Fyrel said, still next to her horse, her cheeks less red now.

"One of the Halflings in hiding that helped others find refuge," Elaran said. "She is one of the founding members of the Rose Road."

My chest tightened with the urge to correct Elaran's mistake. Victoria was Mortal, not a Halfling. Though I could understand the assumption in a world where so few Mortals were willing to risk their lives to ferry Halflings into safety. But something in her gaze told me that correction was best left until the Halflings were safe and not under threat of siege from Damien's sellswords.

"Doesn't explain why we're rushing to Silstra the moment she sends word." Gerarda crossed her arms. "Wouldn't it be safer with more of a plan? I never sent in Shades without at least a week of surveillance."

I tugged on the new fastener at my neck. The gleaming gemstones and the white stone of the Order that we had reclaimed for ourselves. "We aren't Shades any longer."

Gerarda crossed her arms, refusing to move until she had her answer.

I sighed. I had been evading Gerarda's questions since Dynara sent word of Victoria's message two days prior. And anyone willing to put their lives on the line for one of my plans deserved an answer.

"Damien's soldiers are dealing with the chaos that the return of magic unleashed." There had been reports of new plants destroying dwellings and the waters of the Three Sisters rising up and washing livestock away. "That chaos is a distraction we can use to our advantage." I swallowed the lump building in my throat. "Giving Damien time to plot is too dangerous. It's better to move quickly before he has every village under watch."

If he didn't already.

Gerarda's lips were nothing but a thin line across her face. She held my gaze for a long moment then nodded.

Elaran tugged at her partner's bun. "Glad that's settled." She twirled a long, thin blade with two sharpened ends between her fingers. "We should be on our way if we want to make the last portal by dusk."

I shoveled the remaining contents of the meat pouch into my mouth and swallowed. I grabbed the horn of my saddle, ready to mount, but Gwyn grabbed my arm. Her finger was pressed against her lips, and she pointed up to a gap in the foliage where we could see the lightening sky.

Fyrel and Gerarda grabbed their bows and nocked an arrow in perfect unison. They tracked the target as it flew but did not shoot.

Three beautiful birds soared above the tree line. Their feathers were a deep red near their body and burned bright gold at the ends. They had flown over the Pool of Elvera mere hours after the seal had broken and the survivors of Damien's troops had fled.

Laethvaraq. That's what Feron had called them.

He said they were an omen of great prosperity and always flew in a flock of three. Before Aemon had come to Elverath, the *laethvaraq* were seen as a symbol of luck. Then the king had them killed and they were forgotten by all except those old enough to have seen them for themselves.

But that was not what Gerarda and Fyrel had their arrows pointed at. Soaring high above the birds was a small black shadow. It made no sound at all. The only warning was the sudden silence of the wood.

It lingered in the air and, for a moment, I thought it wouldn't strike.

But then it dove.

The small shadow grew in size, almost as large as my eagle form. The *laethvaraq* turned their long necks just in time to see the owl transform into a horrifying beast. Its head slithered from its body like a snake, growing until it was large enough to swallow the lucky birds whole.

We watched in silent horror as its tongue wrapped around the neck of the middle bird. The resounding *snap* echoed through the forest as the owl swallowed the beautiful creature in a single gulp.

Then as quickly as it had transformed, its head shrunk to its original size, and it looked like a normal owl once more.

Gerarda lowered her bow.

"No wonder Syrra hates them," I said under my breath.

"The first shapeshifters." Elaran took a sip from her waterskin. "Many of the Fae who had the gift would take an owl's form."

Like Riven's mother.

I mounted my horse and pushed all thoughts of Riven and his shapeshifting from my mind.

Gwyn's face was solemn. "Feron told me that the *laethvaraq* are born as three. If one dies, two more deaths will swiftly follow."

My chest tightened. I hoped that wasn't an omen too.

"It's amazing," Fyrel said, her arrow still pointed at the sky. "Imagine being able to take whatever form you like."

She turned to me with wide, pondering eyes.

I huffed a laugh. "No shapeshifter has ever known that power. We have one other form, and that is more than enough."

I disappeared into a flash of light and soared across the path, whipping Fyrel's braid with my wing. I perched on my saddle and transformed back to my Fae form with a grin. Fyrel clapped her hands, and Gerarda hit my leg with her shoulder before mounting her own horse.

"Show-off."

CHAPTER TWO

I REFUSED TO LOOK AT THE GROUND where Maerhal had died. Everyone else was focused on readying their blades as we waited for the second sun to fully set. We had spent the day patrolling the King's Road, keeping our ears to the ground for any useful tidbits that would let us know what to expect in Silstra.

The city still smelled of smoke from the fires Damien had set. My body turned to stone, too heavy for my legs to carry, but I stood anyway. Gerarda knew that Maerhal had died in Silstra, and I was certain she told Elaran, but I never told anyone the details.

I never told her that the woman I swore to protect died within the portal's boundary. That only a few weeks earlier, I had come to this city with hope that we could still best Damien and instead left an empty shell. Part of me wished that I had died that day when I opened the seal, that Riven had never helped me, and that I didn't still carry the weight of the war on my shoulders.

"I can't believe that used to be a dam," Gwyn whispered in awe as she stared up at the towering cliff's edge and the thrashing waterfall that now fed the mouth of the Three Sisters below.

Silstra.

Fyrel turned to me. "A few explosions took down a structure that high?"

"Dozens." I swallowed the memory of Nikolai stitching the detonators in a frenzy as we shared a carriage. "And I nearly died doing it."

Fyrel gasped as if she hadn't heard the story half a dozen times on our passage from the Order to the *Faelinth*.

"Tie the horses," I ordered. "It's time."

We walked along the bank of the river with me at the front and Gerarda and Elaran at the back. No one spoke as the first stars dotted the skies and then exploded into a moonless, shimmering tapestry.

The lack of moonlight served us well. We didn't meet a single soul on the steep path up the cliff to the eastern side of Silstra. It was as if the entire city was on edge, checking the skies for another Fae attack.

Of course, they blamed the fires on me and not the man who set them.

Their king.

Bile coated my tongue as the putrid scents of burnt stone and wood filled my lungs. I gazed across the river and saw the ruin of the building I had pulled Collin from. The image of his corpse with the words *Halfling Scum* carved into his chest was imprinted in my mind. It welcomed me every time I closed my eyes and tried to escape into a dreamless sleep where, if only for a few short hours, I could forget all that Damien had done.

What did they do with his body? Had they strung it up along the city center somewhere for residents to gawk at? Or had they thrown it back onto the ruin to rot?

Did Damien stop playing with his toys once they died?

Whatever Damien had done to Collin, I knew what he was doing to Nikolai would be so much worse. How much time did Nikolai have left? I didn't know if I should be counting in hours or days.

Nothing could be done for Nikolai in that moment. I had to trust that Riven would find him or that some other path to his rescue would appear. Guilt tore at my throat, but I needed to push all thoughts of my dear friend from my mind.

We had Halflings to rescue.

We nestled behind one of the large piles of blasted stone at the edge of the city. It was the perfect lookout for Fyrel and Gwyn. I checked their necks for the matching glamours hanging on Elvish chain that Feron had made them. As long as they kept to the shadows and didn't make any obvious movements, they would be hidden from view.

Gerarda let go of Elaran's hand and pulled something from the side pocket of her leathers. She handed thin, silver tubes to Gwyn and Fyrel. Spyglasses. "Watch for movement along the city streets. Signal us with the faebeads I gave you if you spot trouble."

Gwyn's hand wrapped around the spyglass and her lips thinned. "Surely we can be of more help going with you."

She gave Gerarda the sweetest smile.

Fyrel elbowed Gwyn's side, but the girl didn't drop her stare. Despite her years of servitude in the palace, Gwyn had not learned to respect the word *no*. Not that I could blame her—I had done far worse in the dawn of seventeen.

Gerarda leaned three inches to the side to look at me. She always set me up to be the disciplinarian with Gwyn.

"You will do as ordered," I said bluntly.

Gwyn scowled. "I don't need to be coddled."

I raised a brow. "If I was interested in coddling you, you would be in Myrelinth with Vrail. Don't make me regret my decision."

Gwyn turned to Gerarda. She was like a toddler pleading with one parent after the other said no.

Gerarda threw a knife into the air and caught it in the thin holster along her forearm. "Don't turn to me for solace." Her expression was unyielding. "I would have sent you home for arguing against orders the first time."

Gwyn's mouth snapped shut.

Elaran chuckled and stroked Gwyn's cheek and then Fyrel's. "If you're quick enough, you can take a few soldiers during the escape before I get to them."

Fyrel's eyes went wide with anticipation. For someone whose legs had been burned to the bone only a few weeks before, she seemed eager to draw her sword again.

I gritted my teeth. I would not make these girls killers unless absolutely necessary. "The point of the mission is to *avoid* soldiers, Elaran." The scars along my body tightened, pulling at my skin, a thousand tiny reminders of the true cost of a kill.

Elaran gave a coy shrug. "I like my missions a little wild." Her green eyes trailed over me in a way that made me shiver.

Gerarda cleared her throat and handed Elaran a fully stocked quiver. "Dynara's message said that they would expect us at nightfall. The time for quips has ended." There was a slight edge to Gerarda's voice that only seemed to encourage Elaran.

I held a hand to Gwyn's cheek. It was soft and unmarred, unlike her belly. I didn't want her skin marked any more than it already was. "Hold your post." I turned to Fyrel. "No matter what. You're our eyes. Our lives are fully in your hands."

Fyrel straightened and placed her hand over her face and then her chest. "Yes, Mistress."

I raised a brow.

"I mean, Keera."

Gwyn pulled me into a quick embrace. "Don't spare any of them," she whispered. There was a wicked undercurrent to her words, dangerous like the sea on the brink of a storm. It unsettled me how easily the young girl who shook in anticipation of the presents I might bring her now spoke of death. The war had changed her so much. Who would she be at the end of this? If she even survived.

I squeezed her back and nodded.

We slipped under the cover of darkness and stalked along the eastern alleys of the city. Elaran and Gerarda crept behind me, knees bent, darting from shadow to shadow along the empty alleyways.

I held out my hand as we came to a wide street. It was deserted apart from three stragglers who had yet to return to their homes from the pubs and pleasure houses.

Gerarda reached for her sleeping darts, but I stayed her hand. Unconscious bodies would be too easy to spot; we needed a better distraction.

I let my chest fill with the whirlwind magic that came from my lungs and took control of the air around us just enough to create an inconspicuous breeze. With a wave of my hand, the hat flew off the middle man's head and rolled down the street in the opposite direction of our path.

They all chased after it, drunk with ale and laughter, as the three of us crossed the street unseen. Silstra was unusually quiet. It was not one of the larger cities in the kingdom, but there were always people meandering through the streets late into the night.

A sound echoed in the alley, and we all went still.

Elaran pulled the smooth gold pin from her hair. It was sharper than a knife on either end and perfectly balanced. Her fingers tightened around its middle as she pointed to a barrel at the end of the way. She crept along the wall, hidden in shadow, making no sound. I understood why Hildegard had chosen her to spy on Curringham and the other lords for years. She was perfect.

Elaran lifted her tiny spear to strike but froze.

Gerarda nocked an arrow, assuming Elaran had been hit.

But she just stuck the gold rod back into her bountiful curls. She turned, and a small rodent-like creature scurried down the alley behind her. Its tail glowed bright red before it disappeared between a crack in the wooden building.

"Orchard mouse." Gerarda sighed, her shoulders relaxing. They had reappeared across Elverath, continuously searching for their favorite snack—*winvra*—but the magical berries had not replenished as quickly as the mice had returned.

I signaled to keep moving forward. Elaran and Gerarda fell in step behind me as we came to the house that Victoria had been using to hide and feed Halflings. What had once been a house in shambles, with its decrepit roof and rot in the walls, was now a total ruin. Burnt wood covered the ground.

The building had abutted the same house that Damien had thrown Maerhal into. Whether the purple flames had ignited the refuge or Victoria had done it with intent, I didn't know. Dynara's message had been short.

Get there soon was all it had said apart from the instructions on where to find them.

Thankfully Victoria's hideaway had been moved. Tarvelle had seen to it that all the safe houses in Silstra were changed after the last was burned in purple fire. He had done it out of suspicion of me, and ultimately that suspicion had cost him his life. Damien had used his obvious distaste for my past as the perfect scapegoat to hide his true mole among our ranks.

Collin.

He had injected Collin with the same kind of elixir he had put into me. But where Damien had only forged a connection between our minds through dreams, he had given himself full control over Collin's dreamscape. Wearing the face of Killian in Collin's dreams, Damien had gathered all the information he needed to keep watch over his brother's rebellion in the west and use it to his advantage.

Like the locations of our safe houses. I gripped my blade. Even though Damien's soldiers had been scattered in the chaos of recent weeks, I had to be prepared for the possibility that Damien was using these Halflings as a trap.

We were all still stuck in his game.

"It should be around the next bend," Gerarda whispered, pointing to the decrepit temple at the end of the alley.

I ran to the end of the lane and froze. The glamour hiding the safehouse blew away on the evening breeze.

Where a long wooden beam had fallen through the rafters and onto the ground now sat a hole.

Not a hole, but an entrance. Five steps were crudely carved into the dirt leading to a thick stone door. It stood upright, the top of it at ground level, hiding the dugout underneath. Elaran and I walked down the steep steps, both of us stretching our legs and using our hands to climb down. I grazed the divots in the stone door; the hammer that had forged it was quick and imprecise.

My magic stirred, raising the hairs on my neck.

Elaran knocked three times before the door cracked open. A harsh squeal echoed out from the room, and I peered over Elaran's shoulder. Dozens of eyes blinked back at me in the pale starlight. Some held their hands to their faces as though even the night was too bright. From the smell of it, they had locked themselves inside for days.

I held my breath and searched for the only pair of eyes I knew. Deep lines framed her dark brown gaze. Her back had a curve to it now, and her hair was even more gray, but Victoria had nothing but a proud smile across her face as she looked at me.

She hobbled up the steps inside the room. I grabbed her leathered hand. "It has been too long, old friend."

Victoria's round shape had deflated in the months of rations. Knowing her, she had taken less than her share and split it among the children. I scanned the room quickly. There were at least two dozen kids intermixed with the adults.

"Keera." Victoria's voice was shaking as she stepped out of the ground for the first time in what must have been days. Her knee buckled, and I stooped to catch her. "I'm fine—" She stopped, the hand she had raised to shake me off hung in the air, forgotten. Her pupils widened as she noticed my eyes.

No longer silver, but gold.

"Is it truly you?" There was a tone of fear in her voice as she stepped back to put herself between me and the door.

I pulled the medallion from my shirt and tossed it to her. The rose she had helped design was embossed into the metal. I lifted my hand, letting my flames cover my fingers to the delight and shock of the Halflings now climbing out of the safe house. "There is much to be discussed." I let the flames die out. "But there are better places to discuss them."

The bead tied under my braid burned hot, and I froze. Gerarda took hers from under her chest plate, the colorless glass shining bright red. "We need to go now," Gerarda barked, pulling the stragglers from the hole two at a time.

"Keera." Elaran pointed at the upper hill of the city where a troop of soldiers was marching down the alley.

Marching, not running.

"They're only enforcing curfew," Victoria said. "We haven't been spotted."

"Curfew?" I balked. There had been no mention of it in the reports from our scouts or Dynara's message.

Victoria nodded. "The soldiers put it in place the night of the fires. No one is to leave their homes at night. Violators are whipped or hung, depending on the guard who catches you." She curled her tongue as if tasting something bitter.

She didn't need to say the truth. The punishment enforced depended on the color of one's blood.

"We can't ferry out dozens of Halflings without being spotted." Gerarda pointed south to where we needed to take a parade of sixty Halflings without drawing the attention of any of the soldiers or their sentries.

I turned to Victoria. "I take it the Dagger needs no introduction."

Victoria's discerning eyes trailed over Gerarda's short frame. "No, though I reckon the Dagger disliked her title as much as the Blade."

"You can call her Gerarda," Elaran mused, picking up one of the younger Halflings and letting the blond child play with her hair. "And you may call me whatever you like, though I am cordial to *Your Majesty*."

I scoffed and shook my head. "Elaran is the funny one." Gerarda grumbled but didn't correct me.

Elaran smiled smugly.

"Both are excellent warriors in their own right, and they will protect you."

Victoria's smile fell to a deep frown. "Aren't you here to protect us too?"

I shook my head and spread my arms wide. "I'm the bait."

CHAPTER THREE

I SOARED THROUGH THE NIGHT too quickly to be spotted. I landed on the top of the sentry tower—shifting back in a flash of light as I flipped into the room below. I stood straight as the two guards fell with their own blades in their chests and pulled the helmet off the blond.

My heart dropped as I saw Collin's face. Blood pooled from his mouth, and his cheeks were maimed by fire. I fell back, unable to catch my breath for a full minute until the young man's true face came into view.

He looked nothing like Collin.

I shook off the panic and pulled the vapor from the air. A small orb of water grew, taking the form of a male body before freezing to hard ice. I set the helmet on top of my statue and stood beside it. To anyone below, it looked like the guards still stood at their post.

The troop turned down an alley to the center of the city. Small groups broke out from the main march, inspecting the side streets for strays that had gone inside. I scanned the alleys for the poor and homeless who usually filled the streets. My stomach clenched against the truth. They had already been rounded up on the first night of curfew.

A small weed grew in a crack along the tower, its flagrant fight for life almost undetectable. I brushed my finger along the white petal and let that newfound earth magic surge inside me.

The weed grew larger, wrapping around my wrist as its roots scurried down the weather-beaten stone in search of soil. They buried themselves into the earth and I felt it.

I felt everything.

The mountain top had been overwhelming, but this was all-consuming. Like most Fae, I could feel the connection the flower had with the earth, the network of roots and blooms that spanned out across the entire city. But my powers had grown. The land pulsed with life. I could feel every creature walking along the earth and burrowing in the soil; somehow I could feel the cold plunge of every swimmer in every lake and river, the strained muscles of the flyers, big and small, commanding the sky. Everything was connected in a way I could never fathom before. What had once been a useful gift was overwhelming now. It took all my concentration to focus in and glean what I needed from the connection.

It was too much for me to discern any specific being. I didn't have enough control of my gift for such nuance, but I could feel the Halflings and soldiers moving as two giant entities across the city without needing to look.

Gerarda was leading the group toward the eastern side of the river.

I let out two low owl calls. She would know it was a signal for "not that way."

I felt the group shift farther east, taking the alley back to Gwyn and Fyrel, but it would not be enough. The soldiers were crossing the main bridge, and there was no way to disguise a group as large as theirs.

I ducked, hiding the flash of light, but I did not soar into the skies. Instead I let out one long piercing eagle cry.

Run.

I transformed back, the weed wrapping around my ankle as I saw the soldiers searching the sky for a bird. The entire city was expecting me in eagle form.

I tightened my weapons belt. It was time for a show.

I raised my arm and let thin tendrils of water form along the surface of the river. One by one they coiled, readying for an attack. I released the building tension in my stomach, and the tendrils pounced, wrapping around the limbs of the soldiers on the bridge and dragging them into the depths of the canal.

The remaining soldiers shouted and unsheathed their swords as I dragged them over the bridge to join their comrades. By the time they surfaced, the current would be too strong to make it to the riverbank, and they would plummet to their deaths over the falls.

A horn sounded, and one by one the oiled beacons over the sentry towers were engulfed in flames.

I closed my eyes, focusing my gift as best as I could. The Halflings had moved farther south, but a group of soldiers was coming up the hillside pass and another approached the Halflings from the north.

They would be trapped with nowhere to go.

I raised the water from the canal into a towering wave, but I didn't let it fall upon the armored men. Instead I reached my icy hand out and shaped it into a wall of ice that divided the city in two. My powers were draining, but it would slow them down. I needed to get to the Halflings and help them to the portal.

I assessed the situation from the skies. Gwyn and Fyrel were shooting arrows at the men climbing the hillside path while Gerarda and Elaran prepared for a fight in the north.

My heart lurched at the thought of leaving Gwyn, but I had to trust that she could handle herself.

I landed and pushed the soldiers back with one monstrous gust. They fell to the ground in a fit of coughs, Gerarda's throwing knives taking out a dozen before they managed to stand.

The nearest soldiers flinched at the flash of light as I shifted out of my eagle form. I painted bloody streaks across the cobblestone with my boots as my blade carved the last breath from their lungs. The last of them fell and I inspected the stones along the ground. Some were unmarred by time, but others had thick cracks down the middle filled with dirt.

I knelt and placed a palm flat to the ground.

"Now is not the time for prayers, Keera," Gerarda scoffed as she loaded her bow with four arrows and shot.

Elaran charged at a mountain of a man. She flipped through the air with feline grace, twisting to catch the man's neck between her legs. The momentum brought him to the ground with her, and she stuck her hair pin through the back of his neck. "You can pray to me if it helps, Keera." She smirked up at me as she flung a dagger into another man's chest. "I like to see people on their knees." She shot a wink to Gerarda.

Gerarda fired four more arrows, each one landing with deadly accuracy.

"El, I'm the only one who gets to worship you."

Elaran smiled. "Duck!"

Gerarda hit the ground beside me as Elaran lofted a blade over her head. A soldier stumbled back several feet before crumpling to the ground with Gerarda's arrow in his chest. Elaran somersaulted over her kills and landed in a crouch. She pressed a quick kiss to Gerarda's cheek. "Maybe I'll say a prayer to you later."

I cocked my jaw. "I'm trying to concentrate!"

Elaran shrugged and ran toward another soldier. I turned to Gerarda. "Guard me."

She didn't hesitate, turning away and scanning the field of battle. There were two dozen soldiers surrounding us still, but they were hesitant to attack.

A small root twisted around my fingers, and I felt the connection take hold of me once more. The Halflings were scurrying down the mountain, but there were more soldiers in their way.

"Elaran, go to Gwyn and Fyrel now!"

She sliced her spear through a man's throat and ran. Gerarda struck down a brave soldier who charged. I felt a shift in the air. We needed to leave, but something was wrong. The pulsing life I had felt in my earlier connection was gone. No, not gone. Silent. As if every creature close to us had stopped breathing out of fear.

Not of the soldiers.

Not of me.

But of something much worse.

A terrifying shriek split the sky. It echoed like thunder, so loud the sound drummed in my chest. I looked up and could no longer see the stars. They were covered in a thick layer of shadow that swirled like ink in water.

The hair on my neck rose; the soldiers behind me stopped fighting, their heads craning to the sky too. I couldn't see the creature, but I could feel it. The smell of rot and death filled the air, a putrid stench like a victor's field at the height of day.

The wind moved in thick beats, hot and humid enough to pull the sweat from our skin. Along with the darkness had come wings.

I recognized it immediately from Lash's fire stories. The shadowy beasts that had once hunted the Elverin. There was no mistaking the gargantuan body that spanned half the city. Its long, curved neck and even longer beak were just like the shadows Lash had painted by the fireside.

A *waateyshir*.

Its body was made from darkness and smoke. It looked like a bird with a long neck and sharp talons, but its form wasn't rigid. Instead black feathers lined the edges of its wings and back while tendrils of blackness filled its body—a red light pulsing at the center of its chest. Its long beak snapped, lined with teeth as tall as a Mortal man. It was monstrous, emerging from a nightmare rather than a wood. The beast hung in the sky, hovering over the city, terrifying the people who would be its next meal. Tendrils of shadow leaked from its frame as if it was part beast, part smoke.

The *waateyshir* reared back its long neck and its glassy black eyes settled on the line of soldiers behind me. The loose strands of my braid blew toward the beast as it sucked up the air and prepared to attack.

Gerarda's only warning was the flash of light as I transformed. She held up her arms, braced and ready, as my talons wrapped around them, and we sailed just above the ground.

An ear-splitting sound whistled behind us. I heard the last bit of air being pulled from the men's lungs. They were frozen in place, unable to move, unable to do anything except look at the beast.

The whistling stopped. Silence hung in the air for a moment that seemed to stretch much too long. I turned in time for Gerarda and I to witness the true power of the beast. Black flame shot from its beak, illuminated by the soldiers' torches. Their mouths dropped open, but they had no air left to scream before they were turned to ash.

The beast sucked in the ash on its next breath, its pulsing red center glowing brighter as it swallowed its meal.

Gerarda fell from my grasp and took two soldiers down with her as she landed. I changed back to my Fae form, both blades drawn and ready to fight.

"Where's Gwyn?" I shouted to no one in particular. "Fyrel?"

"Down the mountain," someone shouted. I snapped toward the voice and saw Victoria, a sword quivering in her hands as she defended the opening to the hillside path. Her face was already bloodied, red stained her lips and dripped down her neck.

She swung with unskilled brutality, but it was enough to send a soldier lurching back to my waiting knife.

"Victoria, go!" I ordered. "We have this handled. Gwyn and Fyrel can take you to safety."

"There's still one more!" She pointed up on the pile of large rocks where a tiny Halfling boy was hiding among the rubble. His face was caked with dirt except for where rivers of tears had washed the black away.

The *waateyshir* turned its sights on our battle and began to whistle again. Unless we made for the hillside now, we would be nothing but ash in seconds.

My throat ached as I said, "Leave him. Descend now!"

Gerarda followed the order without hesitation. Elaran looked at me with a dubious expression on her face then glanced at the boy.

"El, you are not allowed to die today." Gerarda's voice rattled with desperation as she peered over the cliff's edge.

"Go!" I ordered her. Then I broke into a flash of light and flew directly within the *waateyshir*'s sights.

The beast tracked my movement. Its long beak snapped at me, but my wings were more agile than the giant's. It let out a terrifying caw, and for the moment, it seemed to have forgotten its second meal below.

I flew with all the strength I had left. My magic was mostly depleted, but I needed to lure the beast away. I soared higher and higher, and the *waateyshir* followed. I counted another ten beats of my wings and hoped it was enough.

They had better run.

I tucked my wings in tight and let myself drop into a free fall, lunging between the beast's shadowy wing and long neck. The *waateyshir*'s head snapped in my direction, but it took time for a beast so large to change direction mid-flight. It spread its wings, covering the city in their shadow as it cut a curve across the sky.

The beast's shriek was even more piercing in my eagle form. My vision blurred with the need to concentrate. I opened my wings and felt the air move as the *waateyshir* flapped its own behind me. Gerarda and Elaran ran down the hillside path, only steps from the other Halflings.

But Victoria was not with them.

My stomach plummeted as I opened my wings. She stood on the rubble, holding a little boy and a lit torch. I recognized him as the toddler who had been on her hip the last day I saw her. The Halfling with the stitched ears.

Julian.

She looked up, gave me one decisive nod, and threw the boy over the cliff's edge. All I saw next was her waving arms, catching the attention of the beast as she ran in the direction of the soldiers with a fiery torch flaming above her head.

I dove and snatched the boy from the air. With a flash of light, I was cradling him in one arm as I wrapped a stream of water around our legs, catching us as gently as I could manage.

I grabbed for the cliff edge and the sickening shriek of the *waateyshir* echoed above us. A bone-shattering pain tore through my body as I touched the earth. Not from my magic, but from the connection.

I felt the pulsing life of Victoria and each soldier fade away in an instant. The pain was sharp and hollowing, like someone had carved out my innards.

I stilled, waiting for the *waateyshir* to move toward the Halflings, but it flew toward the barracks in the other direction. The boy giggled and tugged at my braid. I gave him a hollow laugh but did not let go of the cliff.

I hadn't been able to feel the edge of Victoria in the chaos, but now her absence was a hard form I could trace the edges of like a shape cut from a tapestry. Her death was unmistakable. I didn't know if it was my magic or my soul feeling the loss of my dear friend. But it didn't matter because I hadn't felt anything like it before.

The pain of it consumed me. But only Victoria's death, not the soldiers being turned to ash all over Silstra. Only the person I knew. My breath hitched. The feeling was so overwhelming that, had anyone else died since my powers had reached their full strength, I would have felt it.

Which meant Nikolai was alive.

CHAPTER FOUR

"Ow!"

The toddler tugged on my braid hard enough that there were more than a few loose strands between his grubby fingers. He giggled at my grimace and waited for a smile, but I couldn't give him one. My body ached with exhaustion and grief. It took what was left of my energy to pull a thick spout from the thrashing water below and use it to carry us to the edge of the river.

Elaran waited for me at the bottom. "Gerarda already sent word to Feron. He will be ready when we return to discuss . . ." She raised her hand to the sky that was beginning to clear over the wood. The thick bands of stars glimmered through wisps of shadow while the remaining soldiers' shrieks echoed in the distance.

The *waateyshir* would be occupied long enough for us to get to the portal. My back relaxed, and my magic settled to a low simmer under my skin.

Julian giggled in my arms. I wrapped the boy around my shoulders hoping he would leave my braid alone, but his fingers dug in to hold himself steady.

"You're not very motherly," she said, her voice completely deadpan as she wriggled her fingers up at the boy.

"My mother stuffed me in a tree for seven hundred years." I winced as Julian tugged again. "And the only parents I ever saw at the Order were the ones who dropped their daughters off in the middle of the night. None of them were particularly motherly either."

Elaran's teasing smirk faltered. I'd hit a nerve.

Whatever it was, she steeled herself just as quickly. "Why don't we let the grumpy, sullen Fae protect us with her special magic powers while you come with me," she said in an exaggerated high-pitched voice that made my ears hurt. She reached up for the boy, and he opened his arms for her.

"I could have walked him to the portal," I grumbled.

Elaran raised a brow at me. "You have blood all over your face. I'm saving the poor thing from a childhood of nightmares." She tucked him onto her hip, and he immediately rested his head on her shoulder.

"I think maybe the humongous bird of death might have already done that."

Elaran looked at my boots. It took her eyes a long time to make it to my face again. "I refuse to believe that Hildegard taught you to fight with so little grace."

I looked down. My tunic and leathers were covered in thick smears of red. The parts that weren't sticky with blood were stained dark from ash.

I scoffed and opened my mouth to retort, but I couldn't. Minutes after battle and Elaran's leathers were pristine. She wore no shirt underneath her fighting vest but even her tan skin was clean. Not a scratch or drop of blood. Her perfectly done updo held together by her gold weapon only made it more annoying.

She bit her lip knowingly as she smiled.

I cocked my jaw to the side and let my shoulders slump forward. "We need to go."

The boy sucked his thumb. His ears had grown into their round shape with no scar along the front and only a tiny little line of stitching left behind it. If he was lucky enough to survive to adulthood, time would wear the scar away completely.

My skin prickled along the edge of every name I'd collected. If only time could wash away all scars.

"I'm sorry you lost a friend today." There was no pretense to Elaran's words. Her knowing smile had fallen to a straight, serious line across her mouth.

My throat burned hot. I had spent the past two days planning our escape with the Halflings and imagining Victoria's face when she first laid eyes on Myrelinth. I was looking forward to when she'd get to see all the faces of the ones she saved over the years alive and free—at least as well as they could be with Damien still on the throne. Some of them even had children now.

Children Victoria would never get to meet. Something rumbled in that dark, rocky bottom in the depths of myself, the one that I had fought so hard to climb out of. Lash. Maerhal. Nikolai. And now Victoria. Every loss had set a crack along the ground of it, fracturing it little by little. I didn't know how many more losses I could take until that dark place I kept so contained crumbled into a hungry pit that sucked every last bit of hope out of me.

I grew used to the searing pain in my throat; it was a reminder of how much I'd already fought and won. I could fight a little more.

"I'm sorry too." I drew a breath of cold air to ease my throat. "But there's no other way she would have wanted to go. She was a protector to the very end."

Elaran bit her cheek and didn't say anything, but I knew she wasn't one to let words sit on her tongue.

"Say what you wish." I was too riddled with grief for offense, and I didn't have the energy to wonder what Elaran wanted to say.

She glanced at me then down at Julian. "She was hit by one of the soldiers."

I winced. What man would strike a woman so frail?

"He paid a hefty price; she threw him over the edge for it." There was a note of admiration in Elaran's voice that made me smile. "But he split her lip." Elaran paused, running a finger over the curve of Julian's ear. "She was bleeding." Elaran turned to me, her green eyes fierce and serious. "She bled red, not amber."

I huffed a laugh. "That's to be expected. She is—was—Mortal." Tears misted my eyes as I corrected myself.

Elaran stared at the ground in disbelief. Her nostrils flared, trying to sort through which question to ask first.

"But how could you trust her? With something as important as *our* people's lives?" Elaran stopped walking. We were nearing the portal too quickly for her to get the answers she wanted.

She turned, lifting her chin as she looked at me. As she judged me and my decisions. I didn't blame her. If it were anyone else partnering with Mortals, I would have questions too.

I shrugged. "Because she trusted me first."

Elaran's jaw snapped shut, her feet rooted to the ground like she was an earth wielder tethering herself to that spot.

"Before Victoria started her life ferrying Halfling children in and out of hiding, she had her own."

Elaran's sharp nose wrinkled. "Halflings or children?"

"Both." The word sunk to that dark place inside me as the memories of those early years came to the surface.

"Had . . ." Elaran's lips clung to the word for much longer than they needed as she realized what had happened. "They were discovered?"

I nodded. "The eldest was named Idris. He was a young boy when it happened. He was working for an apothecary in town when he nicked his palm shearing some *winvra* leaves. The apothecary saw amber and reported him."

Elaran blinked and her face turned sour. "She married a Halfling?"

I nodded.

"How could she not know?" Elaran said to herself more than to me.

"She did." My throat tightened. "Her husband's name was Landyn. He was a Halfling who escaped the fields in Volcar and somehow convinced his agent that he was dead. He looked Mortal, and no one ever questioned it when he settled in Silstra. Then he walked into the butcher shop looking for a job and found his wife instead. Vic never told me when he told her or how, but she knew before the marriage happened and married him anyway."

Elaran's neck tensed. It was a sad story, but not unheard of. Surely Gerarda had told her of the families we were sent to discipline when such a union was discovered.

Elaran shook her head. "But she lived . . . After her child was discovered, her entire family would have been exposed." Elaran took a step back. "She told the guards that she didn't know. She begged them to spare her while her family paid the consequences of her actions?"

I bit my lip. It had not been a guard who had been begged to. It had been me. Though it was not Victoria who had been on her knees.

"I was the one dispatched to dispense the king's mercy that day."

Elaran's eyes went wide and she stilled, little Julian nestling further into her shoulder to sleep.

"I told the Shades to take the family to the city circle." I cleared my throat. "Aemon liked his punishments to be conducted in public for everyone to see. And fear. It was my blade that cut each of their palms; it was I who discovered Victoria was Mortal and the rest of her family was not."

Elaran's lips snarled. "She trusted you because you spared her."

I scoffed. "No, she hated me for it. It wasn't Victoria who begged for her life that day. She was so calm she would have tied her own noose if I'd asked her." I kicked at the grass and looked up at the city. In almost thirty years, so much had changed and yet so little. "But her husband pleaded first. He swore that Victoria didn't know. That his daughter, who was barely eight, didn't even know. He swore he had deceived them all."

"And she agreed to this?" Elaran pursed her lips in disgust.

"No. Victoria said nothing. But her parents came to her defense. They had never known the truth about their son-in-law or grandchildren. They corroborated his lie."

"And you believed him?"

I shook my head. "Of course not. But why should all three die if I only needed to kill one?"

Elaran's shoulders fell. "Oh, Keera."

"Landyn was killed by my blade and hung in the city circle on my orders." My voice sounded far away, like it wasn't my memories I was divulging but instead some story from long ago. "I made sure the children didn't see it. That was the best I could do for them. The son was given to a kind agent in Cereliath with a small plot of land to farm. He kept his wards' paperwork up to date and allowed them some leave after each harvest so Victoria was still able to see her son."

"And the daughter?"

I met Elaran's gaze. She already knew what happened to young and able-bodied girls in the kingdom. "I let her have her last evening with her mother, and then Willa was brought to the Order to train."

"What happened to them?" Her voice was barely a whisper.

"Idris was stopped by some guards on his way back to Cereliath. His paperwork was in order, but they insisted it was a forgery. He was beaten and left on the edge of his agent's property." I swallowed. "He didn't survive."

A tear rolled down Elaran's cheek. "And Willa?"

"She trained hard. She was a favorite of Myrrah's." I smiled, remembering the ambling little girl who would leap from post to post in the training grounds dreaming of the days when she would get to join the Shield at sea. "She died during her Trials. I brought her body back to Silstra. I thought a mother should see her daughter one last time. Have the chance to bury her properly. She deserved that much."

"How did she ever agree to work with you when you caused her so much pain?" Elaran's words were not hard with judgment but rather breathy with disbelief that someone could be that forgiving.

I shrugged. I didn't know the answer to that either. "I think because she was a mother to Halflings. She loved them with all her heart and saw what choices they had to make—she had to make—to give them the best chance. And then when that was ripped from them, how to make the best choice for their survival. She had been angry at needing to make those choices for so long that by the time I brought her daughter back to her, she could see that I was forced to make hard choices too."

Elaran readjusted Julian on her hip. "How many Mortals have helped you along the way?"

I sighed, tallying them up in my head. "A few, but not many. It was too dangerous to give Mortals the chance to prove themselves.

It puts everything in jeopardy." I beat my palm against the hilt of my dagger. "But Victoria knew of many Mortal parents hiding their Halfling spouses and children over the years. She helped them hide in plain sight and move when they were close to discovery. She even managed to help some hide before the soldiers could get to them once their families had been found out."

Elaran took a deep breath. "She was remarkable. To take all that pain and fight so tirelessly with it. With no care for the consequences."

"She was remarkable." I nodded. "But I think Victoria always knew the path she forged would end with her death. Yet she fought anyway."

Elaran took a step forward, and I was grateful her questions were done. The best parts of Victoria were entangled with the worst parts of me.

"I always thought if we were brave enough to take the kingdom to war that it would end in so much bloodshed either there would be no Halflings left standing or no Mortals. I never pictured a world where our kin won and there would still be Mortals left. Mortals who might not want to fight us."

I froze, unsure of what Elaran was suggesting.

But when she turned to face me, there was nothing but concern etched upon her face. My story had shaken her so completely a few loose curls had fallen from their twist. "What if we win and the survivors don't want to leave but don't want to fight? What do we do with them?"

I shrugged. I had no idea. I had barely begun to imagine a world where I survived winning the war, let alone had the power to make decisions like that. My entire life was a practice of balancing death, not life. I didn't know if I was capable of making decisions that allowed people to do anything other than survive.

That's all I had ever done.

CHAPTER FIVE

"WHO IS THIS?" Gerarda asked in an unrecognizable high pitch as she drummed her fingers in front of Julian's nose. He giggled, grabbing the short length of her hair and tugging. Gerarda laughed and uncurled his fingers one by one. "That's quite the grip strength, little one."

"He does that," I mumbled.

Gerarda ignored me and stood on her tiptoes, waving her hands in front of her face and making expressions I didn't even know she was capable of until that very moment.

"Stop talking like that. You're making the others uncomfortable."

Elaran raised one manicured brow in the direction of the Halflings who were eating and drinking the supplies Fyrel and Gwyn were passing out.

"Fine." I crossed my arms. "You're making *me* uncomfortable."

Gerarda cleared her throat and rested her hands on the hilt of her blade. "I already sent word to Feron about the *waateyshir* attacking the city. He will have everyone convened the moment we arrive in Myrelinth."

I shook my head. "Aralinth."

The Halflings deserved a day to celebrate their safe passage to the *Faelinth* without news of a *waateyshir*'s return darkening that victory.

Gerarda nodded, already pulling the notebook from her saddlebag. "They'll be waiting for us."

I stopped. Feron would call the Elders for the meeting. Myrrah wouldn't know what the *waateyshir* was capable of any more than Gerarda and I, but her experience defending the kingdom as Shield was an invaluable asset. Hopefully, Darythir and Feron could fill in the gaps in our knowledge.

I straightened to my full height, every muscle fiber screeching from fatigue. "Vrail and Syrra should be there."

Gerarda's jaw pulsed but she nodded.

"Tell them it has to do with Nikolai."

Gwyn's head whipped around. She dropped the waterskin and left it for Fyrel to pick up. "If you're planning another mission, I want to go."

I sighed. "One thing at a time, Gwyn. And for now I need you and Fyrel to take the lead bringing the Halflings back to Myrelinth."

Her red brows lifted underneath her curls. "Why us?"

Fyrel fixed the collar of her tunic and stood straight like an initiate awaiting Hildegard's orders.

"You both made recent journeys to the *Faelinth* and have settled well." I turned to the Halflings. They huddled together in one group, whispering, like they were still hidden in the ground instead of shielded by a glamour. "They need to see that now more than ever."

Fyrel nodded. "We will get them home safe."

I turned to Gwyn. She looked less certain. "Make sure they know how to cross through the Singing Wood *before* you go into the forest. The other Fae will be meet you along the trail to escort the group through the darkest part of the path."

Gwyn rolled her eyes. "No sound, no fire." She elbowed me in the side as I scowled. "I'll make sure to give the young ones a drop of sleeping draught to get through the wood."

I looked up at the sky. The guiding star had not yet hit its peak. "If you make haste"—I turned to Gerarda—"you could make the northern portal before dawn."

The knife Gerarda was flipping through her fingers to entertain Julian froze. "You aren't coming?"

I shook my head and wrapped my fingers around the small vial from my saddlebag. "No, I need to sleep." I grabbed the vial of clear liquid. I didn't have the strength to keep Damien from my mind tonight, even though he hadn't tried to visit since I had taken hold of the dreamscape for myself. "I'll fly to Aralinth before dawn."

Elaran hiked the toddler further up her hip. She gave me a knowing look but didn't say anything as she and the two young warriors readied the Halflings for their journey.

Gerarda mounted her horse and was gone with a single nod.

I unlatched the blanket rolled under my saddlebag and walked as far as possible from where Maerhal had died but was still hidden by the glamour. I nestled against a trunk at the edge of the Dead Wood that had sprung back to life. Turquoise dust fluttered down from the leaves, catching along my braid.

I closed my eyes and pretended to sleep so I didn't have to speak to the Halflings as they gasped at the watery veil Fyrel jumped through. What would I say to them? *Enjoy your time in Myrelinth before I bring death to its door?*

They needed hope, but I had to hang on to every drop I had with an iron grip.

As soon as they were all through, I grabbed the notebook Riven had left me from my saddlebag. In the weeks he had been gone, I hadn't received one message apart from his initial note. And I hadn't sent any to him.

There had been no time after the seal broke. The whiplash of Maerhal's death to learning the truth that Riven and Killian were not brothers but the same person barely had time to settle before we left to break the last seal. I had choked down my anger. After all, I had done so much worse than keeping one secret. I'd had no idea if Riven would survive the last seal breaking, and even so, it had almost killed him. I hadn't wanted our last night to be one of anger and arguments.

He had lived, and the anger I had forced into a simmer in the face of death had now come to a boil.

But Riven had left.

No goodbye. No rushed conversation or promise to have one upon his return. He no longer had Killian's face to hide behind, and he was nowhere to be found.

Now that we were fighting two enemies, we needed as many people as we could scrounge, even Riven. I took a soothing breath and swallowed my pride. My pen carved into the notebook like a knife, each stroke a blow sent to Riven. Wherever he was.

Feron needs you home now.

My pen hovered over the page. I didn't know if that would be enough. My stomach twisted. I knew that if I told him that I wanted him to return, needed him, he would. But I didn't know if that was true, and there had already been more than enough lies shared between us. So I wrote the only truth I knew would bring him home.

Nik is alive.

CHAPTER SIX

THE MORNING LIGHT ON MY WINGS felt glorious. I was thankful for the flight to clear my mind. Aralinth glinted in the distance, the giant leaves of Sil'abar came to life with the same auric glow of the Burning Mountains I had already flown over.

I dove for the center of the tree, transforming mid-dive and landing on the top of the giant Elder birch. I stood and let the cool morning breeze brush across my face as I looked out at the city of eternal spring.

I had thought the city beautiful before magic had returned. The flowery canopies that had hung over the alleyways were now so lush and thick they covered every roof and wall in blooms that had not existed before the revival.

Soft pastels smelled of honey, and vibrant jewel tones carried thick, seductive aromas I recognized from Nikolai's prized perfume collection.

I pressed my hand to a thin line in the peeling bark of the trunk. It opened without hesitation, pulling back like a gutted stag to reveal the palace inside. I dropped through the roof and landed on my knee.

Rheih sniffed. "Maybe you should spend more time showering and using the door instead of dropping in through the roof."

I raised a brow. Her own grayed curls were matted with twigs and leaves from that morning's harvest. I wasn't sure the Mage had slept since the return, too many new plants and herbs for her to catalog, but there was no redness in her yellow catlike eyes.

She continued to mutter insults at me as we walked to the end of the hall where the others were waiting.

Feron stood at the far side of the circular room. His hands were pressed to Gerarda's temples. Her eyes unfocused and her jaw went slack. Feron was watching her memory, seeing the *waateyshir* for himself.

He dropped his hands and turned to me. "It is as you expected." He signed what he had witnessed for Darythir, who reeled back in her chair.

She shook her head, annoyed, and signed something too quickly for me to follow. Myrrah tugged on Feron's purple robe. His long twists swayed behind him as he translated for both of us.

"Show them." I nodded to Myrrah and Darythir. Vrail poked her head from a tower of books sitting on the table and my chest heated with delight. Her skin was sallow and dry, and the dark circles under her eyes looked like bruises, but she was here.

I looked for Syrra but Elaran shook her head.

She hadn't come.

The three joined hands as Feron projected the memory for them to see. Darythir's face drained of its warmth.

"It destroyed the entire city." I recounted what I had seen flying over Silstra that morning. Everything was a burnt ruin, though no smoke fanned in the breeze, just sickening ash.

Myrrah turned her chair to face the entire room. "Why would they reappear now?" She looked at Feron but he only shrugged.

"The *waateyshirak* were defeated well before I was born. Thousands and thousands of years before." Feron sat on the edge of the chair he'd crafted with his magic and rested his hand on his cane. "Our histories say that the *niinokwenar* and the Elves had killed the last of them well before Kieran'thara and Ara'linthir gave birth to the first generation of Dark and Light Fae, as you call them."

"It must be connected to the resurgence of magic." Gerarda stood beside Elaran's chair. "That is too big of a coincidence otherwise."

Vrail shook her head so violently I thought she would make herself sick. "That isn't possible. From everything the other Elverin and Rheih have cataloged, breaking the seals only restored the magic that existed when the Light Fae created the siphons. There is no evidence that the return of stored magic was strong enough to bring a creature from millennia ago out of extinction."

All the enthusiastic joy Vrail usually had when explaining something was gone. Her words were hollow and monotone, and there was no life in her apart from her bouncing leg.

Feron considered her answer. "It is strange that the *waateyshirak* are the only foes of our past to resurface. There are other creatures in our histories that have not returned."

"Not yet," Myrrah huffed. "Perhaps they will join . . ." She stumbled on the Elvish word for the shadowy beast and came up with a translation in the King's Tongue. "These Dark Ones."

I bit my cheek and slumped into an empty chair. Vrail was right, this was too much of a coincidence. Just while the Elverin were preparing to vanquish their enemy to the east, a lethal one from their past returned?

"What if it isn't a coincidence?" I sat up, leaning on the table's edge. "What if Kairn did something to that last seal?"

Vrail's brow creased. "A catalyst?"

I nodded. "He stabbed a blade into the seal before I broke it. It was black and laced with something. I had figured it was poison to harm me but—"

"There was a flash of black smoke when the seal broke." Gerarda flipped her knife through her fingers as she addressed Feron. "I witnessed her break each of the other seals, but that had never happened before."

Someone moved against the wall. "Even Damien would know that bringing back the *waateyshirak* would be a death sentence for the entire continent."

My body froze at the sound of Riven's voice. I didn't move as he stepped to take the chair beside me. Everyone else in the room was silent, waiting for one of us to make the first move.

Except for Rheih.

"Are his eyes green?" she whispered loudly to Gerarda.

"I don't think underestimating Damien any more than we already have is a good idea," I said coolly over my shoulder.

Riven's jaw pulsed. It might have taken me a few short weeks to realize that Damien knew about the seals and his father's connection to the magic of Elverath, but it was Riven who was too confident his own brother didn't know his secret. And Riven allowed Damien to use that knowledge to fracture our forces so completely the crevice between us was deeper than the Rift itself.

"If this was Damien's doing, then he knows something that we don't." Gerarda perched on the armrest of Elaran's chair.

I looked to Vrail. "What do you know about the *waateyshirak*? How do we fight them? How many were there in Faelin's time?"

Vrail gave a half-hearted shrug. "Very little." She pointed at the dozens of books in front of her. "There are brief mentions in these texts, but so much of that knowledge was lost in the Blood Purges. Aemon targeted our scrolls as much as he did the Elverin."

My skin itched underneath my tunic. Feron and some of the other Elverin were thousands of years old; had they not read anything useful in the time before Aemon's reign? I turned to him, but he merely shook his head, reading my thoughts.

"All I ever knew were stories." The faelight cast a silvery glow along the top of Feron's dark cheekbones. "The Elves had learned to protect themselves against the *waateyshirak*." He waved his hand and an image appeared across my mind. From the gasps in the room, I knew everyone else was seeing the vision too. A terrifying shadow of a beast flew over the city of Myrelinth. Every burl was dark, the entire city quiet as the beast flew overhead and a spout of fiery light blasted in the distance. "The *waateyshirak* use their scent and hearing to hunt more than their eyes. They can see movement but not details. The Elves took refuge in Myrelinth because the plant life masked their scent. They formed patrols to warn the citizens before the beasts approached."

"The fire was a distraction." Elaran toyed with the gold weapon holding up her curls and laid her head on Gerarda's lap. The ease of their closeness made the distance between me and Riven feel like an ocean.

"Yes." Feron nodded. "It was a useful tool to keep the cities safe while the *waateyshirak* were in their frenzy."

"Frenzy?"

Vrail's leg started bouncing again, though she didn't look at me while she spoke. Her dark eyes just stared out at nothing; she had left part of herself in that library. "The creatures were only active one year for every century. But that year would be chaos, constant attacks all over Elverath, and as the year dragged on the creatures only got larger and more deadly. The Elves named it *bii'agar niibe giizir*—the year of the sleeping sun—because most would reverse their habits to sleeping during the daylight hours so they could be alert all night long."

I leaned forward. "They can only attack at night?"

Vrail nodded, still not looking at me. "Faelin created the second sun to make the nights shorter than they were before. Sunlight is the only true enemy of a *waateyshir*."

Feron leaned on the top of his cane from his seat. "The shortened nights made it harder for the *waateyshirak* to breed. They grew weaker and their numbers began to dwindle as Faelin led attacks into their nests." Feron's full lips fell into a shallow frown. "Her gifts started to wane after she forged the second sun. She faded from the world completely only a few thousand years afterward. But she was a brilliant warrior. She used what was left of her gifts to battle the *waateyshirak* until they were vanquished. And then she was gone."

"Not just her gifts," Vrail interjected. "Faelin's main weapon was her sword."

"Yes." Feron smiled. "Her blade was said to have speared the heart of many *waateyshirak*."

"They have hearts?" Myrrah crossed her arms. "They look to be made of shadow and smoke more than anything else."

"They do." I nodded. "I saw it."

Riven snapped his head to me, his eyes wide with worry as if the beast was flying over our heads at that very moment.

I ignored him and spoke to Myrrah. "When I was leading it away from the Halflings, I flew under its wing. The shadows move and shift like watery feathers, but underneath is a red light. It pulsed bright red the moment before it attacked."

"So we spear it through the heart with a blade?" Gerarda tossed her knife into the air and caught it through the hole in its hilt with her ring finger. "Easy enough."

I scoffed. "Are you volunteering, Gerarda?"

"Scared, Keera?" she replied with a devilish smile.

Riven clenched his armrest.

"You can't use just any blade." Vrail sighed and leaned on the table. "Faelin's sword was blood-bound and so were the other warriors' from *Niikir'na*."

Feron cleared his throat. "We are not alone," he whispered. "Come in."

The wall split immediately with his command. Gwyn and Fyrel stood, the latter's hand still lifted as if she were about to knock.

Gwyn's eyes sparkled with delight. "There is a message from the scouts." She ran a burnt piece of parchment over to me. "The *waateyshir* was spotted making its nest in the north."

Feron took no offense as I read the letter instead of him.

I confirmed the message and slid it across the table for the Elders to read for themselves. "Are the Halflings settling in?" I raised a brow at both of them. They'd had orders to stay in Myrelinth.

Fryel's cheeks burned bright red, but Gwyn grabbed her wrist and shoved the girl behind her. "They were tired and went to sleep in one of the dormitories in the lower city."

I narrowed my eyes. There was something suspicious in Gwyn's tone, but I didn't have the energy to infer what it was. There were more pressing matters at hand.

"Good job, both of you." I nodded in the direction of the door. "Make sure they have food and clothes waiting for them when they wake. Get the other Shades to help you."

Fyrel nodded, but Gwyn glanced around the room.

"Now," I pushed. They stepped back slowly. "I'll come check on you soon."

I waited for Feron to close the doors before I turned back to the group. "The spearing is going to have to wait." I took a deep breath and explained everything that had happened in Silstra. The way my magic had been connected to every living thing in Elverath and the undeniable coldness I felt when Victoria had been killed. "It was too powerful a feeling. I would know if something like that had happened since Elvera."

Riven turned in his seat, his back straight like he was made of stone. "You think you would have felt it if Nik had died?"

"I know I would have."

Riven's eyes were misted with hope. "Can you use it to track him?"

"That had been my plan." I turned to Feron. "To ask you to train me."

Feron nodded without hesitation. Then his brows furrowed. "'Had been' your plan?"

"Dynara has been planning a ball as part of her ruse to get the courtesans and Halflings out of Cereliath." I crossed my arms. "Of course, it's being hosted by the new mistress of the House of Harvest. A celebration in honor of the new king." My lip curled around Damien's title. "Dynara is certain that Damien will not attend but send an emissary in his stead. She has already begun pulling strings to make sure it serves us best."

Riven stilled beside me. "Who does she think will serve as emissary?"

"Kairn."

"Damien could be expecting a ruse." Riven shook his head. "He could kill Nik out of spite in the meantime. Kairn might not show. Waiting for a ball is leaving him too long."

"What better chance do we have?" I turned to Feron. "Even if we trained every hour, it would take me months to be able to find someone across an entire continent. If it's even possible."

Riven crossed his arms. "There's no guarantee that we could get Kairn to talk even if we captured him."

"I could get the man to talk." Myrrah cracked her knuckles. "Don't worry about that."

I stood. "We don't need to get him to tell us anything at all." I looked at Feron. "Do we?"

Feron leaned back in his chair. His shoulders rose as he realized what I was asking of him. He could pluck every memory Kairn had of Nikolai from his mind without a bead of sweat wetting his brow. But I knew Feron didn't like to tamper with minds that had not let him in.

Eventually he met my gaze and nodded. "I will get you what you need."

"And the *waateyshir*?" Vrail asked. "It could attack throughout the night."

"We will set our schedules just as the Elves used to." Darythir nodded with me as Feron interpreted for her. "We sleep through the day in both cities. We have scouts through the Faeland and along the borders to keep watch on its location. Vrail, you work with Gerarda and Elaran to prep the scouts with whatever they will need. Myrrah and the Shades will help break the news as gently as we can to the rest of the Elverin."

Elaran lifted her head. "Why don't we just hunt the beast and end this now?"

Riven answered for me. "Because it might not attack us." There was an unmistakable edge of hope in his words.

"Exactly." I nodded. "If Damien was the heart of this problem, let him deal with it. At the very least it may end up being distracting enough that we escape Cereliath unscathed, with all the Halflings and Kairn in tow."

"And what about the Halflings still in the kingdom?" Myrrah's voice was hard. "What if they are attacked in the middle of the night?"

My throat burned but I swallowed it down. "We always knew we wouldn't save everyone. Splitting our focus will only get more of us killed." I walked toward the door. "We'll meet tomorrow to discuss specifics. Today we need to secure the cities."

Riven followed me like a shadow and grabbed my arm. "We need to talk."

I pulled myself free and shook my head. "We needed to talk three weeks ago."

CHAPTER SEVEN

I flew to Myrelinth. My chest ached with relief when I landed at my burl and saw that Riven was not there waiting for me. I needed a shower. To wash away the swirling thoughts of him and focus on the two enemies we now faced.

I stepped under the branch and let the thoughts run down the drain.

My stomach twisted with guilt for fleeing from him just as he had done to me. But I was home. I was present. And I had been waiting for weeks. Riven could stand to wait a few hours until I knew exactly what I wanted to say to him. Until I knew I could do it without maiming him.

There was someone more important I needed to talk to.

I dressed and plaited my hair into a wet braid. I jumped from the burl, wearing nothing but a pair of training pants and a loose tunic.

I wasn't allowed to bring my weapons into the crypt, and with a couple hours left of sunlight I wouldn't need them.

Fyrel was standing at the base of the tree. Gwyn stood in front of her whispering something into her ear, so close her lips brushed against Fyrel's skin.

I cleared my throat.

Fyrel gasped and shoved Gwyn away. Her stare became permanently fixed on my boots. "We were discussing rooming options for the new Halflings, Mistr—I mean, Keera." Her voice shook with such panic I was surprised the ground wasn't quaking.

I had wondered if those long looks Fyrel gave Gwyn were more than admiration. Though Gwyn's smug smirk hid it better, I could tell she cared for her too.

My stomach lurched. They were both so young, so full of life and hope. I couldn't help but be reminded of Brenna. Of the short time we'd spent whispering into each other's ears and hiding in the shadowed halls of the Order.

At least here they didn't have to hide if they didn't want to. But Fyrel's nervous shaking made it clear that was not a conversation she wanted to have. She picked at the corner of the book she was holding. I recognized it as one of the tomes Vrail had brought to the council.

Gwyn saw how I was dressed, and her face turned serious. "You're visiting the crypt?"

I nodded.

Gwyn's eyes narrowed as she looked up at my burl for the briefest moment before pointing to the closest winding branch of the Myram tree. "There's fresh food in the kitchen from lunch. I doubt she's eaten since yesterday."

"I'll go fetch something for her." I squinted at Fyrel's shoulder and stooped. I pulled the long piece of ribbon that Gwyn used to tie back her curls from the edge of her leathers. "I think this is yours." I passed it to Gwyn.

She smirked. "I was just looking for that," she said too sweetly.

Fyrel looked like she was about to vomit.

I headed to the stairs and heard Fyrel slide to the ground at the bottom of the trunk. "I told you it didn't fall out in the wind. We need to be more careful."

Gwyn's singsong laugh followed me all the way down the stairs.

I found Syrra in the lowest levels of Myrelinth. Only one tunnel led to the crypts. We were far into the Dark Wood, underneath layers of rock that pulsed with turquoise and silver light through its veins.

Stone petals bloomed along the cracks, filling the circular chamber with the fresh scent of river water and honey. With closed eyes, I could imagine that I was outside along the lake and not deep into the earth where it was cool enough to keep bodies before funeral rites were performed.

She had become a statue guarding her sister until then. In the dim light, the scars along her arms looked more like moss, dark and shadowed lichen that grew on stone standing still too long.

A haunted expression was carved forevermore on her face. I'd watched a part of her die the day I brought her sister home in my arms, only weeks after her miraculous return. Since then, the living part of Syrra had slowly begun to fade. Perhaps she truly was a tombstone and not a statue at all.

"The mission was a success," I said in way of a greeting. Even though Syrra's face did not move, I knew she'd heard me approach. "We saved a few dozen Halflings before a *waateyshir* came to Silstra. Well, we saved all but one."

I glanced around the room. Had the beast not turned Victoria's body to ash, I would have given her an Elvish funeral. She had certainly helped enough of us to deserve one.

But life so rarely gave justice to the deserving.

A blink was the only sign that Syrra had heard me. Her hands stayed tucked behind her back, and her eyes were locked on the wrapped linen that covered Maerhal's body. The Elverin had ways of preserving the body, but the longer Syrra waited, the longer Maerhal had to wait to be returned to the earth to join her ancestors.

Feron had wanted to light her pyre alongside Lash's, but Syrra had refused. She would not allow her sister to be buried without her son. It wasn't what Nikolai would have wanted. It was he who would wear her *diizra* and no one else.

My stomach clenched. I wasn't sure Nikolai was capable of wanting anything at all. I was certain he was alive, but that didn't give me any comfort. Damien was too cruel to those in his keep. He had more than one way to make a person wish for death and nothing else.

I fought the urge to run out of the room and fly from city to city until I could feel Nikolai under my feet, but that would be playing directly into Damien's hand. He wanted us fractured; he wanted our focus on our friend instead of our rebellion. He wanted us in a desperate frenzy, but I refused to play his game any longer.

I had trained my entire life for this. Balancing the hardest decisions, choosing between two false choices even though both ripped at my soul. Nikolai just needed to survive long enough for us to have a solid plan of attack.

I owed him that. I would keep my head even as the others lost theirs.

But it would be easier to do it with Syrra in fighting form.

"Feron told me about the Elvish warriors of old." I took a step closer to the stone slab Syrra guarded. "The first ones to fight the *waateyshirak*. The ones who started *Niikir'na* before the palace ever stood on the island."

Syrra's neck tensed but she still didn't speak.

"We need warriors like that again." I stood at the edge of the slab, turning myself so Syrra had no choice but to look at me. "We need you."

Her full lips were set into a frown I thought might be permanently etched into her face. Even her eyes seemed to droop at the corners. She was no longer an Elf, no longer a person, just a shell—and her shell was beginning to collapse.

Tears pooled at the corners of my eyes. She had been there when my sorrows lashed at me and wouldn't let go. She had found me, drowning in my guilt, and reached out her hand until I could breathe on my own again.

I tapped the backs of my fingers along the edge of the slab. It was my turn to find a way to reach her. But how did one make a statue breathe with hope?

"Syrra," I whispered, my desperation echoing against the stone walls. "You have waited long enough. There are so many who are still . . ."

That last word caught in my throat.

Syrra's head turned, curving toward me like the owls she found so frightening. "Alive?"

I nodded. "A warrior protects the living; she doesn't haunt the dead."

"She is not truly dead until her pyre is lit." Syrra's neck flexed. "Until then, my sister rests in the in-between." Her lip trembled.

The in-between was a cold cave, much too close to the hole Maerhal had spent the better part of her life in. She deserved a burial, to have her body turned to ash so it could grow again under the warmth of the sun and the cool of the rain. It was wrong to keep her underground another day.

My fingers turned to a fist along the stone. "Who will save the Elverin if their leaders are caught between grief and hope?"

Syrra scoffed. "I am not certain there is any hope left."

I tapped my fingers again. What good would it do to admit to her that I struggled with the same fear, that each day I woke with a mountain on my chest, burying me under the weight of everything we had to lose, and I was nothing but fractured pieces waiting to fall, praying that the war ended before I did.

I took a deep breath. The damp air smelled of earth and spring water. "If we don't continue the fight, then Maerhal and Lash died for nothing."

Syrra's dark eyes cut to me.

"They died believing that Elverath would be ours again." I lifted my chin to keep my voice from breaking. "They died with the same dream we all had. Of our freedom and our magic, returned to us."

A tear welled along Syrra's bottom lash. I watched it swell and fall onto her cheek, leaving a river of grief along her skin.

She lifted her chin and the tear fell to the ground. "I no longer believe that dream is worth all this suffering."

My heart tore as I reached for her hand. Her skin was cold like stone.

I opened my mouth, but no words came. I had been so sure that breaking that last seal would solve all our problems. I was not thinking of the army that waited for us in every major city. The battles still left to fight, the losses still to come. I had moved forward, focused on one singular goal, but now that the seals were broken and there was still so much left to do, I couldn't help but wonder if Syrra was right.

Had this fight been worth it at all?

CHAPTER EIGHT

RIVEN WAITED FOR ME at the end of the long tunnel that led to the crypt. A small faelight danced around his shoulder and I stilled. He stood in the shadows of the tunnel, and for a moment I thought his powers had returned. His face was that of the Fae I had come to know, come to love, everything exactly the same except for the violet eyes that were now an unmistakable royal green, the only thing left of Killian, his other self. The part of him that had been a lie.

This was the first time I had allowed myself to just look at him.

The new Riven.

The true Riven.

The Halfling with no secrets left to hide behind.

I cast a ball of wind and pushed him into the wall. "I'm not in the mood for conversation."

"There are a thousand different problems raining down on your head, Keera." Riven kept his back against the root-packed earth, but his shoulders curved toward me like a bow around its arrow. "The right mood will never find you. You keep yourself too busy for it to catch up."

"And why is that, Riven?" My words were so hot they stung the dry patches of my lips. "It couldn't be that this rebellion was once led by a council yet I am the *only* one at my post. Nikolai is captured, Vrail and Syrra are too sick with grief to be useful in meetings let alone do their duties, there was a prince who was handling his fair share for a time, but it seems he never truly existed and his real identity *fled*." I'd stalked so close to Riven that I could hear his pulse quicken in his throat. "Perhaps I am busy because everything has fallen to *me*."

Riven's jaw pulsed. "You're right. I'm sorry. I didn't know that I was leaving you with so little support."

I scoffed. "Of course you didn't. You abandoned us. You abandoned me."

There was a surprised gasp at the turn of the tunnel. The outline of three Halflings was visible by their shared faelight. They scurried backward to give us our privacy, but I just started walking down the tunnel.

Riven matched my pace. He grabbed my hand and pulled me right along a fork. We walked in silence until we reached Killian's—Riven's—bedroom door. He yanked open the stone without hesitation and held up an arm for me to go inside.

I looked at it for a long minute. I had a dozen other things I should have been doing, but being distracted by Riven would keep me from doing them well.

Better to get the conversation over with.

I hadn't stepped foot into the bedroom since knowing the truth. There was a coldness to the bed and stacks of books along the floor. Did Riven ever sleep here during his ruse? Or was this just another place for Vrail to spend her nights, glamoured and reading until dawn?

Riven bit his lip. He leaned against the tall bedpost. "The books are mine. I do like to read. I did a lot as a boy, and I still try now."

I swallowed. "Glad to know at least that wasn't part of the lie." There was an edge to the words I couldn't dull. I wasn't sure why I cared. Riven had never presented himself as the bookish one, that was reserved only for Killian.

He had always told me as much of the truth as he could. But now it was my job to stitch those truths together into one form. Like the blanket covering his mattress, violet and jade sewn together with a seam down the middle.

"Did Syrra agree to attend the meeting tomorrow?" Riven's hand hung oddly at his side, caught between stretching and resting.

I leaned against the hardness of his door, keeping as much space between us as possible. "I didn't ask." My jaw pulsed. "She won't leave her sister's side."

Riven's head jolted back. His long black hair spooled over his shoulder, released from his usual half braid. "She didn't care that Nikolai is alive?"

I pocketed my tongue in my cheek and twisted my boot along the ground.

"You didn't tell her?"

"She's a wreck, Riven." My voice cracked as I spoke. "She doesn't have a little hope left—she has none. I'm not going to stoke a dead flame until I have something tangible to give her."

Riven crossed his arms. "She deserves to know."

"She deserves to have a sister who isn't dead!" The words passed my lips before I could think better of them.

Riven recoiled like I had punched him in the jaw. "You do blame me, then?" The rasp in his tone was brooding, dangerous. I felt like a rabbit being circled by a fox, and I didn't know from which direction its pounce would come.

"This has never been about blame, Riven." I slumped against the back of the door and let my body sink to the ground. "I can understand the choice you made and still be angry for what happened."

"Angry at me?" Riven swallowed. "You're angry at me." It wasn't a question but a resigned statement. His sharp features fell flat along his face, like he had been waiting for me to admit just that.

"Yes," I whispered. I wiped my sleeve across my cheek to catch the tears. My throat burned with the need for wine, and my body ached so badly I knew a week's rest wouldn't alleviate it fully. "I'm angry at you for the lie. I'm angry at Damien for the game he played. I'm angry at Feron for not telling me, and I'm angry at Nik, and Vrail, and Syrra for that too. I'm angry that everyone has their part in this, but I'm the only one still fighting."

"I was looking for Nik!" Riven's fangs glinted in the silvery glow of the faelight.

I rolled my eyes. "You left because it was easier. Because it's what you do. You make decisions for people. You decide what they'll think, how they'll feel, and you leave because you can't bear to be proven right."

Riven blinked. "I was always coming back. I would never leave you."

"You didn't stay an hour after we made it back to Aralinth." I huffed a laugh. "You didn't even tell me where you were going."

Riven's mouth snapped shut. He drummed his finger along the post as his jaw pulsed. "I knew what you were going to say."

"No, you didn't." I leaned my head back against the stone. "But enlighten me, my prince. Since you know my mind better than I do."

Riven's brow cast a shadow over his eyes at the mention of his title. For a moment it was almost like his powers had returned. "That you regret it. That without my death hanging overhead, the truth was too much for you to truly forgive. Everything looked different when we made it back. Everything *is* different."

I stood even though the bones in my legs felt like sand. "Regret forgiving you? Or loving you?"

Riven winced. "Both."

It was the most heartbreaking word I'd ever heard.

I walked over to the bed and sat down on the plush mattress. Riven didn't move. His body was rigid, the same way he would be whenever his magic caused him more pain than usual. His brow still twitched even though his powers were gone. The weight of his regrets was more painful than any magic could be.

For the first time since it had been severed, I wished for our bond. That my touch could keep that pain at bay for just a moment. But maybe Elverath had known better when she gave Riven back his life, not as a Fae or Mortal, but as a Halfling. Without the pain of his magic to distract him, he could finally face the pain of his legacy of lies.

I knew better than anyone that journey had to be led by oneself.

I pressed my head against the post Riven had been leaning on. "I chose you." Tears pooled along my lashes, but they didn't fall. "When Damien offered me that deal—Maerhal or you. I chose *you*. Even though I *promised* Nikolai to bring his mother back to him. I made that choice without a second thought."

"If you had known the truth—"

"Stop." I waved my hand through the air and sent a blast of wind into Riven's chest. He slid back against the wall, and his jaw snapped shut.

I pulled myself to the end of the bed. "You do not get to diminish my choice because you regret yours. You kept the truth of your identity a secret, and it cost you. It cost *us*. But that doesn't change that I *chose* you, Riven."

A tear streamed down his face. "I didn't deserve it."

"But I do!" My words echoed against the hard stone of the room. "That choice was taken from me once before." I lifted the arm with Brenna's name etched into the skin. "She didn't give me a choice. I would have plunged that dagger into my own heart a thousand times for her. I would have killed a thousand people to save her, but she took that choice away." The image of Brenna's poison-stained lips flashed across my mind as if I were still trapped inside that moment. As if I were realizing that she was already dead all over again. I cleared my throat and met Riven's hard gaze. "I've had to live with that. I have loved her and resented her for thirty years. I deserved a choice then just as I deserve a choice now—I *earned* it. And I chose you."

Riven's lip trembled but he didn't say anything.

I stood. I had no fight left for this anymore. "You want to earn my forgiveness? You want to make it right? Make it so that choice doesn't go to waste?"

Riven still didn't speak. I turned to leave, I did not have it in me to fight for the both of us. I was almost at the door when Riven's rasp broke the silence. "What if I can't live with that choice? Yours and mine? What if I never get past this?" His jade eyes swam in a pool of tears as I turned back to face him.

I shrugged. I didn't have the answer any more than he did. "You either find a way, or you let it consume you. That choice is yours."

Riven retreated further into himself. His shoulders slumped forward, protecting him, and for the first time I saw the young prince that he had once been.

"You told me once, in Koratha, that you believed you inherited your father's legacy, and it was on you to end the Crown. At whatever cost." I'd thought I had been speaking to the prince about the weight of his crown, but knowing the truth now, it was so easy to see that the Crown never left Riven's head no matter what face he wore. "You said it to me as Killian, but what does it mean for Riven?"

"It changes nothing."

"Doesn't it?" I waved my hand around the room that was very much *not* the kingdom. "Your father came to these lands to conquer the Elverin for his own gain. He killed entire bloodlines that will never resurface."

"I know." His jaw pulsed. "You learned the stories from your tutors at the Order and then from the knowledge keepers here, but I was *four*, hearing my father boast about it over a flank and flagon of wine." Riven's lip pulled back over his fangs.

"If it disgusts you so much, then why do you let your father do the same to you?"

Riven stilled. "What do you mean?"

"You speak of your grand legacy. You give so much credence to your lineage under the Crown, but doesn't your mother deserve just as much? Are you not the son of Laethellia Numenthira just as much as you are Aemon's? Perhaps even more so, since you fight for her kin and not his."

Riven's jaw hung slack.

I swallowed. So much of I wanted to say stormed inside me. For Riven, but also for the younger version of me who ran from my troubles at every chance she got. The hard truths I'd come to learn had to be shared. I owed it to that young girl who was left in the Rift. "You exist because of this war, Riven. And as such, you have been dealt choices no one else has had to make. You will—you have—made mistakes. If you keep running from them, you will always wrestle with that anger. And the others you make angry. But the truth is that you can only do one thing as you move forward."

His word was barely a whisper. "What?"

"Choose better next time. Choose right, one day at a time. Day by day."

Riven picked at the skin around his thumb. "I'm not sure my decisions can be trusted."

"No leader is." My words were heavy but tasted true enough.

Riven bit his cheek and pushed off from the wall as my gust faded. "I am sorry, for leaving like I did." He shifted to step closer to me but then thought better of it. "I know you say you can forgive me, but . . ." Riven paused. "I don't know if I can let you."

His words pierced my belly like a sword, but they did not twist. A clean cut, something that could heal well with enough time and care.

I was willing to give Riven both as long as he kept being honest.

"Okay." I nodded. "The two sides of this war live inside you just as they live on this land, Riven. There's nowhere in the world you could run to hide from that truth. But maybe if you stop running, you'll find that others do not find your truth nearly as frightening as you do."

"And what if I can't?" Riven looked down at the ground. His staying in Myrelinth meant that he would have to come clean about his secret to everyone.

I opened the door and told him the truth he needed to hear. "Then the war will claim you. And likely all who follow you into battle."

Gerarda stood in the grand hall of the lower city when I walked through. The rescued Halflings were trying on the remaining clothes from the selection Nikolai and Dynara had organized weeks prior. My heart tore with guilt seeing their smiles; both of my friends should have witnessed that joy.

"The scouts have been informed and so have the remaining Fae." Gerarda walked at full speed to keep up with my stride. "At least one adult from every dwelling will stay up overnight to respond to any emergencies. And those without immediate kin have been sorted into groups of six."

I grabbed a leaf pad and threw it on top of a large faelight. "Good work." I nodded at the floating orb. "Jump on. I need to grab my weapons belt before we head out on patrol."

Gerarda's lips pursed. She preferred to walk up the height of the Myram than ride a floating ball of light through its hollow center. But she nodded and climbed to one side. "Feron and Darythir have secured Aralinth, and we have informed all residents that no one is allowed to leave the cities after dusk. Even to harvest."

My scoff was silenced by the rush of wind as the faelight caught the current and we were launched toward the upper burls. "Rheih must not be happy."

Gerarda didn't answer. She just shook her head while holding onto the leaf with all her might.

I stepped off the faelight with ease. "I want Gwyn and Fyrel to join you on patrol." I turned as Gerarda slid off the faelight like a cautious cat. I coughed to hide my grin. "Though perhaps we should separate them. Fyrel seems a bit *distracted.* Maybe she should patrol with me."

Gerarda chuckled and nodded. "I've noticed too."

I walked into my burl, ignoring the piles of reports and discarded clothes I hadn't had time to clean. I pulled on my weapons belt and froze.

My dagger was missing.

"What is it?" Gerarda asked when I spun around and started rifling through the sheets.

"My dagger"—I lifted up a pile of dirty clothes—"it's not here."

Gerarda crossed her arms. "If you keep your weapons in the same state as your chambers, this can't be the first time you've misplaced it."

"I don't *misplace* my dagger."

"I took it from you once, and you didn't notice for an entire day."

I shot her a look over my shoulder. "I also had a casket of wine in my belly when you took it—" I stopped mid-sentence as I spied a thin, green ribbon on the ground.

"Damn it." I ran out the door and leaped from the bridge of tangled branches to the grove below. I held out my hand and brought a vine to it.

Elaran staggered out of the way as I landed. "If you wanted to wrestle, Keera, you should've just asked." She shot me a demure smile from where I had rolled on the ground.

I ignored her. "Have you seen them?"

Elaran's smile turned serious at once. "Who?" she asked, already pulling her curls back into her signature twist.

"Gwyn and Fyrel."

Gerarda landed beside me.

"They said they were going to the training field—" Elaran's words went silent in a flash of light. I flew across the city, my eyes darting through the groves looking for red hair or a long brown braid, but I saw neither.

I transformed at the top of the training field and ran inside the equipment room.

"They took two spears, a bow and quiver each, and seven blades between them," I said when Gerarda and Elaran reached me. I grabbed two blades from the wall along with a harness. I didn't have time to go back to my burl.

The portals would be shifting in less than an hour.

"You're sure they took it?" Gerarda asked, loading her own weapons.

Elaran grabbed blades too. "Who took what?"

Gerarda slipped a thin, long blade into the leather slit along her forearm. "Keera's dagger."

Elaran blinked once and then her mouth fell open. "It's bloodbound." She turned to Gerarda. "They couldn't be that stupid?"

Gerarda shrugged. "I would have done anything as an initiate to prove myself."

My worries came crashing down, squeezing my chest until I couldn't breathe. Gerarda was right. Newly honed skills and untested confidence was a deadly combination.

The same combination that convinced me that Brenna and I alone could topple the Crown. The combination that had sent Gwyn and Fyrel north of the Burning Mountains to kill the *waateyshir*.

I grabbed a vial of *winvra* berries from the supply closet and ran toward the portal. I did the math in my head; it was quicker to reach them through the portals than to fly, but we had to leave now.

If I didn't get there in time, Gwyn was going to die.

CHAPTER NINE

GERARDA AND ELARAN HAD THE SENSE to grab horses while I ran on foot to the north side of the lake. Old portals had reawakened when the last seal broke. I only hoped that Gwyn had not taken the time to learn the new paths and that we could catch up with them before they did anything foolish.

Gerarda and Elaran charged at full speed toward two twin rocks that stood touching each other at the top. Gerarda pulled a vial of *winvra* from her pocket and pulled the cork out with her teeth. She dropped the reins of the horse meant for me, and I leaped onto the saddle mid-run, galloping behind them as they ran through the glowing water and into the snowy mountain tops along the southern ridge.

"This way," I shouted, pointing along a winding path that continued south. It was the opposite direction of Gwyn and Fyrel, but at the end of it was a portal that opened along the northern shore of the *Faelinth*.

We just had to reach it before dusk.

I used my fire powers to melt the snow so our horses could run as fast as possible along the mountainous terrain. It was cold, but I used my magic to divert the winds. Our limbs were not completely turned to ice under our clothes.

Orange streaks painted the sky. If we didn't reach the portal soon, I would abandon Elaran and Gerarda and fly through it on my own.

"The scouts reported the beast making a nest along the eastern foothills. The note mentioned a cave," Gerarda shouted over the steady rhythm of hoofbeats.

I knew of it. I hadn't had a chance to visit every rebellion safe house, but Tarvelle's maps had only marked one location this far north. A small cave they would use to rest in while ferrying Halflings across the northern channel instead of through the Burning Mountains.

But as far as I knew, it was glamoured. Gwyn and Fyrel wouldn't know it was there. They wouldn't be able to run to it if they needed to hide.

My stomach was a hard rock, tugging at my ribs with every step my horse took. Then a large stony arch came into view. It was made of the mountain itself, no seams or cracks along the stone, a relic of an earth wielder's magic from long ago.

The veil of water shimmered in the light of the setting suns. We only had minutes until the portals changed from their sunlit paths to their starlit ones.

I yanked on the reins, and my horse slowed to a walk. I tossed enough *winvra* into the water for us all to pass. I held up a fist and ran through first.

Salt filled my lungs. A cold and briny wind passed through the Elder birch trunks. They were thinner here than in the southern parts of the Dark Wood. Even with the new foliage covering the ground, you could see far into the wood.

There was no sign of Gwyn or the *waateyshir*.

I slipped off the saddle and tied my horse along one of the lower branches. The others did the same, our horses happy for the rest after running so long. I called the warmth of my healing magic forward and let it run over each of them, soothing the aches in their legs until all three were happily grazing along the ground.

I pulled out my blades and nodded south. "We will come to a glamoured cave. I've never been there, but Riven told me it opens like a mouth along the edge of the mountain. That should be enough for the glamour to break."

Gerarda and Elaran nodded. The latter took her bow and walked thirty paces to the right of me while Gerarda did the same on the left. We marched forward as a unit, crouching and checking the skies every few feet.

The first stars dotted the deep blue skies. The only light left was along the horizon, but with the coverage of the forest it was already dark.

Dark enough for the *waateyshir* to fly.

We came to a small hill and the salty breeze went dead. I could no longer smell the ocean at all. Only sulfur and ash. I looked down at my boot and the white sprinkling of snow had turned dark. The shrubbery was burnt and black like a fire had blazed through this part of the forest.

The *waateyshir* was close.

A piercing cry split the air. I no longer cared about being cautious. I ran over the hilltop and saw the shadowy creature stretching its long neck and taking flight.

"Gwyn!" Panic shredded through my voice. "Fyrel!"

I was answered by a scream. It wasn't a shriek of fear, but a battle cry.

On the other side of the burnt grove, a small flame grew. My shoulders stiffened, my blades suspended midair, as I realized what it was.

Fyrel ran at full speed with a flaming torch above her head. Behind her were the flapping wings of a second *waateyshir*.

Fyrel did not look back but charged forward. She didn't even shift direction to evade a potential attack.

She wasn't using the torch to defend herself. The shadowy beast wasn't chasing her. She was luring it.

Fyrel was the bait.

The other beast shrieked from the clouds. It circled, watching its kin chase Fyrel. I ran toward the Halfling as the beast behind her reared back its long neck. Smoke and ash leaked from its open beak. The stench of rotting flesh and burnt meat seared my nostrils, but I kept running.

It stretched its wings, lifting its chest upward, and I saw it.

The red glow in the beast's chest flared. Fyrel had seconds until it attacked.

"Move!" I begged at the top of my lungs. To Fyrel, to the beast, to the ground underneath her feet. But none did.

Stray strands of hair blew across my face as the beast took in a deep breath. The liquid black flames spurted from its mouth directly at Fyrel's back.

I called forth as large a gust as I could muster but it did nothing against the stream of black, magical flame. My heart hammered against my chest. I was about to watch Fyrel's bones turn to ash.

A flash of brown swooped in front of the girl just as the black flames licked her ankles. Fyrel fell to the ground, rolling far enough to stamp out the flames crawling up her cloak.

Gerarda shrieked with a desperation I had never heard from her before.

Elaran stood with four arrows nocked along her bow as the beast reared back its neck once more.

Gerarda ran toward her, but there wasn't enough time. Elaran loosed the arrows, and I set the tips of each aflame.

The *waateyshir* shrieked as one passed through its wing. It stopped its attack, flying high enough into the air to get out of reach of Elaran's bow.

Elaran dropped to the ground. The bottom of her pants were singed away, and her skin was blistered and black.

Gerarda slid on her knees and stroked Elaran's hairline as she winced. She pulled a vial from her pocket and dropped some black liquid onto Elaran's parted lips. Hot tears streamed down her face as she whispered, "You foolish woman. You could've died."

Elaran patted her palm against her lover's cheek. "You can't be a hero worth talking about without a little risk, Gerrie."

Gerarda scowled but pressed a kiss to Elaran's head.

I pulled Fyrel to her feet and scanned the ground. There wasn't a red curl in sight.

"Where is she?" I yelled over the sound of my own racing heart.

Fyrel didn't answer, her voice paralyzed from shock. There was no color left in her eyes, only wide black pupils that looked upward to the cliff's edge above us.

The two *waateyshirak* were circling the edge together, staring down at Gwyn, who stood at the top of a small abutment. She held a spear in her hands.

Gwyn held the pointed end to the ground. The blunt end of the handle was wrapped in tight leather binding it to the hilt of my dagger. A makeshift spear with a blood-bound point.

Gwyn was going to try to stab it through the beast's heart.

Her stance was strong, but the arm holding the weapon shook. She hadn't anticipated a second beast.

The largest of the two tilted its head, staring down at Gwyn like a bird watching a worm in the dirt.

"Gwyn, run!" I shouted, and then disappeared in a flash of light.

The beasts' heads snapped toward the ground at the disturbance. My pleas for Gwyn to run became high-pitched eagle calls, and my wings beat as hard as they could.

I soared through the middle of the shadowy circle. Their tendrils of ash burned my feathers as I flew, but the *waateyshirak* took the bait.

A thunderous screech echoed through the trees as they both beat their wings hard enough that the leaves below them shook free of their branches.

I looked down. Both beasts were following me, the smaller trailing after its larger kin. My eagle eyes spotted Gwyn, climbing down the rocky edge with her spear in hand.

We rose above the lowest peaks of the mountain, and a horn blew in the distance. The *waateyshir* closest to me whirled around at the noise. A large flame ignited along the eastern edge of the mountain.

A warning pyre.

The beast flew toward it, and my heartbeat slowed along with my wing beats. I looked down, expecting to see the smaller one following me too, but its attention had been caught by something below.

Gwyn slipped along the rock face. Amber blood covered her arm. The sharp inhale from the creature sounded like thunder in the distance—it could smell her blood.

It didn't wait to attack. Its large wings stretched as it circled to dive.

I dove first.

Its hot breath pulled at my tail feathers as it inhaled, preparing to strike.

I transformed mid-fall. The beast snapped at the flash of light and then reared back as I sent a spiral of flame toward it.

It opened its wings enough to evade the attack. The forest went silent as I fell toward the ground. I looked for Gwyn and saw that she was running.

Not away from the beast, but toward it.

It reared back and the red, pulsing glow in its chest burned brighter. But that was just what Gwyn had wanted. She leaped from the cliff's edge, spear above her head. Her legs circled underneath her, propelling her as close to the beast as possible.

Black smoke pooled from its mouth as Gwyn hurled the spear toward the red, pulsing light. I transformed again and let my wings catch me as I watched the spear cut through the beast. Just short of its heart.

Black shadow leaked from the slice like blood in water. I didn't have time to wonder how such a shapeless thing could bleed. I reached out for Gwyn's leg with my talons. Her body lurched but there was no time to be gentle. The makeshift spear fell to the ground.

The *waateyshir* roared above us as I dropped Gwyn on the forest floor.

I curved through the air like a blade and the beast followed, swooping low enough to burn the tops of the trees with its smoky wings. It snapped at me, but I found the strength to keep myself just out of reach.

"Keera!" Gerarda shouted from below. I glanced and saw that she was cutting my blade free from the spear. She mimed a throw, and I knew we would only have one shot at it.

I let out a high-pitched call and lured the beast higher. Then I dove back toward the ground.

The beast snapped at me again, its hot breath burning the skin on my small legs as I stayed tucked. I plummeted to the ground and Gerarda's frame grew larger. She kissed the hilt of the dagger, holding it by the red blade, and I transformed once more.

The beast reared at the flash of light.

Gerarda snapped her wrist.

I hit the ground. My shoulder and leg snapped as my bones broke, but I didn't hear it. All anyone could hear for a hundred leagues was the shriek of the shadowy creature as the blade shot through its red center. Liquid shadow oozed from the wound and then the beast exploded into a cloud of black ash. My bloodred dagger sank to the ground, its job done. The wounded *waateyshir* roared at the sight and flew over the trees, leaving us and our weapon behind.

Gerarda ran over to me. Amber blood coated her cheeks, but it wasn't hers. I looked for Gwyn, but then a piercing pain shot through my body as Gerarda popped my shoulder back into place.

"Fuck!" I shouted loud enough for my lungs to ache. "What are you doing?"

Gerarda cocked her jaw to the side and pressed into my femur with unnecessary vigor. "Saving your ass, as usual."

The pain was too much for me to roll my eyes. Gerarda grabbed my ankle and twisted. I screamed until my vision blurred.

"That was the last of them." Gerarda held out her hand to me, assessing my newly unbroken body.

I looked at it incredulously. "You expect me to walk on a broken femur."

Gerarda gave my leg a hard pat. I winced but it felt like pain from a bad bruise, not an open fracture. My healing gift now had incredible speed. Magic flared hot under my skin. I didn't feel tired, yet my control was slipping, like there were too many gifts fighting inside my body for release.

"You're the one who decided plummeting to your death was necessary." She stood and wiped her hands on her pants. "Apparently I'm the only one with any sense."

A shriek sounded in the distance. Gerarda and I both froze, waiting for the sound of giant wings, but it did not come. She nodded at the cave, cut into the mountain. "We can hide there until morning. You likely won't be done yelling by then anyway."

CHAPTER TEN

MY NOSTRILS FLARED with steaming breath that dried my lips to the point of cracking. It was as if I had transformed into a beast of fire and ash as I paced in front of the two runaways. The aches in my leg and shoulder no longer existed. All I could focus on was Gwyn and Fyrel huddled up together on the floor.

"You could have been killed!" My voice boomed against the cavern walls. The flames of the fire Gerarda had made twitched and sparked higher for a moment. "What possessed you to go after the *waateyshirak* on your own? With no plan and no backup?"

Fyrel bowed her head. Her own chest was heaving just as much as mine was. At least she had been scared into seeing sense, but Gwyn leaned against the wall, perfectly calm.

She crossed her arms. "We had a plan."

"To lure a beast toward you and fling a spear at it?" Outside, a flock of birds took flight as the sky cracked with a bolt of lightning. I took a deep breath. My rage was overwhelming my powers. My control was a thin thread, stretched and ready to snap.

Gerarda placed a hand on my shoulder. "They're fools"—she shot a disappointed look at both, and only then did Gwyn have the decency to blush—"but they're alive."

A half sob, half grunt ripped from my chest.

Gwyn's hard mouth softened. Fyrel stared at the ground unable to look at me. I just wanted to go a week—*one week*—without the threat of losing someone close to me.

Elaran lifted her chin. She stood on one leg, the other too burned to take her weight. I didn't want to try to heal the skin until Feron and Rheih could inspect it. I'd learned my lesson with Maerhal. Her brow tremored with pain and annoyance at the girls. "Tell us why we shouldn't strip you both of your weapons and never let you join a mission again."

Fyrel's bottom lip quivered but her back straightened against the rock. "We were wrong. We'll accept whatever punishment you see fit."

"No, we fucking won't." Gwyn turned with a look of disgust on her face then snapped her head to me. "At least we were willing to find a way to destroy those creatures."

I chucked what was left of the spear at her feet. "With a makeshift weapon you didn't know would work?"

"But it did."

"She has a point," Gerarda mumbled.

"And yet she wasn't the one who killed the beast. You did." I turned back to Gwyn. "I know you have more sense than this."

"Sense?" Gwyn stood. "Sense to try to fight back instead of hiding in the *Faelinth* while Damien adds more swords to his armies?

I heard you in the meeting room. The *waateyshir* was an obstacle. I was taking care of it."

I pointed at Fyrel's burnt clothes and Elaran's charred leg. "Does that look taken care of to you? You didn't even know if my dagger would work on the *waateyshir*."

"I'm not a complete fool." Gwyn crossed her arms. "I've listened to the stories of Faelin too. She struck down dozens of beasts with her sword. So did the other warriors of *Niikir'na* with their weapons."

I ran my hand through my braid, pulling strands loose that stuck to my sweaty skin like leaches. "Faelin's sword is hanging in pieces in Aralinth. Not to mention the blade is ten times the length of this. And all the others have been lost."

Gwyn's brows creased. "But they were all blood-bound blades. Like yours." She nodded at the dagger lying atop my discarded cloak.

I paused. "You left because you thought a blood-bound blade would kill the beast? Or because you overheard Vrail's untested assumption?

"I *knew* a blood-bound blade would kill it." Gwyn crossed her arms. "And thanks to me, now you all know too."

Gerarda gave a grunt of a laugh. "I think you mean thanks to me."

"Either way." Gwyn scowled as she shrugged. "We know how to kill them now."

I rubbed my brow. "One blade against all the *waateyshirak* is not a plan. We need more weapons than that." My fists shook at my sides as my magic surged to a mountainous peak. I spoke through gritted teeth. "Why not bring your theory to me instead of going out on your own? Your actions almost cost five lives tonight."

Gwyn pinched her arm and pursed her mouth to the side. I stooped and put my hands on her shoulders as gently as I could manage with the magic coursing through me.

Her blue eyes were misted but hard. "You have been so busy and this was just one more thing for you to deal with."

My heart ached. "Gwyn, you needn't worry about that."

"But I do!" Gwyn knocked my arms off her. "The more things distracting you, the longer it takes for us to attack Damien. I'm not some burden that you need to coddle, Keera. I'm not that little girl who used to cry in your chambers anymore. I've fought soldiers and won. I almost killed a *waateyshir* tonight. *That's* what I want. I want to fight. I *need* to fight. I just want this to end."

My entire body shook with anger. Not at Gwyn, but at seeing the same rage that had taken hold of me my entire life come to claim her too. I never wanted to pass on that rage to the next generation of Halflings. They deserved a legacy of hope and peace, to love freely without the shadow of the king haunting their dreams. My hands clenched at my sides as my emotions reached a heated peak to match the swell of my magic.

"Gwyn, you are not and have never been a burden." I choked on the words. My hold on my gifts was waning, but Gwyn needed to hear this. "I've *never* thought that."

A tear welled at the corner of her eye. She reached her hand out for me, but I stepped back. "Don't touch me." My voice shook enough for Gerarda to step between me and Elaran.

"Keera, your eyes."

I didn't need a looking glass to know they were glowing.

They were burning.

Some new kind of power thrashed underneath my skin. It didn't scorch like a burnout, but instead itched like a thousand tiny bugs were burrowing under my skin, vying to get out.

I had no idea what would happen when my hold broke.

I ran out of the cave. The snow cooled my skin but did nothing to damper the competing powers inside my chest.

Gwyn followed me, her face stark with worry as she ripped herself from Fyrel's grasp.

“Keera, I’m sorry!” she shouted through the snowfall.

“Stay back!” I turned with my arm stretched out toward her. There was a loud crack. But no lightning shot from the cloudless sky. Instead a golden bolt shot through my hand and hit Gwyn square in the chest.

The itching ceased but I barely noticed.

Time seemed to stretch. Gwyn crumpled to the ground like a feather, lazily falling until she folded onto the burnt snow. Unmoving.

I screamed at the ground, and the trees behind me burst into flames while the forest floor froze to ice. Above me, large storm clouds appeared, whirling in giant circles as I let my magic drain from me. These gifts were not just overwhelming; they were dangerous.

I was dangerous.

I needed to dull myself.

“Is she dead?” I screeched as a towering wall of stone lifted from the earth and fell back onto the flames, smothering them along with the heightened stores of my magic. I fell forward onto my knees, trying to catch my breath. I couldn’t look at Gwyn’s lifeless body. I just froze, letting fat tears fall onto my bloodied hands.

Gerarda and Elaran ran to Gwyn, pulling her onto Elaran’s lap. From the sideline of my vision, I saw Elaran press her ear to Gwyn’s chest while Gerarda felt for a pulse along her neck.

“She’s alive, Keera,” Gerarda shouted over the storm that my magic had stoked. Lightning flashed in the clouds and a thunderous boom followed a moment later.

My arms collapsed, and my face smacked into the ground with relief. I pushed myself onto my feet, needing to see Gwyn for myself. I slid across the ice and pulled her body onto my lap.

I cupped her cheek in my hand. “Gwyn, I’m so sorry.” I sobbed. “Gwyn, can you hear me? Let me heal you.”

Her hand lifted to mine and I gasped. Her palms were worn and blistered as they had been before, but now her long fingers were radiating with bright light. She tapped the back of my hand and a thin line carved through the air, like a rock marking glass. It lingered for a moment and then faded into nothing, like leaves blowing away on the wind.

"Gwyn?" I turned to Gerarda and Elaran to make sure they were seeing this too.

Gwyn shifted on my lap, and Elaran stepped back in shock.

I turned and saw that Gwyn was already looking up at me.

Her eyes were no longer blue.

They were amber.

CHAPTER ELEVEN

"Don't move!" The warm flow of my healing magic surged forward as I grasped Gwyn's hand. Apart from the bruise that was disappearing in front of my eyes, there was nothing wrong with her. She was perfectly healthy—no, vibrant. Gwyn's body pulsed with a strength I'd never felt in her before. My magic hummed at her touch, the warmth extending down the rest of me.

I blinked. The strength was intoxicating.

"How do you feel?" I asked in awe.

Gwyn looked at her hand again. Her fingers were no longer glowing but she stared at them anyway. "Like I won't need to sleep for days." She snapped her hand into a fist and then unfurled it, the glow returning to her fingertips. "There's something warm and tingling under my skin. I can feel it move and shift."

I dropped my arm. I didn't need to touch her skin to know what that feeling was. "Magic."

Gwyn's newly amber eyes flared bright around the pupils as if the magic pulsing inside her recognized the word.

Gwyn was Fae.

I turned to the others. "I've never heard of amber-eyed Fae before."

Gerarda and Elaran just shrugged as Fyrel tentatively reached out to touch Gwyn's hand. I held my breath, waiting for something to happen, but the glow along her fingertips dissipated as she laced her fingers through Fyrel's.

Gwyn pulled her closer and grabbed the Elvish dagger from Fyrel's weapons belt. She gasped as she saw her eyes in the steel for the very first time.

"How is this possible?" she whispered.

Elaran leaned on the wall with her long arms crossed. "Syrra was right that day you broke the seal. You're a *niinokwenar*, Keera."

I scoffed. "The Faemothers birthed new Fae; they didn't turn Elverin into them." Though something deep in my belly rumbled with fear. Even Feron had thought my eyes turning gold had meant something more than unlocking all my gifts.

"Faelin did not give birth to her daughters," Gerarda reminded me. "She prayed to Elverath to gift her with children, and she woke from her sleep with two babes."

My skin prickled. There were not enough Fae to ensure a win against each of Damien's cities. And I was not going to birth a new generation of Fae fighters to end the Crown. But creating them? That was a power of untold strength.

A power that scared me more than anything else in my life.

"Since when do you believe in children's stories?" I shot over my shoulder.

Gerarda flung the knife in her hand across the cave. The hilt vibrated as it sunk into the rock. "Since when do you have gold eyes and can turn Halflings into Fae?"

I opened my mouth to argue, but Fyrel's panicked gasp made me turn back to Gwyn.

She pressed a dagger to the soft skin of her forearm. I reached for it, but not before she sliced through her flesh and a line of blood dripped down her arm.

Her blood was still amber but shimmered, unmistakably, with gold.

I stood and grabbed the blade Gerarda had thrown at the wall. I sliced a thin line across my own palm. I had just bled amber onto the snow, but now my blood shifted with the same golden glow as Gwyn's. Slowly the glow of my blood faded as my skin healed but Gwyn's remained.

"Fae bleed red," Elaran murmured. "Halflings bleed amber."

Fyrel cut the sleeve of her tunic and wrapped it around Gwyn's arm. Gwyn looked up at me through her curls. "Then what am I?"

Elaran tilted her head to the side, staring at Gwyn with a newfound curiosity that made me nervous. She was not a warrior studying a comrade, or a woman gazing at a young girl; she was a general smiling as the tides of war shifted in her favor.

That fear taking root in my belly burst as Elaran said the truth aloud.

"Something entirely new."

CHAPTER TWELVE

"We need more firewood." I turned to Gerarda. "You can help. We're the only ones not injured."

Gwyn straightened. "I'm not injured!"

"We don't know what you are." I crossed my arms. "But haven't you done enough for one night?"

Fyrel had the good sense to pull Gwyn back to the ground and passed her some of the nuts and dried meat Elaran had found left at the back of the cave.

"Gerarda." I pasted a smile on my face that I hoped was natural enough to avoid suspicion.

She pocketed her knife and stood. "I doubt we'll need two armfuls to make it through the night."

I raised a brow and looked down at her small frame. "Your arms aren't long enough to carry a full load, are they?"

Gerarda jumped into the air from a standstill. She flipped over my head and grasped my shoulders, using the momentum to pull me to the ground as she landed on her feet.

"They're long enough to do that." She smirked and held out her hand to pull me up.

I grabbed for it, but she pulled it back with lightning speed and her smirk grew. A chorus of laughter covered my grumbling as I marched out of the cave. I didn't say anything to Gerarda, but she was on me as soon as we stepped out of earshot.

"You're a terrible liar."

I raised a brow.

Gerarda leaned against one of the Elder birches that hadn't been burned in the fight with the *waateyshirak*. "You wanted to get me alone." She nodded in the direction of the cave. "You're not *that* easy to take down. You let it happen."

I lifted my chin.

Gerarda flipped a thin blade through her fingers. "Why?"

I took a deep breath. "I need you to get Gwyn and Fyrel back to Aralinth. Wait until morning to leave and take your time getting back."

The knife stopped. "You're not staying?"

I swallowed and shook my head.

Gerarda's eyes narrowed until they were thin blades across her face, too sharp and too willing to cut. "What is so important that you need to risk another encounter with the *shirak* to make it there before we do?"

"You know why."

Gerarda shrugged. "I don't see—"

"You're not a fool." I took a few more steps from the cave and lowered my voice so only the trees would hear us. "You know exactly what crossed through Elaran's mind when she saw Gwyn's eyes and hands."

Gerarda pointed her knife at my belly. "El is not a threat!"

I held a hand up to Gerarda's lips to silence her. "She thought it just as you did. Just as I did. Because that is what we are trained to do." Gerarda's shoulders relaxed, and she lowered the knife. "But Gwyn is young. Young and naïve enough to run into the woods with half a plan and no care for the consequences. She has no idea the fights that will be drawn over this. The tensions and the opinions—I will not let desperate people turn that young girl into a pawn for this war."

Gerarda leaned back. "What's your plan? Go back and get Feron to make a glamour for her to keep the truth a secret?" She huffed a laugh. "Such secrets festered so well the last time."

My heart raced. Even though part of me wanted to grab Gwyn and hide her away until this war was over, I knew that wasn't possible. Gwyn would never hide, and she deserved to fight as much as the rest of us if she wanted.

But she didn't need to be an experiment to be poked and prodded, pushed beyond her limits.

That I could prevent.

"This is a matter for the Elders to decide. I need time to gather them all, and then you can sneak Gwyn into the city. Late afternoon while people are still resting."

Gerarda's mouth turned into a sympathetic frown. "What if the Elders do not care? What if they are more than happy to turn Halflings into soldiers to get rid of the Crown for good?"

I looked down at my hands. The same ones that had taken so many lives. I remembered every one, every decision I had to make to not save someone in hopes of saving two on the morrow. Those decisions had marked me in so many other ways than the scars along my body.

This felt the same. This new power festered under my skin, not as a gift but as a curse. Instead of running a blade through the Halflings myself, anyone I turned into a Fae would be reborn with a sword in their hand and a target on their back when the battles broke out. It would be someone else's sword that took their last breath, but my hand would hold the blade either way.

I took a staggering breath and leaned into the tree to hold my weight. "I don't know," I said.

And for the first time, Gerarda looked scared too.

I made it to Aralinth as the suns began to rise. The watery veil between the two twisted trunks in the garden no longer shimmered with silver light but gold. I didn't transform; instead I soared over one of the large canopies and snipped off a dew rose with my beak. I dropped it into the small pool of water along the twisted branches from above and dove through the veil a moment later.

The trail to Myrelinth was just wide enough with my large wings. I soared silently, banking along the last curve. A group of Elverin on patrol jumped back as I came through the end of the trail. I let out a low call in apology and curved left toward my burl.

Riven wasn't in his. No faelight hovered in the window, and a thin layer of dust covered the twisted branches that framed his bed.

He hadn't been here at all.

I spread my wings and dove through the center of the Myram. Panicked shrieks followed by immediate laughter echoed through the hollow tree as I evaded a group of Halflings climbing to the burls on faelight.

I soared through an opening and flew into the grand hall. Hundreds of Elverin looked up at me, apparently no one had felt safe enough to sleep with the *shirak* on the loose. I tilted my wings back and forth as I flew over a group of children, their giggles calming the room as I disappeared down the tunnel toward Killian's chambers.

The flash of light as I transformed made up for my lack of faelight. I knocked on the door, chest gasping from the exertion of my long flight.

Riven pulled it open. One hand on his sword, the other pulling up his boot.

Mumbled voices echoed down the tunnel.

"Quiet." I cupped my hand around his mouth and pushed him back into the room, letting the door slide closed behind us.

I didn't move. I stood on the tips of my toes waiting for the voices to pass.

Riven's jade eyes bore down on me. The heat in them only grew as I slid my fingers away from his mouth.

"Sorry," I said, more to say anything than to apologize.

Riven's lip twitched upward. "You can push me into a dark room anytime you like, Keera." Riven let his gaze trail down my body. "You never need ask."

His regret still hung from him, obvious in his wrinkled clothes and the dark circles under his eyes. But there was something devious in his smirk. Something light and playful too. It was new and familiar all at once.

The face was Riven's. But the mischief and wit in his eyes was all Killian. It was so obvious now, how the prince had watched me the same way Riven had. Just without the pain of his magic. And now without the pain of his secret.

Riven's smirk faded when I didn't speak. His jade eyes glinted as if the magic he had lost was only resting under his skin. My fingers tingled.

Maybe it was.

"Keera, what's wrong?"

I gulped down my panic. There was no time to lose myself in the comfort of Riven's arms even if that's what I wanted. To go to bed and pretend that the world outside of this room did not exist.

"Something happened to Gwyn—"

Riven charged for the door but I grabbed his arm.

He lifted his hand to my cheek. "I'm so sorry, *diizra*." His whisper was even softer than his touch. The sweetness of his name for me sent a warm wave down my skin, soothing the onerous itch.

"She's not dead."

Riven's thumb stilled. "How injured is she?"

"She's not injured either. Not really." I took a breath trying to find the words that would make sense of everything that had happened, but the only ones I found were simple. "She's Fae."

The stillness in Riven's hand traveled up his arm until his whole body was rigid.

I held up my hand in front of him. I didn't dare call that newfound power forward—I wasn't even certain I could control it—but I saw the realization settle into the hard lines of Riven's eyes. "I made her Fae."

I leaned back. Riven's reaction was slow like ice melting until he could finally move enough to ask. "Elverath gave you the power to restore the Light Fae." There was a hint of worry in his awe. I didn't know if that was for himself, for me, or for Gwyn.

I shook my head.

Riven recoiled back. "Her eyes turned violet?"

"Amber." I lifted my chin to meet his gaze. "Her eyes turned amber just like her Halfling blood."

Riven looked down at his own hand. The same thought passed through our minds and we both ignored it.

When he looked up, his jaw was hard and his eyes determined. "Tell me everything."

So I did. I told him about the panic when I realized that the girls were missing, and Riven grabbed my hand. He grabbed the other as I described the attack of the *waateyshirak*. By the time I had finished, his arms were wrapped around me and my cheek was pressed against his chest.

"We worked so hard to get them here." I sighed into the warmth of Riven's body. "I know my magic is meant to be a gift, but this . . ." My voice trailed off. I didn't even want to imagine the decisions that were to come.

Riven tightened his grip on me. He knew there would be bloodshed too. I leaned into his comfort. The anger was still there, but I had to let it go. At least for the moment. Worry broiled at my throat, and if I didn't lean on someone, I would drown my anxieties in wine.

Riven's muscles flexed as if showing he had the strength to help. "What do you need from me?"

I looked up at him. Until that moment, I had been holding the weight of this all on my own. Trusting others still wasn't habit. But whatever else had happened between us, I knew I could trust Riven with this. And in that moment, that was enough.

"I know I said we can take this day by day, and I meant that." I pulled back so Riven could see my entire face. "But today I need you to choose me like I chose you. I need an ally in that room. I need to know someone else is there to protect her."

Riven caressed my bottom lip with his thumb. "Done." He pressed the gentlest, softest kiss to my forehead. "We only have today. And today I choose you, *diizra*."

Those words were enough to slow the hammering inside my chest.

I pulled back and kissed the tip of his nose.

Riven's eyes narrowed suspiciously. "There's another choice you need me to make?"

I tugged on his collar as I lowered myself to the flats of my feet. "Think of it more as a favor."

He raised a brow.

"I need you to talk to Syrra." My jaw pulsed. "I need her to leave the crypt."

Riven let out a long, cold breath. "She might not go willingly."

"She must be there." I fixed my cloak against my shoulder. "I don't have time to drag her out myself."

Riven swallowed but nodded. "Which Elders will you ask for support?"

My hand instinctively wrapped around the hilt of my dagger.

"All of them."

CHAPTER THIRTEEN

The council chambers felt smaller than usual. Sap coursed through the live grain of the walls, and with every pulse, the round edge of the room seemed to get closer and closer.

Riven gave me a nod from where he stood beside Syrra. Her back was as straight as a tree in her chair and her arms bent out at odd angles as if at any moment she would spring forward and run from the room.

I didn't know how much he had told her. But I felt better having her with us.

Someone knocked on the wall.

The grain split in an instant, curving back wide enough for Gerarda and Elaran to step through. Two hooded figures stood behind them, heads bent low so no one could see their faces under the shadow of the cloth.

Rheih walked in behind them. Her curls were held back with two sticks she seemingly plucked from the forest floor.

"Where were you?" I seethed through my teeth as she took the chair beside me. I had searched for her for hours, but the Mage had been nowhere to be found.

Her yellow eyes narrowed to thin slits. "Someone set a curfew on the entire city. With my harvest hours cut in half, I can't be available for every frivolity you see fit to entertain us with."

She clucked her tongue and my hand turned to a fist along the armrest.

"I didn't realize you found me entertaining," I deadpanned.

Rheih sighed and adjusted the smock on top of her robes. "That's the true sadness. I don't."

Feron stood before I could lose everyone's respect for smacking an elderly Mage in the mouth.

"We all agree to keep what is shared in this room private until we come to a consensus?" Feron made a slow circular glance about the room.

Everyone nodded except for one of the hooded figures. I didn't need to see her red curls to know it was Gwyn.

I cleared my throat.

"I swear it," Gwyn chimed in a bored voice.

Feron sat and nodded at Gerarda and Elaran. They both stepped to the side, allowing Fyrel and Gwyn to approach the circular table.

Gwyn pulled back her hood. Then she lifted her hand to expose her glowing fingers and the unmistakable amber color of her eyes.

"Shit." Myrrah leaned forward in her wheelchair for a better view.

Rheih stood from her chair, though it barely added any height to her vantage point. She mumbled under her breath and walked over to the girls to examine Gwyn more closely.

"I thought this was a bore," I quipped at her from across the table. The Mage grunted and grabbed Gwyn's wrist. I turned to the others. "As you can see, something more than an attack happened in those woods."

Syrra's rigid body loosened just enough for her to turn her head to Gwyn. Her unfocused gaze cleared as she watched the girl leave amber streaks of light in the air.

Darythir signed something too quick for me to fully catch. But the quick pulse of her hand in front of her chest was unmistakable.

Blood.

"I wonder too," Rheih answered her. She reached deep into the pockets of her smock and pulled out a needle. Gwyn held out her palm without protest. The Mage pricked the meaty part of her hand and gasped as the amber and gold blood pooled along Gwyn's skin.

Gwyn didn't flinch; she just watched as her blood flooded the crater of her palm. She held it higher for the others to gawk at.

"Extraordinary," Myrrah whispered, stretching in her chair to touch the blood for herself. She rubbed it along her fingertips as if she would be able to feel some physical difference from all the blood she had ever spilled.

I formed a sphere of water from the carafe on the table. Myrrah dipped her fingers into it absentmindedly, the magical blood washing away in thin swirls. She looked to Feron. "There are no stories that speak of such a thing?"

Feron shook his head, interpreting the question for Darythir, who slashed the air once with a flat, tight palm.

Signed Elvish for *no*.

Myrrah's awed expression sprouted into a grin. "This is excellent." She turned to me. "Think of the advantage." Her icy blue eyes glinted as new plans of attack formed behind them.

"Think of the bloodshed." My words were sharp and raw like the feeling in my throat. Not the physical burn of craving, but the habit, the desire. That same guilt I had spent decades dodging was curling its fingers around the end of my braid and with one good tug would drown me with it.

Syrra noticed the flex in my neck. She looked down at her hands, both bulging at the knuckles from how tightly she fisted them. She was standing strong against her desires too.

Elaran perched herself on the armrest of an empty chair. "No matter how or when we attack the capital, there will be bloodshed, Keera." She twisted the end of one of her curls until the slack went straight. "The more Fae soldiers we have, the less there will be."

Gerarda's jaw pulsed behind her lover, but she stood with her arms tucked behind her back. Silent.

"Do you think Gwyn's eyes being amber are a coincidence?" I scoffed, knowing that Elaran was much too smart for that. "It isn't as simple as turning any willing Elverin into Fae. I would be turning Halflings. *Me.* Not you. And the moment their eyes turn amber, I would be carving a target onto their chest."

Fyrel straightened, panic-stricken. "What do you mean?"

Her worried gaze shifted from Gwyn to me.

I flattened my hands onto the table. "Damien will attack the Fae first. As soon as his forces spot anyone using their powers, Damien will attack them with every ship, soldier, and weapon he has. The Fae warriors who remain have trained for centuries; their control over their powers is habit. And they have centuries more experience to know *exactly* what they are signing up for. But the Halflings you want me to turn into Fae?" I took my time to look around the table. "They are not warriors. They will be vulnerable and many, if not all, will die taking Elverath back for the rest of you."

Darythir waved her hand.

"You are certain your gifts only extend to Halflings?" Feron interpreted.

My belly hardened. "Unlike Damien, I do not make it a habit of experimenting on others with magic I do not understand."

"Then you do not know." The age in Darythir's cheeks made her frown even more pronounced. Her dark eyes narrowed at me as she leaned forward on the table.

Syrra stood. Her sudden movement made everyone in the room flinch with surprise. She ignored the reactions, only looking at me. "I volunteer to take this test."

I froze. "Absolutely not."

"Keera, you cannot paddle in both directions." Syrra straightened to her full height, her half braid falling from her shoulder. "I agree with you—this war should not be won by filling our front lines with turned Halflings. There are seasoned warriors among the Elves who would gladly take that burden. Let me be the first to claim it."

I shook my head. "What if it doesn't work?"

"I have been content as an Elf." Syrra hid her hands behind her back. "I do not see why that would change."

"What if the magic is tainted?" I raised a brow and glanced at Riven. "What if my gift does turn you, even though it shouldn't, because we were greedy enough to push our blessings? What if the magic lashes and festers inside you because you were never meant to exist and you carry the pain of that every day?" Riven shifted behind her chair, keeping his head low underneath his cloak, but I kept going. "Could you live with pain like that? Knowing there would be no guarantee you would have a second form to spare you?"

The room went quiet. Darythir's brows furrowed at my words, but it was Riven's place to tell her what I meant.

Riven placed a hand on Syrra's arm. "Keera is right to ask the question, and you would be right to consider it."

Whatever gifts I did possess, I knew I didn't understand them. And though I was not raised in a time or land lush with magic, I knew enough to know that it could always react in unexpected ways.

Some not for the better.

Syrra did not cower. Her neck flexed and her gaze trailed down me like the sharp point of a blade. "Then I shall bear it with gratitude that it was I who volunteered and the burden is not carried by another."

I rubbed the skin along my palm. My magic itched, yearning to be unleashed once more. I stood strong even as the sensation crept down my body until my bones vibrated.

Syrra had answered her question like any warrior would, but now it was my turn. Would I be able to live with the knowledge that my hands had bestowed that pain on another? Not just another, but a friend.

Darythir leaned back in her chair, eyes shifting between me and Syrra. She would not allow the council to assume there were any restraints on my gift until proven otherwise.

There was no path forward without experimenting on someone.

And if not Syrra, who? She had been the one who had spent her life training as a protector of her realm, her people. Her sister, her lover, her child. Syrra more than anyone knew what the cost a decision like this could be, and she had volunteered anyway.

The itching along my palm intensified to a slow, undeniable burn.

"Fine." My answer cut through the tension in the room like one of Gerarda's throwing knives. I nodded to the chair. "You should sit."

Syrra's back tensed and somehow her feet sunk lower into the live grain of the floor.

Gwyn caught on to my annoyance and cleared her throat. "Sitting would be best. I lost consciousness for a moment when I turned."

Syrra narrowed her eyes at Gwyn, but the girl did not waver. She lifted her chin, and her amber eyes glinted with a faint glow.

Syrra nodded once.

"This will be most comfortable," Feron said with a slow wave of his hand. The grain of the wood behind him split open, revealing pink skies and the cool dusk air with it. Two thick branches slithered through, vines curling down them like intertwining snakes until a soft hammock of green hung between them.

Syrra sat along the edge and lay back. Her feet still planted on the floor.

I stepped forward. The power under my skin hissed like a red-hot poker being pulled from a flame, knowing it was about to brand.

I stood over Syrra. Her long waves brushed against my knee. "You're certain?"

The scars along her arms twitched. "As sure as my arrow flies."

Myrrah huffed a laugh but rolled her chair back against the wall. As far away from the magic as possible.

I glanced at the others. "The rest of you should stand back too."

No one spoke as they made their way to the back wall, covering the seam of grain with their half-curious, half-worried faces.

Only when everyone was as far from me as possible did I lift my hand. It hovered over Syrra's chest as I let the power dammed inside me overflow. I touched Syrra's forehead, and the magic rushed forward.

It was different than Gwyn's transformation. Perhaps because I was not panicked, I could control the speed of the magic as it poured out of me in ribbons of gold light. Riven gasped as the light twisted around Syrra's arms, as deft and tangible as his shadows had been.

The light trailed up the length of Syrra's body and then down. It tapped her scars wherever her skin met the air, searching like a mouse for a hole to crawl into.

But it didn't find one.

I held my breath, waiting for the light to sink into Syrra, gripping her the way my magic had with Gwyn, but it didn't come. Instead the gold ribbons began to fade at the end as they retreated back into my palm. The sensation sent a shiver down my spine. My body became a waterfall for magic with no place to go.

The magic felt cooler on its return, unspent and sad.

Syrra opened her eyes. They were as dark as ever.

Darythir clucked her tongue as Rheih inspected Syrra's brown irises. She tugged on her lids until Syrra swatted her hand away.

"Keera's suspicions were correct." The Mage turned back around, the tug of curiosity pulling at her lips. "Only a Halfling can receive her gifts."

I shook my head. "Only a Halfling can receive my curse."

Elaran scoffed and leaned back on her chair so her body was draped over it like silk. "Unfair of you to call it a curse while you stand there with more gifts than any other Fae, living or dead." The room went still. Elaran smiled softly at Gwyn. "Do you feel cursed, lovely?"

Gwyn's body hardened. "Not at all."

"We don't even know what her powers are." My hand clenched.

"Precisely," Elaran said, her face sharp and pinched. "So you cannot decide for her whether it's a curse or not." She flicked her wrist. "Perhaps you shouldn't decide at all."

My jaw snapped shut. Elaran smirked and slowly pulled the sharp pin from her bundle of curls. Riven leaped over the back of the chair in front of him and placed himself between me and her before my hand had fully gripped my dagger.

"So reactive," Elaran purred.

"How else do you expect others to respond to threats?" Riven's nostrils flared wide as his hand grabbed for his own weapon. The shadow of his hood shifting dangerously close to his eyes.

Gerarda stepped in front Elaran without a hint of fear in her face. She looked bored, the smallest staring up at the largest Elverin in the room. "El was not making a threat."

"I was actually." She crossed her arms.

Feron leaned forward on his cane. "I expect this conversation to be civil."

Gerarda plucked the weapon from Elaran's hand before she could issue another threat. "Perhaps we should discuss this later. When everyone's had time to digest what's transpired."

Elaran drummed her fingers along her arm. "What is there to digest other than Keera holds victory in her hand and refuses to use it?"

I pinched the bridge of my nose. "It is not that simple."

Elaran's brows perked upward. "No? Then perhaps you want to keep the magic all for yourself?" She leaned forward, head resting on Gerarda's shoulder, who fought to keep her body between ours. "Scared that if you give away too much of your magic, there'll be nothing left for you?"

My anger broiled. How did Elaran not see that was the least of my worries? If Damien's army was not preparing for war, I would gladly do whatever I needed to be rid of my magic. From the moment my mother placed me in that godforsaken tree, all magic had done was hand me decisions of ruin.

Feron stood with his arm extended to the door. "We should discuss this after breakfast."

I ignored him. "Perhaps it's you who wants it all for herself?" I lifted my hand. The palm was pulsing with golden light. "Don't hide behind the fate of the war when all you want is a taste."

Elaran stepped forward, grabbing my dagger from its sheath. Riven slid his weapon out, but Elaran merely cut a slit through her woven sleeve, exposing her tan skin. "Do it then."

My heart thrummed in my chest, pulsing so heavily it echoed in my skull, drowning out the explosion of voices in the room. The intoxicating warmth of that new magic flooded through me, coaxing me into unleashing it out of spite. To give in to the momentary goodness of that relief.

No.

I swallowed. My days of succumbing to my whims were over. I did not want to do this, so I wouldn't. No matter how much Elaran or my magic pulled me into it.

I opened my mouth to say just that when a thick branch wrapped around my waist and Elaran's too. We were both flung backward, hurtled to opposite sides of the room.

For the first time, I could see true anger on Feron's ancient face. His long twists swayed behind him as he stepped into the middle of the room, his cane knocking against the floor the only sound anyone made at all.

"Enough." His disgust was heavy on his tongue. "I will not have such chaos present at this council." He turned to me. "I agree with Keera."

Elaran huffed a disappointed laugh.

"For now," Feron added. "Until we discern the extent of Gwyn's gifts and their reliability, it is best that Keera does not turn anyone else."

My shoulders eased against Riven's chest.

Feron's eyes glowed violet, unfocusing for the briefest moment. Then his brow flickered and his focus returned to the room. "It seems we have a more pressing matter."

The wall split open just as Feron finished his words, revealing a short Halfling with stitched ears and a fastener along his cloak.

A courier.

Feron held out his hand. The Halfling was holding a letter.

"It's not for you." The Halfling boy bowed his head apologetically to Feron. "It's for her."

He turned to me with an outstretched hand. I flipped the envelope to find the red seal of crossed sheaves of wheat. The sigil of the House of Harvest.

I ripped the envelope open and pulled out a finely dyed piece of parchment.

Lord Kilmor cordially invites you to celebrate
the inauguration of the new king.

Riven peered over my shoulder. "The ball?"

But I wasn't reading the rest of the invitation. I barely noticed the date.

All I saw was the delicate scrawl across the top. It was the same writing that filled my notebooks with frantic messages back and forth for months.

It's time.

Dynara was ready to bring the courtesans home.

CHAPTER FOURTEEN

"THIS IS USELESS!" Gwyn kicked a patch of grass with her boot. The amber glow around her fingertips faded as she stomped the ground, cursing under her breath.

Feron sat on a rock he had pulled from the ground two hours before. He had gotten Gwyn to try every gift he could think of, but her magic hadn't responded to any of it.

Riven pushed my shoulders down to massage my neck. Even though Gwyn insisted she felt no pain when her fingers glowed, every attempt twisted my insides into knots.

What if she never got control of her magic? What if it festered inside of her until it tore at her mind and body, fracturing her like Riven's had? She might not feel pain now, but neither had Riven for the first few years of his life, not until his gift had blossomed and he transformed that first time.

I swallowed. Part of me didn't want Gwyn to discover her powers. I wanted her to stay in that in-between state where she was safe, even if it was for a little while. The other crueler part of me wanted her magic to explode out of her at its peak so I could glimpse the worst to come.

Catastrophizing was torture. I'd seen too much, done too much in my life, to imagine the worst for Gwyn.

I pulled at the collar of my tunic, letting the air cool the sweat from my skin.

"Perhaps the wind is your element." Feron looked at me.

My jaw cocked to the side. Gwyn had started the day trying that gift. But his patient stare got the best of me.

"Stand on your mark," I told Gwyn, pointing at the grass she'd kicked.

She sighed but took her place. I walked her through the exercise, holding my breath as her fingers came to life and waited for a gust or a tiny breeze to blow across my face.

But nothing came.

Gwyn shrieked in rage. A flock of birds nearby scattered like leaves in the wind Gwyn couldn't conjure.

She kicked the back of Feron's rock. "Fuck!"

Gwyn fell to the ground.

Fyrel ran to her side. "Maybe we should try again tomorrow."

"No," Gwyn snapped. "I can do this. I *need* to do this!"

I pulled off her boot. "You need to stay still. You have a broken toe." I pressed my fingers around the rest of her foot, feeling for swelling and breaks along the ankle just as Rheih had taught me. "Look away," I ordered, readying to snap her knuckle back into place.

Gwyn crossed her arms and didn't break my gaze.

I shook my head.

Snap.

She groaned but refused to move. I called my healing gift forward and let it ease her pain as the bones fused back together. I didn't call it back until Gwyn's breathing had settled and her jaw relaxed.

I lifted her foot, checking my work. The scar along her ankle caught the light just like my names did on the rare occasions I let sunlight touch them. The tether that had bound Gwyn to the palace for most of her life hadn't disappeared but settled into a fine silver line.

It had burned into her skin like a brand the day her mother died. And even though the magic was broken, she would carry the relic with her for the rest of her days. No matter how far she got from the kingdom, no matter who won the war I'd started, she would carry that past with her everywhere.

My magic prickled under my skin. But there were things magic couldn't fix.

Gwyn sat up, tucking her chin onto her knees.

"You don't need to be this hard on yourself." I patted her leg.

Her amber eyes flashed. "Yes, I do. I need to be ready."

I stilled. "Ready for what?"

Gwyn picked at the grass, unable to meet my eyes. "To fight." Her jaw pulsed, and I knew she didn't mean fight on the battlefield.

She only had one target in mind.

Her fingers traced the outline of her tether without looking. How many times had she done that in the palace, dreaming of her freedom? Now that she had it, all she could think about was going back and gutting Damien like he had her.

Panic pulled at my ribs until it hurt to breathe. No matter what happened, I would rather die than let Gwyn go after Damien on her own.

"Do that again, child," Feron said. He nodded at Gwyn's fingers on her ankle, tracing the tether.

They were glowing, leaving streaks of amber light in the air over her skin, but this time the light hadn't disappeared. The strokes had fused together into a single symbol waiting for Gwyn to finish.

She stopped and the symbol fizzled out.

"Only draw the lines within that circle," Feron said, eyeing her ankle from his stone seat with glowing irises. He was mapping the pattern along her skin with his magic, feeling the grooves of Gwyn's scar like a river cutting through Elverath.

Gwyn straightened, her fingers hovering over her tether. She took a quick breath and started marking the air with light. The symbol was made of five straight lines encased by a circle. It reminded me of the shapes I had cut into the earth at each seal.

The amber streaks pulsed when Gwyn finally connected the shape. They turned gold, and a thick stone grew from the ground until it pierced the light like a sword through a belly.

Gwyn's eyes went wide with delight.

"I did it."

I stilled, assessing Gwyn for any oncoming pain. "How do you feel?"

"Amazing." Gwyn looked at her fingertips. "Everything inside me is buzzing and warm. Whatever that was, my magic liked it."

"No pain?" Gwyn shook her head and my shoulders finally fell from my ears. "You're an earth wielder."

"Awesome," Fyrel whispered.

"No, she is not," Feron said, his brow tense over the straight line of his mouth. "That symbol on her leg is not just decoration. It is an ancient rune for stone. I assume Aemon used it in his tether to represent the palace of Koratha, as it is carved from a single piece of stone. Gwyn does not have command over the earth like you and me; the stone appeared because she traced the rune to command it."

Riven's voice had that same bookish curiosity that Vrail's used to have. "Like a spell?"

"Much more powerful than anything the Mages or Elves have ever conjured. Together or alone." Feron bit his lip and turned toward Fyrel. "Fetch me a piece of parchment and a glass pen."

She ran to the equipment room, throwing drawers open with lightning speed until she found what he had asked for.

Feron sketched a shape onto the paper. It was made of seven jagged lines also encased in a circle. "Draw this," he said to Gwyn.

The parchment shook in her hand, but the other glowed with the light of her magic. She traced the lines with her finger, finishing in a circular arc. Once more, the amber light pulsed and turned gold the moment the rune was finished. This time, the paper combusted into crimson flames, burning hot and tall before finally falling to the ground and snuffing out.

"Earth and fire?" Riven cocked his head back, impressed. "Those are two powerful gifts."

Feron shook his head. "One gift. Of unknown and untapped potential." He turned to Gwyn. "Do you feel tired at all?"

She smirked and shook her head. "I feel like I never need to sleep again." She drew the fire rune once more and giggled as a ball of flame hung in the air for a few moments before dropping to the ground.

"Do spell wielders grow weary more quickly than other wielders?" I asked. Feron's mindwalking gift took more from him than his earth wielding, just as shifting between forms depleted my own gifts more quickly.

Feron blinked. "There is no such thing as a spell wielder." His lips pursed, studying Gwyn once more. "Until now."

Gwyn's eyes went wide and a sly smile crept up her lips. "Until now," she repeated under her breath.

I froze. "You have never seen magic like this before?"

Feron shook his head. "Mages and some Elves were practiced in the art of spell casting. But it was never like this. Runes were the foundation of the spell, but they would spend weeks waiting for the stars and moon to align as they harvested the correct ingredients. And I never saw a spell that worked so directly as this."

"Not even the Faemothers?" Riven crossed his arms.

Feron shook his head. "None of the *niinokwenar* nor their descendants have ever held this power. At least not to my knowledge." He turned to Gwyn and uttered the same cursed words Elaran had. "You, my child, are something entirely new."

Gwyn lifted her chin and claimed a name for herself. "An Amber Fae."

I bit my cheek. "But what does that mean? If I turn any more Halflings into Fae, they could all have powers that you have never seen?"

Feron gave a noncommittal shrug. "It would appear so. But the blessings of Elverath should never be assumed."

"But what if these new powers are too much? What if they can't be controlled? What if they hurt people?" I started to pace. "What if you and the other Fae can't train them, Feron?"

Gwyn stood. From the way she still stared at her hands, it was clear she hadn't heard a word I said. "I'm going to the library," she shouted, already running toward the tunnel.

Fyrel trailed after her. It would only take them minutes to convince Vrail to give them every book with runes she had.

My stomach hardened. I turned back to Feron.

"How do we help her hone her gift?" My shoulders tightened around my neck once more. "How do we train her for battle with a gift like that?"

Riven and Feron held the same hard expression on their faces. For a moment they looked like father and son instead of distant kin.

Then Feron said the scariest words I had ever heard. "I don't know if we can."

"Is she coming?" Riven asked, leaning against the outside of my burl.

I shook my head. "She didn't even speak to me. She just stared at the wall as I explained the mission. I'm not even sure if she heard me."

Riven grazed my cheek with the back of his hand. "Syrra blames herself."

I rubbed my brow, exhaustion getting the best of me. "She shouldn't."

"No." Riven's voice was hard. "She shouldn't."

I bit my lip. I wanted to console Riven, to tell him that he shouldn't blame himself for Maerhal's death either, but I didn't know if I believed it. I had spent so long wrapped up in my own guilt that I had no measure for what was healthy and what was the darkness digging its talons deeper into me. All I knew for sure was that if my lie had been exploited by Damien and ended with someone dead, I would feel guilty too. More than I already did.

I walked into my burl, discarding my cloak on a chair. Riven lingered in the doorway. I took out my braid and turned back to him. "You can come in."

He stepped through the threshold like a child stepping into unknown waters. So much had happened between us, yet he had spent so little time in my chambers. We were like two people lost at sea, clamoring onto each other to save ourselves from the pain and guilt. I didn't regret it. But we hadn't had the chance to grow slowly together, stacking tiny little moments over the course of years. There hadn't been time, but part of me wished there had been.

"When I first came to Myrelinth, you started to tell me little details about yourself." I unlaced my vest and let it fall to the floor. "Why did you stop?"

Riven swallowed from his seat on the chaise. "Because I ran out of things to tell you without telling you the truth about . . . who I was."

"I know now. Tell me something." I grabbed the back of the chair. I was still dressed but I felt completely naked.

Riven bunched his trousers in his fist. "I know I run away from problems when they arise. I think I convince myself that if no one is dying then it can wait, but making others wait—making you wait—hurts. I know that but I still don't know if I can stop."

I perched on Riven's armrest and tucked a loose strand back into his half braid. "Why run at all?"

Riven leaned his head back to look at me. "All I ever saw was my father cause pain. Pain to his servants, pain to his lords, pain to the people he claimed to love." Riven's jaw pulsed. "Sometimes I wonder if that's all I'm capable of. Hurting people. Sometimes it feels like if anyone spends enough time with me, they will get hurt and that staying far away is the best thing for everyone."

My chest tore at Riven's words; they were too familiar. I had lived that way for thirty years, keeping others at a distance for that very reason. But I'd been wrong.

I sighed. "You run to save them from the hurt, but the leaving is what does it."

Riven's face crumpled and he nodded.

"Thank you for telling me." I pressed a kiss to his forehead.

Riven's eyes widened like he'd thought I would never touch him like that again. "Thank you, *diizra*. For listening and for asking."

"Confess all you like," I said jokingly, but Riven's face hardened.

"I'm scared for Nik."

I caressed his cheek with my hand. "I am too." Every night I went to bed, I hoped that I wasn't woken by a messenger announcing Nik was dead.

"No. Not like that." Riven cleared his throat. "I'm terrified of Nik dying without coming home but I am more scared of him living and never forgiving me." Riven peered up at me. "Is that selfish?"

"A little," I answered, smoothing his hair. "But I don't think it's wrong. You want to make things right, Riven. Your heart is true even if it's a little wanting."

He laid his head on my lap. "Did you get the sleeping draught?"

I pulled a small case out of my pocket. "I had Rheih increase the dosage."

Riven grunted. He opened the case to reveal two small darts inside. "You're certain you don't need more help tomorrow."

I shook my head. "You get Kairn out, and Dynara and I will take care of the rest."

CHAPTER FIFTEEN

The road into Cereliath wasn't lined with the hungry but with soldiers. Rows of tents filled the harvested fields as a makeshift barracks. My jaw clenched. Aemon never had money to house the people dying outside of the city's walls yet the Crown's armies were well covered.

And well stocked from the piles of food and weapons at the center of the tents. A group of young soldiers stood with their armor half on, wrestling over the last piece of meat. The older soldiers sat, sloshing their ale as they cheered.

The men had been here for almost a fortnight with nothing to do but patrol. They were like starved dogs, vying for a fight.

But I wouldn't give it to them.

Yet.

The soldiers paid me no notice as I walked by on the King's Road. I smirked. Riven had insisted on using a glamour but I knew my disguise would be enough. My dress was tattered and covered in mud and manure. I led an ass I had stolen from a nearby field on bare feet and filled its saddle basket with the rotten fruit left in its slough.

I lifted an empty tin toward the soldiers walking on the road, covering my eyes with the hood of my moth-eaten cloak. One averted his eyes, too disgusted to look at me, while the other spat at my feet. Neither suspected that the deadliest blade in the kingdom had just asked them for coin.

I hid my smirk all the way into the city center.

A cast-iron thread and needle hung over the entrance of the house. My knock resounded off the metal-plated door like a rock falling to the bottom of a well. Mistress Augustine did not entertain her guests at the main house, but it was where her most prized girls stayed.

I straightened. There was no noise on the other side of the door. I knocked again and glanced down the street to make sure no one was taking too much notice.

Footsteps so soft no Mortal would be able to hear them approached the door, but it didn't open. I leaned closer.

One heartbeat. I cleared my throat of its rasp. "I'm here to see Miss Dynara. We have an appointment."

The breathing on the other side of the door stopped. I reached for the thin dagger holstered under my skirts.

The door opened to reveal an elegant woman, her gray hair pulled back into a bun without a strand misplaced. The years had turned her hard-lined mouth into a permanent frown and spotted her pale hands. She wore gold rings endowed with impressive jewels of every color so her hands were always grasping her riches. She collected young and beautiful Halflings in the same way, holding them and their youth close as hers faded with every passing day.

None of this surprised me. I'd had many encounters with Mistress Augustine during my tenure as Blade. Her theater was a notorious place for traitors and power-hungry lords to get a bit too drunk and a bit too loud.

What surprised me was seeing her at all. Last I'd heard, she was dead.

Poisoned by Dynara herself.

I bowed my head. "Mistress Augustine."

A smug smile grew along her face. It seemed unnatural for her features, like her mouth was moving in ways it never had before.

"Let her in before she's seen," a familiar voice called from the landing of the wide staircase. Dynara stood at the top of the stairs, her silk robe draped effortlessly over her shoulders and her hair pinned in curls around her head.

Mistress Augustine chuckled and opened the door wide enough for me to slip in.

I looked between the Mistress and Dynara, not sure what I should say. "Not exactly the attire I was expecting, D."

"Not all of us need to use a blade to cause trouble." Mistress Augustine folded her arms and leaned against the banister. "Though I'm glad I only have to rely on my wits this evening and don't need to bathe myself in essence." She sniffed pointedly at the scent of lavender and dew rose that wafted from Dynara's slick skin.

Dynara shook her head. "Keera darling, meet the lovely Crison Clairbelle. She is somehow more stubborn and cross than you've ever been."

Mistress Augustine held out her hand, but it was no longer bent and spotted. Dynara's introduction shattered the glamour, blowing the illusion away like mist in the wind to reveal a much younger-looking and much more beautiful woman underneath. She had a full pout and feline eyes that held a rage behind them.

I spied the faint stitches along her ears as her black hair fell from her face. Not a woman at all. But a Halfling.

I smirked and shook her hand.

"Keera Waateyith'thir," I said. My full name felt foreign on my lips. I'd never introduced myself with it before.

Crison didn't hide her study of me. She let her eyes trail up my body from my bare feet to the mud-caked braid. "Traded your hood for your name, I see." She raised a thick brow at the state of my dress. "I'm starting to think Nara oversold the luxuries of the Faeland."

I huffed a laugh. "Always better to blend than hide." I turned to Dynara. Our voices echoed throughout the house, but I couldn't hear any other voices besides ours. "Speaking of hiding. Where have you hidden them?"

Dynara pulled a thick gold chain from her pocket and locked it around her neck. "Who, dear?" She adjusted the amber stone between her breasts; it was the size of a child's fist.

I blinked. "The courtesans. Gerarda and Elaran are at the safe house. They'll ferry the Halflings to Pirmiith and Feron at the portal as soon as the fire—"

"Portal?" Crison's rounded ears twitched.

I ignored her. "I thought you would have the courtesans here . . ."

"The party can't be a distraction if there are none of us at the party to *distract*." Dynara nodded at the wall, not at the large portrait of Mistress Augustine and her scraggly cat, but at the house at the top of the hill in that direction.

The House of Harvest.

I rubbed my brow. "How many courtesans are going to be joining us tonight?"

"All of them." Dynara crossed her arms.

"How many is that?"

"Two hundred." Crison's lip curled. "Why does she get to come in here and question all our planning?" She sniffed loudly.

"Because I can do this." My fist burst into flames.

Crison merely shrugged. "Nothing I haven't done with a candle and a bottle of mead."

Dynara shook her head and walked down the hall. "Come, Keera, you need to dress," she called down to me.

Crison raced to the stairs to climb them first. I followed her into Dynara's chambers, the vein in my forehead pulsing.

Dynara pointed at the tub of steaming water. "Get in and hurry. It will take ages for us to wash that dirt from your hair."

"Us?" Crison cocked her jaw to the side and leaned against the window.

Dynara ignored her. "The carriage will be here in just over an hour."

I shook my head, partly because I didn't want to disrobe in front of Crison and partly because I wanted to understand how Dynara thought we were going to ferry two hundred courtesans out of the House of Harvest without anyone noticing. "The plan was to get the courtesans out of the city not into the center of it."

"No, that was the *end* of the plan," Dynara replied, almost bored.

Crison shouldered me as she walked past and opened an armoire. It was full of vials and jewelry that concealed dangerous weapons. "First we host a party of our own." She looked at Dynara, disgusted. "You said you trusted her with your life, but it doesn't seem like she pays the same respect to you." She lifted her chin, eyes narrowing in my direction.

My jaw pulsed. "I trust Dynara with my life." I turned to my friend. "But you may have overestimated my abilities."

Dynara shook a few drops of cedar essence into the tub. She leaned toward me and sniffed then poured in half the bottle. "Keera, you told me you needed Kairn and you had no doubt I could do it. Trust me in this too. Every Halfling will make it out of that house but first they have to ensure the lords do not."

Crison grinned and chucked a piece of parchment at me. It was thick and folded along the middle to create the perfect invitation. I'd read the top lines when Dynara had first sent her courier. Now the last two caught my attention.

Mistress Augustine presents: The Dance of Elves.
House of Harvest. Invite only.

"How many lords did you invite?" I looked up at them both.

Dynara's answering grin was feline and deadly. "I invited them all."

CHAPTER SIXTEEN

THE HOUSE OF HARVEST had transformed into a theater. Rich velvet drapes covered every sandstone wall and window. Flickering candles lined the hallways, creating an intimate atmosphere that shouldn't have been possible in such an enormous manor.

I wore a long jade gown that glistened like a tide pool as I walked. It was a custom piece made by Wilden, the local tailor who had designed every dress and suit of leathers I had ever worn as Blade. Dynara must have told him the dress was for me because the fit was perfect and underneath the layered gossamer skirt were matching trousers and boots that went up to the knee. I just had to pull a single ribbon at my hip to detach the skirt and I would be free to run or strike at will.

Wilden had more than outdone himself.

Lords nodded to Dynara as they passed through the entrance hall. Their eyes lingered over her ample bust and the waterfall of curls that perfectly framed her face.

She had always been striking, but in the soft light of the torches surrounded by dozens of dazed men, it was undeniable just how enchanting Dynara truly was. Every movement she made was the perfect blend of grace and seduction. She held her fan with her middle and ring fingers while the index grazed along her collarbone and the pinkie pointed to the high slit in her burgundy skirt. The men's eyes trailed down the length of her, never realizing that they were following a map of Dynara's own making. That they were too focused on her to notice the drapes shifting as people moved behind them.

In another life, Dynara would have done well at the Order.

I hid my mouth behind my own fan. My glamoured bracelet shifted down the sleeve of my gown. Dynara tilted her head to hear me whisper, "Where are the wives?"

We had been stationed at the entrance for almost an hour, and I hadn't seen any of the kingdom's ladies on the arms of the lords. Every person wearing a skirt had a brand along her wrist or arm, many of whom were Halflings pretending to be Mortal. Most of the servants were Halflings too.

Bile coated my tongue. Even though the Crown had outlawed Mortals fraternizing with us, most of the men were delighted at the idea of pleasure houses filled with secret Halflings. I didn't know if it was the servitude or forbidden nature that made Mortal men feral with lust. I supposed it didn't matter. They would lay with Halflings like Dynara without regret, boasting to their friends in a haze of ale and sweat, while making Halflings like me enforce the king's law for the other halfbreeds who dared get caught speaking to a Mortal out of turn. No matter what role the kingdom gave us, the hypocrisy was stifling. My skin itched along my back as if I were a marionette being restrung to obey the kingdom's rule, even just for a night.

For this to work, everyone had to be a puppet one last time.

Dynara ran her bejeweled hand along the length of her hair, twisting the ends of it at her hip. She gave the lords passing by us a demure smile before turning her head toward my neck to hide her answer. "The lords are well aware of who is hosting this event. Most of them would consider their wives an intrusion."

She nodded in the direction of the ballroom doors. Crison, as Mistress Augustine, was speaking to Lord Curringham's replacement—Lord Kilmor. Despite the glamour disguising herself as the Mistress to everyone else, Crison still styled herself as Augustine. Her raven hair was slicked back into Augustine's signature bun, tugging at her skin so much that her thick brows were pulled up toward her hairline.

She turned just enough for me to see the necklace around her throat. I recognized it as the glamour Dynara had taken to Cereliath that first night. I had always assumed she would be the one to play her old Mistress, but Crison played the part well. If I didn't know about the glamour, I would have never believed that the woman heartily laughing at Kilmor's joke was not the actual Augustine. Her mannerisms were perfect, even down to the slight curve of her neck and the hip that jutted to the left.

Dynara pointed at a couple stepping out of their carriage. The lord was handsome with only a streak of gray over his eyebrow. He glanced around at the courtesans milling about the front hall. On his arm was a beautiful blonde with pale, freckled skin. If her husband's eyes were hungry, hers were ravenous.

I recoiled back against the curtain.

Dynara hid the curl of her lip behind her hand. "The only wives who come are the ones who like to partake in their husbands' . . . purchases." Dynara lifted her chin. "And for that, they will burn too."

It was unnerving to see such a sweet smile say such violent words. Dynara nodded at the black carriage pulling up behind them. The coachman wore an Elvish chain around his neck though he looked Mortal enough not to need a glamour. He opened the door, and everyone saw a brown-haired man with hazel eyes and a thick, curling beard. I saw Riven, the glamour shattering for me as soon as I noticed the blue flower pinned to his jacket.

Dynara smirked as Riven's hand grazed my skirt without looking at me. He took his place at the end of the hallway, waiting and ready.

"The green eyes suit him." Dynara pursed her lips, the glamour breaking for her too. My stomach tightened. I had told Riven the truth was his to share, but Dynara had known something was wrong from the moment I wrote to her saying Riven had left. She had started prying before Crison even left the room.

She cocked her jaw to the side, looking away from Riven's sideways glances. As a true friend, she had accepted my choice in forgiving him, but I knew it would be sometime before Dynara forgave Riven—and Killian—for lying to her.

Her chest heaved as the new Lord of Harvest nodded his head and made his way toward us.

To her.

His eyes never left Dynara. "Lord Kilmor," she said with a curtsy. She looked up at the lord through her lashes and gave him a feline smile that would make any man weak in the knees.

"Paxton." He grabbed her hand and pressed his lips to it. "Dynara, don't make me remind you again."

She bit her rouged lip. "You will need to remind me at least one more time before I disgrace a lord in his own house." She waved her hand at the lavish decoration before tracing her middle finger across the top of her breast.

Lord Kilmor was entranced. I didn't know if that made Dynara superbly skilled or him unabashedly pathetic. I glanced at her elegant dress and then to his misbuttoned jacket and knew the answer was both.

"Your mistress's talents for throwing a party are unmatched." Lord Kilmor didn't hold his arm out for Dynara to take but instead looped his through hers. As fixated as he was with her, she was not a lady he was trying to court; she was a prize he wanted the room to watch him claim.

I tucked my hands behind my back to keep from punching him in the jaw.

He walked Dynara toward the great hall, ignoring me trailing behind them as his lips brushed Dynara's ear. "I heard that the king may attend. Though I can't be shocked that such a beautiful creature would entice him all the way from the capital."

I froze beside them as Dynara laughed. "I would be delighted if His Majesty graced us with his presence. We both would, wouldn't we, *Dashir*?" She smiled at me.

Lord Kilmor didn't notice the mischief in it. Dynara hadn't called me by the alias we'd agreed on, but the Elvish word for *rumor*.

The meaning fluttered right over Kilmor's balding head. He had no idea that he had only heard Damien would be attending because that was what Dynara had wanted him to hear. The *rumor* he spoke of was a story that Dynara had sparked and fanned across the kingdom until every important man in Elverath was present.

She had already told me Damien had sent his regrets.

As expected.

Damien's frequent dalliances late into the night had only been part of his guise. Now that he had claimed the throne, he had no need to attend parties. He was attending to much more vile ends.

"Look, there he is now," Lord Kilmor shouted with an embarrassing amount of glee as a royal carriage rolled up onto the curved path at the front of the manor.

Dynara's confident smile dropped as she whipped her head to see who would step out of it. I turned with her, feeling for the hilt of my dagger through my skirts as the door to the carriage opened.

Both our shoulders eased as a towering man dressed in all black stepped onto the stone walkway.

Lord Kilmor stood on the tips of his toes, neck stretching to see if someone else stepped from the carriage. But no other figure appeared behind the gargantuan frame.

My jaw set.

Kairn.

His long black hair flowed loosely behind him as he stomped down the hall. I hid my wrinkled nose behind my fan. There was a sourness to his scent, like he hadn't showered after a week's ride but merely doused himself in perfumed oil.

I glanced at Riven. The sleeping dart was already wedged between his fingers as he meandered through the crowd. "*Wait*," I signed behind my fan. Lord Kilmor might notice if the mountain of a man fell unconscious at his feet.

Kairn handed Kilmor a pristine envelope without a word. The lord gulped in the shadow of Damien's new Blade and didn't say anything to him at all. My gaze fell to Kairn's chest, where an odd pendant was stitched into his leathers. It was round along the top like a gemstone inset into a crown, but it wasn't a jewel at all.

The top layer was made of glass. The bottom was lined with fractured pieces of a pearlescent material that turned deep black around the edge. It was a strange decoration. Damien wasn't someone who would allow his guards to wear something without a purpose, but I had no idea what the purpose was.

"A letter from the king," Kilmor mused to his guests.

He turned the envelope over to reveal the dark purple seal on the back. I peered at the letter as Lord Kilmor struggled to open it. The symbol was still of a crown, but not King Aemon's. It had a single point—not three—and was dripping in blood.

I had to restrain myself from scoffing. Spilling blood had allowed Aemon to make his throne, and spilling more blood was Damien's way of keeping it.

Lord Kilmor's eyes danced across the page, too erratically for him to truly read the words inked into the parchment.

Kairn huffed a breath that smelled of rotten teeth. "His Majesty extends his regrets for being unable to attend your festivities. Though he would like to invite you and your wi—"

Kairn turned to Dynara, realizing too late that she was certainly not the wife of any lord in the kingdom let alone the High Lord of the Harvest. Her revealing dress and the gold ink painted across her eyeline was not appropriate for a lady.

But Dynara was not dressed as herself. She was dressed as the lords' fantasy come to life.

"You can call me Dynara, sire." Her words dripped with honey as she slowly fanned her hand over the thin cut in my bodice that showed every inch of unmarked skin from my breasts to my navel. "And this is *Dashir*." Her lips held no smirk, but her eyes did as she used my newfound alias.

Kairn's gray eye stormed like the sea. The other, marked black from Damien's magic, was flat and unmoving. The amber pupil sat in its midst, a perfect circle that Damien could look through at any point.

I held my breath, waiting for the pupil to contract and reshape. It lingered on me for a fraction longer than Dynara or Kilmor but then settled on the lord.

I forced myself to release a breath. The glamour still dangled from my wrist. It was enough to keep Kairn—or Damien—from recognizing me. There was no reason to believe that the glamour would fail, that Damien had discovered a way to break through it or track me outside of sleep, but my hand rested over the release ribbon of my skirt anyway, ready to attack.

I had learned my lesson in underestimating Damien. One sign of recognition from Kairn, and I would stab my blade into his gut before he could get his sword from its sheath.

A long moment stretched between us, Kairn taking his time as his gaze trailed over me. I forced myself not to look at Riven standing at the table behind him. Though I saw his jaw flex as Kairn smacked his lips at me like a dog begging for a bowl of scrap meat. I smiled widely instead of gutting him. Kairn didn't have an inkling as to who I was.

We still had the upper hand.

"How thoughtful of His Majesty to send such an esteemed member of the Arsenal to protect us," I said with a curtsy and an obvious glance at the giant silver sword fastening Kairn's black cloak. "I feel safer already." I stepped forward and let my finger graze over the silver fastener—the same symbol that had hung from my neck for thirty years. "Though I hope His Majesty understands that even his *sharpest* blades can grow dull without sufficient *relief*." I imitated Dynara's low rasp, letting my words hang in the air like a secret between me and my target.

Kairn blinked. I didn't know if he was shocked by my forwardness or had noticed the jest in my tone.

It didn't matter. His hesitation was enough.

I pressed my chest against him, bending at the knees to widen the distance in our heights. It was strange how the largest of Mortals seemed to prefer the smallest of women. Kairn wrapped his hand around my waist and pressed me even more tightly against him.

I had him.

"I would be most delighted if you would join me for a dance." I looked up at the man who had claimed my post, who had captured Nikolai and did gods knew what with him, and smiled through heavy lashes.

Kairn took my arm with a ghastly grin. I held my breath so I didn't have to smell the stale sweat and dirt that couldn't be covered by the shiniest leather armor. The crowd split as Kairn walked us down the hall. No man wanted to anger the gigantic assassin with a reputation for blood-filled rages. And the courtesans seemed relieved that Kairn had not chosen them.

My stomach hardened. I would never have let his hand touch any of them.

The drapes of fabric that covered the walls ruffled as we walked past. I hid my gaze behind my fan and caught the silhouette of someone running behind the curtains with a heavy bag slung over their shoulders.

The servants were escaping right under Kairn's nose.

Riven followed behind us, ready to strike. Dynara nodded at a black-haired woman standing at the door and she dropped the tray she was carrying.

Riven stuck the dart into Kairn's neck. He smacked his skin, looking for the culprit just as a line of courtesans dressed in feathered costumes exploded out of the side room. Kilmor and Dynara were lost in the wave of chaos, but Riven and I held strong, waiting for the Blade to drop.

But he didn't.

“Out of the way,” Kairn barked, pushing two girls to the ground. He rubbed his brow and leaned against the wall. I turned to Riven with an outstretched hand and he slipped me a second dart.

“Sire, are you well?” I asked, shoving my cleavage into his face as I stuck the dart into his arm.

Kairn swayed again, catching his weight on a table full of drinks. Glass shattered, covering the floor, but Kairn still didn’t fall. He had taken five times the dose to quell the average man and that still wasn’t enough.

I turned back to Riven, ready to catch another dart, but Riven shook his head. My heart stilled. There were none left.

CHAPTER SEVENTEEN

Dynara's eyes went wide as Kairn crashed through the doors to the great hall and stumbled down the stairs. Kilmor trailed after him like a lost puppy with two glasses of wine.

"Why isn't he unconscious?" Dynara asked as a troupe of dancers took the stage at the far end of the room. The lords hollered and clapped, throwing loose coin onto the stage.

"The sleeping draught didn't work." I grabbed a glass of water from a server walking by. "Two oversized doses. I can get him out." I took a sip of my drink. "But it won't be discreet."

Dynara looked up the stairs where Riven was watching Kairn, who still hadn't fallen. "If it hasn't worked now, it isn't working at all." She fanned her neck. "Can you get him out before . . ." She glanced up at the giant amber stone set into the roof of the ballroom.

Dynara checked the bead on the back of her bracelet. It was glass but contained a liquid that would turn bright red when it was time to leave. All the courtesans wore one. "Keera, you don't have much time," she urged.

I swallowed. "I know."

Kairn stood to his full height, seemingly recovered from his momentary dizzy spell. Lord Kilmor threw up his hands and handed the man a drink. They both downed their glasses in a single swallow. Kilmor's cheeks reddened, and he grabbed the server's thigh as he set the empty glass on her tray.

"How you've lasted this long without slapping him is a miracle," I muttered under my breath. Dynara had wormed herself into the House of Harvest with ease. She had been the *special guest* of the new High Lord of the Harvest for weeks. She had more patience than I ever would.

Dynara set down her own drink. "Kilmor is nothing compared to the lords I had to entertain before I freed myself." A sigh slid between her clenched teeth as she smiled across the room. "And none of them were as bad as the mistresses," she said without moving her lips.

Kairn took another drink from a nearby tray, turning toward us. "The pendant he wears on his chest. I've never seen one like it before."

"You think it has some kind of special meaning?" Dynara's eyes tightened over her fan.

I tapped the edge of my glass. "Does Kairn present himself as the type of man interested in flaunting his jewels?"

Dynara's scoff caught in her throat. She raised a dainty wrist to hide her lips. "He barely presents himself as a man who bathes." Her mouth tightened as she came to the same thought I had. "The pendant is from Damien."

"Yes." I chewed my lip. "But gift or tool?" Something flared underneath my skin; it wasn't warm like magic, but cool. The same eerie breeze that blows on one's neck when someone is watching.

I didn't have time to ponder that question. That would have to wait until after—if I managed to get Kairn out without causing a scene.

I grabbed Dynara's wrist, letting our pretense drop with my fan. "This dance needs to happen now." I nodded in the direction of Kairn and Kilmor.

Dynara looked up at the giant bronzed gemstone in the middle of the roof over the dance floor. The last rays of sun were casting beautiful rings of amber and gold onto the patrons below, but soon it would be completely dark.

Then the hall would be alight with something else.

"We can't delay, Keera. And we can't do anything to draw the lords' attention now." Dynara's neck flexed. "I want Kairn as much as you do, but too many lives are depending on us to *stick to the plan*."

I cocked my jaw to the side. The plan had gone up in flames the moment Kairn had stayed conscious from Riven's dart. "I need him alive, D."

She lifted her wrist. The bead was almost red. "You're out of time." She turned to Riven at the landing of the entrance. "He was supposed to be gone five minutes ago," she whispered.

I glanced up at Riven. His face was hard as he paced the landing. There was nothing he could do; he didn't have any magic to subdue Kairn and there was no time left to test who would win on brawn alone. My stomach twisted into knots. I wanted to shout at him. Tell him to leave—to take the carriage without Kairn and make sure the rest of the Halflings got out safe—but that would send a panic through the room.

Instead, I lifted my hand and made three quick, precise movements.

Go. Now. Alone.

My signed Elvish was terrible on the best of days, but from the way Riven froze against the banister I knew he understood.

I wouldn't be going with him to ferry the Halflings to safety. The plan had failed. I was our only chance left.

The old Blade had to dance with the new.

Riven walked backward, never taking his eyes off me until the doors of the landing had shut. No one but Dynara and I heard the soft thud of the locking post being pushed into place behind the wooden doors.

Everyone in the hall was sealed in.

Except for those of us who knew where the servants' entrance was hidden.

Dynara put down her fan. "It's done. We can't change the plan now, Keera."

"This is our only chance to find Nikolai," I pleaded. "I will wait as long as I can, but we need to start *now*."

Dynara didn't need to hear another word. She marched over to Crison and whispered something in her ear.

Crison clanked her ornate silver cane against a glass. "Before the real show begins, I think it best for the lords to get to know my girls with a dance or two." She turned to Kilmor. "Lord Kilmor, if you would be so obliged." She lifted Dynara's hand for him to take.

"It would be my pleasure," he said, stepping forward.

The only hint that he had stepped on her toes was the brief flinch in Dynara's smile.

Crison then nodded her head at the Blade. "My newest attraction is free, sire. Do her the honor of being her first?" Crison's tone made it obvious that she was implying much more than my first dance was up for grabs.

I swallowed down the bile coating my tongue and curtsied.

Kairn licked his lips hungrily and nodded. He crossed the dance floor in three strides and grabbed me by the waist like he was picking up a bale of hay. He did not bow before the music began nor did he keep a respectable distance between our bodies as we twirled around the dance floor. I glanced around the room and saw that all the men were acting the same, draping their partners over themselves in a fashion that would never have been allowed with noble ladies. Not even in Damien's dingiest of after parties.

The courtesans laughed and giggled, well-practiced in the art of making men believe they were enjoying their company. I was glad that this would be their last night of play-acting they would have to suffer through.

"Are you feeling better, sire?" Kairn's steps were sluggish, but I didn't know if that was the sleeping draught making its way through his body or just a lack of grace.

He grunted but said nothing.

"Such a shame that the king could not join us," I pushed. I couldn't pull words out of men easily like Dynara. At least not without my knives. But I had to try. If the pendant on his chest was concealing some kind of weapon, I needed to know. Preferably before the room went up in flames.

Kairn sniffed loudly. "The king has more important matters than attending parties."

"You're the second most important man in the kingdom and yet you're here." I batted my lashes and my pulse raced, fearing I had laid the flattery on too thick. "Who will protect him from an attack if you are not by his side?"

Kairn's scarred lip pursed. "The Arsenal is not his personal guard. We do not travel with the king."

"We?" I raised a brow. "Are your brethren here? I'm sure we could find them escorts that would please them."

Kairn shook his head. "The Arsenal does not travel together. The kingdom is best protected if our strength is spread across the entire continent." He grinned, evidently believing his rehearsed speech made him sound more important than he was. But there was something interesting in those words. That hadn't been how the Arsenal operated when I was Blade. Damien must have made changes for a reason.

"I'm sure my sisters would feel safer with as many of you in the city as possible." I feigned a look of panic and leaned closer to him to whisper. "We are all terrified those monsters will come from the clouds and roast everyone in the city alive."

Kairn pulled me against him. "No need to worry about that." He stuck out his chest like a mating bird. I would have written it off as a poor attempt of wooing, but Kairn's black eye flashed and the amber pupil was no longer a perfect circle.

There were three of us in this dance now.

It could have been a coincidence, but I think something in Kairn's words triggered Damien's worry. Perhaps my gut feeling about the pendant had not been as outlandish as I'd thought.

I waited three seconds. If Damien had recognized me through the glamour, Kairn would have already shoved his sword through my throat, but his eyes were anchored to my breasts. It would be a shame to burn such a lovely bodice, but I already knew I could never stomach wearing it again now that his hands had touched it.

I forced down the urge to vomit as I stroked Kairn's cheek. "What takes more bravery? Fighting off one of the *waateyshirak* or defending us from the Elves in the west?"

Kairn's eyes narrowed. I watched the amber pupil shift from the sideline of my vision as I trailed my hand down Kairn's chest and toyed with his belt.

He grinned. "Those Elves are nothing compared to the shadowy beasts. Our armies will take care of them soon enough."

"They've lived so long. Has that not made them good fighters?" I pressed my chest into his, and it had the exact effect I'd intended.

Kairn's jaw went slack as he stared. Then he straightened as the crescendo hit its peak. "It's the Fae you have to worry about. Elves are just as easy to kill as they are to capture."

I blinked in disbelief. I hadn't even needed to weave Nikolai's capture into the conversation—Kairn was already alluding to it. A sly smile curved up my mouth as I started to ask him about where they could keep such prisoners, but Kairn went rigid. The amber pupil flared across his black eye, and I knew that the Blade was no longer the one in control of his body.

Damien's scowl tugged along Kairn's scar. I thought he had somehow guessed who I was, but he never got the chance to ask.

A loud boom shook the walls.

Everyone turned their attention to the band as if any of their instruments could make such a sound.

Only Damien in Kairn's body looked up and saw the large amber gem come loose and plummet to the floor.

We both backed away with enough time to spare ourselves, but Lord Kilmor was caught in the fall. His body was pinned underneath the giant stone, blood oozing from his mouth. He tried to speak, reaching out with his hand, which still held a wineglass. He groaned and his arm went limp.

Dynara's chest heaved as she screamed. I knew that her terror was not real, but it didn't keep the men from surrounding the fallen gem and their lost lord. Dynara stepped back through the crowd in four deft steps and started up the staircase.

Crison was already standing at the top of the landing, her glamoured pendant around her neck. "I will fetch some servants from their quarters to help clean up this mess at once," she called out to the lords, who were already chattering about who the king would name as the next Lord of the Harvest.

She slipped through the door and waited for Dynara. They needed to secure the entryway again before the lords tried getting out. Crison tugged at Dynara's arm, but Dynara waited, silently pleading with me to follow them and leave Kairn behind.

But I couldn't. He knew where Nikolai was, and I already owed Nik so much. I wouldn't turn my back on him now.

I shook my head and watched Dynara slip through the doors without me. There was a loud bang as the wooden beam dropped into place. None of the lords noticed; they still stood around the gem and Kilmor's broken body.

Only Kairn was looking about the room. "Where are the servants?" he said, more to himself than the lords. "Where are the girls?"

He had noticed what the lords had not. Every courtesan and servant had disappeared. He drew his sword, still glancing about the room, and then his gaze fell on me, amber pupil pulsing and bright.

It was Damien's scowl on his face.

I started to run, and Kairn charged after me. I dashed up the stairs, trying to claim higher ground, but his strides were long enough to catch me. His boots trampled my skirts, pulling the release ribbon free. Kairn reeled back in shock as my outfit transformed in front of his eyes.

Without the burden of cloth swirling around my legs, I jumped up onto the banister and slid behind Kairn, using the momentum to push his shoulder and send him tumbling down the stairs. I tried to reach for the pendant along his chest, but his sword sliced my arm. I cursed and landed in a roll on the floor.

The lords turned around from the commotion, but I didn't care if they saw me now. They were already dead.

Kairn hurled a dagger at my head, and I ducked under it, drawing a dagger of my own.

Something sharp stung my nose.

Smoke trickled underneath the doors. The lords' murmurs turned into surprised shouts as they ran for the stairs.

"It's locked!" someone shouted.

Three men pulled a velvet curtain to the floor. "The windows!" they cried, scratching at the thick sheets of wood that the servants had nailed into the stone exterior.

Kairn cursed from the landing, trying to break through the door with his giant size. He sneered down at me as the first licks of flame crawled up the drapes. "You plan to die with us?"

"Not at all," I said, disappearing into a flash of light.

"She's a bird" was the last thing I heard before the screaming started.

I flapped my wings, soaring high above the growing cloud of smoke. Subduing Kairn without killing him would already be hard enough. I didn't need to fight every lord desperately clinging to life; I would let the smoke make quick work of them.

I circled the manor five times, flying higher with each pass. The screaming stopped. I tucked my wings against my feathered body and plummeted toward the hole in the roof. I closed my eyes as I passed through the smoke, only opening them when I heard faint coughs through the crackling.

Hot flames devoured the walls. The lords who had tried to climb the drapes had fallen to the ground, flesh melting from their bones. The fire licked my feathers, and I transformed back into my Fae form, using my fire wielding to push the flames away.

The men who were still alive were on their knees, coughing too hard to notice me weaving through the floor. A wave of my hand pushed the smoke upward, giving the men momentary relief.

I scanned the room searching for Kairn, but he wasn't among the languishing lords.

An arm reached for my ankle from behind an overturned chaise and pulled me to the ground. My chin smacked against the tile, splitting the skin as Kairn dragged me along the floor.

I twisted, aiming a kick at his face, but he blocked it with his upper arm. I conjured my gusts, trying to pull the air from Kairn's lungs but he stomped on my thigh. I heard the snap of my femur as he broke it. Then I screamed.

Kairn snorted as I writhed in pain, trying to free myself. It was overwhelming—the flames flared higher, stoked by my magic, but I couldn't focus enough to direct them. Kairn straddled my waist. I swiped for his pendant, but he evaded my grasp by leaning back, pressing onto the splintered bone that was sticking out of my skin.

"I thought that's what you were after." Kairn's pupil flared, and I knew Damien was watching as he wrapped his hands around my neck. It flared again, settling on my eyes.

Shock registered on Kairn's face as Damien took control of his body, but then it faded into pure vindication. "Such a disappointing way for this to end, Keera," he rasped as his hands tightened around my throat.

I held the last bit of air in my lungs as I spread my arms, trying to find some kind of weapon. Flames scorched my skin, but I didn't let that stop me.

Metal. Something hard and round. *A goblet.* I pulled it toward me with just my fingertips. The blood vessels in Kairn's natural eye exploded, and a bead of sweat fell off his brow onto my throbbing face. I inched the goblet closer until finally it rolled toward me. I grabbed the rim and jabbed my leg upward.

I howled as the jagged end of my bone pierced Kairn's back. My vision blurred from the pain, but I held on. I refused to die in this place, fighting Damien in a stolen body. I jammed my leg once more, and Kairn's pupil went still as Damien lost control.

Kairn's grip on my throat loosened just enough for me to twist out of his reach. I smacked his temple with the goblet. His head lolled back behind him as he rolled off me, not quite unconscious but dazed.

I snapped my leg into place and let my healing gift fuse the bone as I pushed the flames against the wall. The other lords had fallen to their sides, wheezing loudly as smoke filled their lungs.

The pain in my leg faded to something manageable, and I pounced on Kairn. With a handful of his cloak, I spun around his shoulders, pulling the fabric taut and pinning his arms with my legs. I yanked as tightly as I could, using my control over the air to pull the last of his breath from his lungs.

It only took a moment for him to fall limp.

I wiped my nose and looked around the room. Most of the lords were dead, but not all. Dynara had wanted them to burn in here, and I was not going to risk her desires for mine. Tiny little currents of air formed along each of their lips, pulling the last of their lives from them until all but Kairn lay dead along the manor floor.

I sent the largest gust I was capable directly at the eastern wall. The stone toppled into the garden, and the flames raged with new air to stoke them. I dragged Kairn by his shoulders, and we tumbled onto the grass.

He was too big to carry in my eagle form, so I summoned a root to circle around Kairn's body. It lifted him from the ground, growing out of the soil like a seedling. I walked around the manor toward the city center, ready to fight the soldiers I had seen that afternoon, but there were none. Dynara must have done something to slow them down.

There was a cart by the stables. Kairn groaned as I dropped him into it and pulled out a length of Elvish rope from the pocket of my trousers. His wrists were thick. I tied the rope around three times to secure the binding and cut above the knot with one of my Elvish blades, the only edge sharp enough to slice through the silver rope. I used the rest to bind his legs.

I pulled my hair back into a loose braid and secured it with the rest of the rope. Kairn's pendant still lay across his chest, rising with his shallow breaths.

The top of it was perfectly clear like glass, but the inside was rimmed with a thin concave pearlescent gem. I brushed it with my fingers just as horns called out into the night. Kairn coughed, partially roused by the sound of the battle. His eyelids fluttered and the pendant began to glow.

Then I heard the piercing screech of a *waateyshir*.

CHAPTER EIGHTEEN

THE *WAATEYSHIR* COVERED THE starlit sky with its inky wings. The residents of Cereliath came pouring out of their homes, flooding the streets. Panicked shrieks echoed into the night, and within moments the entire city descended into chaos. Another horn sounded in the distance. The steady rhythm of soldiers marching grew closer, approaching from the west side of the city.

I ran through the street. Dodging women and children howling in their nightdresses and men wielding anything from their kitchens as a weapon. The shadowy beast snapped its beak as it drifted overhead, souring the air with its foul stench. It made no noise. It didn't need to; everyone in the city knew why the creature had come to Cereliath.

To feed.

I jumped over two children cowering in the street. Three men blocked my path, and I shouldered my way between them. My chest heated. I would never reach the beast fighting against the flow of panic.

Higher ground. That's what I need.

I curved in a rounded bank and leaped for a drain on the closest dwelling. I caught it by the tips of my fingers. The shadowy beast let out a screech as I hauled my aching body onto the roof.

My heart hammered against my ribs as I ran, my path completely clear of obstacles apart from the empty air between dwellings. The first was easy enough to jump over, but the second was wider than any gap I had successfully cleared.

I thought about flying, but switching forms used so much more of my magic than my other gifts. And I would need all my strength to keep the *waateyshir* from making a meal of our rescue mission.

I didn't let up. Instead I ran faster, never taking my eyes off the beast that was now circling the city center. I jumped and released that whirling power that came from my chest. I was propelled forward, soaring on my gusts before I crashed down onto the neighboring roof.

"Fire!" someone shouted from below as I rolled out of my leap.

I smirked and lifted my hands. Both were covered in bright crimson flames that tickled my cheeks. I waved my hands in a circle in front of me, uncoiling each tendril of flame into long fiery strands that stretched as I braided them together.

Feron had taught me how to braid the wind, but it worked just as well with flame.

Another horn blew in the distance, but I didn't have time to look as I launched the fiery ball at the beast. It snapped its beak but didn't follow it as I had hoped. Its long neck reared back and it shot a blast of black fire down on the city.

Gerarda ran down the street in the opposite direction of its path, throwing open the doors of the carriages that were now blocked from the crowds and ushering the courtesans and servants out of the city on foot.

I couldn't defend all of them, but I could distract the beast. I disappeared into a flash of light and flew straight up into the air. The *waateyshir* made a slow bank as it turned. I waited until I could taste death on my tongue and transformed back into my Fae form. I dropped in free fall and sent a fiery blast toward the beast.

It worked. The creature fanned its wings and saw the flash of light as I transformed back into a bird. I dove and the beast followed, snapping at my tail feathers. I flew upward, looping back over the *waateyshir* as it tried to follow my path.

A group of soldiers shot a barrage of flaming arrows at the beast. I missed the attack, but the beast did not. The arrows turned to ash as they scraped the shadows leaking from the *waateyshir*. The beast shrieked and dove after them.

I dropped onto the roof and turned back into my Fae form.

"What's the plan?" Gerarda shouted, fighting a soldier on the street below.

I jumped from the roof and landed on another soldier's back. "Get everyone to the portal and hope the beast doesn't follow us." I dodged a third soldier's swing.

Gerarda pounced on his shoulders and stabbed her knife through his throat. I disarmed him as he gurgled his last words and started running toward the train of carriages. The residents had begun to crowd around them, banging on the doors, demanding to be let in, as if some well-polished wood could keep them safe from the shadowy beast that was feasting on a troop of soldiers.

I lit a circle of flame around the middle carriage. The Mortals lurched back in fear of being burned. They saw my golden eyes and ran in the other direction.

I snuffed out the flames and opened the door. Six Halflings trembled inside. Two in servants clothes and the rest dressed for the ball. "Run to the western edge of the city," I told them as I helped the first out of the carriage. "You will find Halflings wearing white pins around their necks. Trust them."

They nodded and ran.

I grabbed a fallen sword and joined Gerarda sparring five soldiers on her own.

"Why did Elaran find the Blade bound and stuffed in a crate?" she asked, pressing her back to mine.

"Duck!" I shouted. We moved as one, avoiding a soldier's swing. I gutted him through the belly with his comrade's sword. "Apparently he's too big for the sleeping draught to work."

Gerarda knelt and swiped a soldier's legs. "Did you only bring one dose?"

"Of course not," I shouted, shoving two soldiers to the ground with their bows jammed through their eyes. "We brought a second. It didn't work either."

Gerarda clenched her teeth. "Was Riven opposed to a third?" She switched to throwing knives, and soldiers started dropping in every direction.

"He's unconscious and in a cart." I rolled my eyes. "Why does it matter how he got there?"

Gerarda rushed forward, the man still on her sword, and pinned a second to the door of someone's house. "Just once, I would like to go on a mission without you complicating it."

"I don't complicate." I slashed my blade across my new opponent's neck as the *waateyshir* rained down black flame from above. "I improvise."

The soldier in front of me dropped to his knees. Dead. Gerarda shot me a look and I held up my hands. "I didn't touch that one."

His upper body crashed to the ground, shaking the long shaft of the spear sticking out from his skull. Vrail stood behind him, her arm still extended from her throw.

"Where did you come from?" I swung my sword. "You're supposed to be in Myrelinth."

A sword sliced the throat of the man I was fighting. "She came with me," Gwyn said with a proud smirk on her face.

My nostrils flared. "We agreed you needed to study your runes."

"Gerarda sent word that there was trouble." Gwyn blocked a loose swing with the axe she held in her other hand. "We passed Riven on the way." My chest heaved with relief. "He got a group of Halflings and a few carriages out of the city before alarms were raised," Gwyn continued. "Says reinforcements will be here soon."

"Soon?" I ducked under Gerarda's swing as she took down two men in one blow. She turned to fight another, and Fyrel had taken my place against her back. I sighed. Of course Gwyn had brought her too. "How did you get here before the reinforcements?"

Vrail looked down at her opponent guiltily, but it wasn't for his death.

My head snapped to Gwyn.

She levied a heavy swing at a soldier. "We might have been studying at the edge of the portal so we would know if you needed help."

"How chivalrous of you." I gritted my teeth. "Gwyn, we can't let Damien's men see your eyes. It's not safe."

She held up her wrist and the glamoured bracelet that dangled from it. "I planned ahead."

My nostrils flared. "I think it's best if—"

"Get mad at them later!" Gerarda shouted. "We need as many people as we can get."

Gwyn laughed but then her face turned dark.

From the shadow of the *waateyshir*.

"Duck!" I shouted as the beast opened its beak to attack. I pulled up as much stone as possible to create a shield over us. The black fire poured over the edges, but no one was hurt.

I lowered the rock back into the ground. Elaran stood on the other side of it with Dynara and Crison. "I found some friends," she said with a smirk.

"Good." I nodded at Gwyn. "You and Fyrel head to the portal to help Riven. Take as many Halflings back with you as you can. Tell Riven not to be a fool. I'm trusting him with your lives and every Halfling we send you."

They nodded and ran.

"There's still courtesans in the other carriages," Dynara said pointing down the road.

My stomach hardened. That was in the opposite direction of the portal.

Dynara lifted her chin. "I haven't worked this hard not to get them to that damned portal, Keera."

I sighed. "Fine, but don't go alone."

"I'll come with you," Vrail shouted, taking down another soldier.

"And the Blade?" Gerarda threw her last knife and moved onto arrows. "He's still unconscious in that cart."

I tracked the *waateyshir* as it circled back for another attack. I had bigger things to attend to. "Can you take care of that, Ger?" I batted my lashes. "Take El with you."

"Always cleaning up your messes," Gerarda muttered. She emptied her quiver in a single pull of her bow and turned in the direction of where I'd left the cart. She paused and I looked to see why.

Kairn was gone.

"He can't have gone far," I called, running for a rooftop. "His hands and legs are bound with Elvish rope."

"You brought rope but no extra sleeping draught?" Gerarda's jaw cocked to the side. "How did Hildegard ever name you Blade?"

I stoked the soldier's torches on the hill. The flames roared, catching the notice of the shadowy beast. "I was her favorite," I teased.

Gerarda shook her head. "That's the only explanation."

The *waateyshir* started feasting on the line of soldiers. My shoulders eased by a fraction as I jumped onto the street once more.

"Down!" Gerarda shouted as she launched a knife directly at my head.

I didn't hesitate. My chest flattened against the ground as Kairn hopped to the right, all his limbs still tied.

Gerarda's throwing knife vibrated in the black wood of the royal carriage, missing him by an inch.

Kairn grinned and angled his arms against the blade. I rose to my feet, unbothered until the Elvish rope fell to the ground.

"I didn't mean to do that," Gerarda said, realizing she had given Kairn an Elvish blade—the only kind sharp enough to cut through his binding.

"This is why she picked me," I shouted. I turned to Kairn, ready to subdue him with my magic when a trail of black flame turned the dwelling beside me to dust.

"Watch out!" I hurled myself on top of Gerarda, knocking her out of its path. We both lay on the ground staring up at the beast as it started to whistle.

Then it stopped.

Mid-attack.

The beast tilted its head as if in a daze.

I looked around, wondering what had caught its attention. The pendant at Kairn's chest pulsed with white light. The shadowy beast bobbed its head to the rhythm.

Kairn could control it.

The pendant wasn't a weapon; it was protection.

I conjured two vines and wrapped Kairn in their hold before he could run. The pendant's light dimmed as he struggled, and the *waateyshir* let out a terrifying shriek.

"Keera!" Dynara yelled as the beast attacked. She ran for me, leaving Crison and Vrail behind and catching the beast's attention.

Panic swelled in my chest. It burst through me, shredding my fear and my control all at once. "No!" I screamed, reaching out my hand and shooting a golden wave in Dynara's direction, catching Crison and Vrail in the wake.

She fell to the ground as someone pushed her out of the way. I turned to Kairn with two fists of flame. "Order it away, and I won't kill you."

He spat at my boot.

I diffused my flames and grabbed my dagger. I yanked his wrist and cut off his ring finger. "Order it away or I will take a different appendage next." I pressed my dagger to his groin to make my message clear.

Kairn bit his lip to keep from crying, but the pendant along his chest started to glow. The *waateyshir* stopped its rampage and soared into the clouds. It shrieked in the distance and left Cereliath in its smoking, burnt wreckage.

Kairn snarled at me. "Good enough?"

"No," I said, before slamming the end of my blade into his face. Kairn crumpled to the ground like all the smaller men I had fought as Blade. I cut the pendant from his chest and tucked it into my pocket. Whatever it was, I knew it was too valuable to let Kairn ever get his hands on it again.

Gerarda came to my side and blew two sleeping darts into his neck. "See how simple it is?"

"He was already unconscious."

"And now he'll *stay* unconscious."

I rolled my eyes. "Put a bag over his head. And a gag and earmuffs to be safe."

Gerarda's smirk fell and she nodded.

I turned around expecting to see the others fending off the few soldiers that were left, but the men had fled. Instead, Crison and Vrail sat on the ground where Dynara had left them. They were conscious but Elaran stared down at them, eyes completely wide.

Crison and Vrail each had amber eyes.

CHAPTER NINETEEN

Pirmiith handed me a change of clothes he'd found at the back of the safe house. Dust shot into the air as I unfurled them but they would do. All I wanted was to get back to Aralinth to check on Vrail and Crison. They had seemed fine traveling to the safe house, great even. But that same uneasiness that settled in my stomach every time I watched Gwyn use her magic twisted my belly now.

But I couldn't do anything for them until we dealt with Kairn. And I would never bring him into the spring city.

There were too many things he could see.

Too many things *Damien* could see.

I took the glamoured wristlet off. It was useless now that Damien and Kairn had broken the enchantment.

My breath hitched as I lifted the shirt from the pile. It wasn't a shirt at all, but armored leathers. A vest with no sleeves.

My jaw clenched.

"We should cover his face before he wakes," Pirmiith said from the other room. Feron had pulled rock from the earth the moment we stepped inside the tunnel. All Damien would see was stone in every direction.

As far as he would know, we were in a cave.

"No need," I called in Elvish from around the stone wall. "He's seen the gold of my eyes. He already knows I'm a *niinokwenar*."

I fidgeted with the gold ring along my middle finger. It felt like Feron had given it to me so long ago. A safety net for when Damien entered my dreams. The glamour kept him from seeing anything he could use against me.

Like my scars.

I hadn't needed it for weeks. The elixir worked well enough, and even on the occasions that I fell into a short sleep without drinking it, Damien never called. As soon as I had learned to take control of the dreams, he lost all interest in the connection he'd forged between us.

The ring would keep my scars hidden from him and Kairn. But I trusted everyone else and knew they would see them. I didn't even know the names of some of the Elverin that Pirmiith had brought, but they would know this truest part of me.

I swallowed the lump in my throat.

Seeing them means they hold no ill will against you, I reminded myself. *You can't hold on to secrets and juggle every decision of this war. You have no use for secrets anymore.*

A warm sureness filled my chest at those words. It was a strange feeling; one I had not felt in a long time. One I thought I would never be able to feel again.

Trust. In myself.

The light was dim with only two faelights hovering along the ceiling. Even still, the moment I stepped around the wall, everyone went quiet.

Riven let out a grunt from under his hood, his fingers reaching for the laces at his throat to untie it, but I shook my head.

This was my choice.

Gerarda smiled smugly from the other side of the slab while Elaran's jaw dropped. Her gaze followed the same path that all the others did, starting at my shoulders before trailing down to the fiery patterns along my wrists. Her nostrils flared as she saw Brenna's name written bigger, and more rigidly, than all the others.

I felt the weight of Riven's stare beside me, but I didn't look at him.

Feron beamed at me. Then he clapped his hands. "Let us begin."

Gerarda pulled out a small vial of blue liquid that I recognized. Unstoppered, it would fill the room with a pungent odor, foul enough to raise Kairn from his unconscious state.

I looked at Feron. "You can't just enter his memory while he's unconscious?"

"It would add a considerable amount of time to the process."

I glanced at Riven, who was still under his hood. Even though I wanted him to be honest about who he truly was with the rest of the Elverin, having Damien announce it to the room by mindwalking into Kairn was not the way it should happen.

Understanding flooded Feron's face. He raised his hand and a root shot from the earth, twisting around his wrist. His lilac eyes glowed for a long moment before he dropped the root back into the ground.

Feron turned to Pirmiith. "There is movement along the eastern edge of the forest. Something big."

"I will bring a group to search." Pirmiith stood straight, his spear already in his hand.

Feron shook his head. "Send two."

Pirmiith frowned. "Do you not need help with the mountain man?" His lip curled as he looked down at an unconscious Kairn.

Feron smiled gently. "I think the five of us can handle one Mortal man." He looked at Riven and me, and then Gerarda and Elaran. The only people in the room who knew the truth about Riven and his connection to Damien.

Pirmiith's grasp tightened on his spear, though he still seemed doubtful.

I cleared my throat. "If it's the *shirak*, we need to know."

Pirmiith's jaw pulsed, but he nodded, leaving with the others.

"I could have left." Riven lowered his hood as the Elverin slipped through the portal.

No one contradicted him. The muscle in his neck tensed. We were not lying for him, but it was too close for Riven's comfort.

"It will anger Damien more that you're here," I said. Anger was a useful emotion. Anything that threw Damien off his collected nature could be helpful. "But put your hood back on."

Riven's lips parted in confusion.

I swallowed but didn't hold back. "He will see your green eyes as a weakness."

It tore at me to see the hurt on Riven's face. Not because he cared what Damien thought, but because me saying it meant I thought the same. I was happy that Riven could live the rest of his life without pain, that his sacrifice hadn't meant he died that day in Elvera, but it was still a loss.

There were no other shadow wielders who could replace him, and that was all his brother would see. A gaping hole in our advantage.

Riven pulled his hood forward and leaned against the wall. In the dim light, the shadows were heavy across his face and body. If I didn't know his powers were gone, I would have believed that he still had command of the darkness.

I turned my attention to the slab in front of me. Each of Kairn's limbs were encased in thick roots that wrapped around the base of the slab. I pulled the pendant from my pocket. "Kairn used this to control the *waateyshir*."

Feron frowned. "That isn't possible."

"Damien has done impossible things before," I said with a shrug. "I saw him use it. It pulsed just before the beast arrived, like it was answering the pendant's call. The beast only fled because I made Kairn use the pendant to send the beast away."

Feron held the pendant in his palm. "Then this is an invaluable asset."

I nodded to Gerarda. "Wake him. I want Damien to know he's lost hold of his secrets and his weapon."

Gerarda opened the vial. The scent of rotten eggs and brine, more intense than any sea I had ever come across, wafted into the air.

Kairn's nose twitched and then his eyes opened. One dark gray. One black.

I used my gusts to send the foul odor out of the room, and his amber pupil pulsed.

Or Damien's, from the way the pupil pulsed brighter and turned in a circle to count the people in the room.

Finally, it landed on me.

I held back a sigh of relief when Kairn's eyes didn't lower to my scars. Instead, a vile grin grew over his thin lips. It was haunting and unnatural, like a creature had taken its time to cut Kairn's flesh from his bones and wear it as a disguise.

"I thought I glimpsed a change in your eyes," Kairn said in a cool tone that was unmistakably Damien. Even though it was the dirty, scarred face of the Blade that looked up at me, all I could see was the man who had carved the scars into my back.

"*Niinokwenar*," Damien spat like the word was poison on his tongue. His gaze shifted to something over my shoulder and his smile turned into a scowl. "You've put your remaining days into an hourglass, Keera." He looked back at me. "Or did you think I would let my brother ride you long enough that your filthy womb could sprout a new Fae?" Damien huffed a laugh. "Or birth an army to rival my forces?"

Kairn's body tried to sit up, but his head barely moved an inch.

Damien noticed Feron standing at the Blade's feet. "How long do you think it will take, Lord Feron, for my men to burn your forest to the ground and seize the cities my father was too lazy to take from you?"

Feron lifted his chin but did not deign to respond.

Damien huffed another laugh and turned back to me. "Is that your plan, then? You gave up being the kingdom's Blade to become Feron's whore?" He turned to Riven. "Do you let him fuck her too, brother? I suppose it needn't matter who fathers the brute as long as it has purple eyes."

Something solid smacked Kairn's jaw. I whipped around to cool Riven's temper, but he hadn't moved.

A bloody root sunk back into the ground. Feron took two menacing steps along the slab and squeezed Kairn's face. "You will not disrespect the *niinokwenar* again."

"Torture this body all you want." Damien shrugged as best he could against his bindings. "It's not me who feels the pain."

Feron's eyes glowed violet. Kairn's body shook against the magic as Feron entered his mind. The ancient Fae's nostrils flared as he rifled through the Blade's mind, searching for something. Or someone.

Kairn let out a high-pitched scream. Feron's lips twitched into a momentary smile as Kairn's body went limp.

Feron let go of him, and his amber pupil was nothing more than a solid, crisp circle. Kairn's head darted in every direction, taking in the room for the first time.

Feron sat on a stool he'd constructed of roots. "Damien will not bother us again."

"That seemed unpleasant." Gerarda crossed her arms.

Feron nodded solemnly. "Mindwalking is a blessing, but like all gifts, it can be sharpened into a powerful weapon when needed." He tugged at the long sleeves of his robe. "Anyone wanting to access the Blade's memories with me must touch his bare skin."

"You're doing that to me?" Kairn's voice shook.

"No." Feron stilled. "How much pain you experience in this process is entirely up to you. A willing participant will feel nothing but warmth. Fight the magic and the more uncomfortable it will become."

My chest tightened. I was the only one in the room who knew just how uncomfortable it was having Feron walk through one's memories.

"Or you could just tell us what other uses your pendant has to Damien." I lifted my brows at Kairn.

Riven's hand clenched. "And where you took Nikolai."

Kairn grunted but didn't say a word.

Feron let the moment stretch for a long while before he stepped toward Kairn's head. "Very well." He placed his hands against the Blade's temples.

Gerarda and Elaran gasped in unison as the warmth of Feron's magic took hold. A slithering feeling looped around our arms and then branched out from our spines.

I closed my eyes and watched as the blackness behind my lids began to swirl.

There was no source of light, but I could see the others standing beside me in the darkness. Kairn kneeled in front of Feron, not bound but silent. He crossed his arms and refused to look at us.

Feron's brow twitched as he sorted through Kairn's memories. The darkness lightened and gray shadows swirled all around us. The memories flew by, too quick and too many for me to understand.

Feron bit his cheek and the shadows became inked with color.

"You make it seem so easy," I murmured as Feron riffled through Kairn's latest memories. It had taken much more than a few moments for him to break in to my mind.

"Some minds are more stubborn than others." He opened one eye at me.

Gerarda laughed. "She's been told that before."

I flicked the back of her head.

She lifted her hand to it, not out of anger, but curiosity that she could feel my touch at all. Inside Kairn's memories, all our minds were connected.

Feron closed his eyes once more and kept searching.

I studied him as he did his work. The fluttering of his eyes behind his eyelids, the small twitches of his head as Feron discarded one memory for another.

There were no restrictions on my powers now. Any gift that a Fae had, I had too as the *niinokwenar*. Even though mindwalking was usually gifted to Dark Fae, Feron was certain that I could master it if I took the time to train.

I looked at my hands and thought of Vrail and Crison. Two more Halflings I had marked for battle the moment their eyes turned amber. I already had one gift that came with too much power. I wasn't interested in gaining more.

Feron let out a short breath. And the colored shadows stilled, finally taking the form of something I recognized.

Elaran gasped as the island of Elvera appeared before us. It floated in the sky, high above the Pool of Elvera below. The newly ignited waterfall poured down in an endless shoot, feeding the lake and the Silstra all at once.

It was the day I broke the last seal.

The memory started. It was as if we were all living through that day again, except this time through Kairn's eyes.

I saw myself trying to cut through the seal and failing. Amber blood poured down my nostrils and throat, so thick I felt the urge to choke again just watching it.

Tears welled in my eyes as Riven came and grabbed my hand. His body fell limp as he gave me every last drop of his magic through the bond. His hand found my shoulder as I cried, reminding me that he'd survived. I watched—both past and present versions of me—as Riven died.

"Take the Elf," Damien's voice called inside Kairn's mind. He glanced at me leaning over Riven and started to run. Kairn grabbed Nikolai by his tunic. Nik kicked but his shouts were muffled by Kairn's meaty hand. I watched myself as I chased after them, spent and broken hearted, but Kairn jumped into the portal. He turned back, looking over his shoulder, and we all saw the blurred image of Vrail pulling me back from the water, telling me not to chase after them. My throat burned.

I could feel Kairn's smugness leeching from the memory. He had abandoned all those soldiers below without remorse. Fled like a coward and called himself a victor because he managed to take a hostage with him.

The sensation made me sick, but I didn't punch Kairn like I wanted to. That would only make Feron's job harder.

Instead, I held my breath and waited to see where Kairn had taken them. Riven's hand on my shoulder tightened. The portal that had reopened in Elvera was a rare treasure. It could bring passersby to any portal in the realm.

Kairn could have gone anywhere. I didn't even know if he understood what the portal was when he had jumped through it. The magic may have taken him to whatever location last flitted through his mind with no conscious effort at all.

But now I had an answer. My hands turned to fists as I watched Kairn drag Nikolai onto the shore of a lake. He kicked him in the head and Nikolai fell. His limbs splayed out at odd angles in the sand, red pooling along his lip.

Kairn panted for breath as he bound Nik's limbs and threw him onto his shoulder like a sack of flour. Then he stood and faced a view I had seen countless times before.

Out of all the places Kairn could have gone, he chose the island that I knew so well.

My teeth gritted against each other. I had been too quick to listen to Vrail that day. She had urged me not to chase Kairn through the portal. She had said that it was useless, too dangerous to justify since we had no way to know where Kairn had gone.

But my instincts had been right.

Where else would a dog go except back to the cage his master had made him?

I pushed the guilt from my mind as I saw Kairn enter the throne room through his own eyes. Damien sat perfectly straight in his gold throne, his blond hair accentuating the cheekbones that had only grown starker since he'd claimed the crown. His jade eye and his black eye tracked Kairn across the marbled tile until the Blade reached the dais. Kairn threw Nikolai to the ground like he was nothing and knelt before his king.

The other members of the Arsenal stood behind the throne, each one wearing a gleaming fastener at the necks of their cloaks. It had only been days in this memory since Gerarda and I had killed the Dagger, Shield, and Bow during the battle of Volcar, but Damien had already appointed three more men. All just as nasty and brutal looking as the last. All with one black eye and amber pupil.

Damien stood. The scar along his magic eye pulled taut as he looked down at Nikolai with disgust. His scowl became a faint smile as he turned his attention back to Kairn.

"Finally, one of my weapons has come home a success." Damien grabbed the canister of wine beside his throne and poured two glasses. He picked up his own goblet, savoring a sip, before motioning for Kairn to pick up his own. The Blade was still a servant, after all.

Damien snapped his hands at the guards stationed along the entry. They moved in unison to pull the tall white doors open just wide enough for a gangly young man with a red velvet cushion to scurry through. He clambered up to Damien on knobby legs that could barely hold his weight. Kairn's gaze focused on the red marks along his skin. The scars looked as if hot oil had dripped along the flesh and was left to burn.

"Look." Riven pointed at something in the memory. Kairn's attention had turned from the young servant to the items on the velvet cushion.

Five gleaming pendants sat on the lush fabric. Each a perfect copy of the one Kairn had worn on his chest.

Damien's lips thinned. "Only five?" He looked like he wanted to spit at the boy. "I told the smith I wanted as many as he could fashion."

The servant paled. "Th-this was all he could do with th-the measurements you gave him."

Damien lifted his chin. "There is nothing left?"

The boy shook his head rather than speaking.

"Nothing left of what?" Elaran murmured but none of us answered her. We just watched as Damien dismissed the servant and let the cushion sit on the table beside his throne.

His long finger traced the edge of the middle pendant. "Our enemy may have regained some semblance of their old power." He tapped the glass covering the pearlescent material inside the pendant. "But I have reawakened an even older enemy."

Kairn's viewpoint shifted as he looked Damien in the eyes. "You expect us to fight this war on two fronts?"

"Not at all." Damien smirked as he picked up a pendant and fastened it to the middle of Kairn's chest. "The *waateyshirak* are the natural enemy of the Fae, and these pendants will make them . . . understand that our objectives are aligned."

Feron took a step forward, his eyes narrowing as he studied Damien. One Elvish word had revealed so much. Damien had meant for the *waateyshirak* to return. And he didn't just know their name or how devastating they were, he thought he could use them to his advantage.

"Can you reason with the *waateyshirak*?" I asked Feron. "Do they speak like us? Do they have some kind of language we don't know?"

Feron didn't answer; he merely took another step forward, refusing to look away from the memory.

Damien pinned three more pendants to his Arsenal. His hand lingered over the fifth before he assessed the last member. The Bow was brawny but young, pocks still dotting his cheeks and only a few hairs growing on his chin.

"You're stationed in Koratha, correct?" Damien asked.

The Bow nodded.

"Then I shall keep this." Damien slipped the pendant into his pocket. "There are only five of them after all."

Kairn looked down at his chest to study his pendant for the first time. I squinted as if that would make Kairn's memory clearer or compel him to ask Damien all the questions I wanted him to answer.

Riven noticed the peculiar sheen of the material inset into the pendant. "What is it?"

Feron shook his head. "I have never seen it before. But I will ask Vrail when we return. She may have come across a description that I do not recall."

Damien addressed the four members who had pendants pinned to their chests. "Keep them on you at all times and use them only when needed."

Kairn cleared his throat. "And what are they needed for, Your Majesty?"

"To protect my armies and send the *waateyshirak* feasting on half-blood meat." Damien sat back down in his throne and took another sip of wine. "If the Faeland is going to commit treason with magic, then I shall defend my kingdom with it."

A cool confidence spread over Damien's face, infecting the Arsenal surrounding him. Even though it wasn't my memory, I could feel the swell of anticipation that had thrashed in Kairn's belly that day. It was sickening.

The memory faded to nothing, and another took its place. This time we were on an island, but it wasn't the Order.

Tall trees spanned across the large expanse in front of Kairn. He stood on a beach of pearls across a narrow passageway with Damien and the rest of the Arsenal. It was one of the northern islands of the Fractured Isles. He looked down and the pendant glowed along his chest as a *waateyshir* opened its beak and rained shadowy death onto the forest below. The forest where the local Halflings had taken refuge after we had destroyed the ports. The ones Gerarda had begged to come with us that day. But they would not abandon their homeland.

Vomit crawled up my throat. Damien had trained his Arsenal on them. As far from our scouts as possible.

In the memory, Kairn muttered something under his breath. I didn't recognize the word as it left his lips, but I was connected to his mind. I knew the meaning because Kairn did.

Burn them.

My stomach knotted. Dynara had talked of burning people too. That was all this war had become: two wildfires coming to a head with nowhere else to burn. Either one would succeed, or we both would be snuffed out, but either way only destruction would be left in our wake.

Syrra's words echoed in my mind. *Is it worth all this suffering?*

The *waateyshir* flapped its wings and wound back its neck. I thought it was going to attack once more, following Kairn's command, but it thrashed its head instead.

The beast was fighting whatever control the pendant had on it.

"Let it go," Damien ordered from his spot along the shore. "We have more important matters than burning a few stolen ships."

Kairn relaxed, wheezing as he bent over his knees—the pendant took a toll to use.

The new Dagger tossed Kairn a towel to wipe his brow.

Damien watched the beast fly away before turning back to the group with a satisfied grin. "Faelin thought herself so clever when she vanquished those beasts. I doubt she realized how powerful the pieces of themselves they'd left behind were."

"Pieces, Your Majesty?" the Shield asked.

"The *waateyshirak* lay eggs like any common bird." Damien tilted his head to the side as the beast disappeared along the horizon, out to feast on the creatures of the sea before the suns rose. "Some of those shells were left behind. Enough to brandish the weapons I made you and the pendants you wear now."

Damien turned on the ball of his foot. "The seal was the perfect catalyst. It was a rebirth of magic back into the land. But why couldn't it birth something else? Magic comes at a cost. If the Fae wanted their magic back, then they would have to take their terrors back too. And with these"—Damien pointed to their pendants—"You can keep those filthy creatures from terrorizing us."

Kairn wiped his brow. "The beasts will still pose a risk when the rebellion is dealt with."

Damien merely shrugged. I could see in his casual confidence that he knew the beasts would only feast for a year. "I will face the brunt of any risk as long as it means I stay seated on my throne." He met Kairn's gaze. "And I will reward anyone who aids in that cause, far above the handsome sums I'm already paying you."

The rest of the Arsenal grinned.

"What did it feel like?" Damien asked Kairn, his black eye pulsing with amber.

"It was like trying to ride a wild stallion. No, an entire herd. All at once," Kairn answered honestly.

The Arsenal paled beside him.

"You must practice then." Damien clutched his own pendant. "I cannot be everywhere at once to protect my kingdom. They are powerful beasts. I doubt true control is possible, but if we can keep them from attacking our cities, then I can rest easy with whatever damage they do."

Feron and I shared a worried glance before he waved his hand and launched us out of Kairn's mind. I had what I needed. Damien only had five pendants, and we now had one.

We could use it to protect our cities from the *shirak* just as he had planned to do himself.

I turned to Riven, and for the first time in weeks, his eyes were filled with hope. Not at the idea of protecting our borders and the Elverin inside them, but of having something Damien wanted.

Badly enough to trade for.

CHAPTER TWENTY

"WE CAN'T ABANDON HIM!" Riven shouted, his hood slipping as he paced along the wall. "Nik has done too much for the rebellion for us to leave him with Damien. What if he kills him?"

"Or tortures him," Vrail added, her leg bouncing in her chair.

Dynara bit her lip. "Or worse."

I rubbed my brow. "I am not saying that we should abandon him. We know he's in Koratha. Now we have better options—"

"It seems the surest way to get my nephew back is to give Damien what he wants most." Syrra's knuckles bulged over the end of her armrest. "And that is the pendant."

I shook my head. "Riven, you saw what that pendant can do. We can't relinquish something so powerful to save one life. This could keep the Elverin safe from the *shirak* for the rest of their cycle. Hundreds—no, thousands of lives are at stake."

Riven jutted his chin from under the shadow of his hood. "None of them are locked in Damien's dungeons."

Feron stood. "We have been talking in circles for hours and it helps no one." His head made a slow turn about the room as he addressed us all. "We must act. I propose a vote."

Syrra's lip twitched. "A true Elverin would never vote to leave a soul behind."

"A true warrior would never sacrifice a shield that can protect save cities for one life," Gerarda retorted from behind me.

I tugged at the roots of my braid. This was senseless. "Why is this one way or another. We can offer Damien the pendant but not give it to him."

"So he can kill my nephew in front of us for deceiving him?" Syrra's jaw hardened.

I drummed my fingers on the round table. "We could make a forgery. Give him a lookalike in exchange for Nikolai." I turned to Riven. "Then you can get him out of there before Damien learns the truth."

Elaran shook her head. "He would suspect that. He would test the pendant immediately and then none of us can be sure what he would do."

"That's why we need to give him the pendant. The real one." Riven crossed his arms and leaned against the wall. "I won't abandon my friend."

"That's what you think I'm doing?" I stood, leaning on the table. "This is what Damien wants. This is why he had Kairn take Nikolai in the first place. He wants us squabbling over one life while he makes moves to take thousands. We can't lose focus. I won't allow it."

"Nik would come for you." Riven seethed. "If it was you in Damien's keep."

My head hung between my shoulder blades. "I would hope he wouldn't. I would hope that if I were captured and my friends had something that could protect the Elverin I have spent my entire life fighting for, they would know that I would *never* want them to sacrifice it for me." My nostrils flared. I pointed to Gerarda and Myrrah. "We are the only ones in this room who have been prisoners in the kingdom, and I know they would share that same hope."

Gerarda and Myrrah nodded.

"Damien made a grave mistake letting us get a hold of this," Myrrah said, eyeing the pendant at the middle of the table. "We can't afford not to exploit it."

Darythir shook her head as Feron interpreted the conversation for her. "This is just another circle. Let us vote," she signed.

Feron nodded. "I don't think we need faelights to cast this vote. We can raise our hands." He tucked a loose twist behind his ear. "Who believes that we should trade this pendant in exchange for Nikolai?"

My chest tightened. Riven and Vrail's hands shot into the air. Syrra was slower but just as adamant, her jaw set as she stared down the table at me. Dynara swallowed, her eyes glued to the table as she raised her hand.

Rheih gasped as Feron raised his own hand. "I did not expect that, old friend."

"It is not an easy choice." Feron placed both hands on the top of his cane. "But I am not convinced these pendants are great protection. Damien's Arsenal already struggles to use them to control the *waateyshirak* and they are still young. As they grow, they will only become harder to control. I am not willing to sacrifice an opportunity to return Nikolai to us on a tool I am convinced will fail."

I looked around the room to see if anyone else would raise their hand after Feron's speech but no one did.

Feron cleared his throat. "And who believes that we should offer a trade but not forfeit the pendant?"

Gerarda and Elaran raised theirs together, followed swiftly by Myrrah. Rheih waved her hand over her shoulder, her eagle-like eyes narrowing on me. My breath hitched as Darythir also raised her hand.

The vote was split. Five to five.

"It seems the *niinokwenar* is to be the tiebreaker," Rheih mused.

I raised my hand and Riven sank to the floor.

Syrra stood. "Very well, the *niinokwenar* has spoken." She walked out the door, back to her sister's crypt.

My throat tightened, but I knew I could not leave this conversation here. I looked to Vrail and Riven. "I expect you both want to join us on the trade."

They nodded.

"And can I trust that you will follow the plan even though you voted against it?" I flexed my fingers against the tabletop.

Vrail's brow wrinkled over her reddening cheeks. "No. I don't think I could." Tears welled in her eyes.

My heart broke at her honesty. "Then you will stay here. Help Rheih prepare the infirmary for when we get Nikolai home."

I turned to Riven. My stomach swelled like a raging sea. We had been through so much in our short time together, but always from the same front. Now that we stood on opposing sides, I didn't know what choice Riven would make. I trusted him with my life, but I didn't know if I could trust him to choose me over his friend—over his guilt.

Riven's jaw flexed and he stood. When he spoke, there was no malice in his tone, not even defeat. It was gentle and sincere. "I will do whatever you say, *diizra*."

I found Gwyn in her burl. She'd claimed one in our grove when she first arrived in Myrelinth, but Gwyn had never moved in, preferring the lower city to keep as far away from me as possible. I was glad that storm had passed. I liked having Gwyn close by, in the same grove that held everyone I considered family.

"I need your help," I said, knocking on her open door.

She was twisted on the floor like a braided loaf. I raised my brow—I couldn't imagine a mission where she would end up in such a position. The exercise was definitely one she'd learned from Gerarda. Gwyn's head popped up from between her legs. "With what?"

"Magic."

Her amber eyes glowed as she unknotted herself and stood. "Lead the way."

We crept through the groves, which were quiet in the early morning now that most had gone to bed. We turned into the Dark Wood and Gwyn's walk transformed into a skip. "Where are we going? Volcar?" Her eyes went wide and she licked her lips.

Gwyn had been wanting to visit Volcar ever since the magic had been restored. Before then, really. Ever since I gave her that perfume and described the snow and smoke to her on our makeshift beach. My stomach clenched. That seemed like a lifetime ago now.

I shook my head. "Aralinth."

The excitement faded from Gwyn's face and three little lines appeared between her brow.

I crossed my arms. "If it's too dull, you needn't come."

Gwyn shook her head like a sheet blowing in the wind. "I'm coming."

"Good." In truth, I couldn't do it without her. But Gwyn had already shown how inflated her self-confidence had become. I didn't want to add to it until I knew she could humble herself on the field of battle.

I grabbed a vial of pressed flowers from my bag and dropped two blue lilies into the small pool tucked into the branches of the portal. The color reminded me of Gwyn's eyes. Or what her eyes used to be.

We stepped out into the gardens of Aralinth. Magic had only intensified the eternal spring in the city. The canopies that hung over every part of the city were thicker and held blooms I had never seen before.

Even the grasses in the garden sprung blooms as far as we could see. Darythir had said that the moment the seal broke, they could feel the magic surge beneath their feet like a wave and the gardens became a meadow, restored to their former beauty.

Gwyn leaned her head on my shoulder and looped her arm through mine. "It's the city your mother would have known."

My jaw went slack, unsure what to say to that. Until now I had only caught glimpses of what the Elverath of old had been, what Aemon had destroyed. I was determined to restore its glory fully before fate claimed me. Even if it was the last thing I did.

And to do that we needed a weapon that could kill the *waateyshirak* once and for all.

The large split in Sil'abar opened as we walked through the entrance. A gentle breeze blew through the giant trunk of the Elder birch, carrying the scent of sap and freshwater from where the liquids pulsed in the live grain walls.

I led us to the display room without trouble. Cereliath had been a success, but I was not foolish enough to know that luck had been on our side. As much as I wanted to fight this war alone, I could not. But I wanted to give those who fought alongside me something stronger than faith or luck to fight with. I wanted to give them something that had been chipped away with each loss we bore.

Hope.

Gwyn's jaw went slack as she stared up at the shattered sword hanging on the wall. "It's Faelin's." She pressed her hand against the glass case, tracing the outline of the largest pieces of the blade. "I recognize it from your book."

I nodded. "The only other blood-bound blade we have." I grabbed the frame and yanked it off the wall.

"Are you allowed to do that?"

I shrugged. "I'd rather ask for forgiveness."

A mischievous smirk sprouted on Gwyn's lips. "We could fit the smaller pieces as arrowheads. The larger may work as throwing knives."

I grabbed an axe from the wall and wedged the blade behind the frame. The snap echoed down the hall as I wrenched the case open. I paused, expecting a rush of footsteps, but there was just silence.

"We're not making arrows and knives." I lifted the glass top from the case. "We're making *one* weapon."

"What kind?" Gwyn's gaze never left the golden steel.

I fanned my hand above the pieces. They had sat, undisturbed, for millennia, but now they were to be reforged. I picked up the smallest piece and held it up to the faelight. "The one it was always meant to be."

The glass creaked against the wood floor as Gwyn leaned it against one of the other display cases. I caressed the hilt of the sword. It hummed under my touch, the magic of the weapon recognizing the magic in me.

"I can feel it," Gwyn whispered, touching one of the shattered pieces of blade. "It's almost like it's quivering very *very* fast."

I grabbed my own dagger and cut my hand. The amber blood glinted with gold as I wrapped my fingers around the hilt. "I need you to cast a binding spell."

Gwyn ran a hand through her red curls. "I don't know how."

"Yes, you do." There was no doubt in my voice as I nodded to Gwyn's chest. "You pore over those books every spare moment you have. You know the runes. Trust yourself."

Gwyn's cheeks flushed. "Memorizing runes isn't the same as spell casting. Feron says that art will take me decades to master."

My stomach clenched. We didn't have years. No one did while the threat of Damien and the *shirak* loomed overhead. I tighten my grip around the hilt and it warmed under my touch. This was the right path. I knew it and so did my magic. "The Elverin believe that blood carries memories." I set the hilt back into the case. "That magic lives through every living thing and passes through the generations—an endless cycle."

"*Giiwithara'biizan kwenar*," Gwyn interjected with an unconvinced nod. "Darythir and Rheih explained it to me."

"The Fae of old are your ancestors as much as they are mine. So are the Elves who wrote the first spells." I grabbed her hand. "Trust yourself. Let your instincts guide you, and you will carve the right path. Give the ancestors a chance to answer your call."

"And if they don't?" Gwyn's eyes lined with tears. I didn't know if she was worried that the ancestors would ignore her or that they didn't exist.

My chest tightened. I had struggled with that question for so long. Life had been too hard to believe that those of the past watched over us. But after seeing my mother's sacrifice—the Light Fae and what they had done for their kin—I couldn't deny the truth any longer. Our ancestors were not only watching over us, but they shared in our pain. They hadn't wanted any of this to happen either.

It only served Aemon and his son to forget that.

"They've always been with you, Gwyn." I tightened my grip on her hand. "Just as they've always been with me. And they haven't failed either of us yet."

Her lips disappeared as she inhaled deeply through her nose. She let out the breath and her fingertips glowed with amber light. Gwyn closed her eyes and started carving a circle into the air. There was no pattern to her movement, but it flowed like a river cutting through a mountain.

Suddenly Gwyn's fingertips pulsed brighter. Her face relaxed as she let the rush of the river carry her and painted the air with her magic. She combined four runes, layering them over top of one another until the circle encasing them shifted from amber to gold.

Gwyn opened her eyes and pushed the spell onto the shattered pieces with her palm. Her voice echoed as she spoke, like all her foremothers were speaking with her. "*Ozithir*."

The blade responded immediately. My arm lifted with the hilt, pulled upward by some unseeable force. The magic gripped my hand, keeping me in its hold just as the seals had done each time I'd planted my dagger into the ground. One by one, the shattered pieces rose into the air too—rearranging themselves into their original order, the space between them growing closer and closer until not even a hair could fit. The spell folded around the pieces like a blanket, fusing the blade together with a flash of amber light.

There was a final pulse of magic, and the hilt burned my skin. I cursed, letting go of the blade. The metal clanked against the empty case. Gwyn gasped as I stepped back.

The gold color of the blade had faded to a common silver.

Gwyn's brows furrowed. "Did I do something wrong?"

I shook my head, touching the hilt with just my fingertips. It was hot but no longer burned. "Blood-bound blades choose their wielder. This blade has not chosen me."

My stomach twisted into knots. I didn't want any more responsibility in this war, but I had assumed the sword would recognize the similarities between me and Faelin, its previous wielder. Now someone else would have to claim the blade and the responsibility that such a weapon carried.

Gwyn took a deep breath and reached for the hilt herself. She closed her eyes as her fingers wrapped around it, head turned away as if that would keep her hand from burning. After several long moments, she opened a single eye. The blade was still silver.

I burst into a fit of laughter. Gwyn shoved my shoulder. "It could have been me!" Her offense gave way to her own hearty laugh.

I sheathed the sword in its case and strapped it to my back.

Gwyn's gaze still lingered on the hilt. "Who do you think it will choose?"

We walked out of the room together, ready to head back through the portal to Myrelinth. "Fyrel," I answered only because I knew it would annoy her most.

Gwyn's eyes stormed with envy. "I would never hear the end of it."

I laughed but its aftertaste was sour. Whoever the sword chose would have the only other weapon against the *shirak*. The moment the blade turned gold, they would be a target. For the shadow beasts and Damien's Arsenal.

I just hoped whoever Faelin's sword chose didn't have to die.

CHAPTER TWENTY-ONE

Syrra still stood guard over Maerhal. Her legs were stone anchoring her to the ground above her sister's head. Only her eyes tracked me across the room as I took my usual spot along the middle of the stone slab.

Syrra swallowed as I placed a bouquet of moonflowers across Maerhal's chest. Nikolai had spent centuries bringing flowers to her statue whenever he was home; it felt only right that I should continue the tradition while he was gone. "I thought Vrail had been leaving them," she whispered, eyes teary.

My head dropped low. "I don't think Vrail can step foot into this room without crying. She spends all her time trying to find a way to locate Nikolai."

Syrra's teeth gritted together. The only thing that made her feel more useless than knowing she hadn't been there to protect her sister was being reminded that her own nephew had been taken under her watch.

She nodded at the bouquet. "You have shown your hand too easily. You have kept this up for weeks without letting me know it was you bringing the bouquets. You did not come here to lay flowers."

"No," I sighed, tucking Maerhal's bandaged arms over the stems. "But this way we both get to enjoy the blooms."

"Her favorites," we said at the same time.

The tears lining Syrra's eyes began to well, but they did not fall. She lifted her head, refusing to blink. "What have you come to ask of me?"

I appreciated Syrra's tact. She never wasted time, always cutting straight to the point. It reminded me of Hildegard.

"You still believe that changing Halflings into Fae is the only way to win this war?"

Syrra nodded. "Not just the war. But the *waateyshirak* are a contentious threat, especially when our numbers are so small."

"Feron has agreed to train the new Fae in their powers." My hands balled into fists at my sides. "I'm hoping Riven will too."

Syrra didn't move. She was a statue again, a soldier cast in stone for failing her post.

"They will need to be trained in combat too." I made a point of letting my gaze trail over Syrra's scars, each a mark of her skills and victories on the fields of battle. "Trained by someone who has fought alongside Fae and won."

"Pirmiith is a warrior in his own right." Syrra's neck flexed. "He fought in all of Aemon's wars while I was left useless."

"And he shall again, if he wishes." I grabbed Syrra's hand. "But we both know he is not who should lead this army. We have sat fractured long enough. It is time that *all* our leaders step up to the helm again."

A single tear dropped from Syrra's eye, missing her cheek and wetting her full lip instead. "You saw for yourself. Elverath rejected the chance to bless me. Perhaps I am meant to step *back*."

I shook my head. "For someone so old, you are absolutely ridiculous."

Syrra didn't laugh.

I changed tactics. "Perhaps Elverath didn't find it fitting to make you Fae because you have already been blessed."

She scoffed, her hands waving over her sister. "Any blessings given to me have rotted away." Her jaw dropped as she turned and saw what I held in my hand. The blade was still wrapped in my cloak, but Syrra recognized its hilt.

I knew she had stared at that blade for hours, as a girl, as a warrior in training, even as a seasoned one. I knew she had haunted the equipment room in Sil'abar to stare at the relics of storied warriors because I had done the same at the Order. I stared into the stony eyes of the statues that had not been destroyed, devouring every story I heard of them, not knowing that one day I would meet one of those statues come to life.

With a blade more powerful than any other.

I pulled out the sword, a glorious *ring* echoing through the room as if the steel conducted its own music from the air. Syrra gasped as she saw the blade forged anew, but silver.

"Faelin's blade did not choose me." I kneeled and presented the sword to her. "I think it had another, *wiser* warrior in mind."

Syrra blinked down in disbelief, no quick retort finding her lips. She reached her hand out but did not dare touch the blade. Her fingers shook over the steel.

"How did you reforge it?" she croaked. "Those arts have long been lost to us."

"We asked and Elverath answered." I lifted the blade a few inches higher.

Syrra pulled her hand back. "What . . . what if it doesn't choose me?"

"Then no one beyond these walls will ever know." Syrra was strong, but I knew a soldier could only take so many hits before her shield shattered and her blade began to dull. Maerhal, Nikolai, Lash. Her blood rejecting the chance to turn Fae.

Syrra needed a win.

We all did.

And I hoped I was right that this would give us one.

She took a deep breath and reached for the hilt. Her hand moved like snowmelt, barely at all and then all at once. Her fingers wrapped around the hilt, and the steel shone brighter than the suns with her touch.

Syrra hoisted the blade high over her head. It carved a trench in the rock with just a scratch. The blade was sharper than any other in existence. Syrra's eyes went wide as the bright glow of the blade faded and the weapon's true color returned.

Gold. The same color the blade had been while wielded by Faelin.

But the sword was no longer the Faemother's.

It was Syrra's.

For the first time in weeks, a smile crept along Syrra's mouth. It was not one of joy or pride, but one of vengeance.

CHAPTER TWENTY-TWO

Calling Damien into my dream was as easy as breathing. Whatever connection he had formed between our minds was second nature now. I smirked down at him from his precious golden throne when he appeared, kneeling on the floor of the throne room.

"I knew you would be tempted." Damien's magic eye flared as he pushed himself off the marble floor. He pulled on the bottom of his waistcoat so it sat straight across his hip.

I snarled at him and used my control over the dream to set the throne aflame. I stayed in the seat as the gold started to drip onto the floor. "I've come to propose a trade."

Damien scoffed. He tucked his hands behind his back though he didn't hide his surprise quite enough. "You have nothing that interests me."

"I don't?" I raised a brow. "How disappointed Kairn will be that his master thinks so little of him."

Damien's eye narrowed by a fraction. A hairline wrinkle appeared between his brows but it disappeared as he adjusted the circlet that appeared on his head. "Blades are useful but they can always be *replaced*." He emphasized the last word as he scowled up at me. "Why walk through a battle to collect a new weapon when I have my choice of blacksmiths here in the capital?" His tone was cool and collected, but I recognized it for the mask it was.

"You may forge new Blades at will, but you can't forge new pendants, can you?" I waved my hand and Kairn's pendant was conjured along the front of my leathers. I twisted on the throne so both my legs were folded over one armrest, completely encased in the burning flames.

Damien's lip curled. "If you know what it does, then I doubt I have anything that could tempt you to part with it."

I pulled one of my smaller blades from my belt and scraped the molten gold from the back of the throne. Damien flinched.

"Now, Damien," I said in my best imitation of his condescending tone. "You are too smart to think that's true." I waved my arm out to the room in front of us. "I pulled you into this dream for a reason. And it wasn't just to see that scar on your face."

Damien traced a finger down the scar Gwyn had given him. "Tell Gwyn I send my regards. I'm looking forward to seeing her again."

My bones turned to ice. I took a deep breath and reminded myself that Gwyn was safe in the *Faelinth* with me. Damien couldn't reach her. I lifted my chin in his direction, toying with my knife. "She certainly has improved from the horrific state you left her in." Bile coated my tongue as I remembered Gwyn's gaping wounds, but I didn't let my disgust show.

The amber pupil of Damien's black eye flared at my lack of a reaction. "I'll make sure to enjoy her death even more the second time." Damien's lip quivered in anticipation. "Perhaps, I'll have you watch."

I flung the knife into Damien's shoulder. He lurched from the force, but there was no pain. It was his dream as much as it was mine.

"We will give you Kairn and his precious pendant in exchange for Nikolai." I gritted my teeth as Damien yanked out the knife and stanched the bleeding with a handkerchief from his breast pocket.

"Who?" Damien fluttered his lashes like a lady at court.

I rolled my eyes. "The Elf you stole from us. Do we have a deal or not?"

Damien took a step forward and shrugged. "I hung an Elf along the wall by that name. We do not let traitors live long in the capital, especially not ones who are trying to kill me."

I kept my face still. Damien was trying to bait me, to see if I would reveal how much information I knew. The truth was I didn't know anything about Nikolai. I only knew Damien. And he would have made sure that Nikolai's death had been whispered about in the farthest reaches of the kingdom. It would have been brutal and public, as much a punishment for me and Riven as it was for Nik.

"We have ways of knowing when one of our soldiers is killed." I shot Damien a hard look, rising from the molten throne to stand over him. "You know Nikolai is alive just as well as we do."

Damien's jaw fettered from side to side. "How do I know you will return the pendant?"

"You don't." Damien was too clever to assume that we would give the pendant over so easily, but I knew he might be desperate enough to try anyway. And that was all I needed.

Damien's lips thinned but he nodded. "When?"

"Full moon," I answered. It was three days away but with the *shirak* around, I preferred to work under as much moonlight as possible.

Damien pulled at his sleeves. "Or I could extend a peace treaty for the night and you can send your rebels to the palace to make the trade."

"Absolutely not."

I flicked my ring finger with my thumb. The location had to be a place that didn't give Damien a heavy advantage but one he would still agree to.

"The edge of the Dead Wood outside Koratha." I stepped from the dais and the chair turned to ash behind me. "Let me make myself clear." I took another step. I was standing so close to Damien, the heat of his breath landed on my chin. "If Nikolai or any of my people are injured during this transaction, I will wreak havoc on your city until I find you quivering in the palace, and then I will fillet you alive."

Damien rolled his eyes. "No need for dramatics. Give me my pendant and you can have your precious Elf back. With no *other* injuries than the ones he's already sustained." Damien took the knife I had embedded in his shoulder and slowly grazed it down his throat to the middle of his chest. I didn't know if it was a threat or a reenactment of what he had done to Nikolai, but he plunged the hilt of the knife through his chest and the dream ended.

CHAPTER TWENTY-THREE

"THIS ISN'T WORKING." Vrail sank to the ground, wiping the sweat from her brow. Feron used a root to pass her a waterskin. "We've been at this for days it isn't going to happen."

Feron turned to Gwyn. "Do you remember what it felt like when you drew that first rune?" He glanced down at her ankle where the tether was marked.

Gwyn shook her head. "I wasn't thinking at all. I was too exhausted."

"They're never going to let us leave," Crison wheezed, snatching the waterskin from Vrail's hand.

Feron's eyes narrowed. "Perhaps it was not the exhaustion but the clear mind." He gestured for the two new Fae to sit up straight along the grass.

Crison groaned but did it. Feron reached for both their hands and sat with them on a bench made from his roots. His eyes started to glow and his voice went deep. "Let the warmth fill your body and your mind. Concentrate on that warmth, let it overwhelm you until it is all you can feel."

I stilled beside Gwyn, waiting for something to happen. I crossed my arms in frustration but Gwyn pointed at Crison's relaxed shoulders. Her eyes glowed behind her eyelids. A small songbird flew from a nearby tree and perched on her shoulder.

Something jumped out of the lake. I turned and my jaw dropped. All across the glassy water were animals of every kind. Birds, turtles, otters. All of them were swimming closer to shore, closer to Crison.

The tree line was full of animals too. Mostly small rodents, but there were a few foxes sitting curiously. Their presence didn't scare the small animals away—I wasn't even sure they noticed the predators beside them. All the animals were focused on Crison.

Vrail's leg bounced and her eyes shot open. She gasped as she saw Crison's arms stretched out to the sides, holding every songbird in the Dark Wood. Crison opened her own eyes, pupils glowing bright amber, and smiled.

"I called and they came."

"Is this a new gift too?" I asked Feron as Gwyn knelt down to pet one of the birds.

His brows raised. "Yes. I have never heard of such a power before." He reached out and pet a bird on Crison's other arm. It chirped and didn't move. "It seems Elverath has given you an extraordinary gift, Keera."

I scoffed. "To curse Halflings?"

"Do Gwyn and Crison seem cursed to you?" Feron tilted his head at Crison's wide smile.

"Well perhaps it is me who is cursed," Vrail muttered. "Cursed to never discover my gift at all."

"They've arrived." Elaran nodded in the direction of the three giant shadows riding down the King's Road.

I bent to the ground where we were still huddled along the edge of the Dead Wood, hidden from the approaching Arsenal's view. I flattened my hand along the soil and closed my eyes as my magic coursed through the network of interconnected roots. It was slow at first, then exploded in all directions.

I could feel every living creature within ten leagues of us. Every mouse, every flower, and the dozens of soldiers Damien had hidden beyond the ridge of the hill, the beach, and the far reaches of the Dead Wood. "And they brought friends." I stood, and from the hard sets of everyone's jaws, I knew my golden eyes were glowing in the darkness. "Prepare yourselves," I said with a glance at Syrra.

She nodded, the hilt of Faelin's sword gleaming behind her back. Gerarda gripped a blade in each hand while Elaran took her place between them with an arrow already nocked. They were a fierce trio. There were no others I would trust to protect us from the *shirak* if the Arsenal called in some reinforcements.

I stepped out onto the road. My cloak drifted behind me in the evening breeze as something curled around my hand. I gripped the warmth. My body still expected to feel the softness of shadow but instead I found Riven's calloused hand.

His jade eyes were dark and hard as he squeezed mine back. "They don't deserve mercy, but make it quick, *diizra*. Nikolai has been gone long enough."

I pulled his hand to my lips as if I could drain his worry with a single kiss, but I knew nothing would settle Riven's fears until his dearest friend was back in the safety of our homeland. Even though he disagreed with how I had planned this mission, he still had faith in me.

I could not disappoint him.

The Arsenal stopped their approach still on their mounts a few hundred feet from the tree line. I walked alone to meet them, holding no weapon; the threat of my glowing eyes was enough.

"Do you have the pendant?" the burly rider in the middle rasped. In the moonlight, I could see three scars running across his face. They glistened like silver rivers against his pale skin. I knew Damien had chosen the most fearsome-looking warriors to fill his Arsenal, but while such scars may have struck fear into the hearts of city folk, all I saw was a man who didn't protect his face in battle.

Such a man could never strike fear in me.

"I do," I answered back with a casual wave of my arm to the forest behind me. "I have your first in command too." I eyed the shiny Dagger at the man's throat. He stood between the Arrow and a titleless soldier with one black eye. The Bow and Shield were missing from the escort. Damien had only sent enough to ensure that their two pendants outnumbered the one we held.

The Dagger grunted, showing as little concern for Kairn's life as Damien had. Though I knew that was because the return of the Blade meant that the Dagger would be sheathed once more. The same jealousy that had plagued Gerarda for decades danced in the new Dagger's eyes now. He hadn't even had his post for a month and he already craved the taste of power only the Blade would provide.

"No trade without proof of the pendant." The Dagger raised his chin, looking down at me from the spaces between his scars.

"I don't even know your name and you're already making demands of me." I toyed with Feron's glamoured ring on my finger.

"Quinton," the Dagger answered. "And we have been instructed—"

"Your *instructions* don't mean shit to me." I raised my hand and the clouds crackled. "I am in charge of this trade, and if you listen to *me*, you shall leave with your heads."

Quinton's jaw pulsed but he nodded.

"Good boy." I pointed at the large group of soldiers waiting at the crest of the hill. "We need proof of life to move forward. Bring out your hostage and we'll bring ours and your precious pendant."

Quinton turned to the Arrow beside him and nodded once. The Arrow was taller and leaner than the Dagger, but still one of the largest Mortals I had ever seen. His dark eyes never left my body as he leaned down and pulled something from his saddlebag. He uncorked the lid of a tiny glass vial and threw the open container directly in the air above his head.

A cloud of purple fog oozed out from the vial, only visible to me because it was lit from the full moon behind it. He lifted the torch in his hand and tossed it into the thick cloud. The fog erupted into purple flames, hot enough to pull the sweat from our brows.

The entourage started galloping in the darkness. I bent down, pretending to tie my boot, and let my finger graze the soil. My shoulders eased as I felt Nikolai's presence in the midst of the herd. He was injured and sore. He would need more medical attention than I could give him, but he was alive and his heartbeat was strong enough.

I encircled the purple flames with my gusts, herding them into a small ball. My magic thrashed in my belly as I pulled water from the air to create a larger sphere around the flames. I froze it before the purple fire turned the water to steam. The flames puttered out, trapped inside with no air to feed them.

The ball dropped and shattered in front of the Dagger's horse. It reared onto its hind legs. The Dagger cursed, slipping low in his saddle, but he did not fall off.

Quinton sneered. "You expect me to be impressed by your signal?" The rasp in his voice was tighter, higher pitched.

I lifted a brow. "That wasn't my signal. I just didn't want yours to wreck the effect." I raised my hand once more and flames flowed up my arm and into the sky like a geyser rush. With three simple waves, the flames tightened and rearranged themselves into the shape of an owl mid-flight. I cooed as loudly as I could, the fiery bird flapping its wings above me.

The three men looked up in awe at my display of magic. Each of their throats bobbed as I waved my hand and my flames dissipated into the wind.

Gwyn and Fyrel rode out from the tree line. Behind them was Riven pulling Kairn down the King's Road by an Elvish rope. The bag was still over his head so he staggered like a drunkard walking home after the pub. Syrra rode behind them all, her head scanning the field for a threat from any direction.

Quinton's lip disappeared behind his teeth. "That could be anyone," he said loud enough for Riven to hear.

I turned to Riven and nodded at the bag. His jaw clamped shut as he stared up at the Arsenal, but he ripped the bag off Kairn's head and shoved him to his knees. Kairn coughed against the gag in his mouth. When he looked up at the Arsenal, his thick brows knitted in confusion.

They didn't realize he didn't recognize any of them. He barely remembered his own name after Feron had finished with him.

"He lost his fastener?" Quinton asked with a smug look at Kairn's empty throat. "And what about the pendant?"

I pulled the Elvish chain from underneath my tunic and held up the forgery Feron had made. "It stays with me until the exchange is done."

"King Damien never agreed to those terms—"

Quinton's objection was cut off mid-sentence by a thunderous crack. His head was split in two from the heavy axe that was now embedded into the base of his skull. I turned to Riven as the Dagger's lifeless body collapsed to the ground, twitching. His hood slipped back from his face just enough for me to see that his eyes were more deadly than I had ever seen them.

Riven's nostrils flared as he tugged his hood back in place. "My brother is not here, and I do not give a fuck about his terms."

The Arrow glanced at his surviving comrades. Damien had kept the truth of Riven's lineage a secret from his closest guards. But it didn't matter. Their gazes lingered over the bloody pool of their leader as they waved at the entourage to complete their approach.

The four men stopped their horses a safe distance from Riven. The two in the front dismounted their saddles and walked to the black carriage door. One reached in and dragged Nikolai onto the ground. He groaned as his shoulder was pinned under his body. My chest heaved with relief, but I stood strong.

Flames flared behind me. "Treat him with gentle hands or Quinton will not be the only one with an axe in his head."

They scoffed until the Arrow's voice boomed overhead. "Do it."

He dismounted his saddle and grabbed Nikolai with one arm. He dragged him, closing the distance between us in five paces. Nikolai was beaten and bruised, barely conscious as they threw him to the ground. I was used to being taller than Mortals, even the men, but the Arrow towered over me.

"The pendant." He held out his hand. "Now."

Riven shoved Kairn into the soldiers' midst. He fell down and the leaf-bound eye patch fell from his eye and was left discarded on the ground. The amber ring in his black eye flared, and when I turned back to the Arrow, his ring had shrunk.

Damien was here. Jumping from Arrow to Blade at will.

"I know you're watching," I called out, now looking at Damien through Kairn's face. "Call back your soldiers, and I will give your Arrow the pendant."

The ring in the Arrow's eye flared once more. This time when he spoke, I knew it was Damien who said the words.

"Why would I do that, Keera, when you've already killed my most beloved Dagger?" The cadence of the Arrow's voice had changed completely, its roughness smoothed to the highest pedigree befitting a king. Even his facial expression had turned hard and calculating instead of brutish and ruthless.

"You didn't give a shit about him." I lifted my chin to the Arrow, wondering if he could still hear me while his master controlled his mind. "Just like you don't care about this one."

Damien didn't even pretend to deny it. "That's of little consequence. The soldiers stay."

He jumped into the mind of the young man beside the Arrow. He snatched the pendant from my hand and place it around his neck. He closed his eyes and tried to call a *waateyshir* forward with the pendant.

But he couldn't.

Panic swelled in my chest as the soldier's amber pupil flared with rage. I turned back to the others. "Get Nikolai back now!"

Riven didn't need to be told twice. He ran for Nik but the soldiers held him back long enough for the Arrow to press a blade to Nikolai's throat. Red blood pooled along the steel as Nikolai choked on his gag.

"A forgery?" the Arrow spat, though it was Damien who was truly speaking. "I will gut your filthy Elf, and then I will call every beast for miles to burn everyone you love to the ground."

The pendant in the Arrow's chest began to glow. Damien lifted the blade over his soldier's head, ready to plunge into Nikolai's chest.

"Enough." Syrra stepped from the group. "Drop your blade and let my nephew go." She pulled something from her pocket and tossed it onto the ground.

The pendant.

The real one.

The amber pupil flared bright as Damien's glance darted between Nikolai's limp body and the pendant on the ground. He dropped the blade and dove for the pendant. Riven was there before the Arrow hit the ground. He scooped Nikolai in to his arms and ran for the portal hidden in the tree line.

"You broke your vow." I turned to Syrra. "And you may have just cost us the war."

"I made no vow to you." Her neck flexed. "You may not be willing to trade one life to save many, but my sister's line will not die because of you." There was no hostility in her words, just truth. Syrra had known what she was going to do from the moment we took that vote.

The Arrow stood with the second pendant around his neck. "Arm yourselves!" he shouted to the soldiers Riven hadn't struck down. "And fight for your king."

Damien's unmistakable smirk crept up the Arrow's freckled face. Both the pendants in his hands glowed bright.

And the ground shook with the piercing calls of the *shirak*.

Fyrel and Gwyn stepped beside me, swords already drawn in their hands. Another piercing cry rang out. Torches were lit along the ridge, illuminating just how much force Damien had brought to take that pendant. He didn't care if his men were caught in the devastation. The body he controlled would be safe as long as it held that pendant, and if it wasn't, Damien was secure in his palace with a pendant of his own.

I flicked my wrist and a wall of flames cut the Arrow off from his horse. A foul smell permeated the air, and the wind blew upward. The beast was right above our heads, disguised by the darkening skies.

"Move!" I shouted to Fyrel and Gwyn as I leaped away from the shadowy blast. The soldiers surrounding Kairn had not been so quick. Their bodies writhed in pain as the shadowy ash ate their flesh and turned their bones to dust. The shadows of their skeletons fell to the ground. Kairn crouched just outside of the wake with wide eyes.

An owl call echoed from behind me as Elaran and Gerarda charged forward. The soldiers that had been guarding Nikolai fled toward the hills, but their screams only drew the beast's attention.

"Get that pendant," I told Gerarda. "Syrra and I will kill the beast."

Syrra drew her sword and pointed up at the beast setting the fleeing soldiers aflame. I opened my waterskin, and Syrra ran forward without hesitation. I pulled the water from the spout in a giant floating orb and dissected it into tiny spheres. With a wave of my hand, they each flattened into discs that I sent hurling into the air.

Syrra leaped and I froze the first disc to ice. Each step, I froze another disc until Syrra was running through the sky, climbing higher and higher toward the beast. It scanned the ground, looking for more men to devour.

Syrra let out a feral battle cry and the creature turned its billowing head. Its red eyes flashed bright as it saw Syrra charging after it. I lifted the last disc, propelling Syrra high enough to jump onto the beast's back. She wielded her sword above her head, ready to pierce it through, but the beast dodged her strike.

It snapped at Syrra as she fell, nearly cutting her in two. Panic pulled at my chest as I tried to conjure enough water to catch her fall. I missed, but Syrra reached out and plunged her free hand through the orb.

That was all I needed. Syrra held her breath and let the water envelop her completely while my magic gently lowered her to the ground. Sweat pooled at my brow. The heat of death radiated from the beast as it banked along the air toward us.

I bit my cheek. I could distract the beast—lead it to Syrra's blade in my eagle form—but I couldn't use magic in that form. I would leave everyone too exposed.

The beast opened its beak, whistling as it sucked the air into its belly. The Arrow, still controlled by Damien, ran around the flames for his horse. Both pendants glowed around his neck, the one encrusted in his leathers and the one Syrra had given him.

I raised my hand, but Gerarda got there first. There was a metallic *ring* as her throwing blade grazed over the bottom belt of the saddle, slicing through the leather completely but leaving the horse unharmed. The Arrow collapsed into a dazed pile as soon as his foot hit the stirrup.

Elaran released an arrow of her own, pinning Damien's host to the ground by his cloak. "We have this."

"Aid Syrra," Gerarda shouted over her shoulder as they ran after the pendant.

Syrra erupted from water.

"Keera, pin it with pillars!" Gwyn shouted as she and Fyrel battled with the three soldiers who hadn't fled.

Syrra brandished her sword above her head and let out another cry. The beast whipped its head and soared low toward her.

I shot three stone pillars into the air, and the beast banked to the left.

I lifted three more, and the *waateyshir* dodged again as the towers curved overhead, trapping it from flying higher.

Smaller pillars shot from the ground and Syrra's dance began. She moved through the air with fluid grace, feet barely touching each landing point as she floated to the next.

The beast shot black flame from between the pillars. Syrra dodged but the flames were long enough to reach Elaran. Gerarda leaped over the fire, pushing her lover safely to the ground.

Damien smirked as he realized there was no one left to pursue him. He grabbed the Dagger's body and slung it over the bare back of the Arrow's horse. Then he jumped on and rode toward the hill. Two pendants were encrusted in Arsenal leathers, and one was hanging from his fist.

I clamped my jaw as the beast snapped at Syrra's feet. Its talons scraped at the earth as it started to walk backward out of the snare of pillars.

I raised my hands to close the cage, but Syrra held up a fist. She darted across the long-arched pillar, readying her trap.

I held my breath as the *waateyshir* freed itself and opened its wings. It let out a screech of victory and stretched its long body toward the sky.

That was what Syrra had been waiting for. She leaped from the stone with her golden blade high above her head.

Her blade struck true.

The beast let out a horrible wail as Syrra's blade tore through its chest. Tendrils of shadows leaked from the wound until nothing of the beast remained except for the scorched circle of earth where it fell.

I transformed in a flash of light. I beat my wings as hard as I could to get as high as possible before the Arrow crested over the hillside. The glowing pendants were easy to spot with my eagle vision. I tucked in my wings and dove.

Damien cursed as I scratched the Arrow's face with my talons. His horse reared, and his soldier had no saddle to steady him.

The pendant dangled from my talons. I did not tempt fate by trying for another with more *shirak* on the way. I dropped it over Fyrel's head. She caught it in her hand as I transformed back to my Fae form.

I grabbed for a dagger, but I was not wearing any weapons.

Flames covered my hands, ready to fire, but Gwyn snatched the pendant first and placed herself between the Blade and Fyrel.

Kairn's amber eye pulsed. He feigned a reach for Gwyn but dropped and swiped her legs instead. Kairn smirked as he picked Gwyn up by her curls and pressed a thin blade to her throat.

"Let her go!" I shouted as I made three quick signs with my hand at my hip.

Damien's magic eye didn't notice the movement but Gwyn did.

Kairn's lip curled. "She's not an Elf but she will do." His blade pressed against Gwyn's throat as she thrusted both her elbows back with all the force she had.

The air in Kairn's lungs released in a cough. Gwyn rolled out of his grasp and stood.

The pendant swung from Kairn's fist, but Damien didn't make his soldier flee. Gwyn stooped for a rock, but Damien made Kairn dodge the blow. The Blade's jaw hung slack, the amber pupil flared as he saw Gwyn's face.

Her glamoured necklace lay on the ground, discarded, along with Kairn's small blade.

Gwyn lifted her chin; fully lit from the moon, she didn't balk. Damien had already seen the truth.

Her amber eyes.

Damien's host snarled. Pale light glowed from the pendant as he called another beast forward. Gerarda shot an arrow through his shoulder but the damage was already done. In the distance, a shrieking call beckoned.

Kairn yanked the arrow from his flesh and stabbed the sharp end through the glowing pendant. The light flickered, like a candle at the end of its wick.

Gwyn stepped toward Damien, a small sword in her hand. "I can still gut you," Damien snapped as he made Kairn reach for the blade on the ground.

Her face was emotionless as she pierced her blade through the mountainous man's heart. The amber pupil pulsed once and then went dark.

Gwyn turned, leaving her blade in Kairn's chest. "Let's get to the portal before the *shirak* arrive."

CHAPTER TWENTY-FOUR

WE TRAVELED TO ARALINTH. It was quicker to get to, and Rheih and Feron were already there. Syrra had not left Riven and Nikolai's side from the moment we stepped back into the Dead Wood. Tears streamed down her face as she caressed Nikolai's hair, ignoring the way the shorn sides of his head had started to grow out in thick, pressed chunks.

I didn't use my healing gift. I wouldn't do anything without instruction. My gifts were powerful, but solely relying on them had cost Nikolai his mother. I wouldn't let desperation take him too.

Vrail waited at the edge of the city. The golden leaves of Sil'abar cast warm streaks of light on her face as she ran for us. For Nikolai.

"Is he alive?" she croaked, tripping on her long robe as her black braid trailed behind her.

I nodded but Vrail didn't see it.

"Someone tell me he's alive!" she screamed, falling to her knees.

"He is," Riven answered, stooping down so Vrail could see Nikolai's bruised face and the faint rise of his chest.

"He's home." Riven's voice gave way to a sob just as Feron and Rheih walked out of Sil'abar.

I put my hand on Riven's shoulder, feeling the weight of his rasps under my skin. "Let's bring him to Feron and Rheih. They will be able to tell us what Damien did to him."

Riven nodded and carried Nikolai's limp body to the healer's quarters inside. No one spoke as Rheih completed her inspection. She poked and prodded. She used instruments I didn't even know the names of to check inside his ears and up his nose. "Was he conscious when you got him?" She pulled open his lips and checked his gums.

I nodded. "I used my healing gift to put him to sleep." I turned to Feron. "Just like you taught me. And then I numbed his pain, and he hasn't woken since."

"That's all?" Rheih's yellow eyes stared up at me over Nikolai's matted coils.

I swallowed. "Yes." Fear slipped into the word; it came out breathy and unsettled.

Rheih stepped back from the white stone slab Riven had placed Nikolai on and started rifling through her shelves. Vrail grabbed his hand and refused to move even while Rheih muttered under her breath and walked around the seat Feron had made for the Halfling.

Rheih pricked Nikolai's arm with a tiny rod. She studied the red drop of blood, sniffing it twice before bringing it to her lips.

She lashed her tongue and spat on the ground.

"What's wrong with it?" Riven tensed.

Rheih pushed a gray curl back into her braid and started examining Nikolai's body. Vrail flinched when she ripped through his shirt with a blade and revealed the bruises that covered his brown skin. "He's ingested some kind of magical additive . . ."

I froze. "Damien gave him an elixir too?" The one Damien had given me had allowed him to peer into my dreams. What if his experiments on Nikolai had been worse than that?

"Perhaps." Rheih tilted her head to the side, clucking her tongue. "Magic can affect the taste of blood. Sweet for blessings and sour—" Rheih's face fell. Nikolai had not been blessed.

Gerarda crossed her arms. "A trap Damien set? Maybe he planned for Keera to heal Nikolai only for it to trigger something that would kill him."

The blood drained from my face. I had never been so happy to have not used my powers since they'd awakened. "Is that possible?"

"Theoretically . . ." Rheih muttered to herself. "But I've tasted something similar before. I just need to find"—she lifted up Nikolai's left wrist—"the marking."

Gwyn stepped backward into Syrra, her eyes bulging at the sight of Nikolai's now exposed wrist. The skin was swollen and red around the pattern, but it would settle to a pale silver. Just like hers.

Similar markings were now branded into his skin.

"I will kill him," I seethed before my thoughts caught up with me. "But how was Nikolai able to leave the palace if Damien tethered him there?"

Feron's hold on his cane tightened as he leaned in closer, examining the tether marking for himself. "A tether can have many uses. Gwyn was tied to the palace but that does not mean that is what Nikolai is tied to." He muttered something to Rheih in Elvish.

Her yellow eyes were wide. "I did not know a Mortal could set such powerful magic."

"He's using Halfling blood to do it." Bile crawled up my throat.

Rheih tilted her head. "Blood is a powerful catalyst, but it's never been used to bind a life to—"

"There's never been blood like the Halflings' before." I turned to Feron. "That day in the Rift, my mother said she didn't know why Halfling blood had turned amber. I never cared to ask then, but before their sacrifice, Halflings bled red, didn't they?"

Feron paused. "I cannot be sure. Halflings were not unheard of before the Blood Purges, but they were very rare—and all were born to our eastern kin where the Mortals had landed and settled. There was not much time between those years and the start of Aemon's Purges. And by then, almost all the Halflings who had been born were slain or died protecting their people. I do not think I learned of amber blood until after the Treaty was signed."

"What if the reason I can turn Halflings into Amber Fae isn't because I have the power to give them gifts, but the power to *awaken* them?"

Feron blinked. "Their blood is already—"

"Imbued with magic. A living capsule of the Light Fae's magic in the only people who had the hope of surviving Aemon's plot to kill the Elves and Fae entirely."

"That doesn't answer the question though," Vrail interrupted, not showing any interest in the discovery we had just made. She only had eyes for the Elf in front of her. "What did Damien tie Nikolai to?"

Rheih lifted Nikolai's wrist to Feron, pointing at something in the markings. She nodded at Gwyn. "Show me your ankle."

Gwyn stilled but pulled off her boot and sock. She lifted her foot to the edge of the slab for Rheih to inspect.

"Ancient runes," she mumbled, running to the wall to grab a large piece of glass. Its edges were rounded and it bulged out on one side so it looked like a giant raindrop when she pressed it to Gwyn's scar.

Gwyn winced from the cool glass. Rheih studied the markings around her ankle and then Nikolai's wrist, the pattern magnified under her tool. She nodded at Feron. "Can you read them?"

Feron crouched down, putting all his weight on his cane. When he looked up, his eyes were wide. "*Ziiba*," he whispered. "And the other?" Rheih lifted Gwyn's ankle only an inch but it was enough to throw her off balance. Fyrel caught her.

"*Asiina*," Feron said with a sorrowful look on his face.

"Water and stone?" Riven started to pace along the slab. "That's all we have to go on?"

Syrra's inhale was sharp as she put the meaning together. I turned and saw the worry in her eyes. "Stone is one of two symbols our ancestors used to represent a city or a home. The other is that of a tree."

Like the burls of Myrelinth and the stone dwellings of Aralinth. The two ways the Elverin had always built their homes.

"So Gwyn was tethered to a place, and Nikolai is tethered to . . . the sea?"

A thick tear dropped from Vrail's cheek and landed on Nikolai's forehead. "These runes are rudimentary, translating them properly without the full context is much more likely to be wrong than it is to be right." Vrail pointed at the rune. "This could mean water, yes. But it could be any body of water. It could be a vial that Damien could smash at any time." Vrail's chest broke into a small sob, but she forced herself to push through. "But it could also be less literal. Water is used to represent things that flow or have a cycle. Magic or spring, for example."

My stomach plummeted through the floor. "Look again, there must be more information than just that!" Panic struck my heart; it hammered in my chest like a caged beast vying to get out.

But Vrail's expression was pure defeat. "I can't translate a spell from a single rune, Keera."

I turned to Feron and Rheih, but they both shook their heads.

Gwyn pulled on her boot. "We might not know how to decode the spell that set the tether, but we know the man who did it. Damien wouldn't create it in the first place if he couldn't use it somehow." She lifted her chin. "It gives him an edge."

Riven scoffed. "Or it is nothing but a puzzle with no answer to waste our time."

Elaran tugged on one of her curls. "What would have happened if Keera had blown up the palace of Koratha instead of the dam at Silstra?" She nodded at Gwyn's ankle.

Feron's mouth went flat. "A tether is made of two parts. If the bond is not severed and one of the parts is destroyed, so is the other."

Gwyn's bottom lip protruded, more fascinated than worried. "So I would have died."

I fought the urge to vomit as Feron nodded.

"That's the threat." Gerarda stopped toying with her blade. "Damien wants us to know that at any moment—"

"He can take Nikolai from us." Riven finished for her. "Permanently."

My shoulders wilted. "So he would have tethered it to something small enough to move and break." I swallowed. "It could be anything."

Syrra caressed her nephew's face. "I will storm Koratha and gut the pretender myself."

"He would destroy it the moment you walked through the door out of spite." Riven punched the stony wall hard enough that his knuckles bled.

Gerarda scowled. "We do anything that displeases Damien and we risk killing our friend?"

Riven wiped the blood on his cloak. "Or wait for Damien to destroy the tether—and Nik with it—just before the battle starts. He has used chaos and grief as weapons already." Riven looked down at his friend. I didn't know what was eating at him more, the guilt or the grief.

I held back my own tears. That had always been Damien's tactic. Careful chess moves that ensured he had a way of bringing our rebellion to its knees at his whim. We could transform every Halfling in our ranks to fight him, but Damien knew we would be distracted with such a threat hanging over our heads.

Nikolai's life was in Damien's hands, and it was only a matter of time before Damien would claim it.

CHAPTER TWENTY-FIVE

Riven hovered over Nikolai's sick bed. Deep bags were set under his eyes and his half braid was loose and tangled.

"When's the last time you ate?" I asked, standing beside him.

Riven ignored the question. "Why hasn't he woken up yet?"

I rubbed his shoulder. "Rheih said it would take time. He's been through a lot—"

"We don't know what he's been through, he hasn't said anything—" Riven took a deep breath. "I just don't know what to do to help." He turned to me with tears in his eyes. "How do I help him?"

I leaned my head on his shoulder. "You're already doing it. You got him out, Riven. You're here at his bedside."

"You're making an insufferable amount of noise," Nikolai murmured.

Riven reared back in shock. He sat down in the chair next to Nik's bed and grabbed his hand. "I'm so glad you're okay."

Nikolai slid his hand out of Riven's grasp. "Is that what you call this?" His lip curled in disgust; it looked unnatural on his gentle face. "I may be alive, Riventh, but I am most certainly *not* okay."

Riven leaned forward. "Nik—"

"I don't want to hear it." Nikolai crossed his arms. "Did you think getting captured would change the fact that my mother is *dead*? That it would change how it was your inability to trust yourself, your need to keep the parts of yourself *you* didn't like hidden away, that got her *killed*?" Nikolai swallowed. "You want to know what your brother did to me? He threw me into the same pit my mother was kept in for my entire life. The daily beatings were a relief because at least for that hour I wouldn't have to face the reality of what my mother lived with. What she barely got to forget before *your brother* and *your lies* killed her."

Riven's chin trembled. "Nik, I am so sorry. If I could go back—"

"But you can't." Nikolai raised his chin and eyed the black cloak hanging over the chair. His gaze turned venomous. "My mother is dead and you still haven't told anyone who you are."

Riven winced.

Nikolai shook his head in disgust. "Get out of my sight."

"Nik—"

"Go!" Nikolai shouted, pointing at the door.

I stepped from the bed but Nik settled back. "You don't need to go, Keera dear. If anything, you should be angry at me." Tears welled in his eyes.

I glanced back at the door, heart torn from all the pain in the room. I grabbed Nik's hand. "Anger doesn't help me defeat Damien. And that's what I need to do." My throat tightened. I didn't add the rest. That it was what I needed to do to make this all worth it. The lives I'd taken, Brenna, Hildegard, Maerhal. If I lost focus on my mission, their deaths and all the pain they caused, would be for naught.

Nikolai sat up. "I need to get dressed."

"You are dressed."

He looked down at the simple trousers and tunic I had picked out for Rheih to change him into. "This is a misery." He lifted his hand. "Now heal me so I feel a little less miserable and can leave this room for good."

I rolled my eyes and pushed his shoulders back down onto the bed. "You need your rest, Nik. You need to heal."

"Exactly." He lifted his other hand, the one with the tether along his wrist.

I didn't move. "Nik. I can't."

His face fell. "I can't just sit in this room, Keera. Underground. There's too much to do, too much to prepare." His voice cracked. "A funeral to plan."

I sat down in the chair. "Nik, Rheih said you will be fine a few days. But I have no idea what will happen to you if I use my magic now that you have *that*." I nodded at his tether.

Nik grabbed his wrist. He stared at the brand along his skin, caressing it with his fingers. "How did you survive it?" he asked without looking up.

My back tensed. "Survive what?"

"The pit Aemon put you in." A tear fell from Nikolai's eye as he looked up at me. "You were only a child. And my mother—"

"She's how I survived it," I whispered. "She would speak to me through the walls. Tell me stories. But mostly she just listened. She listened to me sing, she listened to me cry, she always made sure I knew that even though I couldn't see my own hand in front of my face that I was never alone."

"She wrote your name in a stone. Did she tell you that?" Nikolai wiped his cheek.

I froze. "No. She never said anything."

"I felt it one night, lying on the ground. At first I thought it was just a brick or a piece of stone that had fallen away over time . . . maybe it was, but it was etched with your name. Dozens of them. Keera, Keera, Keera, Keera. Like she knew one day you'd come back for her." Nikolai's brow trembled and he picked a loose thread from the blanket over his legs. "She carved them with her fingernails."

My throat burned so hot I didn't know if I could speak. "That must have taken her a long time."

"Years, I'd imagine." Nikolai took a deep breath. "But nothing compared to the walls. She carved my name into them hundreds of times. As high up as I could reach, I could feel the carvings." He looked up at me. "Strange that you would be housed together, with her writing names into the walls of her cage and you carving names into your skin."

I swallowed. "No one leaves the darkness unchanged."

Nikolai sighed and leaned back on the pillow. He was more than distraught; he was broken.

I grabbed his hand. "But the light is healing. Just give it time."

"You swear it?" Nikolai raised a brow. "You're not just saying that so I don't start moping around and wearing outfits like this everywhere I go."

"I picked that outfit, you know."

"You spent seven hundred years locked in a tree and then five more stuffed in a hole in the ground, Keera dear. Of course you developed an atrocious sense of fashion."

I barked a laugh and tossed the spare pillow at Nikolai's head.

"Laughing is a good sign," Gwyn cheered from the doorway with a plate of food. "Riven told me you might be hungry."

Nikolai's face soured. "Not really."

"Are you sure?" Gwyn removed the lid from a bowl of stew and fresh bread. "The kitchen just finished."

Nikolai's pupils widened, and he nodded at the table beside his bed. Gwyn set the tray down but her eyes were locked on Nikolai's wrist. "I'm so sorry that he did that to you." Her eyes glowed bright. "He will die for it."

A perplexed look crossed Nikolai's face. His lips parted, trying to find the words to ask what had happened in the weeks he had been gone. But there would be time for that. He rubbed at his wrist like if he only pressed harder the brand would rub away.

I leaned back in my chair. "What did it feel like?"

Gwyn went completely still.

"It just burned." Nikolai sighed and stopped rubbing his wrist. "And then it felt like my life would never be mine again."

My stomach clenched. "Do you know what he tethered you to?"

"No." Nikolai shook his head. "He just chanted the same word over and over again."

Gwyn's fists flexed. "What word?"

"*Moroq*." Nikolai shrugged. "It sounds old Elvish to me."

"Maybe Vrail knows." I turned to Gwyn to see if she had come across it in her books, but all I saw were red curls bouncing out of the room.

CHAPTER TWENTY-SIX

"What's going on?" I asked Orrin, the youngest Shade we'd rescued from the Order, when I got to Myrelinth. She swung along the vines with other children, racing to the Myram tree.

"There's an announcement." She giggled, flipping through the air as she caught her next vine.

"Announcement?"

The entire city had gathered, as well as some Elverin from Aralinth. They crowded around the Myram, bubbling with concern and excitement. Riven stood at the base of the tree waiting for the crowd to quiet.

His fingers pulled at the laces of his cloak.

I went completely still. This is not what Nikolai had meant. This is not what Riven wanted. He needed time. I stepped forward but someone grabbed my arm.

"Let him do this, Keera," Gerarda said, appearing at my side.

I yanked my arm free. "He's only doing this because he thinks it will appease Nikolai."

She shrugged. "Does the reason matter? He needs to stop hiding and face what he's done." There was no hardness in Gerarda's voice, just blunt truth.

Riven swallowed. He took a step forward, moving closer to the crowd so they could see the jade color of his eyes as his cloak fell to the ground.

They erupted into shocked whispers. Some pointed at Riven's eyes, other backed away as if the Elverin standing before them was an imposter and not the Riven they had come to know.

He cleared his throat. "There is something I have been keeping from all of you." He spoke in shaky Elvish, his vowels clipped and his consonants too harsh for the words. He stopped, taking a breath, and when he spoke again, it was in the King's Tongue. "Some of you may have noticed my absence. I needed time to decide how to tell you this, to know what to say." Riven's head drooped for a moment but then he stood tall.

My body yearned to reach out for him, to pull him back into the safety of the shadows. But he needed to do this. He needed it, and so did I.

"The day Keera Waateyith'thir broke the last seal and returned the magic to our lands, the Fae you knew as Riventh Numenthira died." A united gasp broke through the crowd. "I used the last of my powers to help Keera break the seal and my life ended." Riven's brows furrowed, like he wanted to add something else to that part of the story but he stopped himself. "But Elverath saw fit to bless me with a new life. A life where I could live as a Halfling."

"His eyes are green," someone whispered from the back of the crowd.

Riven nodded. "My eyes are green. And my blood is amber. And my shadows are gone."

Uldrath sat on Pirmiith's shoulders with a confused look on his face. "Why a Halfling?" He looked down at the veins in his own hand pulsing with amber blood. "Why wouldn't the magic bring you back as you were? Or an Elf?"

Riven picked at the skin around his thumb. "Because Riventh the Fae was not the only one who died that day."

The crowd's gasp was even louder than the first.

"I'm not sure what reasons the others have given you to explain Killian's absence." Riven's hands shook. "But he has not been scouting or studying in the libraries of Volcar or meeting with any of the lords in the kingdom. Those were—and always have been—lies. Or at least only half the truth."

Riven's eyes searched for something in the crowd. I didn't know what it was until I saw her. Vrail, creating an aisle through the crowd as she walked toward the Myram tree, the glamoured necklace hanging from her neck. For the first time, I saw what all the others must have seen before. The striking red of the jacket Vrail always wore as Killian gave color to her cheeks, but wasn't tailored to her body like the rest of her clothes. It was the costume she wore as she played her part.

But everyone else saw Killian.

Vrail's leg bounced as she took her spot beside Riven. He gave her a short nod and kept speaking. "The prince you knew also died that day. But only because the prince you knew never existed at all."

Vrail pulled at the necklace and the clasp broke. The crowd went silent as the glamour shattered and Vrail stood before them—short, black-haired, and definitely *not* Killian.

The Elverin exploded into shouts and angry questions. "Why would you do this?" someone shouted from the bridges above the grove.

"How did this happen?" shouted another.

"Did Feron know?"

Riven raised a hand to silence the barrage of questions. "For those of you old enough to remember her, my mother was a gifted healer and a form shifter. She passed one of those gifts on to me. Her son. The prince."

Jaws fell one by one as the Elverin began to comprehend the ruse. "I was born Killian son of Aemon and Laethellia. I was not born a Halfling, but a Mortal with red blood to prove it true. But as I grew older, my magic grew stronger until eventually I transformed into my other form. Not an owl like my mother, but a Fae. A shadow wielder. From that day forward, I was both Riven the Fae and Killian the prince. Vrail took on the task of pretending to be me when my father sent me away to the tutors of Volcar, while Feron trained me and my powers in Vellinth. After a decade, he thought me fit enough to join the Elverin and I met all of you."

Feron stepped forward, his cane creaking against a rock in the soil. His lids were heavy and his eyes more sunken as he told the crowd what he had done. The memories he had placed in their minds. The lies he and Riven had spun together.

By the time he was done, thick tears had carved rivers down his cheeks and the crowd was silent.

"Why did you lie to us?" Uldrath asked in the innocent tone only a child could master.

Riven cleared his throat. "Because I wanted to keep you safe." His voice cracked. "And I'm sorry I didn't." He stalked through the crowd, passing Gerarda and me.

I followed him out to the edge of the city. "Where are you going?"

Riven froze, hearing the desperation in my voice. He walked back and grabbed my hand. "I'm not leaving you, *diizra*." He pressed a kiss to my forehead. "I'm not even leaving the city. I just need an hour alone to let this settle." He held up his hand, which was shaking uncontrollably.

There was pain and regret in his eyes, but not deception. He wasn't running away again without saying a word. He wasn't leaving with no message for when he would return. Even though I could tell that is what he wanted more than anything else, he was staying.

He was trying.

All he needed was some time, and I could give him that. I dropped his hand. "Thank you for telling me," I said, and he walked into the Dark Wood without his secret.

CHAPTER TWENTY-SEVEN

RHEIH AND FERON HAD SPENT the night assessing Gwyn, Vrail, and Crison to make their report to the rest of the council. Thankfully, none showed any signs of pain, but they still needed to learn how to control their new gifts. Or discover them.

My muscles ached from lack of sleep, but the meeting couldn't wait. Not even for Syrra, who refused to leave Nikolai's side, or Riven, who was secretly making sure all of Nikolai's wishes for his mother's funeral were getting done.

Darythir already sat in the room, with a deep frown that made it obvious she was angry. No, furious. Her eyes narrowed as I entered the room and she stopped signing. My status as a Fae-mother was something not even the eldest of the Elverin were quick to forget.

Feron walked into the room with Myrrah, the two chatting as if they hadn't been up all night too: Feron in the infirmary with me and Myrrah at watch, looking for signs of *shirak* in the skies.

She gave me a small smile before locking her chair next to the ornately carved table. "What is this about, Keera? I want to be asleep by midday."

I cleared my throat and told her that Darythir was concerned about me changing the two newest Fae. "They should have been dead but instead they're Fae?" Myrrah deadpanned. "I don't understand the problem. You should be kicking your heels but you look like you're preparing for a funeral."

I scoffed. "I only delayed their deaths. If we go to war with new, unpracticed magic wielders, who do you think will be the first ones Damien strikes down? They won't last an hour."

Myrrah shrugged. "They may choose not to fight."

I didn't dignify that with a response.

"Then they practice." She slapped her hand on the table. "Starting today."

Feron nodded. "We have already had a few sessions. They haven't mastered their gifts yet. It could become dangerous very quickly."

Darythir signed something too fast for me to catch. There was a dramatic flair in her wrist as her hands finally came to rest.

Feron interpreted for her. "She says that it would help if they were given warning instead of suddenly transforming from Halfling to Fae."

I threw my cloak onto the chair, pacing behind it. If I sat down, I would fall asleep in the middle of our meeting, and we would really get nowhere. "Do you think I meant to? I can't control it."

Feron's brows wrinkled. "But your control has been masterful since you became the *niinokwenar*. You work your earth wielding as well as I do."

I doubted that was true. "The other gifts are fine. I always feel in control. But this"—I lifted my hands and stared at them like they held some secret they refused to tell me—"this is different. It's like being on the brink of burnout, but there's no pain, just this surge of magic I can't hold back."

Gerarda flipped a blade through her fingers. "Both times it's happened you've been scared shitless. Not for you but for the ones you changed. The night you turned Gwyn, you thought she was going to get hurt when you lost control of your magic, and you thought the latest to change were about to die."

Elaran perched on Gerarda's armrest. "Why would that matter?"

Gerarda shrugged. "You can't learn to control something if you never use it. Perhaps if you used this gift *voluntarily*, you wouldn't lose control of it in moments of panic."

My belly hardened with betrayal. "You want me to turn *more* Halflings into Fae."

"It would give us an advantage in the fight against Damien." Myrrah drummed her short, calloused fingers along the table.

"That's optimistic." I ran a shaking hand along the top of my braid. "Look at the Dark Fae. Out of the ten who survived until Damien's crowning, only three were warriors. Riven can still pick up a sword, but he has no shadows to command and Lash is dead. Turning someone Fae does not make them a warrior."

Feron cleared his throat. "There seems to only be one solution." He leaned forward onto his cane, his twists falling from his shoulders to frame his face. "I agree with Gerarda. This gift you have must be used—it was given to you for a reason."

I opened my mouth to protest but Feron held up his hand. "But you do not wish to turn any more Halflings unwillingly, so we must ask for volunteers."

Myrrah's lip pursed in thought. "That would work."

"Are you serious?" I slumped down into the chair, the exhaustion winning out. "We have *shirak* flying overhead, burning our outposts to the ground, not to mention the false king would like to personally behead me and anyone who has given me so much as a smile in the past year."

Darythir waved at Feron, signing something with one hand.

Feron dipped his head in annoyance. "She asks you to make your point."

I threw up my hands. "Every Halfling dreams of revenge. Almost all of them will volunteer to fight but that does not shed the responsibility. It does not shed *me* of it."

"You fought for their freedom, dearie," Myrrah whispered, leaning on the armrest of her chair. "Youthful overconfidence is part of that." She lifted a brow at me. "A big part."

The weight of Darythir's stare did not leave me. Her lips pursed. "Then you can select the candidates from the list of volunteers," she said through Feron.

My blood turned cold. Choosing any name off that list would be just like all the choices I had made before: who should live and who should die. I would be carving a target onto every candidate's back that I selected.

My hands shook. I didn't trust myself to make that choice. I had only ever led because I had to, not because I was good at it. Certainly not because I wanted it. And after weeks of feeling like I was on my own, all I wanted to do was run away and drown myself in wine so I didn't have to be the one who made the choice.

But that wouldn't help. I needed to find a third option, the path I'd always been too impatient to search for. To find others to lean on and take some share of the weight.

"You decide, not me."

Feron stood. "Me?"

"The council." I made a point to look up at them all. "Whoever walks onto the field of battle with glowing eyes will be made a target. I will carve it into whoever I need to, but you shall pick the names. The blood that will be spilled should cover all our hands."

A solemn silence fell over the room. It stretched, like a note held too long, then faded.

I hadn't even realized Darythir was speaking until Feron cut in to interpret. "If everyone was a target, then none would be. We could mark them all."

Myrrah tilted her head, running the numbers of how many Halflings lived in the two Elvish cities. I already knew it was too many.

I wouldn't force a single person to turn. I already felt bad enough about cursing my own friends.

"No." I rapped my knuckles against the wood of my chair. "It would work in theory, but not practice. The new Fae have to be trained, every day. Turn too many and our resources will be spread too thin. Someone will get hurt."

Or worse.

Feron nodded. "I agree with Keera. I will meet with the other Fae and get their opinions on how many we could reasonably train."

"And Riven," I added shyly.

Feron's back straightened. "Are you sure he will want to be near so many magic wielders after losing his powers?"

I shrugged. "Elverath gifted me the ability to control my powers much more quickly than most. Riven is a Fae who has most recently trained. His insight was invaluable to me, and I am certain it will be again to whoever you choose."

And whoever I curse.

Feron's lips curled into a small smile. "I am always delighted to have an excuse to visit my nephew. I shall ask him this afternoon."

My chest heaved with relief. I had been willing to do it, but if Feron wanted to try I wouldn't stop him. Maybe he would succeed where I had all but failed.

Feron stood. "Then it is settled."

Darythir waved her hand, stopping him. She turned to me, asking her question by hand while Feron provided it by tongue.

"I understand not wanting to carry that decision on your own, but why not claim your spot on the council? It is your seat to take." She waved her arm in the direction of the empty chair beside Feron.

My cheeks went hot, tugging on my throat until the words came out heavy and wet. "My expertise is on the battlefield. Doing the best for our people is yours."

CHAPTER TWENTY-EIGHT

I FOUND VRAIL IN THE LIBRARY though it didn't seem to spark the same vibrance in her it once had. She sat surrounded by piles of unshelved books and scrolls. They didn't notice me enter the room—Gwyn's nose was an inch from the page at the end of the table. She whispered to herself as she read, purposely ignoring me while Vrail's gaze was locked on the wall, staring at nothing.

"Any luck?" I waved my hand in front of Vrail's face. I had asked her to find me as many sources as she could about Faelin and her defeat of the *shirak*. Vrail had started researching it the night of the first attack, but she could barely stay focused enough to read.

Her head jerked up, and her newly amber eyes focused on me. "Yes!" She jumped and cleared her throat. "I just need to find where I put it."

"I have one," Gwyn interjected from the end of the table. She pulled a brown leather-bound book from the small stack beside her and lifted it for me to take.

Her arms shielded the page she was reading, but I recognized the book as the one Vrail had stolen from the libraries of Koratha. The book full of runes.

My eyes narrowed. "What are you reading?"

Gwyn snapped the book shut, but not before I caught a glimpse of the illustration of several corpses underneath a vicious-looking rune. "I want to know as many runes as I can. Feron says it's the best way to hone my gift." She fluttered her glowing fingertips.

"There are many ways to sharpen a blade, Gwyn." I reached for the book. "But not all of them are safe."

She pinned the cover to her chest and leaned back. "It's just a book, Keera."

I could tell from her flushed cheeks that she was keeping something from me, but Vrail had taken the other tome from Gwyn and opened it to an illustration of a Fae with voluminous, tight coils and welcoming golden eyes.

"That's the book that Kil—Riven gave me when I first went to Aralinth." My finger dragged over the illustration. "I never ended up finishing it."

Vrail nodded. "Riven does love his books." She flipped the page and there was a small sketch of a *waateyshir* coiling around a giant Elder birch. Its talons had scorched the trunk, and two bodies hung limply from its sharp, shadowy beak.

"Not much is known about the defeat of the *waateyshirak*." Vrail pursed her lips. "So many of our story holders were lost during Aemon's siege, and he destroyed much of what had been written down. But this story outlines the basic elements. The Elves took care of Elverath for millennia, letting its magic flourish and grow.

But they could not defeat the *shirak* on their own, too many of their warriors were lost in their attempts. Finally, they prayed and danced to Elverath herself, hoping for something that would help turn the tide in their favor. And the great Elder birch of Aralinth sprouted from their dancing grounds and five moons later, Faelin emerged from it. She was born from Sil'abar, as the first *niinokwenar*"—Vrail's eyes shifted to me—"and protector of our people from their greatest enemy."

"The *waateyshirak*," Gwyn said, her voice full of awe.

Vrail nodded.

I tilted my head, still studying the illustration. Faelin was standing in front of the beast with a sword, no trace of her gifts being used at all. "She killed them with her magic?"

Vrail shrugged. "That much isn't clear. She studied at *Niikir'na* for many years and eventually was chosen as the wielder of one of the blood-bound blades. It is said that it turned gold the day she slew the first *waateyshir* with it."

"But we already knew that blood-bound blades could hurt them," I said with a sideways look at Gwyn.

Vrail turned the page and there was another illustration, but this time of a giant nest. Two eggs, as black as night, were tucked into the twisted branches as a *waateyshir* flew over the forest in the distance.

Vrail's finger swiped over the page and the egg moved.

Gwyn shrieked. "What was that?"

"Vrail, your hands." I pointed to her fingertips. They were completely dark, as if stained by ink.

The egg moved again, and this time the entire image came to life. It sprung from the page, ink leaking into the air until a moving painting formed. The shadowy beast screeched in the background, while figures of Elves surrounded the nest right next to us.

Vrail's jaw hung slack. "It's showing the story."

We watched as a group of warriors climbed into the gigantic nest and approached the shaking egg. In the distance a fire roared tall over the forest, disappearing as quickly as it came, as another group of Elverin lit pyres.

"Fire wielders," I whispered, recognizing the move I had done dozens of times myself.

Gwyn pointed at the flapping beast. "They're distracting it."

The warriors inside the nest waited as the egg began to crack. The ink wafted through the air, moving in punctuated motions like hundreds of sketches were flashing in front of our eyes.

One of the figures brandished their sword. There was no gold ink to mark the blade for Faelin's, but the *niinokwenar* had a long Elder birch carved into her shoulder and a mane of tightly coiled hair.

The moment the beak burst through its shell, she ran her blade straight through the pulsing chest.

Its shrieks filled the library, dust filling the air as the shelves shook. In the background of the story, the *waateyshir* roared and levied a shadowy death on the fire wielders below before growing larger, coming closer to protect its last egg.

My heartbeat pounded in my chest as if I were watching real warriors at work instead of a story of old being inked into the air. The second hatchling broke through with only three pecks against its shell.

It was dead before it even had the chance to squeak.

Gwyn's brow furrowed. "They're collecting it." She nodded down at the warriors who hammered the egg shells into pieces small enough for them to carry. The same eggshells that now filled Damien's pendants.

"They're going to fashion weapons from it," I said.

Vrail snapped her head to me. "How do you know that?"

"An easy assumption," I said.

The warriors climbed down from the nest and left the *waateyshir* to its sorrows. Only then did the ink fall back onto the page, slithering like snakes until it returned to its original form.

"Are you certain they were all fire wielders?" Gwyn tilted her head. "I couldn't tell with the black ink, but some spouts looked different than others."

I cocked my jaw to the side. "It looked like flame to me"

Vrail studied the book as if more dancing figurines would spring from the page, but her fingers were no longer dark. "There are references to Faelin's daughter, Kieran'thara, having a power that could either kill or scare the *waateyshirak*—the translation is ambiguous. Most believe it is a reference to her fire wielding gift but perhaps not."

I nodded at the shelves. "We should find every reference to her gifts we have. Perhaps your new magic can show us more than what's on the page."

"I don't even know what that was." Vrail stared at her own hand. "I've never heard of such gifts."

I shrugged. "Perhaps there weren't any. Gwyn can write spells from runes. That is not a gift previously held by the Fae."

Vrail nodded. "Spell weaver."

"Ink wielder," Gwyn whispered back at her in wonder.

Vrail's eyes went wide and she tried the words for herself.

I nodded at the book. "Is there anything more to the story?"

Vrail shook her head. "Only that the *shirak* faded shortly after Faelin created the shadow sun. Though the definition of *shortly* is relative. Now we might consider that to be instantaneous, but one must remember that these books were scribed by Elves and Fae. Their concept of short is much different than ours—"

I raised my hand, cutting off Vrail before she could start a full ramble. "Shadow sun?"

Vrail pointed to the ceiling of the library as if we could see the two suns that hung in the skies.

I rubbed my brow. "I know there are two suns, Vrail. But do the records call it a *shadow* sun?"

Gwyn squinted like there was true sunlight in her eyes and shrugged. "I've only ever called it the second sun."

I nodded in agreement.

Vrail's bottom lip protruded. "Yes, it's the phrase that's used the most in the texts." She lifted her left fist and followed it closely with the right. "There is only one true sun. The second that we see is not real but a projection that Faelin created with her magic. It lengthened each day so the *waateyshirak* could never feast to their full strength. It follows the real one like a shadow, forevermore tethered to it."

I bit my lip. "But why would Faelin expend most of her power to create it?"

"I can't be sure." Vrail brushed her finger along the edge of the book. "The *shirak* were numerous and every cycle grew more deadly. When Faelin arrived, her gifts offered protection, but she was just a single Fae. Perhaps she thought the shadow sun would protect the Elverin best." Vrail shrugged. "Aemon destroyed so much of the knowledge they left for us we may never be certain." She sighed, closing the book. "All I know is that whatever purpose Faelin had, it drained her substantially. It is said that her gifts continued to fade until she died only a few centuries after she created the shadow sun."

"A few centuries," Gwyn balked.

"An unimaginable amount of time for ones as young as us," Vrail agreed with a stoic nod. "But several millennia before her time."

"Leaders do not often live long," I said to no one in particular.

Gwyn's nose wrinkled, and she grabbed my hand. She knew my days would come to an end soon too.

CHAPTER TWENTY-NINE

Every halfling in the *Faelinth* circled the Myram tree. The crowd covered the entire grove and the neighboring ones. Some climbed up the trunks to listen from the lower burls and branches.

Their whispers fell silent as I walked through the crowd with Feron and the other council members directly behind me.

"I will be brief but do not mistake that for apathy." I took a moment to scan the entire crowd. "What I am about to say must be considered with the utmost care." The orb of water hanging from my mouth propelled my voice through a larger orb suspended in the center of the grove. Beside it was another, projecting the image of Nikolai as he interpreted everything I said with his crutches tucked underneath his arms.

"You have heard rumblings of Halflings who have been made into Fae. I am here to set those rumors to rest."

A disappointed murmur moved through the crowd.

"It is true."

The murmur changed to an excited buzz. I raised my hand and the Halflings fell silent once more.

"Elverath has given me the ability to transform anyone with amber blood into Fae." The crowd broke into a chorus of surprised gasps. "Not one of the Light Fae you have heard about or one of the Dark you have met, but something new."

Orrin broke through the front of the crowd. "Will we have fire magic like you?"

Everyone laughed as the little girl tugged on her braids, but my stomach hardened. "I cannot say, young one." I turned back to the crowd. "I cannot promise you what magic you will or will not be able to wield. I *can* say that it will not be easy. If you choose to join us in the fight for Elverath, you will have to train relentlessly to control your powers. Day and night, every waking hour until the battles come. You will not rest. And if you volunteer for this, you must know that you may live in pain every day of your life."

I paused, evaluating the response of the crowd. There were much more excited faces than solemn ones. A wave of nausea flooded through me, and I gripped the root holding up my notes.

"In battle, you will be marked as a threat above the rest." I looked down at my boots, refusing to imagine which wide eyes would be forever changed. "If you choose to fight, you may very well die."

"But aren't we better protected with magic?" someone shouted from the back, his voice young and full of wanting.

My hands turned to fists. I knew how easy it was in youth to misjudge the severity of a decision, to be unable to comprehend the weight of it. I took a deep breath and hoped the council would see it unwise to choose someone as young and eager as that.

"Magic is not the solution to all your problems. In many ways it will cause more hardship in your life than it will alleviate. Your magic can hurt you—use too much too quickly and you will suffer the most painful death." The crowd's whispers turned dark. "But that is not the worst of it," I continued. "Lose control and you can maim, even kill, someone you love."

The crowd fell silent.

"Any Halfling, who is of age, may volunteer their name." I lifted a long sheath of parchment on the pedestal Feron had formed beside me. "Mark your name, and you shall be considered. But the decision of who and how many of you shall be chosen lies with the council." I waved my hand at the Elders standing behind me. Each of them scanned the crowd with observant, knowing eyes.

I turned to the young, eager Halfling who already had his hand raised. "Their word is final."

He dropped his hand.

I set the list down. No one parted from the crowd, too many unsure if they wanted to be the first. But then an auburn-haired Halfling I recognized from the Order stepped forward. She wrote her name in quick, assured strokes at the very top of the page. She put the glass pen back in its holder and bowed her head to me.

"It would be an honor to protect this land and save the Halflings who remain lost to us." She lifted a palm to her face and then her chest. I returned the gesture. When I dropped my hand, a line stood behind her.

Gerarda was at the helm, dressed in all black so she looked like the Dagger she once was. She smirked up at the Elders as she wrote her name beside the other Shade's. My breath caught as she handed the pen to the next Halfling in line. Every eligible Halfling we had rescued from the Order stood behind her, ready to write their names. The pins Myrrah had crafted for us glinted in the firelight at their necks.

I glanced around the crowd, looking for Riven in the sea of Halflings. But he was nowhere to be found. My stomach tightened though I didn't know if it was with relief or knowing the only reason Riven didn't write his name was because he still carried too much guilt to do so. He blamed himself for Maerhal's death, and Nikolai blamed him too. He did not think he deserved his magic back, and maybe he was right.

Other Halflings joined the line. Some I recognized as those who trained with Elaran and Gerarda. Some were scouts who had been living in the *Faelinth* for decades already.

Elaran came up behind me and pressed a kiss to my cheek. "Picturing me with amber eyes?"

"No, yours are already so pretty," I deadpanned as Elaran cut in line to write her own name. "Though I can't say I'm surprised you're volunteering." I didn't dull the edge of my tone. I hadn't forgotten Elaran's allegations about me keeping my magic to myself.

She tapped the end of my nose. "Let's not dwell on old storms, Keera. Not when we are about to be Fae together."

I raised a brow. "You think the council will select you."

"Absolutely." Elaran shot them a wink. "They are wise and I am a wise decision." She held out her hand for me to take. "Might as well do it now. I'd like to know what kind of magic I'd get. I'm already so—"

"Presumptuous?" I finished for her.

She tugged on a loose curl. "Can't be presumptuous when I exceed the expectations."

I huffed a laugh. "And those are?"

"Lethal talent, impeccable self-control, and most importantly I have—"

"Delusions?"

Elaran gave me a sly smirk. "The color palette to pull off amber eyes." She brandished her hand across the full-length gown she'd decided was appropriate for the occasion. "You think I'm insufferable now, just wait, Keera dear."

"You didn't have the patience to wait in line, let alone control your . . ." I trailed off as I turned back to the list.

Dynara raised her chin. She didn't say a word, just set down the glass pen and walked away without looking at me. Her name was already inked onto the parchment.

CHAPTER THIRTY

Sil'abar swayed high above us, its golden leaves almost dusty under the gray skies of the morning. The Elders had held their vote at first light, and a crowd was now waiting to hear who would be named as candidates and who would not.

My stomach knotted. Fyrel and Gerarda paced beside me, silent and anxious. My hands were damp as I rubbed them against my thighs.

I had never presided over a Trial as Blade. I had refused, leaving such displeasures to Hildegard to contend with. But now I understood the true weight of what she had done. None of the Halflings circling the giant Elder birch were going to die today, but their fates would be decided for them.

I wouldn't bestow a hood upon their head, but I would change some of their lives—and likely not for the better. What if I did something wrong and their gifts were left fractured like Riven's had been, afflicted with a pain that would never subside for the rest of their lives? And for those whose gifts settled as well as Gwyn's had, they would have the weight of the war on their shoulders.

Feron was the first to exit Sil'abar. His steps were slow, but the crowd didn't dare make a sound. The clack of his cane marked a count as he grew closer. Behind him, Darythir looped her arm through Syrra's as she pushed Myrrah's chair. Rheih followed after them, hands stuffed in the pockets of her smock.

Each of the five Elders held their mouths in a straight line. A small orb of water floated by Feron's mouth and another soared above the crowd ready to hear their decision.

"After much deliberation, my fellow Elders and I have reached a consensus." He lifted his arm and a thick root shot from the ground making a curved seat for him to lean on as he spoke. "We will nominate four Halflings to be bestowed with gifts from the *niinokwenar*."

The crowd broke into a chorus of gasps and outraged shouts. My chest eased as I looked around. I would only be marking four for death out of hundreds. Still four more than I wanted, but the Elders had balanced the scales to a sum I could live with.

Feron lifted his hand and the crowd fell silent. "While it is tempting to turn any willing Halfling, our resources to train new magic wielders are too limited. Restricting the number to four will ensure that we do not spread our resources too thin training the new Fae and those already bestowed with gifts." His eyes drifted over the crowd to find Gwyn, Vrail, and Crison huddled together.

Darythir stepped forward with a piece of parchment in her hand. Feron created a podium for her with a simple wave of his hand. She addressed the crowd, and Feron used his projected voice to interpret for her.

"This was not an easy choice, but it is a choice that each one of us stands by." Her wrinkled eyes were sharp as she stared down the first line of the crowd. "As these new Fae will be key soldiers in the battles to come, we have chosen to select our candidates from the Halflings who have already received extensive training on self-control, combat, and self-defense."

A low murmur echoed through the crowd as the Halflings who had been rescued from the kingdom realized they would not be chosen.

They were picking from the Shades.

My mouth went dry as Darythir continued. "To make it clear, we do not make these decisions lightly"—she glanced at me—"the first candidate to be selected is one of the Elders." Darythir bowed her head, and Myrrah thrust herself forward from their line. The crowd clapped and nodded in approval at the first choice.

Gerarda straightened her back beside me, her hands twisting into knots behind it.

But Darythir did not name her. "The second candidate we have selected is Elaran."

Darythir waved her hand in our direction. Elaran squeezed Gerarda's shoulder before stepping apart from the crowd. She lifted a hand to her face and then her chest before kneeling in front of the Elders.

"I am honored to be chosen," she said in her raspy tone. "I will not disappoint."

Gerarda's teeth gritted together as she lifted her chin. I could see the worry creeping along the corners of her eyes. Concern for her lover and concern for herself—there were only two nominations left.

Darythir took a deep breath before continuing. "The third candidate was not selected for her prowess with a blade but her sharp wit and dedication to the Elverin within the *Faelinth* and outside of it." She paused and smiled at someone in the front row. "Dynara."

I gasped along with the crowd as Dynara stepped forward. She was wearing a long gown cinched at the waist by a bodice made of pearls. But her face was stern, determined as she bowed to the Elders and accepted her post. "Thank you for granting me this honor."

My chest heated. Dynara had not said anything about her decision to add her name to the list of volunteers. And I had jumped at the opportunity to ignore it, knowing I would say the wrong thing and foolishly believing the Elders would never choose her as a candidate.

Gerarda's fist pulsed beside me in sets of four. She only let herself inhale after one set, pulsing again before finally exhaling. A breathing tactic we had been taught at the Order.

I grabbed her hand and squeezed it. There was no one else they would nominate. Her spot had always been secure.

Darythir met my gaze before glancing at the short, determined Halfling beside me. "The final nomination," she signed with shaking hands, "was long discussed but the decision was ultimately unanimous."

My shoulders relaxed, and I patted Gerarda on the back.

"The Elders have selected Fyrel."

Gwyn jumped up onto Fyrel's back with excitement and pressed a kiss to her cheek. The young Halfling stumbled backward, dazed, as the crowd erupted into applause. Gwyn let her go and claim her place in front of the Elders, but I didn't hear a word she said to them. All I saw was Gerarda's black cloak disappearing through the crowd without a sound.

CHAPTER THIRTY-ONE

FERON KNEW ENOUGH TO GET ME in a room far away from the others. He sealed the doorway with a single touch, the live wood snapping together, sealing me in with him and the rest of the Elders.

I turned to Syrra and Myrrah. "You put the life of a child on the line before a seasoned warrior?"

Syrra's arms crossed, strong and tight like a shield held between me and them. "You said you would respect the council's decision. You made this request of us."

I gritted my teeth. "Had I known you would send a girl of barely seventeen to the front lines, perhaps I would not have made such a foolish choice." My breath seared my nostrils. I turned to Myrrah. "Have you not sent enough children to their deaths? You need to send one more?"

Feron raised his hand and the floor underneath me popped upward, knocking me to the ground. "That is enough." His eyes glowed bright lilac, boring down on me like sails on a ship, anchoring me through the swells of my rage. "We weighed this decision for *days*, Keera, and none of us are strangers to the plights of war. Our concerns were greater than just the battles to come."

Darythir signed something with one hand, slow enough for me to make some sense of it.

"Gerarda is a brilliant soldier," I spat. "She would have made a fearsome Fae."

Darythir shook her head, her hands waving at her sides, wordless.

"She would have been a powerful weapon." Syrra kneeled in front of me. "But we interviewed each candidate thoroughly. Do you know what Gerarda said when we asked how she envisioned her life as a Fae *after* the battle was won?"

I leaned back against the wall and shrugged. Gerarda's mind had always been a mystery to me. One she revealed slowly and at her leisure.

Syrra swallowed as the scars of branches along her shoulders tensed, the leaves almost fluttering. "She said she could not conceive of a life after the war. That her only focus was defeating the Crown."

I lifted my chin. "I wouldn't have expected any less from her."

Myrrah pushed her chair beside Syrra. "Aemon forged us into weapons with no regard for who we would be when his battles were won. With no care if we rusted, if we dented, if we were left discarded on the field of battle. All he wanted was us to be sharp and at the ready. How could I ever agree to change someone in such a powerful way—much more powerful than anything Aemon could have devised—when all she can comprehend herself to be is a dagger.

What if the *after* comes and she realizes that she made a rash choice? A choice she regrets and cannot take back?"

I slumped into a chair, the hold of Feron's stare loosening as my rage faded into the grief. The grief I had for my past and Gerarda's too.

I ran a hand over the top of my braid, not caring as long strands fell loose around my face. "But you judge Fyrel as strong enough to handle that choice."

Feron nodded. "The young are more resilient than we give them credit for."

"And there is no future where Fyrel is not chasing after Gwyn." Syrra huffed. "At least this way she will have a better chance at protecting herself."

I scoffed and stood. "Gerarda will appeal your decision." I turned to Darythir and Feron.

The old Elf signed something quick and short.

"As is her right," Feron interpreted in a soft voice. "Though our decision will stand."

I rubbed my neck, my new gift tingling under my skin, knowing it would soon be unleashed again. "When shall we do it then?"

Darythir held one arm across her chest and slowly lifted the other behind it, her fingers curved into the shape of a circle. I didn't need Feron to interpret.

Sunrise.

⚔

"I know you're there." My voice grated against my throat. I didn't turn toward Gerarda as she stepped in front of the wreckage. I had thought abiding by the council's decision would be easy, but I hadn't expected them to nominate every Halfling I considered family to fight alongside me. I needed an outlet to let my anger simmer. The grove outside of Aralinth worked well enough.

Gerarda kicked a branch I had set aflame away from my knees.

"Turn me." She tucked her hands behind her back and kept her eyes focused on the forest above my head. In that moment, she wasn't my friend or even my adversary—she was a soldier.

Just like the council had said. A weapon too dangerous to sharpen any more than she already was.

I fell back to the ground and pulled my arm around my earth-stained knees. "That decision isn't mine to make."

Gerarda's jaw pulsed. "The decision to shoot lies with the archer and not the bow."

I huffed a laugh. "Is that how you trained your Shades? That they were making the decisions instead of following your orders, or Hildegard's orders, or Aemon's?"

"No." Her voice was crisp as it sliced through the air. "My job was to strip them of their will, to make it so they wouldn't have the slightest hesitation at following a command."

I swallowed, hearing the disgrace Gerarda carried for herself in her voice. Even now the choices we had to make under Aemon's rule haunted us. "You did your job well."

She nodded. "I did, but we both know it wasn't right." She finally lowered her gaze to me. Her black eyes smoldering with contempt.

I scraped my finger along the dirt, creating a grooved line between us. "It's not the same."

"Fuck you saying it's not." Gerarda spun on her left toe and began to pace, her rage boiling off her like steam. "And fuck the council for their decision. We both did what needed to be done to survive, to *save* others from that wretched island. And we succeeded. Why should I be punished for how I endured it?"

I gritted my teeth. "Had the council been given the chance, I doubt they would've bestowed these gifts to me either." My skin tightened at those words, worried that the magic coursing through Elverath had made a mistake in choosing me.

"But that's exactly my point." Gerarda ran a hand over her hair. "They didn't get a vote. *You* were chosen for this, Keera. The Light Fae chose you to keep their bloodline alive, and then Elverath herself chose you to be the next *niinokwenar*. I know you balk at the mention of a *savior,* but this path has been set in front of *your* feet. Not the council's."

I stood with a fiery rage in my chest. "And what would you have me do? Make you a Fae out of spite? This is the Elvish way. This is how decisions are made."

Gerarda crossed her arms. "The Elvish way died the day the first Halfling was born." She took a step closer to me. "Tell me you agree with them. Tell me that you think me unfit, and I will never say another word about it."

I clenched my jaw but did not open my lips.

She smirked. "I knew it. You were just as surprised by their decision as I was."

"Gerarda, they have lived *lifetimes* longer than you or I." I took a deep breath. "Perhaps they know something we do not."

"And maybe they know nothing!" Her voice cracked and echoed through the trees. Her next words were more controlled, but no less fiery. "The council did not start the rebellion. That was you, Riven, and the Guild. The council did not even join our ranks until the return of their precious magic was threatened. They did not live under Aemon. *We* did. And we may not have lived through millennia, but none of them have the blood of the dead and the beaten coursing through their veins. Only the Halflings do."

Tears welled along my eyes. "And what if you're wrong? What if Elverath uses my gift to curse you for disobeying their ways? You could spend your life as Riven did—or worse."

Gerarda lifted her chin. "Then so be it. But at least I will live out the last of my days knowing I did *everything* I could to protect my people, to fight for their freedom, to fight for more than just myself to survive." She swallowed and her dark eyes bore into mine, unwavering. "After all we have been through together, Keera, you owe me that. Don't take my chance to do my best from me. Not again."

A hot tear rolled down Gerarda's cheek, and she was no longer the seasoned soldier I had come to respect and care for. She was a lost, lonely girl, trying to do everything she could to save her sister.

Fate had taken that from her.

I would not do the same.

"Yes."

Gerarda fell back onto her heels. "Yes?" The warmth drained from her face as her jaw fell open.

"Having second thoughts, Vallaqar?"

Her black eyes narrowed. "Not at all."

"Where do you want to do it?"

Gerarda waved her arms across the clearing. "Here is good enough for me."

"You don't want to fetch Elaran first?"

Gerarda gulped and she shook her head. "Nothing she would say would change my mind. And I would rather do it before the Elders get suspicious."

I pulled a faebead from the inner pocket of my vest and cracked it with my boot. A large faelight bloomed beside us, and I threw my cloak over top of it. "Lay down."

Gerarda undid her weapons belt and set it on the ground. She twisted her hands over and over again before letting her head fall back onto the makeshift bed. "I'm ready," she said with a nod.

I called my gift forward. Gerarda's black eyes widened for the last time as mine were lit with an auric glow. I reached out and placed my palm over the width of her forehead.

For a moment, nothing happened, as if Gerarda's mind was fighting against the magic. But she took a deep breath, and all her defenses dropped. Her body went limp. Then the rush of my magic overwhelmed her, thick ribbons wrapping around her body like a cocoon.

The warmth faded away and I could breathe normally once more. I looked down at Gerarda, and when her eyes opened, they were gleaming orbs of amber.

I took a step back as Gerarda stood. A gasp ripped from my chest. Inky black shadows leaked from her limbs, twirling along the ground like dusty wisps of wind. Tendrils of darkness, just like Riven's shadows had been.

"Are you in pain?" My voice shook with fear of what I had done to my friend.

Gerarda blinked. "No." She laughed, a single pure note that sounded more like song than joy. "I feel incredible. Though this is not a new power."

I shrugged. I didn't understand the magic any more than she did.

Gerarda fluttered her fingers and strands of shadow shot from her fingertips. I burst into a fit of laughter that didn't settle until Gerarda hurled a shadow at my face.

"Don't lose control or you'll have to train with Riven."

Gerarda cursed under her breath.

CHAPTER THIRTY-TWO

I WAS GRATEFUL THAT no one followed me back to Myrelinth. Fyrel was sitting in the garden near the portal. She waved, covering her flushed cheeks when she saw me. Gwyn turned, her curls splayed across Fyrel's lap as she lay in the sun, her amber eyes glinting under the golden hue of Sil'abar.

My throat went dry. Tomorrow Fyrel's eyes would be just as amber.

I gave them a stiff nod and tossed a dried bulb into the portal to pass into the Dark Wood. Perhaps Syrra and Myrrah were right. The two of them had become inseparable since Gwyn had found her voice again. Fyrel would follow Gwyn to the front lines no matter what.

With magic or without it. Halfling or Fae.

It wouldn't matter.

That truth did little to quell my anxieties as I hiked through the trail and into the quiet city. The news of the selection had not yet made it to Myrelinth since most of its residents had made the journey to the spring city to hear it for themselves.

I hiked up one of the spiraling branches of the Myram tree. My muscles ached as I climbed, my worries dripping onto the teal moss with my sweat. By the time I reached the top of the tree, my fears were not completely exhausted but faded enough that I might fall asleep.

I heard a heartbeat as I passed over Riven's burl. He was home. My legs carried me there instead. My body knew that tonight was not one I wanted to spend alone. Riven lay across the carpet, black trousers untied with no tunic on. His olive brown skin gleamed under the small faelight that twirled overhead. His eyes were not closed, but fixed on the ceiling of the burl, deep in thought.

I dropped my cloak and weapons without a word and lay on the floor beside him. He still refused to sleep in a bed even though his mattress sat just to his left. "You didn't attend the council decision." It wasn't a question or a judgment.

He cleared his throat and tilted his chin upward, showcasing the sharp angles of his face. "There was no need." Riven's flat hand turned to a fist on his chest. "I knew my name would not be called."

I drew a deep breath. I had suspected as much when Riven didn't show to the announcement. "You didn't put forth your name for consideration." Again, not a question.

Riven was quiet for a long moment that I let stretch between us. I didn't tense at the silence like I used to but instead relaxed along the floor as Riven found the words. Another influence of the Elverin, I supposed.

My magic hummed under my skin, not with quite the same warmth that once existed between us, but close. Like a hand pressed against a window of a memory, I could still feel the shadow of the bond between us.

Riven finally turned to me, his jade eyes misted and narrow. "Do you think less of me for it?"

I grabbed Riven's fist and flattened it, lacing my fingers through his and resting both our hands on his chest. "No." I pressed a kiss to his shoulder. "Though I would like to know why you didn't."

His throat bobbed but he said nothing.

"Are you scared the pain will return alongside your shadows?" I rubbed my thumb along his hand. "Or are you worried you won't have shadow magic at all?"

Riven's mouth straightened. His other hand caressed my wrist absentmindedly as he weighed the question. "Those were worries, but small ones." Riven bit his lip.

I toyed with his half braid but eventually my patience waned. "You can ask me."

Riven turned his head in surprise.

I pulled his bottom lip from between his teeth. "You only bite your lip and frown when you're concerned that speaking your mind will hurt whomever you speak it to."

I trailed my finger along the arch of his nose and tapped the point. "It would hurt me more if you stayed silent." I bit my own lip, our agreement echoing wordlessly between us.

Riven nipped my finger, snatching my wrist to press a kiss against it, before he turned on his side too. His actions were playful, but his gaze was weighted. "You wore your title of Blade for so long it became a mask." His grip on my hand tightened. "How did you keep the edges of yourself and the character you had to play from blending into one?"

My lips parted, but I had no answer for him. Riven saw me more fully than I had ever seen myself. Not because he could hold space for the dark parts of me I preferred to ignore, but because to him I was *whole*. That was why I loved him so, why his presence brought me so much comfort, because he gave me faith that one day I would feel whole too.

But maybe he had always worked so hard for me to feel that way because he never had. I had shattered myself into pieces with every choice I had to make, and Riven had shattered himself, too, every time he had to lie about who he was. My chest ached for us both. For the people we could have been if we never had to try to stitch ourselves back together.

If we ever did.

"I didn't." It wasn't the answer Riven wanted to hear, but it was true. A simple answer, though a storm raged behind those words. Riven's jaw clenched, and I knew he had his own storm to contend with. Perhaps sharing mine would help.

"I had one truth, that was all I could hold on to. One promise." My throat constricted against each word so they came out ragged and beaten. "The only true part of me was the part that wanted to kill the king to protect the Shades. Everything else was the Blade."

Riven's brows pinched. "You don't give yourself enough credit. You cared for Gwyn. For Hildegard."

I bit the inside of my cheek, suddenly unable to meet Riven's gaze. "I did, but not in the way I could have if the threat of their deaths weren't haunting my every moment." My chest ached as I sighed. "I loved them as well as I knew how to. As well as I could. But I had cut off so much of myself that it could never have been a full love. Not the kind of love you see here."

"And now?" Riven grabbed the end of my braid and held it under his nose.

My lips twitched to the side. "I'm learning, but it still hurts."

He frowned.

"It's a good kind of hurt though," I continued. "Being the Blade, doing the things I had to do, made it impossible to be a person.

I don't have a favorite color. I don't have any skills apart from killing and spying, no hobbies, no books I've read again and again. I'm missing all those little layers that blend to make a full portrait of someone."

"The deceit leeched you of all your color." Riven's voice was hoarse and his gaze far away, as if he were speaking more about himself than me. "Leaving only shadow."

My heart tore for Riven. For me. I remembered Gwyn's wise words from the day I learned the truth about him. That his choices might have been different than mine, but that our secrets had isolated us in the same way. Erected walls around us that had to fall but were a torment to break. We were two children who had grown, set apart from those around them, burdened with choices no other before them had to make.

Finding each other was almost enough for me to believe in fate. Two souls bound in shadow, two people who yearned for something other than darkness.

"Yes," I whispered. "I know how to be a weapon. I know how to fight." I pushed a loose strand of Riven's hair back into his long mane. "And I know how to steal a tender moment here and there." My finger trailed over the long point of his ear. "But how to maintain joy—to be truly content? To be a *person* apart from all of this"—I waved my hand over our heads, sending the faelight swirling—"that is something I do not know much of. But I learn more of it every day."

Riven grabbed my hand and pressed the back of it against his mouth. Then he laced our fingers together and rested them on his chest. My breath fell into the rhythm of its steady rise and fall. It was my own healer's drum.

"I know nothing of it." A thick tear fell from the corner of Riven's eye and trickled down his neck. I caught it against my lips and nestled my head on his shoulder. "I don't remember much of being a boy. I always felt different—perhaps I knew I was—even before that first time I shifted forms. But from that day, I have lived in secret. From that day, I've tainted every relationship I've ever had with the lies I've told. Each lie drained my life of color until there was nothing much left. And it has cost those I care for so much more."

His voice cracked. All I wanted was to wrap my arms around him and press my lips to his, but Rheih had taught me well. Poisons needed to be leeched, and some could only be drained by speaking the bitter truth of them.

"I didn't put my name down for consideration because I feel like Elverath has given me a second chance to make things right." Riven's neck flexed. He stared up at the ceiling but kept speaking. "For decades, I've wished that I'd just been born a Halfling. That I never had to hide myself away. No crown, no magic, no mask. Just the same path as every other Halfling." His jaw pulsed. He knew that life was much harder than that of a prince. Riven had said as much himself—or as Killian rather—in the safe house in Koratha. It shamed him to hold onto that wish, but shame didn't change the truth; it only burrowed it deeper inside.

"But no other Halfling could have led the rebellion."

Riven pulled back to look at me in disbelief.

I shook my head, refusing to let himself diminish all that he had done. "I could never have done it without you. Whatever lies we told, whatever masks we wore, this path we're on has always been a shared one."

Riven's hand cupped my cheek. His lips pressed against my forehead. "And I am happy to share it, *diizra*. But I want to do so in this body. This version of me that never wore the crown or hid from it." He cleared his throat and met my gaze. "I didn't make choices I was proud of when I was a Fae—perhaps this time I will make better ones. Redeem myself. Learn how to be a person again too."

I rested my hand against Riven's cheek, and we lay there staring at each other. My magic hummed beneath my skin, and I swore his jade eyes glowed just a little. The golden flecks within their depths shone as they looked at me. A glimpse of the color oozing back into him.

So much of Riven was still clouded in darkness. I recognized it because the same shadows had only begun to fade around me. They were still stirred by the weight of Damien and his armies, of knowing the losses that would come, but I could see the horizon well enough.

But Riven's shadows were still thick clouds of grief. He needed time. Time to heal enough to believe a version of himself he was proud of could exist. Time to believe he was worthy of the love we all held for him.

I knew too well how much time that would take.

I pressed my lips to his, as gentle and comforting a touch I could offer. I would wait for as many lifetimes as he needed. And I would hold faith that the light would come and banish the shadows away for both of us until then.

"Make me a promise," I whispered against Riven's cheek.

He froze. His hand dropped to my waist and slowly pushed me away from him. His eyes narrowed, scanning the door and then my face. "What do you have planned?"

I rubbed my thumb over his brow until it relaxed. "Not a promise made in blood." I pressed my forehead against his. "Promise me, that after this is over, when we can let ourselves become dull and useless without our people dying, that we will *try*." Tears formed at the corners of my eyes. "Promise me, that even when the war is won, we won't let the darkness win. We will carve out a little bit of joy for ourselves each day no matter what happens until it is all we know. Until our bellies ache from laughing and our rooms are filled with relics of half-drawn hobbies, and we can sleep without a faelight overhead to keep the darkness from catching us again."

Rivers of want flowed down my face. I yearned for that future in a way I had never allowed myself before. For both of us. A future that was stitched and healed, where our scars barely itched, because we were whole.

Because we were the people we were meant to be.

Riven wiped my eyes with calloused hands. "And if the darkness never clears?" His words shook with a fear that only lovers got to witness.

I kissed his wrist and then his palm. "It will. I know it, *rovaa*."

My choice.

Riven's pupils flared at my name for him. He gripped the back of my head and pulled me into a wanton kiss. His fangs grazed my flesh, almost cutting, as he devoured me.

I gave into his need. Mine had been lingering just below my skin, and Riven's touch had awakened it. I nipped at his lip as our hands unlaced each other's trousers. Riven grunted at the double knot I'd tied and slipped a knife from his pocket.

"Do you want to stop?" he asked, somehow finding the restraint to hold the knife against the lace but not cut.

"Do you?" I gasped into his ear.

Riven pulled my leg tighter against his hip so I had no doubt how much he wanted this.

I raised a smug brow. "Then cut it."

His knife sliced through the laces on my trousers like they were made of air. In one motion, Riven tugged my trousers down my thighs, his lips never leaving my skin. He hiked my leg onto his hip, making quick work of my boot—it was still tied as he slipped it off.

I barely caught my breath before the second one was gone. Riven lifted me into the air, fingers dimpling my hips, and he lowered me onto his mouth.

I gasped and my gusts filled the room, trapping Riven's hungry murmurs and my feral moans in his burl for only us to hear. The tip of his tongue circled around that tender spot, never quite touching it, until it had swelled to the point of pain.

"Riven, please," I begged, my hips bucking against his chin.

He looked up at me, his teeth sinking into the skin of my upper thigh, disappearing beneath the curls. Then he licked me just where I needed and did not relent.

"Fuck," I groaned as his speed increased. I grabbed the small table beside the bed we were not using and bucked my hips. My thighs squeezed Riven's head, but I didn't care if he could draw a breath. And neither did he. From the hungry way his hands roamed my body, clutching at me like I was life itself, I knew that Riven believed he could be sustained on me alone.

He grazed my skin with his teeth, intensifying the pressure building between my legs. Riven groaned and palmed my breast underneath my tunic. My head collapsed backward at the force of his touch.

Riven paused, concerned that he had hurt me. I grabbed his hand through my shirt and squeezed. "Keep going," I rasped. I held onto Riven, letting his touch ground me as the first wave of pleasure shot through my body like a bolt of lightning.

I collapsed but Riven bent his knees for me to lean on as he continued his feast. The pressure built again. Riven scratched my skin as his hand trailed down my body and fell out of my shirt. His fingers laced through mine as he carried me through a second wave of pleasure. And then a third.

My head dropped forward, almost spent. But Riven had others plans. He pulled me into a kiss, letting me taste the passion he had coaxed from me. His tongue was hungry, his touch starved. His new body craved me just as much as his other forms had. Maybe even more so, now that Riven the Fae and Killian the prince could have me all at once.

Riven lifted me again, this time lowering me onto his hips. He pulled his own trousers down, just enough for me to feel the hardness of him. "I can return the favor." I raised a brow at his half-removed trousers.

"No time." Riven shook his head, jaw locked. He pulled at the hem of my tunic and I lifted it over my head. His eyes trailed over my naked body as he spoke. "I need to taste you as I have you."

I leaned forward, flattening my palms on either side of Riven's head. He turned, scraping his fangs against my forearm as I leaned down. Our noses touched. Riven's chest stilled, waiting.

But I held us there, pinned to that moment as it stretched. The candle on the nightstand melted in a ball of flame as the carpet froze, my magic spilling out of me as the tension hit its peak.

Riven winced as my wetness touched him for the first time. His head craned up and I bit his neck, claiming him as mine. "*Diizra*," he whispered, fully at my command. He fisted my hair and pulled me from his neck. His pupils were dark and wide with want. "I need you."

I grabbed a handful of Riven's hair too and pulled him upward so he sat beneath me and my legs wrapped around his torso. He lifted me by my hips one more time, only enough to line our bodies just so.

I moaned as he entered me, but Riven captured the sound with his tongue. His teeth nipped at my lips until they were swollen. His hand reached around my back as he thrust, and my nails left scratches down his. Somehow we were closer without the bond between us. This war had already taken so much from us that we were both split open. Raw and vulnerable. Starved and willing.

He kissed my scars and murmured sweet nothings against my skin. I ran my fingers through his hair and stared into the depths of his jade eyes. In that moment, we were not warriors protecting our home or leaders with the fate of our kin on our shoulders. We were just two people, and that was more than we had ever been.

I leaned back and Riven grabbed my hips, gliding me across him as my body gave way to another wave of pleasure. He was not gentle. His hand spanned the width of my thigh, inching closer to that tender spot.

I cursed as Riven touched me there. He nipped my breast with his teeth, claiming me in every way he could. His thumb flicked again, and I moaned his name.

"Fuck," Riven grunted. His arm wrapped around me as he flipped us without missing a thrust. Riven's hand laced through mine once more. "Keera," he groaned as his teeth grazed my shoulder. "I will never tire of this. As long as you'll have me—"

His words were lost as we both collapsed into a storm of pleasure. Riven fell on top of me like a heavy blanket on a cold winter's night. When he came back to himself, he tried to push off me, but I held on. I liked the solidness of him.

Finally, I let Riven cradle me in the crook of his arm and chest. "That wasn't a promise," I teased, half-heartedly. I was too exhausted to speak, but I didn't want our conversation to be left forgotten.

Riven tucked his chin against my head and stroked my hair in silence. My breaths matched his once more and the rhythm coaxed me to the brink of sleep.

"I promise, *diizra*," Riven whispered, not knowing if I could hear his words.

But I did. "I promise too," I said as I fell asleep with the hope that this one wouldn't cost me.

CHAPTER THIRTY-THREE

"You are certain this is what you want?" I stared down at the four Halflings in front of me.

Elaran twisted one of her curls through her fingers. "We've had the lecture three times now, Keera. Potential pain and suffering, death, and assassination."

"Don't forget the regret and added responsibility," Dynara added with a smirk.

Elaran laughed but Myrrah and Fyrel straightened under my gaze.

Myrrah wheeled forward. "It would be my honor, Keera."

"Mine too." Fyrel nodded.

I turned to Feron.

He lifted his hand and constructed four hammocks of vines and roots. Gwyn and Vrail laid blankets and pillows on top to make them more comfortable. Feron turned to Myrrah as the others sat down in theirs. "Would you like some help?"

Myrrah raised a brow at Feron's cane. "Not sure how much help you can offer."

Feron smirked and two thick roots raised from the ground. One looped behind Myrrah's knees and the other secured her back. They gently lifted her from her wheelchair and onto the hammock.

Myrrah nodded at me. "Can I have what he's got?"

"I can't—"

"Choose what kind of gifts you receive," Gwyn finished for me. "She knows that, Keera. It was a jest."

Myrrah nodded.

"Sorry." I rubbed my brow. "I'm a little tense."

"Then do the others first, Keera dear," Elaran said in a singsong voice. "I want you nimble and calm when you work on me." She winked. "That's how you get the best results."

I rolled my eyes. "Lay back. All of you."

Riven stepped from the wall and grabbed my hand. "You have this, *diizra*," he whispered in my ear.

I took a deep breath, leaning into his touch. I settled there for a minute, enjoying the final moments of before I would be responsible, in part, for my friends' fates on the battlefield.

My skin itched, my new gift already glowing at my palms. I stepped between Myrrah and Fyrel and pressed one hand to each of their foreheads, letting the magic do the work. It flowed out of me and sunk into their skin, filling their body with warm, golden light.

I let go and stepped between Dynara and Elaran. The change worked even more quickly, my magic rushing out of me like a waterfall.

"Open your eyes."

Four pairs of amber irises glowed back at me.

Elaran stood first, checking to see if her fingers glowed like Gwyn. She looked up at me, bewildered, and blinked.

"Whoa," Gwyn and Fyrel said at the same time.

Elaran looked back down at her hands. "What?"

"It's not your hands," I said. "It's your eyes."

They were no longer amber but gold. She looked at Feron and blinked again. This time her eyes were purple.

Vrail tilted her head. "A shapeshifter?"

Elaran matched Vrail's mannerisms and her hair straightened and formed a long, black braid in front of our eyes. "How did I do that?" Elaran took a step back, the vein in her neck pulsing.

Feron grabbed her hand, calming her with his magic. "Do not fret. You will learn to control it as you train with me and the others."

Elaran's shoulders relaxed. She looked at the other new Fae, but none had shown any signs of their gifts yet. "You will help all four of us?"

Feron nodded.

"Five." I cleared my throat. "Feron will train all five of you."

Fyrel held up her hand, recounting the number of cots in the room.

Dynara squinted at me with her fiercely amber eyes. "What do you mean, Keera?"

"She means me." Gerarda walked through the split grain in the wall. She lowered her hood to reveal her amber eyes.

Feron turned to me. "The council will not like this."

"What is done is done," Syrra said from the corner. She walked over to Gerarda and put her hand on her shoulder. "And we need every warrior we can get."

Gerarda's eyes fell to Syrra's scars. "Does that mean I can get one of those?" She chewed on her lip, unable to look away as Syrra laughed.

"You must master your magic first."

I crossed my arms. "And win a war."

"Challenge accepted." Shadows leaked out of Gerarda's hands as she lifted her chin. She looked over my shoulder at Riven, who stared at the shadows like they were ghosts. "And you're going to help me."

"Are you certain?" I asked Syrra through the looking glass.

She swallowed. "I trust you will not cut me?"

My lip trembled as I lifted the curved shearing blade to Syrra's shoulders. Her long black tresses hung over the back of the chair in a braid.

"You needn't cut it all, *Raava*," Nikolai said softly, holding two bundles of his own curls in his lap. All his hair was now the same short length as the sides of his head.

Syrra's teeth gritted together so loudly Vrail flinched. "Do it. Now."

I took a deep breath and gathered Syrra's thick locks together. The leather fastener could only loop around the strands twice before I had to tie it. I lifted the thin blade and held it against Syrra's scalp.

I looked at her through the looking glass once more. She nodded. I pulled back on the blade. The Elvish steel was so sharp it left no trace of the hair behind, only bare, brown skin in the middle of Syrra's head. I took another breath and did it again.

And again.

Seven passes was all it took to remove a warrior fully of her braid. I passed the bundle of her hair to Syrra without a word. She ran a hand across her scalp and nodded. "It is tradition that the one who cuts a mourner's hair is the one to accompany them." Syrra's voice cracked, somehow turning deeper than before. "Will you do that for me today?"

My chest tightened, unbelievably touched that Syrra would ask me. "Of course, my friend," I said in Elvish, grasping Syrra's hand as tightly as I could. "It would be my honor."

Syrra opened her mouth to say something, but a shadow appeared in the doorway of her burl. Nikolai's immediate scowl told me who it was before I turned around.

Riven.

"I just came to see if anyone needed anything," he said, staring at his boots after a quick glance at Nikolai.

Nik grabbed a canister of water from the table and hurled it at Riven's head. Riven didn't even duck out of the way, letting the metal crash into his chest and the water soak through his stained clothes.

"How dare you show your face here." Nikolai's voice was feral; there was nothing familiar in the way his mouth seemed to leak poison as he spoke. "Have you not done enough?"

The words fell to the floor of the burl like a fallen tree, smashing through the dwelling to create a line, us on one side and Riven on the other.

Riven's neck flexed as he tried to find the words but knew there was nothing that would appease Nik. Not today.

"I'm sorry," he whispered to both of them, but Nikolai had already turned away, unable look at his best friend for a second longer than he needed to.

I wanted to run to Riven, to grab his hand and fix the fracture between us all. But he had told me to stay out of it, that he would have to find a way to do so on his own. He sulked away, bent at the middle like a soldier wounded in battle, and I let him go.

Soft drums sounded in the distance and Vrail stood from the bed. "It's time." She lifted her hand to Nikolai and sighed with relief when he took it.

I held out my arm to Syrra. She held her hair in one hand but looped her other arm through mine. We marched in silence toward the Myram tree where the pyre was waiting. The entire *Faelinth* had convened for the ceremony. They stood draped in red like the branches above us, waiting for the closest kin to arrive.

Syrra's grip on my arm tightened as we approached the pyre. Even though she had been standing guard over her sister's body for weeks, even though she had seen the wrappings dozens of times, there was nothing to prepare even the strongest Elf for a moment like this.

Thick tears streamed down her cheeks as she beheld her sister for the last time. Her hair was no longer singed and shorn, but frayed out in every direction with thin braids. It wasn't braided with the living vine that Syrra had painstakingly woven into her hair after her return but with the strands of hair from every person who loved her.

I noticed the braid I had made that morning was overlaid with a thicker one. I looked up trying to find Riven in the crowd of Elverin, but he was not there. He had taken Nikolai at his word and stayed away.

Nikolai and Syrra knelt, each taking one of the strands of Maerhal's hair that had been left for them at the center of her face. Syrra's shoulders shook as she braided every last strand of her hair into her sister's head—as she let Maerhal take everything she had left to grieve.

I handed her a piece of teal fabric from Maerhal's favorite cloak to tie the braid. Nikolai finished his and gently laid it over his mother's cheek. Her skin was untarnished, not a blemish or burn to be found. With the ghost of a smile that still clung to her lips, it was like she was asleep and not dead.

The braids along her crown were too numerous to count. Some were so tiny they appeared to be nothing more than a few strands of hair.

Nikolai walked over to Elaran, who was holding a bouquet of Maerhal's favorite flowers. It was three times the size of the bouquets that Nikolai had left along his mother's statue. A final gift for her to carry with her to the ancestors, so she should be forever shrouded in the scent of moonflowers. Nikolai placed the stems into her hands with rasping breaths.

My own breaths thinned as I watched him. The tears cutting into his cheeks sliced my own heart. The guilt I had been holding onto for months bubbled up as I remembered Maerhal's final moments. Calling out to me, thinking I was her son, telling him she loved him and she was scared. I had been so sure in the comfort I gave her, so confident that I would return her home to her son in a chorus of laughter and joy.

But I hadn't thought to clear her lungs of soot. And she'd died alone on the grass, merely a few feet away from me. She died in pain, the same way she had lived for most of her life. I would carry that mistake with me until it was my body on the pyre.

Nikolai pressed a final kiss to his mother's forehead and backed away. Syrra pulled something small from her pocket. A doll, stitched and patched beyond recognition. A toy shared between sisters and kept for centuries even after Syrra had thought she was the only one of them left alive.

Now she truly was.

Nikolai sobbed as Syrra tucked the doll under Maerhal's soft hands. Another token for her to carry to the ancestors until Syrra could join her there.

"May Favrel and Aydar welcome you," Syrra whispered in Maerhal's ear. Tears scattered across both their faces as Syrra pressed her last wish against her sister's brow. She had to trust that her wife and child would greet Maerhal with open arms in the world to come.

Feron stepped forward with Darythir on the other side of the pyre. He cleared his throat and waited until both Nikolai and Syrra nodded. Then I raised my hands and waited for the story ritual to begin.

I had been practicing since Lash's funeral. I had little of his mastery of fire weaving, but I could create crude images to pair along with Darythir's story. Her hands waved through the air, slow and rounded as she tried to keep her own tears at bay. Feron's voice boomed over the crowds as he interpreted her signs.

"The Elves were the first people of this land," he said, his purple eyes darker than I had ever seen them. "We were not born of prayer like the Fae or of love like the Halflings. We were sculpted by Elverath herself. From her own lands she made us, from the sand on the beaches, and the earth in the mountains, and the clay in the deserts, she made a people of caretakers to watch over the land and help her magic grow."

I painted the sky with my flames. Large mountains of smoke lured behind fiery figures emerging from the ground itself, sprouting like trees. Sweat covered my brow from the heat and the concentration, but not a tendril of flame flickered.

"Elverath granted us long lives to laugh and sing, to cry and love, but ultimately when the day came that our lives should end, the Elves must return to the earth from which they came so they can sprout again."

Darythir's hand lifted from the middle of her belly over her head. Behind her, my tiny seedling grew into a tree that rivaled the height of the Myram.

"The ashes of our loved ones are collected in a *diizra*. It is the most precious keepsake one can hold, and hold it they shall for one year. A year to grieve the one they have lost while their memory rests along their chest."

I glanced at Myrrah. Her cheeks were red, and her hand was wrapped around her own sealed pendant that carried Hildegard's ashes. She had followed tradition and hadn't taken it off since the day Syrra settled the cord around her neck.

"And now we watch as our beloved is turned back into the earth she's made from and placed into her *diizra* to wait for the world to come." Darythir dropped her hands, and Feron nodded at Gerarda.

She stepped forward, dressed in the black leather chest piece that Syrra and Nikolai had made for her. Her short hair tied back in an elaborate braid with a piece cut to the scalp just above her ear.

"Ish'kavra diiz'bithir ish'kavra." Gerarda's voice boomed from her chest with the power of the sea, flooding the grove with its cadence as the drummers hastened their beat. It was heart-piercing melancholy, but there was a beauty to it too. Just like the Elverin's ritual for saying goodbye. It was not without pain, but it would always end in hope and new life.

Gerarda's funeral song came to a close. I faced Nikolai's and Syrra's tearstained faces. My fingers were covered in flames, but I wouldn't light the pyre until they were ready.

Syrra's back straightened and she gave me one stiff nod. Her dark eyes cast above the pyre, unwilling to watch it light.

I turned to Nikolai; his bottom lip quivered as he shakily nodded his head. I touched my hand to the pyre and stoked the flames until every piece of driftwood was alight.

Nikolai fell to his knees. A ghastly shriek tore through his throat, so painful I was sure his lungs were bleeding. His wails echoed through the city as the flames burned hot and Maerhal was returned to the earth once more.

Vrail knelt and wrapped her arms around Nikolai as he sobbed. I looked over at the shaking pile of limbs they had become and saw

Riven standing at the back of the crowd. He was sobbing too, so silently no one else knew to turn around to witness it. But I did. I saw the guilt pouring from his face as he cried. The tall flames reflected in his jade eyes as he watched the mistake he could never fix burn away.

Dark circles hung under his eyes. I doubted he had slept an hour since the funeral was announced. I wanted to cross through the crowd and wipe his tears away, but I knew he wouldn't let me. He would never stop trying to atone for the lives his lies had cost, and that started with making sure I was there to comfort our friends while he could not be.

I stood tall and gave him a small nod as we cried looking at each other, separated by mountains of grief and guilt. I only hoped we wouldn't be lost in a landslide before Riven managed his way through it.

He turned and walked away as if he could hear my prayer and couldn't bear to tell me that today would not be that day.

The entire city watched until the pyre had burned through. Feron brought a leather-bound box and placed it on a root next to Syrra. She wiped her face and opened it to reveal a small golden pouch with a metal shovel and brush. The gold chain hung from the bottom as she passed it to Nikolai. Then she brushed her sister's ashes into the basin of the shovel and poured her remnants into the pouch.

Gerarda grabbed her blade from the fire I had left burning at the edge of the pyre and sealed the top of the pouch with the red-hot steel. It melted together, taking the shape of a closed bloom waiting for the suns to shine on it.

Feron took hold of the chain and lifted it up. His hand hung in the air, stuck between Syrra and Nikolai, unsure who should hold it for the year to come.

Sister or son.

I bit my cheek. "Can't we make two of them?"

"No." Syrra shook her head. "She must be whole for her tree to bloom." The strong Elf turned to her nephew and placed a heavy hand on his shoulder. "She was your mother. It is only right that you hold her safe, Miiran."

Nikolai pulled out a handkerchief and blew his nose. He looked up at Syrra and Feron, like a lost, little boy who didn't know what to do. "I knew her for only a few short months," he said when his airway cleared enough. "You knew her all her life. It should be you who carries her. As you always have."

Syrra's mouth dipped but she nodded. Too touched to speak.

Nikolai nodded at Feron to place the gold chain around Syrra's neck. Feron held up the *diizra* and Syrra bowed her head, but Nikolai rubbed his brow. "No," he shouted, standing up from the ground. "This isn't right." Nikolai snatched the *diizra* from Feron's grasp and ran out of the grove.

He didn't turn back as we shouted after him. Nikolai kept moving through the groves, shouldering past worried onlookers, toward the field where his son's tree stood over his mother's statue.

Feron called a root from the ground and had it hoist himself into the air, using his magic to keep up with all of us.

Nikolai didn't halt until he reached the statue. The place he had marked as the new grove of his kin. It was where he would be buried and where his mother was always meant to be.

He dropped to his knees and started to dig. Syrra grabbed his shoulder, but he shook her off, the *diizra* sitting safely under the stone carving of Maerhal and her toddler-aged son.

"This is not right, Miiran," Syrra pleaded. "We are meant to wait a year to grieve before we give her back to the ancestors."

Nikolai scowled. "I have grieved my entire life for my mother. Seven hundred years of mourning is more than enough." Nikolai wiped his nose on his sleeve. "She spent seventy decades—seven Mortal lifetimes—in darkness. I will not have her wait one more day for peace. I do not need it, and I will not bear it."

Nikolai's eyes were red as he turned back to his aunt in utter desperation. Syrra ran her hand along her shorn head and nodded.

Nikolai turned to Feron, who had placed himself on the ground, though the root still hovered beside him. "Are you going to deny my mother her rest?"

Feron stood perfectly still. His pulse flared along his temple, visible from where he had cut off one of his twists to braid into Maerhal's hair.

"Will you?" Nikolai pressed, his rage bubbling over as he threw a handful of dirt at Feron's boots.

"No," Feron answered hoarsely. "I will not."

Nikolai dug the hole with his bare hands, finally getting deep enough to place the *diizra* at the bottom of it.

Feron lifted his hand and the earth fell back on the gold pouch. The grass sprouted through the dark earth as if Nikolai had never clawed into it at all.

"What are you doing?" I asked Feron quietly.

He nodded at the grave. "It has always been the responsibility of an earth wielder to bring our dead back to life. The magic is what causes the *diizra* to bloom and grow."

I bit my lip. Maerhal had saved me as a young girl, kept my mind strong when all I wanted was to succumb to the darkness. I hadn't been able to save her in the end, but this I could do.

"Can I?" I asked, to Feron or the others I didn't know. I wasn't familiar enough with our people's customs to know whose decision this was.

Syrra turned to me and nodded. "It would be an honor for my sister to be blessed into the next life by a *niinokwenar*."

My throat tightened with worry that now my idea wouldn't work. I didn't have the same control over earth and plants that Feron had from his countless years of practice.

I glanced at Nikolai, who nodded, leaning back against Vrail's legs, his tears finally drying.

I knelt beside the patch of new grass, watering it with my own tears as I spanned my hand across the earth. The magic pulsed underneath me, steady and strong like a heartbeat.

Maerhal—alive once more, just in a different form.

I leaned so close to the ground that the blades of grass tickled my lips as I whispered a final goodbye to the Elf who had saved me in more ways than one.

"Biimaadizir roq waateyak miinawa, mikan."

May you never live in darkness again, dear friend.

My magic anchored me to the ground as it penetrated the earth. Heat pulsed through my veins and into the roots that I could feel sprouting underneath me. A small silver seedling sprang from the earth, growing into a tree before our very eyes.

Within seconds, it was standing high above our heads, higher even than Davan's tree—Nikolai's son. The trunk was unlike anything I'd ever seen. Thin silver bark covered the thick trunk, fraying at some parts like a birch tree, but the inside was not blushed and wooden. It glowed with golden grain that spelled Maerhal's name and all her foremothers.

Flowers sprouted from the leaves as they bore thick, round fruit wrapped in gold flesh. The blooms I recognized immediately.

Moonflowers.

Just as I had pictured. Maerhal had been given a second life as a tree that would glow bright under darkness. The light coming from the tree herself.

Nikolai stood in awe as he beheld the tree I had grown. The tree I had made. I did not need to be as well studied as Vrail or Feron to know that this was the only specimen of its kind. Though the shock on their faces confirmed it.

"Extraordinary," Vrail whispered. She started positing questions about the magic to Feron, but I didn't hear her.

All I heard was the rush of Nikolai's arms wrapping around me in an embrace so tight it pushed the air from my lungs. "Thank you" was all he managed to utter, but it was enough. More than enough.

Syrra wrapped her arms around the both of us. Vrail flattened her palm against the dense bark and gasped.

"Maava?" Nikolai croaked, his eyes wide and terrified.

Syrra went rigid. Even Feron didn't move as he stared at something behind me. I turned and my breath left my lungs. Maerhal was standing there. Her hair longer than I had ever seen it and her eyes filled with more joy than I could ever imagine.

I turned to Vrail. Her hands glowed bright where she touched the tree. "You did this?"

Vrail shrugged, her eyes as round as the suns. "I have no idea how."

Maerhal laughed and it sounded like a song. "Elverath has watched your thirst for knowledge, your hunger for stories, Vrail. It has blessed you with a way to reclaim both."

Nikolai took a cautious step toward his mother but didn't touch her.

Vrail looked down at her hand that wasn't pressed against the tree. "I can speak with the ancestors?" Excitement crinkled her eyes until they disappeared.

Syrra fell to her knees. "You're well, sister?" she asked in Elvish.

"I am." Maerhal smiled and nodded. "I am with our family now." There was a small giggle and a child appeared from behind Maerhal's legs.

A sob cracked through Syrra's chest. "Aydar."

The child beamed and twirled in her yellow robe.

Maerhal turned to Feron and me. "I would like to have some time with my son." She nodded at Vrail. "Her gifts will grow, but for now we only have a short time."

Feron nodded, and we walked out of the field together.

Tears clung to my lashes. "It's true." I cleared the tightness in my throat. "Once a *diizra* is planted, the dead join the ancestors. There is life beyond this."

Feron nodded. "There is always an after, Keera."

I just hoped it was happier than this.

CHAPTER THIRTY-FOUR

My tears had dried to salty lines down my cheeks just like the scars that had been cut through Brenna's eyes. They itched as I made the journey through the portals from Myrelinth to the Order, but I didn't wipe them away.

The brine of the surrounding sea slapped my face as I stepped out of the lake portal and cut across the field to the north side of the island. My chest ached from losing Maerhal, for Nikolai, for Syrra, for myself. But just as Hildegard's funeral had brought the Shades together in our grief, Maerhal's had stitched our bleeding hearts just enough to feel something other than the gash in our chests.

Brenna deserved the same.

We had come to save the Shades, but we had left one behind. I wasn't going to leave her buried on that island alone, completely cut off from anyone who ever cared for her, any ancestors her bones might recognize in the kingdom.

Even if the *Faelinth* ended in ash and flame, Brenna should make it to those lands as we'd dreamed we would.

I pulled the empty *diizra* I had stolen from my pocket as I approached the side of the hill where I had buried her. The waves crashed against the cliff's edge, scraping the rock with their watery claws and filling the air with their mist.

My palm flattened against the earth until I could feel the pulse of life underneath me. Every blade of grass, every wildflower, was connected to a web that pulsed through me like a shared heartbeat.

Brenna's bones didn't pulse. They were cold and dead just as she was, but I could sense the absence of life through the web. I traced the shape of their coldness, inking a shadow of them in my mind. I used the earth gift Elverath had given me to pull them from the soil.

One by one, pillars of every size lifted from the ground, each holding a piece of my first love. I blew a gentle gust across them, sprinkling the dirt through the air until the white shone through. A spout of sea water rose over the cliff's edge by my command, washing them clean.

The bones shone under the night sky, more precious than any metal I had ever held. I let my powers leak out of me as I cried, leaving a trail of blossoms and shrubs with every step I took.

The training field was now a meadow. I lingered over each bushel of blooms, plucking one from every bush until I had a soft bed of petals covering the ground.

I picked up the bones one by one, starting with her feet, and placed them on the blooms. The salt seared my throat as I sobbed. The bones that had once been Brenna—the person who had been larger and brighter than anyone I'd ever known—was now a pile small enough to fit in one of Rheih's berry baskets.

I looked down at the them but I no longer saw bones laid on petals. Brenna was lying on the bed of flowers, blooms poked through her blond curls that splayed out like sunrays lit behind her. The same curls I would have braided my own hair into if I had been able to bury her properly the first time.

Without thinking, I pulled the white hilt from its sheath and grabbed the length of my braid. The end trailed past my weapons belt as I held it in front of me. All those years, all those memories woven together at the ends. The last part of me she'd touched. I lifted the bloodstone dagger to the side of my face and sliced through my braid at my shoulders.

The freshly cut ends untangled in the wind as I circled the braid around Brenna. My hair was now the same length it had been the day Brenna and I met. A worthy amount for me to give to her while leaving enough length for Riven to braid his hair into mine if this war ended the way Damien wanted.

That was how it had always been. Brenna got everything I could give her, and Riven got the pieces that were left. It was unfair. Cruel to both of us. But my heart had been half dead for decades.

Something moved behind me. I turned around on my knee, dagger still in hand. The rock that Gerarda had kicked rolled to a stop beside my boot. With the rage of the sea, I hadn't heard her approach.

"What are you doing here?" My words were sharper than I'd meant them.

Gerarda's amber eyes lingered on my cut braid. There was a sheen over them as she finally looked at me. "This is not a ritual one does alone, Keera." She swallowed thickly. "And Brenna deserves more than one person at her funeral."

My lips trembled. "Almost everyone who knew her is dead."

Gerarda's jaw pulsed four times. "You, me, and Myrrah." She pulled something from her pocket. Her palm opened, and I choked on a laugh.

"She kept it all this time?" I took the tiny ship from Gerarda's hand and caressed the folds Brenna had made in the parchment. A reminder for Myrrah that she would set sail again.

Gerarda nodded. "I asked Myrrah if she wanted to come but she said she would only slow my journey." She gave me a knowing look. Myrrah never slowed anyone down.

"She's had her fill of funerals." I placed the paper ship onto the pile and stood again. "So have I."

"Indeed." Gerarda stood silently over the pile with me, waiting for me to fill the silence, but I had already told Brenna everything I needed to. In my dreams, in my nightmares, in Vellinth with Syrra at my side. I was filled only with grief, but it was no longer cold and trying to drown me. There was a warmth to it, a fullness, it was my love for her persisting in a way that finally let me carry on.

"I actually don't know the words to the song." I turned to Gerarda. "Will you sing it?"

She placed her palm over her face and then her chest. "It would be my honor."

Ish'kavra diiz'bithir ish'kavra.

From flame to ash to flame again.

Gerarda's voice was powerful. It rose to heights that she held like birdsong through the highest treetops before lowering to a turbulent trill. Somehow the words sounded different; at Hildegard's funeral she had sung with grace and refinement, but now her voice shook with the rage that had fueled Brenna every day on this island. It crashed and rolled with the tempo of the sea just as Brenna's love had ebbed and flowed through my life.

Only when Gerarda sliced her hood from her cloak did I realize she was wearing black. It was not the black garb given to us as Shades, but Elvish-spun linen that held its darkness even after decades of wear.

It was a symbol—the hood Brenna never got to claim. Gerarda sliced her hand as she sang, coating the hood in her blood before passing it to me. The hood that had rightfully been Brenna's, the one Damien had taken from her.

I sliced my own palm with my bloodstone blade and turned toward the palace of Koratha. I looked up at the middle tower topped in gold and wondered if Damien was watching us through his magnifying window. Part of me hoped he was, that he had to bear witness to this last act of defiance Brenna and I were doing together.

Gerarda and I lay the hood over the pile of bones. She laced her bloodied palm through mine and my magic seeped into her, stitching the flesh back together without a conscious thought. The last words of the funeral song hung from her lips like a final farewell and then the world went silent.

"*Ish'kavra diiz'bithir ish'kavra*," I whispered, and then I set the pyre aflame.

We stood as the hood and bones burned away, singeing the petals underneath it before they too turned to ash. Gerarda drew a circle on the grass with her foot. "Light another fire here," she said, pulling a knife from her belt.

The flames ignited in an instant. Gerarda placed the blade in the fire before grabbing the *diizra* from my hand and opening the top of it.

I could have used my magic to lift Brenna's ashes into the small satchel, but that wasn't intimate enough. Instead, I scooped what was left of her in my hands and let the ashes roll down my fingers into her new resting place. When the job was done, I used wind to blow the dust from my palms too. The particles whirled together in a tight braid before dropping through the mouth of the *diizra*.

Gerarda folded the opening into an intricate roll that reminded me of a flower still tucked into its bud. Then she pulled the red-hot knife from the fire beside us and sealed the edge of the golden bag for good.

She pulled the chain from the other end free and held it up for my head to slip through. When she let go, Brenna's ashes fell directly over my heart.

I gasped. "It's warm." The *diizra* had been cold in my hand but now it almost pulsed against the bare skin of my chest.

Gerarda nodded. "That life is now yours to carry. For a year until it will be yours to let go."

I lifted my hand to my chest, the palm acting like a shield even though there was no threat nearby. "What if I don't survive the year?"

Gerarda only shrugged and started walking back toward the lake where Riven waited for us both. "You have to."

The training field was cloaked in shadow. Thick tendrils licked at my feet as I walked, climbing to my hips.

Thin vines of shadow twisted around my wrists like snakes, tightening as they coiled until I was held in place. Someone appeared from the darkness in front of me.

Feron.

He walked without need for a cane, his violet eyes glowing, but no ground shifted underneath my feet.

I smirked. "Impressive, Elaran."

Feron's face contorted, skin fading to a light brown. I was staring at myself. "Not as impressive as me," Elaran said in a mocking tone before shifting back to herself. "And not nearly as impressive as that." She pointed to Fyrel, whose eyes glowed amber before she transformed into a fox and then a badger and then a wolverine. Each form progressively bigger than the last.

She ran her furry body between my legs and flopped onto her back. I knelt and scratched her belly. "Is it draining to maintain the different forms?"

There was a flash of light and Fyrel was herself again with my hand on her stomach. "The smaller the animal the easier it is to maintain. I could spend all day as a field mouse and not feel tired, but shifting between different creatures is draining. And the bigger forms." Determination flashed across Fyrel's face.

"Don't overextend yourself," I told her. "This gift is already useful; you don't need to push it further."

Fyrel nodded with a quick glance at Gwyn.

She was standing at the bow of a small boat. It soared through the water with no sail, just Myrrah at the stern shifting the currents of the lake with amber glowing hands. In just a short time, everyone had made so much progress.

I turned back to the others. Crison had a flock of birds flying over the field, and Vrail was using her gift and books to learn anything that could help us win against the *shirak*.

I nodded at Gerarda. "Where's Dynara?"

Gerarda waved her hand and her shadows disappeared to reveal the open training field. The real Feron smiled at me from his seat, but Dynara was nowhere to be found. "They have come far in a short amount of time."

Gerarda crossed her arms. "Not far enough."

"We are better off than when we first saw the *waateyshir* in Silstra." I surveyed the field again. "Where is Dynara?"

A thin gold line appeared in the air next to me. It stretched downward, carving a circle into nothing. I held my breath as the circle closed and a thin watery veil appeared with the golden leaves of Sil'abar glowing on the other side of it.

Dynara stepped through.

"A portal maker," I said in disbelief.

Dynara smirked, waving her amber glowing fingers. "Not a very offensive gift." She turned to Gerarda and Feron.

"But a very powerful one," I said, stretching my arm through the portal. The sunlight warmed my palm even though the day in Myrelinth was overcast and cool. "This changes everything."

Feron's smile widened, and he nodded.

Dynara blinked. "You think it's useful?"

"Yes." I pulled my hand back. "How many can you make before reaching your limit?"

"A couple dozen or so." Dynara tucked her hair behind her rounded ear. "Less if I have to close every one." She raised a glowing fist and punched it through the portal she had just made. The veil froze and then shattered to the ground. "You can use me in battle?" she asked, doubtful.

I smirked. "We can use you to ferry us in and ferry Halflings out. Damien will never know when we'll attack."

Dynara's frown grew into a mischievous smirk.

CHAPTER THIRTY-FIVE

PIRMIITH FOUND US on the training grounds. His eyes were red with tears and Syrra ran for him. "Is it Uldrath? Noemdra? What is wrong, miikan?"

He took a sip from Syrra's waterskin. We stood in silence as he wiped his mouth into a frown. "Damien has raided three of the villages. He took all the Halflings."

I punched the training post beside me. Gerarda's shadows spooled out of her, lashing along the ground. "It's not what we'd planned, but we can liberate them when the war is won."

Pirmiith looked like he was going to be sick.

Gerarda's confidence dropped with her shoulders.

"No," Elaran said, tears pooling in her eyes.

Pirmiith nodded his head. "He killed them all. Slew them in the streets. Even the children."

Gerarda ran from the training ground without a word. Elaran moved to follow her, but I grabbed her arm. "It isn't safe. Let her drain her magic first."

I dropped to my knees, but no sobs came.

Riven shook his head. "But how will he pay for his ships and armies if he has no weapons to sell? He must still need Halfling blood."

Syrra's neck tensed. "He has an entire city to bleed."

"Kairn saw Gwyn's eyes. Damien did too." I tossed my blade onto the grass. "He must have put together what I can do."

Vrail's lip curled in disgust. "He would rather have every Halfling slain than give you the chance to turn them? You would never force that upon a child."

I shrugged, too exhausted by grief and loss for any more rage. "I don't know if Damien is capable of believing that. He assumes everyone would make the same choices he would for power and immortality." I swallowed. It was why I always ended up disappointing him in the games he'd made me play.

We were both willing to be as ruthless as we needed to be. But what we considered *necessary* had never been the same.

I turned to Pirmiith. "Where are the scouts?"

"At their posts." He stood up from the rock. "Except for two who are watching the squadrons led by Arsenal members."

"Who?" I asked.

"The Dagger and the Arrow." Damien had already replaced his dead with new.

Riven grabbed my arm. "They're traveling separately or together?"

"Separately."

My chest tightened. That meant twice as many villages could burn.

I wiped my eyes. "Call in as many as you can."

Elaran scoffed. "You could send the scouts to warn them. Instead, you'd have them leave the Halflings for dead?"

"No." I crossed my arms. "But we have to have a plan or they will die too. We'll decide which villages can be evacuated the quickest. Some of Victoria's contacts are still harboring Halflings." I turned to Dynara. "You will send word, ask them how many they can help escape if we can't get there in time."

Dynara nodded and ran.

I turned to Gwyn. "Are you ready to test your powers?"

"Absolutely." She grinned.

"Good." I nodded her off the field. "Go get rest. We'll fetch you when we have a plan."

Gwyn looped her arm through Fyrel's. "If I'm going, then she is."

Fyrel's cheeks turned pink but she didn't shrug Gwyn off.

My eyes narrowed. "No transformations. No bravery. You must follow orders."

Fyrel's back straightened and she nodded.

"Then get to bed too."

They took off, giggling as if I hadn't just given them permission to risk their lives.

"And what about the cities?" Vrail asked, her face flushed with rage. "There's hundreds of Halflings in Volcar, and Damien's fleet is right there. He could kill them tonight if he wanted."

My mouth tightened. "Then we pray that he doesn't."

None of the Amber Fae had enough control over their powers to fight—that was what Damien was placing his bets on, no doubt. He wanted to force our hand, to make us play, before our magical numbers grew too high and their gifts too strong.

Vrail's voice cracked. "We could evacuate Volcar too."

I shook my head. "We aren't ready. It would spread our resources too thin." I turned to Syrra. "He may not attack the city. He has no way of knowing if we would come to Volcar's aid or use the opportunity to attack the capital."

"A risk." Syrra nodded. "But a balanced one."

Her approval didn't loosen the knots in my stomach.

"So, we just wait?" Vrail scoffed. "Like ducklings along the river knowing there are foxes about?"

"Villages are one thing, cities another." Vrail's disappointment stung, but I knew this was right. Damien wanted us to run in, unprepared, so he had the chance to smite us. We had to fight against that instinct, or we would lose. "We'll send word and supplies, but until Damien does otherwise, we have a responsibility to protect the people already here."

Vrail stomped her foot on the grass, scattering Gerarda's shadows. "I hate this."

So did I.

Vrail met me at Sil'abar. She had found a vacant room secluded enough so we wouldn't be interrupted.

"How certain are you that this will work?" I asked, biting my cheek. My palms were tacky with sweat as I undid my weapons belt and sat on the cushion Vrail had put on the floor.

Her face fell to a deadpan stare. "You know I only deal in probabilities."

"How probable is it then?" I gave her the most dashing smile I could manage, but it felt uneven and misshapen on my lips.

Vrail shook her head. "Probable enough for me to try. It will either work or it won't."

I swallowed thickly. "No chance that I will see anyone else then?" Nikolai had gotten so much healing from speaking with his mother through Vrail's gift, but I knew that some of the ghosts who could be waiting for me would be enough to send me into a spiral of wine-sodden grief.

Vrail's gaze fell to Brenna's name on my arm and then her *diizra* around my neck. "No," she said, more softly than before. "But you don't need to be the one to do this. I could—"

"I do." My jaw snapped shut. Vrail was right; anyone could ask Faelin about her past but I *needed* to. The weight of everyone's fate tore at my shoulders, and I wasn't sure how much longer I would be able to stand. If I fell, how long would it take for the Elverin to tumble with me?

I hoped she could help. Give me answers, yes, but also reinvigorate the part of me that clung to every doubt when our people needed decisive action.

Vrail's lip twitched but she didn't argue. Instead, she patted the pillow and gestured for me to lie back. I did, the soft linen caressing my cheek as my head sunk to the floor.

Vrail looked down at me. "Are you ready then?" She held out her hand for me to grasp.

"Yes," I breathed, clasping my fingers around hers.

Vrail's magic was not the slow, warm creep of Feron's mindwalking ability. It was a jolt. I flinched like I'd been hit by lightning, but there was no pain. When I opened my eyes, I was no longer inside Sil'abar.

There were no dwellings encircling the giant tree, only a wide meadow lush with flowers edged by a thick forest in all directions. The wind blew through my short hair, the jagged ends blowing across my cheek as I stood from the soft ground.

Vrail stood beside me. She squeezed my hand and pointed in the direction of the Dark Wood. "I'll let you speak on your own."

"Thank you, young one," a gentle rumble of a voice sounded beside me.

I turned and saw her. Faelin, the first of the Fae, mother to all our kind. Her coiled hair was long and voluminous, tight spirals encircling her striking face. Eyes of liquid gold complemented the rich brown of her skin. Her high cheekbones were only made sharper by the soft, flat bridge of her nose and round, full lips.

I dropped to my knees. "*Niinokwenar.*"

"One Faemother should not kneel for another. Stand, Keera Waateyith'thir." She gave me a dazzling smile.

I blinked. "You can speak the King's Tongue?"

Faelin's lips twitched. "I can speak whatever tongue my descendants do, for I live in you," she answered in Elvish.

I stood, the top of my head barely reaching Faelin's chin. Her shoulder was marked with the same Elder birch branch that was carved into Syrra's shoulder. The branch of the tree that gave her life.

"Ask what you must." Faelin turned toward the Dark Wood. "It drains your friends' gift greatly to keep me here."

"The *waateyshirak*." I faltered, trying to catch my thoughts. "You banished them by creating the second sun."

Faelin's thick brows furrowed. "I created the shadow sun to lengthen the day and shorten the shadows. But you already know this, Keera."

I tilted my head. "The story we found in Vrail's book. You led hunts to destroy their nests. To kill them one by one. But if you had so many gifts, why not kill them all yourself and keep your magic?"

"All magic has its limits." Faelin took a deep breath. "I had a choice. My powers were great but only great enough to choose between destroying many *waateyshirak* at once or weakening them all. Perhaps if there had been more Fae in those early years, I would have chosen differently, but lessening their strength gave every clan a chance to fight them, even when I could not be there."

"A choice you made with the future Elverin in mind." I ran a hand through my hair. I was trying to make the same choice, but I didn't know what gave the Elverin the best chance. "Could it be done again? Would another shadow sun keep the *waateyshirak* at bay long enough to end Damien's reign?"

Faelin lifted her chin. "Perhaps, but that would come with great sacrifice and no guarantee that the Elverin could vanquish the *waateyshirak* for a second time."

I looked up in the sky, but only one sun shone down on us. Here the *shirak* didn't exist; there was no need for Faelin's protection. "It took all your magic to create the shadow sun? Feron says creating it cost you your gifts and you died."

"Most of it." Faelin gave me a small smile. "Though Fae cannot create magic. Only use it or store it away." She glanced up at the sky.

My heart stilled. "The shadow sun is a seal? It stores your magic still?"

"A powerful spell that took weeks to weave." Faelin nodded. "And one that protects our people still."

"And what if it was broken?" My eyes narrowed. "Would that release enough magic to kill the *shirak* for good?"

Faelin's lips thinned. "Many of them, but not all."

My stomach fell to the ground. It wasn't worth risking the only protection we had against them if it didn't ensure their destruction.

Faelin's stare hardened. "Breaking a seal comes with its own cost." She clasped her hands, her long sleeves billowing in the light breeze. "The last one you broke almost cost you your life."

"Elverath gifted me great power." My hands fisted at my sides. "Perhaps this is how I'm meant to use it."

"Or perhaps Elverath gave you and your kin the gifts to rebuild after the war is won."

I scoffed. "How are we to fight Damien's armies and the *shirak* at once?"

"You will find a way." Faelin's eyes glowed gold. "You always have."

I cocked my jaw. "What is the point of being able to talk to the ancestors if you don't tell me what to do?"

She laughed. "We do not have all the answers, Keera. We never have." Faelin placed a heavy hand on my shoulder. "Your ancestors have already fought this battle and lost. Do not chain yourself to their choices but learn from them."

I bit my cheek. "If I stall, people die. If I make the wrong choice, all our people may die."

"Yes," Faelin answered as if that wasn't the most horrifying word she could say. "Create a second shadow sun, destroy the first, do neither—the choice is yours, and I trust you will make the right one. But know that to create a spell like that—or destroy one—takes measurable strength." Faelin's hand squeezed my shoulder. "Strong enough, and one may do it on their own. But the burden can be shared. Split between many gifts." Faelin leaned closer to me, her eyes lit by an auric glow.

My back tensed. "I can't ask the other Fae to do that."

"Your mother did." Faelin raised a brow.

I stepped out of her grasp. "And that only delayed the conflict. The Elverin are done living under the shadow of the throne. Elverath is theirs, and they will get it back now or die trying. Not seven hundred years from now."

Faelin stepped forward and put her hand to my face. "You have learned so much, Keera. Trust yourself." Her eyes flicked behind me where Vrail was stumbling through the meadow. "Our visit has come to an end for now." She stood tall as the edges of the landscape began to fade. "Know this, Keera Waateyith'thir, there is healing in the past when you are ready to search for it."

I reached out, wanting to know what she meant, but Vrail collapsed on the ground and everything around us went black.

I opened my eyes and saw we were back in the empty room. Vrail panted as she crawled on the floor, reaching for her waterskin. I passed it to her and squeezed her knee.

"Thank you for holding on as long as you did."

Vrail nodded through rasping breaths. "Did she tell you anything that could help us?"

I shook my head.

"At least we tried." Vrail collapsed back onto the floor.

"We did." I cleared my throat and stood so Vrail couldn't see the guilt on my face. I was not going to let the council or any of my friends deliberate on this. Faelin had gifted her knowledge to me, and it was mine to use.

Though hopefully I wouldn't have to.

CHAPTER THIRTY-SIX

WE GATHERED IN FERON'S ROOM to feast when Pirmiith rushed in through the open door. He sped past Riven, who was standing to eat his dinner after Nikolai made a point of dragging his chair away from the table.

"We were wrong," Pirmiith said through a deep breath, waving a report in his hands.

I swallowed the rabbit Syrra had made and grabbed the parchment from him. "About what?"

"The next target is not one of the small villages," Dynara answered for him, her face grave as she passed Pirmiith a goblet of water.

He stood to his full height, his long brown hair tied back into a half braid behind his head. "Damien has ships docking at the ports as we speak. He's attacking Volcar."

Syrra peered over my shoulder to read the note. "He may just be protecting it. It would be foolish to concentrate his entire army so far from the capital."

He shook his head. "He brought ten thousand men with orders for all Mortals to hand over any Halflings in their service to the Crown."

My throat went dry. "Volcar is the second largest city in the kingdom." I turned to Vrail. "How many Halflings would you guess?"

"Thousands," she answered without hesitation. Her leg started to bounce. "But those are only the Halflings with the papers to prove it. Volcar is the easiest place for the amber-blooded to hide. Mortals from every realm congregated there once Aemon established his rule. Elvish features are easier to pass for Mortal."

Gwyn ripped her bread into tiny pieces. "Not when Damien orders his men to prick the palm of every resident—man, woman, and child."

"He goes from raiding villages to an entire city?" I stood and started pacing in front of the hearth. The flames flared as my control slipped.

"It's a trap." Dynara crossed her arms. "He is trying to lure us out to battle at his convenience."

Riven nodded. "Ten thousand men is not even a quarter of his army."

"Dynara is right." Syrra threw her napkin onto her plate. The news was enough to turn even her voracious appetite. "Damien wishes to lure us into a fight so he can observe our strengths before we come for his city."

I cocked my jaw to the side. "He wants to see what kind of magic we have."

"Exactly."

"And kill the Halflings before you can turn them," Riven added.

Fyrel's face soured. "He'll harvest their blood first." She rubbed her arm where Damien's men had prodded her for weeks.

Gerarda grabbed Elaran's thigh protectively as if Damien's soldiers were about to storm through the door. "He won't care how many of his men die. He just wants to watch. To count how many Fae we have and give himself enough time to strategize how best to protect his city."

Elaran wrapped her arm along the back of the chair they shared. "There will be no way to hide it. He could have hundreds of soldiers with magic eyes at this point. Anything we do we must expect him to see."

Gerarda's lip curled over her sharp teeth. "He's using the Halflings as bait. And he will use this as an excuse to kill as many of us as he can."

Nikolai dropped his fork. It clattered against the table. "Unless we do not answer the call."

The entire room went silent. I didn't know if they were more shocked by the suggestion or that it was Nikolai who had been the one to suggest it.

Riven's mouth hung open. "You would have us sit here and do nothing while thousands of our kin are murdered."

"If it means losing the advantage in the war, then perhaps it's the best call." Nikolai shrugged his shoulders. "Preventing their deaths only for Damien to keep control in the end damns us all."

Riven shook his head. "You do not mean that. You have been by my side risking your life for the Halflings from the very start of this rebellion, and now you want to stand by while thousands more than we've ever saved are slaughtered?"

Nikolai's mouth hardened. "Don't judge me, Riventh. Not when I learned how to risk the lives of others to suit my needs from *you*."

"Enough! This feud helps no one." Vrail stood and flung her napkin between them like a flag.

I turned to her. "How many more Halflings are in the capital?"

Vrail froze. "Twice as many, at least."

Riven's frown deepened, and as he leaned back against the wall, he nodded to Syrra. "How long would we need to recuperate from battle before we could attack the capital?"

The Elf bit her lip as she did the calculations. "Assuming none of the Fae were gravely injured, a fortnight at least."

Riven's shoulders fell. "More than enough time for Damien to devise a defense."

"Or an attack," Gerarda interjected.

Syrra lifted her chin. "I agree with my nephew. It is our duty to ensure we defeat Damien. We cannot spread our resources thin now."

Nikolai gave her a sniff nod.

Vrail crossed her arms, her leg still bouncing. "I want to fight." She gave Nikolai an apologetic look. "For the Halflings and for the burial sites. They cover the mountains of Volcar, all from my clan. If Damien destroys them, then I cannot use my gifts to reclaim that history. We'd be losing more than lives."

"There will be nothing left for you to reclaim if Damien holds onto his reign." Riven stepped forward from the wall, the tendons in his neck flexing as he nodded at Nikolai. "I concur with Nik. Defeat must be our priority. Our *only* priority."

Something softened in Nikolai's brow for a moment but then it was gone, his mouth hard and tight once more.

"The Faemother gave me my gifts." Elaran stood from her seat. "I shall use them as she commands."

Gerarda nodded in agreement. "My sword will swing wherever Keera needs it."

Myrrah pushed her chair back from the table. She had been entirely silent since Pirmiith and Dynara walked in.

She made her way to me and grabbed my hand. "It is unfair that so many choices have been left to you in this fight. The one who wins the battle is not always the smartest, but the one who can swing their blade swiftly and with confidence." Her fingers squeezed mine. "There is no one else I would trust to make those decisions than you, Keera. My sails are yours to command."

My lip trembled as I looked up at Feron. In the dim light from the hearth, I could see the years that had marked his face. The ages of loss he had lived through and the decisions he had made to survive them.

"What say you?" I asked, ignoring the way the words shook along my tongue.

Feron leaned on his cane, his brows pinched as he considered the question. "I would say that I am not a seer, but I am someone who once had to choose between fighting for all and saving a few." A tear fell from Feron's cheek, his voice cracking before he spoke again. "And I have lived with those regrets every day since, yet my people have survived. I have no way of knowing if making a different choice would have meant the end of us."

"How did you decide before?" I turned to Vrail and Nikolai. They could give us the exact numbers to analyze if we gave them enough time. But every minute wasted would mean more Halflings lost.

Feron let out a deep breath. "Nothing but my intuition. That is all you ever truly have."

Myrrah squeezed my hand and gave me a pointed look. Who else had been balancing these decisions for decades and who else knew Damien as well as I did? My gut was not a blunt object, but a sharpened weapon, specifically honed for a moment such as this.

There was no time to convene a council. There was not even enough time for more debate. Someone had to make the decision, and I was not going to back down from the choice this time. I didn't care that Elverath had marked me as a leader the day my eyes turned gold, or if the Light Fae had the day they sealed me in that tree, none of those choices mattered.

But this one did. Because it was mine.

I turned to Syrra and Gerarda, my decision made.

"Prepare everyone." I tightened my weapons belt and walked toward the door. "We leave at midday."

Riven grabbed my arm. "Where are you going?"

"To talk to Damien."

CHAPTER THIRTY-SEVEN

DAMIEN WAS EXPECTING MY VISIT; he pulled me into his dream the moment the elixir put me to sleep. I appeared sitting in a chair in the grandest inn in Volcar. It had been one of Damien's favorite haunts when he was a young prince. I didn't want to think about any of the activities he had gotten up to in this very room.

"Why are we here?" I seethed, looking at the falling snow outside of the wide wall of windows.

Damien lifted his chin so his breath fogged the chilled glass. "A good leader always watches over his men on the eve of battle."

I crossed my legs and leaned back in the chair. "You're not really here."

Damien turned to the table behind him and poured himself a cup of wine. He poured a second goblet, filling it and pushing it to my side of the table. I didn't touch it.

He itched the scar above his magic eye. "I'm here in spirit."

"But not in person." I tucked my hands behind my head. "Meaning by your measure, you are *not* a good leader."

Damien shot me an annoyed look. "You have come to make your plea?"

"You wouldn't grant my plea even if it was to your benefit." I leaned forward on my knees as he sipped from his goblet. "Why attack Volcar and leave your city unguarded?"

Damien huffed a laugh. "My city is *very* well guarded, I assure you." He tucked a hand behind his back, looking up at the smoking mountain. "But Volcar is crawling with vermin."

"Even you can see that attacking Volcar is not the strategic play."

Damien raised the brow over his black eye. "Isn't it?" He turned to me. "I have a full armada and ten thousand soldiers ready to invade every home, nook, and cranny. They will find every Halfling within a league of Volcar." He sipped his wine. "And they're paid too handsomely to leave any for you to turn against me."

"Turn against you?" I scoffed. "I can spot one of your ploys, Damien. You can't bait us into battling you in Volcar so you can observe what gifts my *Halflings* have been given."

His lip twitched, but the rest of his face remained entirely resolved. "You won't leave an entire city to burn in smoke and ash. You aren't ruthless enough to make that call." Damien's tone was a mix of disappointed judgment.

I gritted my teeth. "Don't tempt me, Damien. We both know I have the strength to fight you in Volcar tomorrow and Koratha the next."

"Perhaps," he conceded. "But will Gerarda make it there? That worthless Shield? Would they survive? What if one of your comrades is struck down mid-battle?" Damien licked his lips. His last question wasn't just coy banter, but a threat. He knew what we had found along Nikolai's wrist.

He smirked into his wineglass and sat down.

"They will not fall." I lifted my chin. I wouldn't let them.

Damien's grin turned wicked. "And what about Gwyn? What if I order one of my beasts to cut her through the belly for all of you to watch?"

"She will fight alongside me until I take your last breath."

Damien giggled. "Is *that* what you've been fighting for? My head on a spike?" He paced across the room to fill his cup with more wine. "Not very original, Keera."

His eyes lingered on my arm as he sipped, and I knew that he could see the name written there because I was allowing it. He could finally see some part of the truth.

But not all of it.

"Is that why you switched sides?" He jutted his chin at my forearm. "The guilt of what you did finally broke you? One taste of my brother's half-breed lips, and you swap allegiances to fight against your king?"

I blinked in disbelief. Damien was not so self-assured to not see the truth. But as I studied him, it was obvious that Brenna's name was the only one he could see. Feron's ring continued to mask the rest.

I huffed a laugh. "You think that is when I switched sides?" Now it was me pacing around the room, carving a large circle around him so Damien had no choice but to be pinned to the chair. "I was *never* a loyal servant. Not to your father and certainly not to you."

His jade eye glinted with curiosity. He licked his lips as he looked at me in a new light. "You mean to tell me that you killed your roommate, your dearest friend, your *lover*, to falsify your loyalties?" Damien broke into a sarcastic grin. "I've never thought so well of you, Keera. Masterfully devious."

I returned his grin. "It was. But I can't take credit—it wasn't my idea."

Damien's mouth fell to a straight line as he realized this was not a jest.

"Brenna was the one who figured it out," I continued. "The night before the Trial." A twinge of satisfaction pulled across my chest as Damien scowled. "She knew that you thought we were too strong as a pair, that you would convince your father of it. She knew you well enough to devise just how vile you would be."

Damien waved his goblet across his mouth but didn't drink. "And yet she is the one who is dead."

I stopped pacing. "Because she decided to be."

His breath caught.

"You think I made that decision easily? That I chose myself in that moment instead of her?" I snorted. "She had made the decision before either of us had stepped into that room. She had swallowed a poison and stained her lips just enough for me to see." I lifted my chin. "She was dead before you ever tied her to that chair."

"That can't be true," Damien sputtered.

"But it is. I made the only move I could—I pierced that dagger through her chest before you could discover the truth. So that I could live to carry out our promise."

"Your promise?"

"To end the Crown."

Damien scoffed but it was airy and feeble. "A child's dream."

"Yes, a child's promise turned into a vow the night you gave me that dagger." I lifted my chin. "The night you gave me my scars."

Damien's black eye flashed with amber at the memory of cutting my back. I let him linger on the joy of it before I revealed the last part of that story.

"But I made a promise to myself that night too." I grabbed the mage pen from my pocket, magically conjuring it into the dream. "I took the blade you cut me with and carved Brenna's name into my arm so I would never forget the vow I made. So I would never stop fighting for our freedom." I cut the smooth skin of my arm with the pen just as I had all those year ago, my blood dripping onto the floor in a thick pool that Damien couldn't look away from.

"A fight that spanned thirty years before the battles began?" Damien snorted, finally meeting my gaze. "How much preparation did you need?"

"One Halfling cannot topple what your father built on her own. I needed to learn that lesson. But the resistance never faltered." I slipped the ring from my finger and reveled in Damien's gasp. "I never stopped carving names, you see. Every time I was forced to slaughter a family or kill an innocent at the Crown's behest, I marked their name into my flesh. Reminder after reminder, year after year, of the lives you would answer for when that reckoning came."

Damien's eyes widened as he saw me—truly—for the first time. I wore only a simple leather vest with an open back that showed every scar along my torso. The ones he had carved and the ones I had.

I allowed him to see me completely, the decades of treachery carved into my skin.

Finally.

"You traitorous snake," Damien spat.

I smacked his goblet from his hand. "Attack as many cities as you wish. But I've been preparing for this fight for a long time. I will not lose."

Damien tried to stand but I shoved him back into his chair. It creaked as I leaned over him, lurking like death over a sickbed ready to claim him. I toyed with the dagger at my belt, a quick escape from this nightmare, but there was one question I couldn't keep myself from asking.

"How does it feel to know that you were bested so long ago?"

"You have not beat me yet." Damien's breath fell hot on my neck as he scowled.

I shook my head. "Not me. Brenna."

"I would hardly call her death a victory," Damien grumbled.

"And that is precisely why she beat you." I placed my hand on the back of his chair. "Because she made a play that you never would. That you're incapable of. She was willing to die to make sure her successor had a chance of winning."

"A true master does not prepare for a successor."

"A master doesn't, but a leader does."

Damien's lip recoiled. "Yet Elverath is *my* kingdom, not Brenna's. This land is mine."

I shook my head. "Land does not belong to the person who claims it, but the one who is willing to die for it." I shoved a knife into his chest, enjoying the way the air wheezed out of the cavity even though it caused him no pain. "And you shall die for nothing."

CHAPTER THIRTY-EIGHT

THE SUNS HAD SET by the time we reached the mountain slope outside the city of Volcar. Damien's men circled the perimeter of the city—the line a dozen soldiers deep. Their ships waited in the channel behind them, stocked and armed.

I stood high along the hill with the Fae lined beside me while Riven and Pimiirth waited in the nearby woods with the rest of the Elverin, ready to attack once the path was clear.

I scanned the ships with my spyglass. My eye caught on a young man with a tiny dagger fastening his black cloak.

Damien had a new Arsenal every week. The new Dagger was the leanest so far, though from the way his dark eyes shifted around the crowd, noticing every hint of movement, I knew he was a sharp shot. His short frame was deceiving, but Gerarda had proven that a Dagger didn't need to be large to be deadly.

He stood at the top of the tallest mast in the armada, his ship still docked at port. He took out his own spyglass and held it up to his eye. One dark brown, the other black. At least until Damien decided to peer through it.

The glass glinted in the orange light of the evening suns as his scope landed on me. I waved. The Dagger scowled behind the spyglass, the amber pupil flaring bright inside it. His gaze stayed on me, trailing down the lengths of my arms and torso. There was no reason to hide my scars any longer. Damien knew the truth of it now.

I could tell by the way his lips curled that it was Damien who was watching me, not the Dagger. His body straightened and he shouted something to the men on the lower decks. Still, he did not set the spyglass down nor did he turn away from me.

I smirked, hoping he could see it, and raised my dagger above my head with Brenna's name in full view. I let it linger in the air before lowering the blade and pointing it directly at Damien's stolen face.

His lip curled back over his teeth, and when he opened his mouth, the ground shook under my feet, his voice echoing across the entire city. I turned to the others behind me. Was this some kind of new invention? Some kind of bastardization of the water spells the Elverin used to project their voices?

Vrail pointed down at the soldiers below.

It was worse.

Every soldier had mismatched eyes. One natural and one black as night with an amber ring as a pupil.

My stomach turned.

They all spoke as one terrifying unit. "There's an enemy in our midst," the chorus of voices boomed so loud small balls of snow rolled down the snowy peaks.

My throat tightened. Damien wasn't speaking to us. He was delivering his message directly to the citizens of Volcar. With no chance of interruption and no doubt that even the hardest of hearing would feel the tremble of his words.

"My most loyal and adoring subjects, this is your king speaking." A wave of shocked gasps echoed through Volcar. "The traitorous Blade who killed my father, your most kind and loving king, has come to set siege to our city. She plans to kill your children, your wives, your neighbors. And believe me when I say a vile creature like her will delight in your cries."

My teeth creaked as they ground together, but there was nothing I could do to stop his speech.

"But you needn't fret." Damien's smirk crawled up his Dagger's face. "My soldiers and armada will more than match their forces. And the *waateyshirak* circling the smoking mountain answer only to me."

The pendant on the Dagger's chest glowed bright. In the distance, an ear-splitting screech split the skies.

The blood drained from my face as the *waateyshir* appeared from behind the smoking, snow-capped mountain. It soared through the smoke without hesitation, the burning air scorching its belly like a soft caress keeping it safe from the last rays of sunlight. It dove deep into its pit and emerged with a second *waateyshir* chasing its billowing black tail.

"But the traitor has come for more than just your screams," Damien continued. "She is here to turn every single Halfling into an evil creature that will feast on your bones. Her golden eyes mark her for the terror that she is." Some of the soldiers shifted to get a better look at me, as if their Mortal eyes could see the details of my face from across the valley. "So hand over every Halfling known to you so my guard can protect them from her vicious hand. Name them now and no one need be harmed except for the traitors in the north."

The Dagger's lip twitched as panic erupted across the streets of Volcar. Mortals shoved people out of the way, women shrieked, pointing at Halflings as they clutched their children to their breasts.

"Surrender and I will not harm them," Damien offered in ten thousand whispers.

I stepped forward. I didn't need my spyglass to know the Dagger smiled and his amber pupil pulsed as I raised my hand. Damien waited for me to drop my weapon, a symbol of surrender, but instead a thin spout of water breached the surface of the sea next to his boat and floated upward at my command in a twisting spiral.

It formed a large sphere above the ships, filling itself with water from the channel until it grew to twice the size of the *miikibi'thir* orb in Vellinth. The crowds hushed; they had no words for magic like this. It hadn't existed in their lifetimes.

With an easy wave of my hand, I pulled a tiny droplet from the orb and sent it soaring toward my mouth. If Damien wanted to make speeches, I could make one too.

I paused to make sure the *shirak* were staying close to their mountain. Their beaks snapped and their talons stretched, but Damien had not commanded them to attack. The suns had not surrendered their protection.

Yet.

I cleared my throat, and my voice boomed across the entire city. I smiled as the ground shook more than it had for Damien's speech. "To the Mortals, I have only one thing to say and that is that your king lies to you." Broken shrieks echoed through the skies as the city dwellers pointed up at the large orb of water that projected my voice as well as my likeness. It was like a gigantic looking glass had been suspended in the air and I was looking out from it. My pointed ears, golden eyes, and scars on full display.

I was a creature they and their foremothers had never seen. The past come to reclaim its land from their clutches.

"Damien doesn't care how many of you die. He does not care if every one of you perish as long as he remains upon the throne." I lifted my chin and let the glow in my eyes simmer. "He killed his own father to claim that chair, and he will kill you too. The sides have been drawn. Choose yours carefully, for history will be decided soon."

I cleared my throat, letting my voice soften before I addressed the people I most cared for. "For the Halflings, you know the Crown has never offered us true protection. You can taste the falsehoods in Damien's words just as well as I. But you should know that he has come for you now because he knows what waits for you when the rebellion wins."

I flicked my wrist and the image in the orb changed from my face to memories of Halflings singing together in Myrelinth, laughing and celebrating as the children danced and swung in the trees. Image after image, Halfling after Halfling, I let them see what freedom looked like.

Half of the people in the streets froze, unable to look away from the sky.

I looked down the line at the Amber Fae who joined me. I nodded and each of their eyes began to glow.

"He comes for you because he knows the power you hold." The images changed once more, no longer memories but what I was witnessing now. Gerarda's amber eyes were even brighter as the shadows curled around her body, lashing out like thrown blades. Elaran changed her face into Gerarda's and then into the Dagger's before transforming into Damien himself, the glowing amber eyes the only sign that she was not truly him.

"He knows what you can become," I said, my eyes never leaving the Dagger's face. "And he would rather kill you for it than see you turn against him." I raised my hand and another spout splashed the Dagger in the face. "I will not accept your offer. Today, tomorrow, or ever after. Because no Halfling, Elf, or Fae will ever submit to you again. We shall fight."

Parts of the crowd cheered, and the soldiers readied their swords for an attack. Damien spat salty water onto the deck below, wiping his host's face with his black cloak.

The Dagger waved his hand. A horn blew in the distance as the *shirak* shrieked from the mountain. The soldiers began their march, not toward us but into the city. Their belts filled with blades to slay Halflings in the street.

The pendant on the Dagger's chest began to glow.

"As you wish." The chorus of voices boomed, drowning out the panicked screams from inside the city walls. The Dagger leaned over the crow's nest and lifted his blade in the air, as he shouted his king's final command. "Kill the Halflings on sight!"

CHAPTER THIRTY-NINE

"FERON!" I SHOUTED, POINTING TO the soldiers marching on Volcar. Feron sat high on a slab of rock he'd pulled from the ground, his eyes glowing bright violet.

He lifted his hands, and a wall of stone broke from the ground, blocking access to the city from the main road. Damien's army broke apart immediately, anticipating the maneuver, and lined the stone that now created a wall around the entire city.

"Again!" I roared but Feron didn't move his hand. He let it hang in the air, frozen in time as ashy snow fell across his face. Only when the soldiers had thinned their lines to three men deep did he act.

His fist shook as he pulled his arm down with all his might. He let out a guttural scream, the veins in his neck threatening to rupture as he used his gift to split the ground in two.

Bodies tumbled into the chasm that now divided the new city wall from the outer fields. Some men ran back. Others clutched roots and dirt to keep from falling in, but they were swallowed by the sea as the channel waters came rushing into the rift. The waves thrashed against the banks, spraying salty mist into the faces of the survivors.

A thick root wrapped around my waist and as well as the others', carrying us to the field of battle below. We dropped onto the ground, and I saw Feron collapsed against his seat, chest rising as his violet eyes dimmed.

Men flooded the port and released the lines holding their ships. The sound of creaking wood boomed against the mountain as the thrashing waters split the port in two. My stomach hardened. The vessel manned by the Dagger fought the currents. The three ships ahead of his fled as the rest carried into the chasm. The crews jumped into the water, hoping to swim to shore, but instead fell onto the jagged rocks that now punctured the sea.

My head snapped to Feron, his eyes glowing purple once more.

But the Dagger survived. He leaped the grand mast, his fingernails clinging to the edge of the chasm instead of falling to his death. My nose wrinkled as he climbed onto the soft grass on the Volcar side of the chasm. The pendant pulsed against his chest.

Gerarda aimed her bow at him but I grabbed her arrow. I nodded at the eastern horizon that was now completely dark. "That pendant is the only thing keeping the *shirak* from laying the city to waste."

Her jaw jutted to the side. "I will kill my successor if I so wish."

"As is your right." I nodded. "Get that pendant and kill him however many times you like."

Gerarda's answering smile was sharp like the point of her drawn arrow. "A little help." She smirked.

I braided a length of gust around the end of the bolt. She let it fly—farther than any arrow should. A soldier climbing over the city wall fell to his doom and took three others with him.

The ground shook as a piercing cry split the skies.

The Dagger lifted his arm, and one of the *shirak* descended upon us. I grit my teeth. My powers flared as I pushed my gusts beyond moving air. A small cloud formed under the belly of the *waateyshir* and expanded underneath as it flew toward us. Lightning flashed inside and I raised my arms, pushing the growing storm higher and the *waateyshir* with it. It tried to fly through it, but the swirling hail thrashed at its wings. The beast flew higher, waiting for an opening.

Soldiers carried ladders from stockpiles on the beach. Damien had suspected Feron's line of attack and planned a countermove. He had everything he needed to build a bridge over the moat. The soldiers charged forward and shoved the gigantic ladders across the gap. I glanced at Feron, but he was slumped over, chest heaving and brow slick with sweat.

Soldiers surrounded the Dagger with their shields as he doubled over, clutching the pendant at his chest. The beast shrieked high above the storm. I turned to Gerarda and Syrra as I created a hole through the center of the swirling clouds. "We may only have one shot at this," I told them.

They grinned at each other.

"One shot is all I need," Syrra said.

The Dagger stood tall and hoisted his sword arm into the air. His pendant glowed like a beacon, ushering his beast toward the ground. The *waateyshir* tucked its wings and plummeted through the storm's eye.

Gerarda released her shadows. They sprawled from her limbs in thick sheets, covering the battlefield in a blanket of darkness. She lifted her hands, and the shadows grew thicker, rising above our heads until not a single Elverin or soldier could see anything at all.

The beast began to whistle. Rot and sulfur filled my nostrils as loose strands of hair were sucked upward along my cheek.

"Now!" I shouted, preparing myself to shield as many as I could with my earth wielding. But there was no need.

Fyrel had transformed herself into a gargantuan beast. She snarled, spit dripping from fangs that were larger than me as she stood on her hind legs. She was taller than the masts of the ships, taller than the trees that grew in the frostbitten soil of Volcar. Tall and large enough to throw a thick spear toward the *waateyshir*.

But it was no spear.

Syrra was perfectly aligned—body straight as an arrow—as Fyrel launched her toward the sky. The beast opened its wings in shock, just as Syrra had wanted. She twisted midair and swung her golden sword into the beast's red center.

But the *waateyshir* snapped its beak. It caught Syrra's boot and flung her to the left. The edge of her blade scraped the beast's wing, and it erupted into a terrifying screech. The air turned hot as inky shadows leaked from its wing. It hung its head like it was in pain, but there was no blood leaking from its body, only hot tendrils of darkness that scorched the ground as they fell.

Everyone went still. Not a soul moved in the city or the battlefield outside of it. None except for the Dagger, who was waving his arm with a hand against his chest. The pendant's glow had begun to fade as the beast thrashed and flapped.

Syrra twisted in the air before hitting the ground. She spread her arms wide and thick flaps of leather snapped taut between her vest and wrist guards. Nikolai's latest invention. I stoked my gusts under her belly and she caught flight on the current. She leaned, dodging the leaking shadow from the beast that raged overhead. She landed and winced. The top of her boot was burned away.

Gwyn pulled it off, ripping a layer of skin with it. Syrra's scream was drowned out by the low call of a horn.

I looked to the channel. The horn was not one of Damien's but ours. Myrrah's ships circled the island and were rounding on the eastern side of the channel. They moved fast and without sails, floating on the currents that Myrrah directed from the middle ship. Crison stood at the top of the middle mast, arms pointing to the sky.

The two other shadowy beasts no longer circled the smoking mountain but were coming to defend their kin. I searched for the Dagger and found him in a crowd of soldiers—the pendant on his chest completely dark.

We were *all* under attack.

Syrra's eyes widened, tracking the beast. She pointed to her leg. "Heal it!"

I assessed her wound. Her brown skin was bubbled and black, covered in dirt and ash. "I can't heal it without cleaning it first. The beast's magic still lingers. I know how to get rid of it."

Syrra opened her mouth to argue but Gwyn stuffed one of Nikolai's handkerchiefs between her lips. The Elf grunted as Gwyn poured water over the wound. Syrra clamped down on the cloth, the tendons in her neck flexing as she screamed into her gag. Gwyn raised a glowing finger and looked up at Nikolai and Elaran.

"Hold her." She glanced at Syrra, whose shorn head was covered with sweat as her chest pumped violently against her leathers. Gwyn's mouth fell to a straight line. "Tightly. This is going to hurt much worse."

She drew the rune directly onto Syrra's open flesh. The amber glow inked itself onto the bloodied and burnt skin like it was paper.

"What are you doing?" I asked, horrified at the vessels popping in Syrra's eyes.

"Debriding the wound." Gwyn finished the spell and Syrra went limp. "The elixirs that clean the wound of an Unnamed One were also used to debride wounds left by the *shirak*, but the death rune works in a pinch."

Nikolai tugged his hair. "Death rune?"

Gwyn nodded. "It kills anything that may contaminate the wound. You can heal her now. There won't be any adverse effects."

"That's dark magic, Gwyn." I couldn't hide the worry in my voice.

She only shrugged.

"Magic takes its toll." I frowned. "You're not exempt from that."

Gwyn raised a brow at Syrra's cleaned leg. "I will gladly pay it."

"And what happens when the cost is too high?"

Gwyn just shrugged.

I grabbed her arm and whispered, "What happens if it is someone else who pays it?" I turned her shoulders so she was facing Fyrel. Gwyn's cheeks heated. Her gaze dropped to Brenna's name along my arm. She knew enough of my past to know how high that cost could be.

"The Halflings!" Elaran shouted, drawing her sword as the first of the new beasts attacked. Black fire and ash rained down on the city of Volcar, smashing through the wall that Feron had created and taking out everyone within the blast radius. Damien's soldiers moved as one, as if he were controlling all theirs minds at once. They ran toward the city with their swords drawn.

"He doesn't care about the beasts," I balked. "As long as his men slaughter every Halfling in the city." Panic struck my chest. Damien hadn't sent the Dagger to use the *shirak* to attack us—he knew one pendant wouldn't be enough to control them for long. They were merely a distraction. Something we had to fight while his men stormed the city. And he didn't care if his men died during the siege.

He wanted a bloodbath.

"Attack with everything you have. Fyrel, we'll try to draw the beasts away from the city." They all nodded at me. Fyrel lowered so

Syrra could climb on as she blew her horn. Fyrel reared back and they rode toward the city as brumal bear and rider.

Pirmiith's horn answered Syrra's call. He and Riven led the charge of Elverin on horseback. The front line clung to their horses with their thighs and shot arrow after arrow at the closest soldiers.

My stomach hardened watching Riven's black cloak disappear into the chaos as Gerarda's shadows faded. I turned to Dynara. "You work to get as many Halflings out of the city as you can. Portal them to safety. Take these two with you; they're excellent fighters." Gwyn beamed as I looked at her and Elaran. "Don't use your powers in front of the soldiers."

Gwyn's brows furrowed. "Why not?"

Elaran wrapped her arm around her neck. "Because Keera is saving the best in her beast form for last, Ring."

I nodded, watching the skies as another fiery blast rained down on Volcar. "This is not our last battle. Damien can't have time to plan around every one of our advantages—some of our strength needs to be a surprise." Gwyn's lip twitched but she nodded.

Dynara's eyes glowed amber and she opened a portal. A thin veil of mist formed over the circle but we could see the devastation on the other side. Dwellings were burning. Children and parents were screaming, tripping over each other as people began pointing their fingers at anyone they thought was Halfling. The stone streets were already wet with amber blood.

The three slipped through the portal and Dynara closed it behind them. I turned to the battlefield. Syrra and Fyrel had lured one of the *shirak* onto the field of battle. A bone-shaking whistle echoed through the grounds as it aimed its attack along Damien's ranks.

Another horn blew from the sea—Myrrah was in trouble. The three ships that had survived the channel were heading them off before they got to Volcar and another six had circled around the island behind Myrrah's fleet.

"Go." Gerarda nodded in the direction of the sea. "Feron and I can protect the ranks here." She lifted her shadow-covered hand.

Guilt tore at my throat. I just needed to do *something*. Make swift decisions before any more people died. I transformed into my eagle form and set off to Myrrah's ship. I soared over the battle, watching as Syrra launched another attack against the injured *waateyshir*. Dodging stray arrows was easy but leaving Riven alone to fight three soldiers at once took all the willpower I had.

I landed on the eagle's nest of Myrrah's ship. Crison stepped aside as I transformed back into my Fae form.

"Can you sink these ships?" I called down to Myrrah, who had parked her chair in front of the large wooden wheel of the ship.

"What does it look like I'm doing?" Myrrah said, her face red and puffy. Two of Damien's ships began to swirl, caught in the whirlpools Myrrah had created underneath their hulls. "You just going to sit up there and watch?" She shouted up at me.

I stepped over the banister—ready to transform—but Crison grabbed my arm. "I can take three." She looked up. Above the thin storm clouds that lingered from my magic was something bigger and scarier.

A gigantic flock of gulls. Crison's eyes glowed, commanding them all. She had beckoned them from the coast their entire sail and now they circled overhead, poised for an attack.

I nodded and that's all Crison needed. The birds descended and the three farthest ships disappeared into a haze of white wings. The vessels slowed as the gulls tore through their sails. The crew's shouts of frustration turned to screams of horror as the birds descended on them, pecking at their flesh and eyes.

Sweat pooled along Crison's brow but she didn't relent—not until the cries of pain over the water had silenced. I transformed and landed on the top sail of a remaining ship. There was a flash of light, and I stabbed my dagger through the largest sail and jumped, slicing through it all the way down. The men couldn't grab their swords quick enough. I sucked the air from each of their throats until their bodies crumpled to the deck, dead and already forgotten.

"Keera!" Myrrah called as I destroyed a third ship. I turned and saw that Myrrah had not captured the last of hers. Instead, it sailed at full speed toward the city. I transformed but the ship crashed onto the shore before I could reach it.

Soldiers spilled out of the hull like ants invading the beach.

The Elverin split and met the soldiers head-on. The heavy clanks of swords were accented by the groans of fallen men—some dressed in leather, some in metal. The casualties climbed on both sides. I climbed too, flapping my wings until I thought they would fall off. A black mass appeared below, soaring on the same gust of wind that I was, silent and lurking. I held my breath to keep the stench of death from choking me. The red center of the *waateyshir* pulsed through its back, teasing and so, so close.

All I needed was one perfect hit.

I banked right. The *waateyshir* showed no signs that it knew I was there. I took a deep breath and plunged. I passed through the space between its wing and neck and then I transformed. It reared back from the flash of light, opening its chest. I grabbed for my dagger and plunged it into . . .

. . . thin air.

I missed. By less than a foot. I plummeted to the ground trying to stow my dagger before I transformed again, but the sheath was flapping in the rush of air. The open chasm grew closer, but I refused to let go of the dagger. It still needed to claim Damien's life with it. I was not going to let it sink to the bottom of the ocean.

The *waateyshir* shrieked in anger, blasting another attack onto the city. I gripped the handle and prepared myself for an icy drop into the sea as a spout of water rose to catch me. But it never did.

Instead, soft fur skimmed my face, and I instinctively grabbed for anything I could. I held onto Fyrel's fur as she leaped across the chasm. She landed, swatting her giants paws and knocking dozens of soldiers into the water.

I slid down her back and stowed my dagger as Fyrel chased more soldiers away. My skin heated with my flames as I launched balls of fire at the soldiers' throats. Another cry echoed from above as one of the *shirak* dove toward us. It whistled and its throat filled with black fire. I groaned and a wall of stone erupted from the earth, shielding everyone underneath it. I turned and saw a similar shield of stone over the northside of the city as another beast spouted its deadly flames onto those below. It crumbled as it fell back into the earth. Feron was at the ends of his magic.

A portal appeared beside me. Dynara stepped through dragging Gerarda with her.

"I have an idea." She wiped her hair from her face.

Gerarda's eyes immediately fell to Dynara. "Where is El?"

"She's alive," Dynara answered. "Gwyn too."

Relief flood through my chest.

Dynara grabbed Gerarda by her vest. "Can you cover the field in blackness like you did before? As tall and as wide as you can manage."

"Yes." Gerarda's brow crinkled. "But not for long."

Dynara opened another portal and yanked Crison through it. The rage in her face broke the instant she saw Dynara. "How many Unnamed could you summon with your gift?" Dynara asked her.

Crison's face paled. She had only heard of the Unnamed but had never faced one yet. "Several. But I don't know how much control I would have over beasts like that."

Dynara smiled. "You won't need to."

She let out a low whistle in two long tones followed by two short ones. It was the same signal that the scouts along the portal at Myrelinth used when the Unnamed Ones were spotted along the trail in the Singing Wood. Every Elverin fighter who could retreated for the higher plains, abandoning the valley completely. The ground began to rumble, and one by one our remaining fighters were pushed into the air far above our heads on towers of rock too strong for even the Unnamed's claws to strike through.

My chest tightened with concern for Feron, but I couldn't let it crowd my thoughts. Nikolai would take care of him. He had too.

"Be silent." Dynara ordered as she opened a portal. It was almost completely black on the other side, but I could see the twisted trunks of the Singing Wood through the layers of shadow. A soft breeze blew through them, and a child's giggle echoed through the field.

The soldiers turned toward the sound.

"Now!" Dynara shouted to both Crison and Gerarda.

Dynara grabbed my hand and broke into a run, Fyrel following close behind as Gerarda covered the field in darkness. It settled like a dense fog, claiming each of the soldiers until the entire battlefield was covered and the city was left untouched. I knelt, feeling for Gerarda through the earth and pushed her out of the darkness on a pillar of stone.

Crison stood beside Dynara, her eyes amber beacons in the darkness as she called the Unnamed Ones toward the portal. They stalked on four legs, with fangs as long as the antlers on their heads. Rotten flesh left their jaws and ribs exposed—tender spots they would defend with their sharp, black claws.

Soldiers shouted and lit their torches as the first guttural cries from the Unnamed sounded in the valley. I wrapped my arms around Dynara, Crison, and Fyrel and shielded us in a circle of stone. I left a sliver of space to watch from, but there was nothing to see. All we could hear were the screams.

In every direction, the soldiers shouted and cried, not realizing they were beckoning a bloody death toward them every time they struck a match. That was enough to ignite a deadly rampage. Within minutes, the shouts had gone silent. Gerarda's shadows thinned. An Unnamed hissed as the moonlight hit its skin and ran for thicker shadow. The darkness around us dissipated and I dropped our shield.

Crison's eyes glowed once more and she and Gerarda worked together to send the Unnamed back through the portal, Crison with her magic nudging and Gerarda by creating snakelike paths of darkness that converged at the mouth of the portal threshold. I touched the ground and felt the last of the beasts step back into their wood.

Dynara silently maneuvered around shredded bodies and over scattered armor. I held my breath as she smashed her fist through the portal and it shattered. I exhaled, knowing the Unnamed couldn't make their way back onto the field.

Torn bodies covered the grass in every direction. Most were in pieces too small to recognize, but all oozed with black decay. I lowered the stone pillars holding the Elverin back to the ground as a *waateyshir* circled overhead, cautious and quiet.

Dynara opened a portal to the city center. A soldier backed away from the mist in fear. He spotted the amber glow of Dynara's eyes and raised his sword, but Elaran pounced on his shoulder. His sword fell to the ground and so did he.

El ran through the portal to Gerarda. She pulled her into a quick embrace before addressing the rest of us. "The Halflings that were in the streets are back in Myrelinth with Rheih." She turned to Dynara. "The portal is still open." Dynara nodded and ran into the streets of Volcar to close it.

Gerarda wiped the single streak of blood from Elaran's cheek as Dynara ran back through the portal with Riven. My chest heaved with relief. His face was splattered with blood and ash, but he was alive.

His eyes locked on me, filling with the same relief, but then settled on something over my shoulder. A pile of torn-apart bodies began to move and from it stood the Dagger. His magic eye was thick and pulsed amber. It seemed as though Damien had enough knowledge of the Unnamed Ones to hide his host in a pile of dead soldiers. The Dagger smirked, the pendant along his chest glowing bright once again.

That was why the *waateyshirak* had stalled their attacks. I glanced up and saw all three circling in orbit above us: one leaking fiery shadow from its bent wing and the others hungry and waiting. My eyes fell to the pendant. It was our only chance to save whatever Halflings were left in the city.

I ran without thinking. The others shouted behind me, but I couldn't stop. I grabbed a handful of arrows from my full quiver and shot them at the Dagger, my gusts carrying them toward his head. He rolled onto the grass, using the body of a dead boy to block my shot.

The amber pupil went still at the impact. I snarled as the Dagger, now in control of his own body, started to run. I picked up a spear mid-stride and threw it at him. The shaft reverberated, hitting the ground right where he would have been, but he stopped. He turned to face me once more, his pendant glowing once again. I recognized Damien's smirk as the three *shirak* screeched and dove toward Volcar.

He pulled the pendant from the Dagger's leathers and threw it to the ground.

"No!" I screamed, stumbling on a piece of armor.

Damien slammed the sword down onto the pendant. The glow pulsed but the glass didn't break. Damien raised his arm again. The blade was long and covered in the sticky black venom.

My breath hitched as the thin thread of a portal appeared behind him. Riven slipped through, reaching for the pendant.

Damien's lips didn't even twitch as he swung his arms back down. This time his target wasn't the pendant, but Riven's arm. I looked over my shoulder and saw Dynara standing with the others, but they stood around the portal watching Riven reach for it instead of what Damien was doing. I shot a gust, trying to stop Damien's blade but it hit too low. It blew against his feet, throwing them into the air, but Damien was already through his swing. The Dagger's body fell to the ground and the inky blade severed Riven's forearm.

Riven crumpled to the ground behind me in shouts of pain as Damien laughed. He stabbed the pendant with the blunt end of a dagger and it shattered into pieces.

I hurled myself at his host. Damien was still laughing as I knocked him back to the ground. "Do you see it now?" he mused in a voice much too low to be his own. "You attack me, and we all lose. There can only be one king of Elverath and it will be—"

I snapped the Dagger's neck before Damien could speak another word. His body crumpled into a pile of nothing. I ran to Riven. Amber blood splattered along the ground as he coughed. His arm had been cut a few inches below the elbow and lay discarded a few feet from him through the portal.

The decay from the Unnamed One's saliva was already eating through the flesh.

My chin shook as I tried to find the words. "I need to get you to Rheih," I choked.

"*Diizra*," Riven coughed. "There's no time."

"No. We can fix this." My vision blurred. "I just need Rheih. No, Gwyn. Gwyn!" I looked at Dynara.

Dynara opened a portal to a group of Halflings in Myrelinth. She pulled Gwyn through and closed the portal behind them.

Gwyn paled as she saw Riven.

"*Diizra*, there's no time—"

"Yes, there is. We can fix this." I turned to Gwyn. "Fix him and I can heal his arm back together."

Gwyn shook her head. "I can't."

"Use the debriding spell. I just watched you do it." My hands shook as I wiped the hair from Riven's face.

"Keera," Riven said with as much force as he could manage. "You need to h-heal it now or it will f-fester. You have a m-minute at th-the most."

I froze. "Or what?"

"Or he dies," Gwyn answered. "You can debride a cut made by the Unnamed One's claws but this"—she pointed at the sword dripping in thick, black liquid—"is Unnamed saliva. It's too potent to debride."

Riven groaned. The saliva was eating through the end of his detached arm. "What about this?" I waved my hand over Riven's wound that was also lined in black saliva.

Gwyn's face was hard. "We amputate."

"No."

"Do it, *diizra,*" Riven urged.

My throat tightened. I couldn't do it. I couldn't maim Riven even more than he already was. My mind understood the logic, but my body resisted.

Gerarda stepped forward. "I will do it."

Gwyn cut the tongue of a discarded boot and stuffed it into Riven's mouth. Tears streamed down my face as Gerarda blanketed me with her shadows so I couldn't see anything except the raise of her sword.

The shadows disappeared. Gerarda had only taken a couple inches, leaving his elbow intact but discarding the rest of the rotting flesh and bone.

"You have to heal the amputation, Keera." Gwyn knelt and placed a hand on my back. "Now before he loses more blood."

There was a deafening shriek. I turned and saw the injured *waateyshir* explode into pieces above the stone wall. Syrra's golden sword sticking from its chest. The others roared in rage descending on Syrra.

"Dynara, take Fyrel." I nodded at the *shirak*. "And Gerarda and Elaran too."

She nodded. "I'll be right back for Riven."

I took in a shaky breath as my hands grasped Riven's bleeding arm. My healing gift surged forward the moment my skin met his. It swirled around the length of his arm, as if looking for what had been cut away, and finally healed over the blunt end that would never hold a hand again.

A *waateyshir* fired an attack onto the city and people fled back into the field to avoid the blast. Commoners and soldiers alike ran, each desperate to put as much distance between them and the *shirak* as possible. I looked at the shattered pendant on the ground. There was no hope of controlling the beasts now. And there was no chance we could hold them off until the suns rose.

Dynara reappeared through a portal. "Take Crison and Gwyn—"

"But I want to fight!" Gwyn cut in.

My jaw hardened. "Gwyn, that's an order."

Her mouth snapped shut. She didn't need to be told again.

I turned back to Dynara. "Get Riven back. Gwyn and Crison can help gather Feron and the injured."

Dynara swallowed. "And what about them?" she pointed at the shadowy beasts.

"The rest of us can handle them."

Riven reached for me with his unsevered arm. "*Diizra*, I can—"

I knelt down and stole a quick kiss from his lips. "I cannot get everyone out of here safely if I am worried for you. And even you, Riven, cannot fight one-handed with no training."

"He didn't take my sword arm," Riven grumbled, but conceded, rolling through the portal before Dynara closed it behind them all.

A flash of light and I was a bird again. I studied the battle from the skies. Fyrel defended citizens in bear form, swiping at what was left of Damien's ranks. Elaran fought beside her, her form wider and more muscled than normal to add extra power behind her strikes. Gerarda and Syrra fought four opponents only a few feet away. Gerarda's small blades rang like bells while Syrra's golden blade whistled through the air.

I watched the skies, looking for another opportunity to attack when I saw one of the soldiers below nock an arrow. He aimed it directly at Elaran's chest. I screamed, calling for my gusts to blow the arrows away, but this form had no magic. My scream echoed as an eagle call, piercing the sky with a desperation that could be heard no matter what form I took. Gerarda turned, seeing the soldier just as I avoided a fiery blast from one of the *shirak*. I tucked in my wings, diving to the ground. The soldier released his arrows one after another. A flash of light and I tumbled to the ground with my arm extended, casting the strongest gust I could manage at the arrows.

But it was too late. The first had already embedded itself in Gerarda's back. She had wrapped her body around her love's, covering as much of the Fae as she could as the second arrow struck her through the shoulder. Gerarda groaned as a third one hit.

Then the air began to whistle. Gerarda's short hair was sucked backward, and she looked up at the open beak of the third *waateyshir* with the second just behind it. I ran, heart pounding as I grabbed my dagger. Syrra rode on Fyrel, beast and warrior desperate to reach Gerarda too.

But none of us did.

The inky blast pummeled down on top of them. Gerarda gripped Elaran and screamed. Not in agony. Not in fear of her own death, but the death of her love. My heart tore, knowing the pain of such a cry.

I collapsed onto the ground in grief. Fyrel roared and reared back on her hind legs as a beam of pure white light shot upward, burrowing a hole in the pulsing red chest of the creature. It let out one final scream and its body exploded into tiny fragments of shadow.

I froze. Tendrils of light pooled from Gerarda, mixing with her shadows as her amber eyes glowed brighter than I had ever seen them. She stood, blood dripping down her nose and ear. She lifted her arms and released a battle cry. A second beam shot upward and its aim was just as true.

The shadowy beast let out one final, ragged cry as its shadows leaked from its body. Within seconds the beast was gone, ash blown away to nothing on the wind.

The few remaining soldiers all snapped straight at the same time, their united voices capturing Damien's cadence perfectly as he spoke through each of them. "You steal my Dagger, coerce her into abandoning her post, and then you taint her with powers to threaten the Crown? That will be the last threat that traitorous bitch ever makes."

"I doubt it," I said proudly before the soldiers fell limp without Damien to fill them. Gerarda stood and snapped the ends from the arrows in her back and shoulder.

Elaran stood, uninjured and brushing the dirt from her knees. "You stupid, asinine . . ."

"Hero?" Gerarda quipped with a grin.

Thick tears fell from Elaran's eyes as Gerarda wiped them from her cheek. "We told each other not to make foolish decisions."

"Saving you could never be a foolish decision, Ran," Gerarda said, pressing a kiss to Elaran's hand.

I raised a brow. "I didn't realize you were so . . . romantic."

"Fuck off and heal me." Gerarda dug her fingers into her own shoulder and pulled the broken end of the arrow through it. I washed it out with water and checked the wound before healing it. Only when Gerarda showed me she had full function of her shoulder and arm did I fix the one on her back.

"How did you know how to attack the beast?" I asked as I wiped the blood from her skin.

Gerarda swallowed thickly. "I didn't. I just wanted to protect El with everything I had." She lifted her palms; one was covered in shadow and one was encased in pure light.

I huffed a laugh. "The gift of shadow and the power to destroy it."

"Damien and his *waateyshirak* are not the threat they were yesterday," Gerarda mused with a proud smirk on her face. I nodded but my throat tightened. Gerarda was right—those were only the first of the beasts she would kill with her gift. But that also meant something else. Damien knew what power she held. She had just become his biggest target in the battle for the capital. Elaran's eyes filled with worry as she came to the same realization. Her grip on Gerarda's arm tightened, but she pasted a smile onto her face. Tomorrow's sorrows were not going to steal this victory from us.

CHAPTER FORTY

NIKOLAI RAN INTO THE INFIRMARY, cheeks puffy and breaths ragged. Rheih tutted her tongue as she inspected Riven's newly healed stump.

"Fine job, Keera," she said approvingly as her eagle eyes assessed the thinnest scar along the amputation. Guilt thrashed in my throat at the pride that swelled in my chest at her approval. Riven squeezed my hand with the one he still had. I had expected him to turn sullen as the reality of his changed body washed over him, but he seemed elated. Eerily so.

I didn't have time to contemplate that because Nikolai threw himself onto Riven's lap. His chest heaved through his sobs as he cried, "I'm so happy you are alive."

"As am I." Riven laughed. There was a sincerity to his words that set my worries at ease.

Nikolai wiped his cheeks with his sleeve. He hadn't even changed into something that wasn't stained with ash or blood.

"I just kept thinking that if you had died, you would have died with me angry at you." He lifted his head, thick tears pooling down his cheeks as his lips trembled.

"But he didn't die, Nik," I whispered, trying to calm him.

He swatted my hand away. "But he *could have* and I would have spent centuries wondering if giving him my favor could have prevented it."

I crossed my arms. "Prevented a sword cutting through his bone and skin?"

"No need to dwell on the details, Keera dear." His lip curled over his fangs as he sniffled into a handkerchief. He turned his attention back to Riven, who was staring down at the Elf with round, misted eyes. "I shouldn't have let my anger cause a split between us—"

"Nik, my decisions took everything from you."

Tears welled along Nikolai's lashes. "Not everything." He wiped his eye. "And while I can still be angry at the decisions you made, it would be unfair of me not to be angry at myself. I could have told Keera the truth just as well as you. I did not have to keep your secret. I *chose* to." He took a deep breath, his brows trembling. "And it is a choice I will have to learn to live with."

Riven sat up. Rheih threw up her hands in annoyance, walking back to her station of herbs where they could not annoy her. Nikolai's hand caressed the smooth skin at the end of Riven's arm.

Nikolai gasped as Riven pulled him into a tight embrace, refusing to let him go even after a long second had passed. "I am the one who is sorry, more deeply than you could ever know." Riven leaned back, his hand still squeezing Nikolai's shoulder. "I know that the divide I created between us cannot be stitched back together quickly, but I will spend a year for every lie I told making it up to you if that's what it takes. And I will fight with everything I have to ensure we both survive this war so I will have the time to show you the truth of those words."

Nikolai collapsed. His fingers lingered around the amputated limb and he shook his head. "My mother has told me many things. She left this life for one with the ancestors."

Riven and I both froze, not daring to move as Nikolai finally spoke of Maerhal.

"She said that after this war there will be a new beginning," he continued. "Cleansed in smoke and blood, fire and water, a new world will grow from the ashes." Nikolai met Riven's gaze with a forlorn look that tore at my soul. "I do not want to build a world that dwells on the pain of the past. Our people deserve better." He looked up at me and squeezed Riven's shoulder "*We* deserve better. I want to grow a new world for our people that sprouts from a soil of trust and forgiveness. Where friends live as close as brothers because to the Elverin we are all kin."

Nikolai held out his hand for Riven to shake. "It would be an honor to fight for that future by your side, miijin."

My brother.

Riven took a ragged breath and shook Nik's hand before pulling him in for another embrace.

"I can make you something useful for your arm," Nikolai mumbled through their limbs.

Gerarda leaned against the door with her arms crossed, so silent I hadn't realized she was there. She rolled her eyes at the two still wrapped in each other's arms. "So dramatic."

"You could tell me." Gerarda's voice sounded out from the burl she shared with Elaran. "I can just act surprised when we get there."

Elaran smiled down at where Gerarda sat in the chair in front of her. She had transformed Gerarda's stoic room into something warm and soft despite the countless blades scattered across the walls and tables. She reached for a leather strap to tie off Gerarda's braid, noticing me in the doorway. She smirked as Gerarda crossed her arms, her back to me.

"My lips are sealed, my love."

Elaran's amber eyes flashed to mine, but Gerarda didn't notice. Instead, she grabbed Elaran by the waist of her trousers and pulled her between her knees. "I have a dozen tricks that could part those lips in a minute, *loqva*."

I cleared my throat.

Gerarda spun around, her face half shocked, half horrified.

I ran my tongue across my teeth like I had been presented with something sweet. "My *guiding star*?" I raised a brow. "I never considered you a romantic, Gerrie."

Gerarda's lips were as thin as her blades. "I'm not."

"Liar," Elaran said, wrapping her arms around Gerarda and pulling her back against her chest. "You should hear the poems she writes me," she cooed over Gerarda's shoulder.

I laughed. This was better than cake. "A poet too?"

"That was one time." Gerarda shoved herself free of Elaran's arms.

"Dozens," El mouthed, though she covered it with a smile when the tiny Fae whipped around on her.

"If this is how tonight is going to be, I'd rather Keera hit me over the head." Gerarda tied her weapons belt around her waist and readjusted her chest piece. "I gave you the courtesy of being unconscious when I abducted you."

"My captives would never dare run." I grinned. "No need for extra work."

Gerarda answered me with a deadpan stare.

I waved them out the door. "Hurry, we're going to be late." I looked out to the skyline.

Gerarda clocked it immediately. "We're traveling by portal then."

I dug a vial of dried blue flowers from my pocket and handed it to her. "Just one."

Her eyes narrowed at the flower. There was only one portal nearby that preferred blooms to berries. We made our way through the Dark Wood in silence, though Gerarda watched everything Elaran and I did for some unspoken clue.

We made it to the gardens of Sil'abar when Elaran started recounting a line from one of Gerarda's poems.

"I will go back home and burn every letter if you utter another word." Gerarda's short, sharp ears were flushed the same color as her cheeks.

Elaran spun around and tapped Gerarda on the nose. "I have them memorized, *aamozhi*."

"Honey tap?" I snorted and collapsed at the middle, holding my stomach.

Gerarda shoved me onto the grass and stalked into the giant tree without looking back.

Elaran stretched out her hand for me to take. "You will pay for that later," I mused. "Ger is not one to forget."

Her amber eyes glowed and for a moment the ends of her hair turned black. "I like her a little feisty. Keeps things fun." She looped her arm around mine and walked me into the palace. "Not that she will remember any of that once she realizes what's about to happen."

"I don't think I'll forget *honey tap* even if we live a thousand years."

Elaran elbowed me in the side. "The story is better than the name, I assure you." Her playful smile fell as we stepped into the palace and the live grain split to reveal a staircase sinking into the ground.

My heart hammered with anticipation. I had barely been able to contain myself since Syrra brought the idea forward.

Gerarda eyed our joined arms suspiciously. "If this is just some ploy to make me—"

"Jealous?" Elaran finished for her with a slow tilt of her head. She even raked one of her fingernails down my arm.

Gerarda almost looked bored. "Keera doesn't have sophisticated enough taste to be enamored with you, my sweet."

"True."

I dropped El's arm. "I don't know if I should be offended or relieved."

"Both," Gerarda answered, lacing her fingers through Elaran's with a smug smile.

I shook my head and nodded at the stairs. Gerarda's nose wrinkled at the scent of cedar smoke and took the first step. I followed her to a landing that widened to a hallway and then to the room at the end of it. There were no windows, only a small hole along the ceiling for the smoke from burning leaves to escape through.

Syrra turned, her golden sword stowed along her back. Her jaw was hard as she spoke to me. "Did you bring it?"

I nodded and tossed her the contents of my trouser pocket.

"What is going on?" Gerarda's eyes widened as Syrra opened her palm to reveal the thin, gold tube I'd given her. "Is that . . ." Gerarda's voice cracked then trailed off.

Rheih added more Elder birch leaves to her bowl. "A mage pen."

Gerarda's lip quirked to the side. "I've always wanted to see the ceremony done." She turned to Rheih. "Do you pick where to cut or does she?"

Everyone in the room fell silent. Elaran squeezed Gerarda's hand. "Dearest, I think you've misunderstood—"

"I have earned enough branches." Syrra lifted her chin. "Today it is you who shall receive their markings."

Gerarda's mouth clamped shut.

Rheih snickered. "The little one finally has nothing to say."

Gerarda ignored her comment and turned to me. "Was this your idea?"

"Not at all." My lips stretched into a wide smile, sincere and proud. "Though I will be the one to imbue it."

Tears welled at the corners of Gerarda's eyes. "How do we begin?"

Rheih waved her hand over Gerarda's torso as she mulched thick purple leaves in a wooden bowl. "Take off the vest and your shirt too."

Gerarda's hands froze.

"Rheih and I can leave until the end if that's more comfortable for you," I interjected, ignoring the old Mage's grumbling.

Gerarda's amber eyes raked over my arms and then Syrra's, our scars proudly showing. She shook her head and started unlacing the ties down the side of her vest. "No need."

She handed the chest plate to Elaran and then her tunic too. Gerarda was well-muscled for her small stature, her round shoulders pressed against the wrap she wore across her chest. She swallowed as she looked at Syrra. "Is this enough or should I remove this too?"

Syrra shook her head. "That is fine, child." She grabbed a pillow from the trunk along the wall and placed it on the ground for

Gerarda to sit on. "Rheih will wash your skin with water then with smoke and then we shall begin."

Elaran and I stood shoulder to shoulder as we watched the Mage work over Gerarda's back and shoulders. I winced seeing the thin scar under Gerarda's left bicep knowing I had caused it. A rage-filled day training together at the Order.

"This ceremony is usually done at *Niikir'na* but this will have to do. It is important that this ritual is passed on and not another loss for Aemon's line to claim."

My stomach clenched at those words, wondering what Syrra meant by them, but she didn't look at me. All I could see was the light reflecting from her shorn head as Syrra grabbed the mage pen. She cleansed the sharp blade in the smoke from Rheih's bowl. "Are you ready?"

Gerarda held the second pillow across her stomach. Her arms tightened, denting the cushion, but she nodded.

"Every warrior is marked with the branch of an Elder birch along their right shoulder. It is what brands us as protectors of our people." Syrra dabbed a damped cloth over Gerarda's shoulder. I looked at the long branch with thin, wilting bark and jagged oval leaves cut into Syrra's shoulder in the same place.

"Usually, this mark is given when you graduate from *Niikir'na*, but I think your time training at the Order is sufficient."

Gerarda didn't flinch as Syrra made the first cut. Her breaths remained slow and even while my own skin itched along my scars. I knew exactly how the slice of the mage pen was piercing at first but then became smooth like a slow pour of water on a hot summer's day. Rheih exchanged Syrra's cloth for a clean one as the first filled with Gerarda's auric-amber blood. I took the muddled leaves from Rheih's bowl. The thick paste carried a heavy scent of birch and cedar root.

"Just like we practiced," Syrra told me with a small nod.

I rubbed the paste over the fresh cut and said the first phrase Syrra had taught me and Vrail had helped me perfect. "*Niikir maashith'kazii roq waabathir.*"

May this warrior's strength never waver.

Gerarda gritted her teeth as Rheih wafted the smoke over the paste and it began to bubble.

"Is something wrong?" Elaran asked, dropping to her knees in front of Gerarda.

"The marking has set." Syrra wiped away the paste and Gerarda's skin had completely healed. Her scar was more iridescent than the unmarked flesh, but it was barely raised at all.

Syrra assessed our work and smiled. "This marking will increase your stamina in times of battle. I do not know if it will affect your powers, but you will be able to fight for a full day without dropping your weapon if you must."

Gerarda looked down to inspect her own skin. Her smile grew as her fingers trailed over the curving branch. "Excellent."

Syrra moved to the second shoulder. She washed it and then Rheih cleansed the skin with smoke. Syrra bit her lip as she marked the starting and ending points of another design with the paste. Her sharp eyes flitted back and forth between Gerarda's shoulders to ensure the two markings would be even. When she was satisfied, she let the mage pen blade rest atop the smoking bowl.

"The second cut is made on the opposite shoulder. It is always claimed by the warrior being marked, a sigil of their own making." Syrra leaned over Gerarda's shoulder to look at her. "What branch should mark your act of bravery for killing the *waateyshirak*?"

Gerarda blinked. "I get to choose?"

"Yes, *maashir*." Syrra's throat tightened as she said the final word.

Gerarda's face flushed. *Strong one* was a term of endearment only used between the warriors of *Nikiir'na*. Syrra hadn't been able to call anyone that in centuries. Gerarda was the start of a new legacy. The pride in the room swelled until it was hard to breathe. Elaran gripped Gerarda's hand tighter, a happy tear falling from her lashes.

Gerarda swallowed. "Then the branch of the *minisabiq*."

"*Minisabiq*?" I had never heard of such a tree.

But Syrra smiled and uncapped the mage pen. "It is a tree that only grows on the smallest island of the Fractured Isles."

Gerarda nodded. "That island was my home. If one shoulder should mark my devotion to the home I have today, then the other should represent the one I lost."

"The tree bears small fruits, if I remember correctly?"

Gerarda nodded. "Round berries the color of the sea at dawn."

Syrra picked up the mage pen and let the side of her hand rest on Gerarda's skin, ready to cut. "Then I shall carve one branch holding three berries. One for each of the *waateyshirak* you vanquished."

Syrra carved the mark into Gerarda's skin with the decisive strokes of a painter. Within minutes the thick, bent branch and berries were realized so completely I was sure I could reach out and wrap my hand around it.

Gerarda moved to stand, but Rheih shoved her back down on the pillow. "Stay."

"That hurt," she snapped.

Rheih's long, grayed brows shot beneath her frizzy mane. "Perhaps your second gift should be to whine less." She shoved a new bowl of paste at me.

Gerarda turned to Syrra. "I didn't think all markings received a gift."

"Only the first is guaranteed." Syrra stood, her job complete. "Any beyond that are at the discretion of the Fae who gives it."

Gerarda's eyes misted as she turned to me. "You asked for this?"

My throat was too tight to speak so I nodded. I knelt and started rubbing the paste into her skin. This time Gerarda didn't even flinch. "Vrail and Syrra told me about the blessings Faelin bestowed on the three warriors she left to lead *Niikir'na* when she knew she was in the twilight of her years." I massaged the thick purple grit into Gerarda's skin, making sure every part of the new wound was covered. "She gave them each a singular gift to help them lead their people. The first was a gift of foresight, so all the student warriors would remain safe under their trainer's care. The second was a gift of projection so all the warriors would hear their steward's call." I set the bowl next to Gerarda's knee and flattened my palm across her shoulder. "And the last gift was given to the Elf who became their leader after Faelin passed." I cleared my throat. "That is the gift I am giving you."

Gerarda's chin trembled. She opened her mouth to speak but no words came.

The pulsing light of my magic swelled in my chest and spread down my hands. I pressed the flat of my palm into the paste and I said the words that Vrail had taught me. *"Babiimithir el aaniko'biithir niiwaaka'win."*

May the ancestors guide your wisdom.

Gerarda sucked in a breath as the paste burned and set.

I wiped her skin clean. Gerarda's second scar was gold as if the molten metal had fused her flesh back together. Her hand shook as she touched the branches that represented both the homes that had raised her. A tear caught along the corner of her eye as she looked at me. "You claim no branches or gifts for yourself?"

I laughed. "I have more gifts and scars than I could ever need." I cleared my throat so there was no taste of humor in my words as I said them. "You have always had the best interest of the Halflings stitched into your heart, and you have always used all your strength to fight for them. I can think of no one more deserving to receive this gift."

I stood and Syrra stepped beside me.

"Rise, Warrior Vallaqar." Syrra lifted her palm to her eyes and then her chest. *"Elverinth il niikir Ganawiithir zaabi."*

May the world see you and call you Protector, forevermore.

CHAPTER FORTY-ONE

I CHOSE THE SETTING FOR THE DREAM. The white stone wall that circled the outer banks of the capital glistened under my boots. I washed the stone of its bloodstains so it was as pristinely white as it would have been in the days before Aemon or his foul son had ever stepped foot upon our shores.

Damien gasped as he was pulled into the dream. I didn't know how I'd done it—I had tugged at some unknown magic in my mind as I fell asleep and demanded his presence. I could see it from his red and puffed cheeks and open shirt that he had not been expecting the call. A moment earlier, he had likely been strewn over his bed or chaise, sipping the wine I could smell on his lips. Now he was standing along the top of the wall, not safely tucked away in one of the towers but forced to stand sideways on the narrow stone just as the Shades who had guarded the city had done. His arms flailed out at the sides as he took in the high plummet. His body still panicked even though we both knew that no harm could come to either of us here. Unfortunately.

"Surrender." I brandished no sword. I didn't even dip the word in malice before I said it. I cast the image of our army of Elverin out into the grasses that surrounded Koratha. After Volcar, Damien's forces were no match for a fresh and seasoned army.

"Surrender," I said again as Damien straightened the sleeves of his shirt and turned to me, his legs twisting underneath him as he tried not to shake.

"I will never." Damien's black eye glowed from its amber pupil.

I extended my arm over the wall, pointing at our forces, while taking slow, masterful steps toward Damien. "You cannot win this siege."

"Perhaps not." Damien's tone was too calm, too even for the loss he faced.

My eyes narrowed. "So why not surrender? Spare your soldiers and your people the need to die for you."

Damien lifted his chin. There was nothing warm about him, his pale skin was flat and sallow, his sharp cheeks and pointed lips had been unsheathed of their beauty in the past months. Now they were only weapons.

Damien's lip pulled back over his teeth. "I will not spare a soul."

My blood turned to ice. There was still a spark of hope in Damien's eyes. He had not completely given up. But the numbers were against him now. Even if he had some secret weapon to use against us, it would be no match for our legion of Fae.

Unless . . .

"You cannot control them," I seethed.

Damien's nose twitched. "I would rather play a game of chance with the *waateyshirak* than surrender myself to you and my brother." He spat the last word from his tongue.

I shook my head. "But they will wipe out just as many of your forces as they will ours. Endless blood will be spilled on both sides."

"But not mine." Damien's smile was cruel.

I fought the urge to hurl him from the wall. "You mean to stow yourself away while the beasts you conjured feast on *everyone*—your people, soldiers, and your enemies—with no distinction."

Damien tucked his arm behind his back. He stepped along the wall, his muscles tensing as he attempted to be as graceful as a Shade and failed. "How many times must you learn this lesson?" Damien tilted his head to the side, a gleeful smile anchoring his balance. "I play for my opponent to lose, Keera. That is the difference between you and me."

"Brutality."

Damien nodded. "You could never stand back and watch your rebels fight the *waateyshirak* without you. You could never order your newly made Fae to stay away from the field of battle to ensure you had magic left to defeat *me.* The first cry of terror would have you and Riven and all your loyal followers marching into battle. You may kill a few of the beasts, but the *waateyshirak* will kill your people too. We will see which side holds the greatest numbers then."

"You would sacrifice an entire city just to keep yourself in some chair?" Venom dripped from my lips.

"I would send every man, woman, and child to their deaths if it secured me your defeat."

"And be a king of no one?"

Damien shrugged. "There would be some survivors." He jutted his chin toward the sea. "And there are always men from other realms who hunger to discover riches and treasure in worlds unknown to them."

I gritted my teeth. Damien wanted to do exactly what his father had done. Except this time, he would ensure that every Fae, Elf, and

Halfling was dead before he oversaw the rebuilding of his kingdom. He would be the only one with any knowledge of magic. He would set himself apart from the rest not merely as a king, but as a god.

I closed the distance between us and grabbed Damien's neck. "I will break your body until you are on the cusp of death, and then I will hang you from your ankles along this wall. One day for every life you have taken. And when that time is done, when the suns have baked your skin and the crows have pecked gashes between your ribs, I will ram my dagger through your chest, throw your body out to sea, and melt your throne to feed the people you have starved. You will die as you deserve, crownless and in never-ending pain."

Fear flashed across Damien's face but he didn't let it settle.

"May the cleverest prevail," he said and jumped off the wall.

CHAPTER FORTY-TWO

EVERYONE WAITED IN THE COUNCIL ROOM. Elaran and Gerarda shared a chair. El had not left Gerarda's side since Volcar. Riven didn't take a seat at the table but stood behind me, the hand he had left resting on my shoulder as I waited for Nikolai and Vrail to stop whispering in their seats.

"Quiet," Myrrah chided when they didn't cease.

Vrail's cheeks flushed and she tucked her chin into her red collar. "Apologies."

Nikolai only grabbed some loose nuts from his lap and tossed them into the air.

Gwyn and Fyrel grinned at each other in the chairs beside Syrra, who merely shook her head.

"The scouts have returned with bad news," I said to Feron seated directly across from me.

He leaned forward on the stone table. "How many *waateyshirak* did they see?"

"Three dozen at least."

Nikolai's hand froze mid-toss, letting the nuts cascade to the ground.

"That's too many." Vrail shook her head so quickly her face blurred. "He only has three pendants left. Extrapolating for the loss of control in Volcar, he has—"

"Tripled the amount of *shirak* he can control safely," I finished for her with a stern nod. "It seems that Damien doesn't care about that. Even now the beasts are tempted to feast on the city. All the residents have been instructed to stay inside."

"He expects Syrra and I to take down more than a few," Gerarda quipped, a thin blade twirling through her knuckles. Only she could find the compliment in such grave news.

"Most likely." I sighed, leaning back into my chair. Riven squeezed my shoulder, and I rested my head against his arm. "Even then it's ten more than I thought he would dare bring into his city. Our armies have not yet arrived, and he has already put every single person's life in jeopardy."

Elaran spun a curl around her fingers. "Damien is past the point of caring. He's either going to keep his seat on that throne, or take as many lives as possible with him when we push him off it."

"Into a pool of jagged spikes," Gwyn added under her breath. The purple bags under her eyes seemed to darken at the idea of it, and I was not certain she was kidding.

Fyrel shot her a worried smile. "It will be hard to kill him with three dozen snapping beaks in our way. They'll lay the city to rubble before we ever breach the wall."

"A stolen throne to rule over broken stones." Gerarda huffed a laugh. "A miserable song for the bards to sing."

"That's not all." I laid a map of Koratha down on the table for all to see. "Damien has the majority of his armada stationed here." I pointed along the opening of the channel south of the Order. It was within firing range of the field where our warriors would be fending off attacks from the *shirak*.

"Easy enough to handle," Myrrah said with a shrug.

Pirmiith clicked his tongue. "Each of Damien's ships are connected underneath by a net of some kind. It extends far out." His finger grazed over the parchment past the boundary of the Order. "The scouts can't be certain what it's for, but they caught the crews loading barrels of violet dust aboard each ship."

"The violet fire," Myrrah whispered. Untamable by wind or water wielding, and so wild that it took the last bit of Lash's magic to clear it for just a few seconds. We would waste all our resources just trying to protect Myrrah's crew.

"So invasion by sea is not an option." Nikolai's nose crinkled as he looked at the map.

"Not for us." Riven's voice was firm but worried. "Though we must prepare for those crews to come ashore to face us."

"I will have ways to stop that for a period of time." Feron's gaze cut to me. "Though we will need to be quick. It will only serve Damien's advantage if we overextend ourselves."

"I agree." I stood and marked the perimeter of the sea net with the bowl of ash that sat on the table. "Myrrah, you and half the Shades will take down as many ships as you can without breaching this threshold. Do not let Damien lure you into his trap."

"Cautious but deadly." Myrrah nodded. "I can do that."

Syrra gave the Fae a knowing grin.

"If you need to retreat or we call you back in, double back around the fleet to safety. Rushing will only get us killed."

Myrrah's playful smirk fell to a straight line as she nodded again.

"The rest of us"—I marked the area outside of the city gates—"will be stationed here in four units. Syrra, you will lead one and take Fyrel with you. If you get your chance to slay one of the *shirak*, take it."

Fyrel stood and flattened her palm over her face and then her chest. Syrra was less formal, only giving a nod.

I turned to Gerarda. "You will command a unit of your own. Pirmiith will protect you on the ground and Feron will protect you from behind the lines."

Gerarda scowled. "Why should I be so well protected while the others are left to fend for themselves?"

"Because you're our biggest asset." I crossed my arms. "We lose you, we lose the war."

Gerarda's mouth opened, but she had no words.

Elaran wrapped her arm around Gerarda's neck protectively. "Dynara and I can work together to confuse the soldiers from inside the castle." She turned to Dynara, who was toying with a small, curved blade.

"I portal us in, take a leader, and El takes their place." Dynara's smile grew. "In all the chaos it'll work a few times before they catch on."

Elaran nodded. "And by then, they'll lose trust in anyone giving orders."

"I like it," I said.

Nikolai turned to Gerarda. "If you can hold off on your light show—"

"Light show?" Gerarda's eyes started to glow and dark sheets of shadow poured from her limbs.

Nikolai rolled his eyes. "Apologies. Your terribly fearsome sunlight blast." He raised a brow. "Better?"

"Marginally."

Nikolai ignored her and continued his point. "If Gerarda can hold off revealing herself, then perhaps the *shirak* will disperse, attack our troops evenly. It would give Syrra and Keera the best chance to land a kill of their own before Gerarda blasts them from the sky."

"If I can prevent an attack, I will. But I can't face all the beasts on my own." Her fist glowed bright. "Even my gifts have limits."

"How many could you reasonably kill before you risked burning through your magic?" I asked.

Gerarda considered the question. "Ten. A dozen would be pushing it."

"Even with two kills each, that is still more than twenty to contend with," Riven murmured, though the entire room could hear his calculations.

Crison stepped from behind Dynara's seat. "I can take care of the rest."

"Your gifts are great, child, but even you cannot command that many," Syrra said in a gentle tone.

Crison gave her a sideways grin. "I don't need to control them all at once. Just long enough for you or Keera to get there." She shot a look at Riven. "Two kills a piece is an underestimate even without me."

Fyrel snorted on accident, and she hid her face in the collar of her shirt without looking at Riven.

"We can always try to kill as many *waateyshirak* as we can and then retreat," Feron said, turning to Dynara. "With strategic portals, our army could disperse very quickly."

Dynara nodded her approval.

"What about the rest of us?" Vrail stepped forward. "We haven't been given assignments."

"You and Riven will stay behind in the healer's tents with Rheih." I eyed the tether around Nikolai's wrist. "You too. If anything happens, I want Rheih close by to help." Nikolai's face hardened as his fingers brushed the tether but he nodded. I turned to the others. "Anyone else can choose to fight where they wish."

Vrail stood as Riven stepped around my chair.

"Absolutely not," they echoed together.

I rubbed my brow, already tired from the arguments I knew were coming. I addressed Vrail first. "You are a skilled warrior, one I would happily have fighting alongside me." Vrail's back straightened at the compliment, her eyes disappearing between her full-cheeked smile. "But"—Vrail's smile fell flat—"your gifts are too precious to risk on the field of battle."

Vrail crossed her arms. "That is not an excuse—"

The flames in the hearth flared and Vrail stopped mid-ramble. One of my hands spewed crimson flames while the other was frozen into a chunk of ice. I took a deep breath and calmed myself.

"We have no way of knowing how many we will lose tomorrow." I looked around the room. "We have already lost so much. Elverath knew that we would need a way to connect the new generation with those of old. A bridge from the past to the future we wish to build." My throat tightened as I looked at the wondrous beauty that was my friend. She had no idea how much of a gift she was. "That bridge is you, Vrail. I will not give Damien the chance to smash it."

"And me?" Riven held up his arm with the sleeve and bolt Nikolai had fitted for him. "Have I not proven myself able to fight?"

I gritted my teeth. "We have already given Damien two targets with Gerarda and me on the battlefield. Giving him a third will only make the fight more dangerous for everyone."

"Damien does not care about me. He already—"

"He cut off your arm!" My face was only inches from Riven's. "He cut off your arm with absolute glee just because he could. Just because he knew it would hurt me. He is your *brother*, Riven, of course he will take notice the moment you step forward to face him." I cleared my throat. "You will do us all a favor by staying in that tent."

"*Diizra*, let me be a soldier," he whispered. It broke my heart to see the pride melt from his face, but my decision was made.

"If we are able to handle the *shirak*, then you may fight as much as you like, but until then your only job will be to tend to the wounded and protect Rheih with all your strength." My brows furrowed. The reasons I gave were enough, but there was more to it. Everything had stopped in that moment when Damien cut Riven's arm. I wasn't watching the battle, I wasn't protecting the others. And Damien had seen it. Riven was a distraction. Damien would use that to his advantage unless we took it off the table.

Riven understood the dismissal for what it was. He straightened and nodded. "As you wish, *diizra*."

My back eased at the addition of his special name for me. Even though he disagreed, even though he yearned to join the fight, Riven would not hold it against me.

Nikolai plopped another nut into his mouth. "What do we do now?"

"Prepare the Elverin for war." I placed my palms flat against the table. "I want every willing person holding a weapon in each hand and a third strung along their back."

CHAPTER FORTY-THREE

Riven found me at the weapons tent, inspecting the edges of the swords with the tips of my fingernails. He leaned against one of towering piles of crates and watched as I finished.

"There is nothing more that you can do," he said, his gravel voice soft but firm. "You must rest, *diizra*."

I shook my head. "I cannot rest here. There are too many tasks to be done. Too many things to inspect."

"Then we will leave." Riven closed the distance between us.

I scoffed. "The glamour concealing our ranks could break. Damien would be foolish to let us attack at dawn, which means I need to be alert and ready the entire night. I can't leave the scouts—"

"You can and you will." Riven clasped his hand around mine. "You cannot lead the Elverin into battle unless you are rested. And you just said that will not happen here."

I opened my mouth to protest, but Riven's finger pressed against my lips. "Syrra and Feron will be here to receive the scouts' reports. They will call us if anything happens."

"Us?" I mumbled through Riven's finger.

Dynara cleared her throat behind him. She stood at the entrance of the tent, her fingers already glowing.

"No." I stepped back. "You're not portaling me away on the eve of battle." My voice cracked. I reached for the table to my left and grabbed a blade.

Riven grabbed my wrist and pulled it away from the swords. "Even your magic has its limits, *diizra.* Taking the night to recover could mean the difference between life or death. Yours or others."

My breath stopped. Riven's mouth curved into a knowing grin. He had me.

I leaned around him, staring Dynara down. "You will portal us back the *moment* anything goes awry."

She crossed her arms, already bored. "Of course I will." She swirled her arms along the inside of the tent and a portal opened. "Now hurry before the night comes and goes," she said with a grin as she tossed a bag through the portal.

Riven pulled me toward it but I let go of his hand and pulled Dynara in for an embrace. Her body stiffened and then relaxed into mine. "Be safe," I told her.

She pressed a kiss to my cheek. "After tomorrow we won't have to be."

She didn't say the haunting part aloud.

If we survived.

Riven tugged on my hand, only his forearm still in the tent with us. I laughed and waved goodbye as Dynara closed the portal behind me.

Riven stooped to pick up the bag with his hook as I realized where we were. The ghost city was silent. Not even the wind dared to breathe as Riven led us to a large tree on the western edge of Vellinth.

The large orb of water hung above us, glowing silver in the full moonlight, casting long stripes along the dwellings in the trunks of the trees. All of them sat empty, except for the one directly ahead. A small faelight hovered around us as we walked up the steps. I gasped as I took in the dwelling. It was small, but lived in. A well-worn carpet covered the floor in a circle to match the shape of the room. On one edge sat a large bed with soft green coverlets and on the other two alcoves. One filled with Riven's clothes and one with mine. I turned to him.

"I had it stocked at the same time as your burl in Myrelinth." Riven looked down at his boots.

"But you didn't show this to me the last time we were here."

His brow went as straight as his mouth. His jade eyes settled on me, heavy and protective. "I didn't want your ghosts to haunt this place too. Not when I planned . . ." He took in a deep breath as his words trailed off.

I tilted my head. "When you planned what, *rovaa*?"

Riven's body melted around mine at the sound of my pet name for him. I gave into his warmth. We were two wicks of the same candle, burning together.

"This is the only place that I ever truly felt at home." Riven swallowed against my ear before pulling back. He pushed a stray hair behind the point of my ear and cupped my cheek. The callouses along his palm scratched at my skin, but I loved their roughness. "This is the only place where I never had to hide. Everyone who came here, everyone who has ever stood by my side in this city knew my secret."

"It's home." My lips quivered as I looked around the room again. The embroidered tapestry over the bed was stitched crooked, a gift from Vrail or Nikolai most likely. The swords and daggers that hung along the wall were well worn, some dented. They were bookended by two curved blades that almost made a circle of steel, identical to Syrra's. The same thin layer of dust that covered them covered the piles of books and the two full shelves that sat on either side of the bed. The room was a true representation of Riven—where the warrior Fae and the studious prince rested wearing whatever face he had liked.

"I hoped it would be ours." Riven's thumb ran along my jaw, calling my attention back to him. "I dreamed of days when my focus could be rebuilding this city, creating a safe haven for Halflings. I had lived through so many fantasies of it when I trained here, I could picture the full houses and the laughter, and Darythir happily teaching signed Elvish to all the newcomers. But from that day in Cereliath, those dreams changed. I just wanted to bring you here, to watch you turn it into something beautiful."

I scoffed. "I don't think I've made anything beautiful in my entire life." I looked down at my hands.

Riven's brows creased as he stared down at me. He pressed a kiss over one of my eyes and then the other. "Elverath herself saw the beauty you had inside you, the beauty you've always had inside you. Why else do you think you were given such gifts?"

I shook my head. "To bring magic and the Fae back."

Now Riven shook his head. "You have focused too long on destroying the Crown. You forget your goal was always to build something better in its place. To build something just and fair and free." Riven put his hand over mine like they were the most precious jewels in the continent. "Ensuring the Shades wore color as soon as they could." Riven's breath caught in his throat. "Designing spectacles for Maerhal so she didn't spend any more days in darkness. Forgiving me for deceiving you because you saw strength and hope in forgiveness where I saw none." Riven kissed the back of my palm.

"You focus only on what your blade has cut and ended, but you forget how much you have fostered and grown, Keera Waateyith'thir."

Riven stared at me with nothing but awe in his eyes. It was palpable, addictive even, as I breathed that hope into my lungs. But each breath was tinged with fear too. "And what if I can't build anything after tomorrow?"

Riven's hand tightened on mine. "Don't say something like that, *diizra*." He could only manage a whisper.

I shook my head. It wasn't dying for my people that scared me. "What if we survive the battle, but after everything we've done, after everyone we've *lost*—" My breath hitched. "What if it all scars me too much, leaves me sullen and useless forever?"

Riven caressed my cheek. "Then you will be sullen and useless. For as long as you need. But then when you have fretted long enough, we can step out of the shadows. Together."

My lip quivered against his thumb. "Together," I repeated. The promise we had made each other wrapped around me like a lifeline, one I knew Riven would never stop tossing down to me if I fell back into that pit of darkness.

I pulled him into a kiss. This time he was not the hungry and desperate one. I tore at his tunic until it lay on the floor in two ragged pieces without letting my mouth leave his. Pressing my body against his chest wasn't enough. I needed to be closer.

Riven met my hunger with his own. He pulled my shirt over my head—sharp and swift. We didn't have a moment to spare. We breathed each other in instead of air, Riven's hand tangled in my hair, mine scratching his back, his chest, his arm.

I stopped. Riven was still wearing his sleeve. His jaw pulsed as I pressed a kiss to his shoulder, trailing my lips down what was left of his arm as I undid the fasteners.

Riven grunted. "I can do it, *diizra.*" But I shook my head. Riven had always been so gentle with my scars, from the very first moment he had seen them he never made me feel ashamed or embarrassed by the difference of my body. I wanted to do the same for him. I slipped off his sleeve and caressed the healed end where his arm had been.

Riven's neck flexed as I pressed my lips to it and then pulled it to my chest. His eyes shifted away from me, but I grabbed his cheek and pulled him into a kiss. Riven groaned into my mouth, wrapping his arm around my back as he pulled me into him. His lips curved around mine like strokes of ink, decisive and well-practiced. His mouth moved to my throat and I claimed his shoulder.

We wrote each other letters with our lips. All the words we didn't have time to say, all the dreams we hoped to share, we scribbled along every part of each other. Riven's arms tightened around me, biceps squeezing my ribs. I looped my legs around his torso as he lifted me onto the mattress, my hands making quick work of both our trousers.

He licked away my tears, and I pulled his hair from the base of his neck, nipping his skin so forcefully I tasted blood. My healing gift exploded. The warmth of it wrapped around us until we were cocooned inside my magic where no one could hurt us—not even each other.

Riven's lips trailed along my stomach, catching on my navel as he spread my knees.

"Tell me you need this as much as I do." His hot breath burned my skin with need.

I stretched my legs, needing to touch more of him, but he nipped my ankle. "*Diizra.*" He pressed a kiss to the inside of my thigh. "Tell me you need this."

Riven's eyes bore down on me. He wouldn't go any further without my approval.

But there was too much meaning packed into those five simple words. I didn't know how to answer him. Nothing I could say seemed big enough, seemed accurate enough, to explain all the ways I needed him.

Riven's thumb brushed against that pulsing point once. He raised a brow.

"Yes," I groaned. "I need you. I need this."

Riven smirked as he devoured me. There were no gentle licks or swirls of his tongue. He pushed my legs into my chest and claimed me as his own. Feasted on me until my body shook and the wind outside whistled through the trees, silencing my moans.

Riven removed his fingers after the third spell with a devilish grin on his face. "You're divine," he whispered, lowering his head for one last taste.

It was too much. I couldn't bear it any longer.

I hooked my leg around his waist and twisted. I captured Riven's laugh with my mouth as I claimed my place on top of him, tasting his joy as it transformed into a groan. I lowered my hips. I didn't have the patience for slow and teasing strokes. I grabbed Riven's arm, using it as an anchor as I ground my hips into him. Riven reached for my neck with his hand, trying to pull me into a kiss, but I leaned back out of reach. He settled for my breast, tugging at my nipple.

"Fuck, Keera," he moaned, his gaze locked on the spot where our bodies met.

I leaned forward. Close enough to kiss and lengthening the depth of my strokes. Riven's eyes shot to me, wanton and feral. His tongue brushed my bottom lip as he whispered my name again.

He matched my hips with thrusts of his own. I whimpered into his ear as a towering wave of pleasure built inside me, much more powerful than the ones before. The faelights in the room swirled on tiny gusts as my body exploded. Riven tensed as he rolled me onto my back with his hand under my hair.

He pressed a kiss to my nose, letting his weight sink into me the way he knew I liked. Our breaths were ragged and my lungs ached, but I reveled in the pain. I closed my eyes and noted every detail of that moment, every scent, every touch, clinging to it with all the strength I had, because for one more night we were alive.

But tomorrow that could change.

CHAPTER FORTY-FOUR

THE HEALING POOLS WERE only a short distance from Vellinth. As soon as the suns had begun to set, Riven pulled me from our bed, dressed me in a matching robe, and carried me there. Not a word was shared between us, in part because the Singing Wood was filled with creatures who would come running at any sound, but also because we both knew the talk would turn to the battle to come and neither of us wanted to waste our final night on that.

The cavern glimmered with rivers of gold and turquoise that expanded across the black rock. He set me down on a dry patch of stone and pulled a carved pin from his robe. He twirled his finger through the air and I turned. Riven gathered what was left of my hair and twisted it onto the top of my head with one hand. He pulled the hair pin from his mouth, and I held the twist as he secured my hair. He pressed a kiss to my bare neck and pulled the robe from my shoulders.

Riven's eyes feasted over my naked body as if he had gone months without it instead of mere minutes. He licked his lips as I dipped my foot into the healing waters, slowly lowering myself until only my collarbone was visible.

My magic hummed underneath my skin—that was the only way to describe it. The pool's effect was immediate. Even though I should be sleeping, I felt like I could fly for days without stopping.

Riven somersaulted into the deep end of the pool, his splash and my laugh echoing down the cavern as he surfaced. Thick strands clung to Riven's face, but he didn't move them. His long lashes clumped together too, the auric light illuminating the gold flecks in his eyes. He just watched as the ribbons of magic swirled around my body, stoking my powers until I vibrated, sending tiny ripples throughout the pool. I tensed. My powers felt like they were going to explode.

Riven reached for a vial at the edge of the pool and dabbed the sweet liquid on my lips. The urge to release my magic faded, but I could still feel the weight of that power stored underneath my skin. Waiting for the release that would come at dawn.

Riven scooped me up and lay me back on the surface of the water so I was floating. He floated beside me, touching cheek to cheek, and looped his smallest finger through mine. Tiny touches, barely any contact at all after what we had just done in our bed, but in that pool, I could feel every part of him. A current ten times stronger than the bond that had once been between us coursed through my body and into Riven's. I could feel every breath he took, every fear he had as our cheeks brushed together. We had an all-consuming love that I'd only felt once before. That I had believed for so long I would never feel again.

I grabbed Brenna's *diizra* that still hung around my neck. No matter what Damien did tomorrow, no matter what or who he took from me, he couldn't take that truth from me. If I died protecting my people, I would die as someone healing, as someone with the capacity to love even though the fear of losing it chilled me to the bone. I may die wielding a blade, but I wouldn't die as one. A tear trickled down my cheek and into the water. Riven sensed it through whatever magic connected us and turned to kiss it away.

"We should try to get a few hours' rest," he whispered, his lips trailing across my ear. I tilted my head into his touch and nodded. Riven stepped out of the pool first and picked up both our robes in his hand. I hung mine from my shoulders and helped Riven thread his arm through the sleeve. The healed end poked through the wide circle of fabric, and I pressed a quick kiss to the scar.

Riven lifted my arm and kissed my elbow with a boyish grin on his face. I laughed and Riven's smile widened.

"You're still the most exquisite creature I've ever seen." My cheeks warmed at his words, and Riven grabbed my wrist and twirled me down the tunnel just as he had in Cereliath. Then we had been two allies barely able to trust each other, but now I would give him everything I held dear without a single doubt.

I twirled back to him, crashing into his chest. Riven caught me with a kiss and hoisted me over his shoulder. I stifled my laughs with my sleeve as Riven carried me through the Singing Wood. The scent of birchwood and dew enveloped me as I let my head rest on Riven's shoulder.

The person I trusted more than any other.

He laid me on the bed and fetched an amber nightgown from his closet. I lifted my brow. "How many of these did you buy?" Between this house and both our burls in Myrelinth, I seemed to have nightgowns in every color the Elverin could dye.

Riven's voice was rough and hoarse. "Ten."

I bit my lip, counting the colors in my head.

"Dozen," he added.

I chucked a pillow at him. "Why would I ever need so many?"

Riven pulled on a soft pair of sleeping trousers and crawled into bed beside me, his chest still bare. He eyed our ripped tunics covering the entrance of his home. "I have a habit of rendering them useless." I elbowed him in the side before turning to lay on his chest. His skin was as warm as a hearth on a cool night, safe and welcome.

Riven nipped my ear before curling a loose strand around his finger. "In truth, when Nikolai asked for a color selection, I told him *all of them*."

"Why?"

Riven shrugged. "You had worn black for so long. I didn't know what colors you liked. I didn't even know if *you* knew which colors you liked. I wanted you to have the chance to choose."

My heart exploded in my chest. I had no doubt that Riven cared for me in the big ways, the ways I needed, but the small ones still took me by surprise. He seemed to know how to love me in ways I hadn't even imagined for myself.

"Green," I whispered against his chest before tapping his nose.

His jade eyes widened knowing exactly what hue of green I meant. Riven cleared his throat. "You do look fantastic in green."

I chuckled. Then that patient silence settled between us, almost enough to lure me to sleep. But there was still one thing I needed to do before sunrise. Something I would only trust Riven with.

I sat up and crossed my leg over Riven's. "I need you to do something for me."

"Anything," he answered without hesitation. His black mane covered the pillow completely like a bird about to take flight, ready to fly toward whatever task I gave him.

I swallowed and grabbed the small pouch at my chest. "I want you to wear this for me tomorrow," I said, slipping the gold chain from my neck.

Riven shook his head. "No." He sat up, kneeling beside me on the bed. "I will not let you go into battle believing you will die. We promised each other."

I silenced him with a gentle kiss. Tears pricked my eyes as I pulled away, placing the *diizra* in his hand. "I promised you I will fight with everything I have, and I *will*." My voice shook with adamant resolve. "But you and I both saw how Damien reacted in Volcar. *If* he bests me, he will take great pleasure in destroying this, and I won't leave that to chance. Brenna died tangled in one of his sick games. Her death will not fall victim to one too."

I wiped the rivers at my cheeks as Riven sat frozen. I grabbed for both his hands, forgetting one was gone. "Damien targeted us both in Volcar and he will do the same in Koratha. But this time—"

"I will not be on the front lines," Riven finished for me, his hardness cracking.

I nodded. "Brenna deserves to be free. She deserves to be reconnected with our kin, even if it's only in death. And right now, you are the better fit to give her that. To protect her and her freedom."

Riven's fingers closed around the *diizra*. "But I didn't know her. Myrrah, Gerarda—"

"Will be targeted too." I reached up and cupped Riven's cheek in my hand. His body shook under my touch as his fears raged inside him. "I can think of no one better to protect the legacy of my first love than the one who loves me now. The one I love. The one I *chose*."

Riven's lip quivered but no words came. My breath hitched thinking he would still say no, but he nodded his head. I sighed in relief and looped the delicate chain through my fingers and over Riven's head. Brenna's *diizra* sat over his heart, the same place that would hold my ashes if Damien got his way. I pushed that thought from my mind and pressed my forehead against Riven's shoulder. He wrapped his arm around me and pulled me back into bed, this time the exhaustion of the choices we had to make pushing us to the brink of sleep. I lay my head on Riven, letting the beat of his heart and rhythm of his breath beckon our dreams toward us.

My hand reached for the pouch on his chest. It was just as warm as it had been laying across my skin. Riven closed his hand over mine and we fell asleep clutching the *diizra* as we clutched each other, with all our promises between us.

CHAPTER FORTY-FIVE

"KEERA, WE NEED TO GO." Dynara's voice sounded far away like she was speaking to me from across a long room and refused to shout. Riven's arm tightened along my chest, still asleep, as Dynara poured a skin of water over both of us. Riven roared awake, the bedsheets flying to the floor.

Dynara tried to hold in a laugh as she realized we weren't dressed, but Gerarda only crossed her arms through the other side of the portal that had opened in the middle of the room. "Classic but effective."

Riven chucked a pillow through the portal and stood to change clothes. Dynara turned around but didn't leave, hiding her giggles behind a cough.

Gerarda's lip curled back in annoyance at my sleepy pace. "The Dead Wood is on fire."

I yanked my leathers on in a fit of panic. "Next time," I said to them, pulling on my boot, "you lead with that."

Riven grabbed a tunic from his closet and handed it to me.

"Don't need it." I shook my head, pulling on my leather vest. "I want Damien to see my scars when I kill him."

Gerarda flipped her blade in her hand, the smell of smoke drifting through the portal. "We have a lot of soldiers to get through first."

I stepped through the portal trying to braid my hair, but it was too short. Gerarda pulled half of it back and secured it into a small knot. "That should hold well enough." She nodded at the end of the tent. "Syrra and El already took the troops to the wall."

Gwyn cleared her throat.

"With the help of Ring," Gerarda added.

I turned to Gwyn. "You need to conserve your energy. The march wasn't that far and we were supposed to wait until dawn."

"There won't be a dawn," Gwyn said darkly as she pulled open the tent. "The suns rose an hour ago."

The sky was black. Not a ray of sunlight or star could be seen through the thick purple smoke that rose as high as the tallest clouds and cast the new morning into never-ending shadow. The *shirak* circled the Order and Koratha with no signs of leaving. Their wide wings made wind so strong I could feel it along the tree line. My nostrils burned and my mouth dried at the taste of ashen wood and death.

Tears welled in my eyes as I saw the Dead Wood. The forest that had sprung back to life was once again black and burnt. The entire wood was alit with violet flame. I gritted my teeth. Damien's purple fire shielded the *shirak* from the sun, losing us our advantage.

My stomach churned as I tried to quell the flames, but all I managed was to drain my power. I sent a gust, trying to push through the thick clouds of smoke, but whatever magic Damien had tainted the fire with made it almost impossible.

"Enough, *diizra*." Riven grabbed my arm. "Lash died fighting Damien's violet flames."

I sighed and took in the sight below. The white wall of Koratha was lined with soldiers, two dozen thick at least. They held torches in their shield hands; it was the only reason I could count their number at all. Tiny little matches in the darkness. Dynara opened another portal and brought us to the tents behind our army. It was not nearly as big as what Damien had amassed. I doubted we had more than a quarter of his men.

But we had more than a dozen Fae who would not be taken by surprise like our foremothers had been. We were here to fight.

"Should we light the faebeads?" Syrra asked in way of greeting.

I looked out at our ranks. Every soldier was standing tall, holding weapons that had only been smithed the day before. Some wore dark ink along their faces like Syrra did, and others decorated their brows with thin strands of gold that were pinned to the backs of their braids.

"Do it." I nodded at Syrra, and she gave the command in Elvish, lifting her golden sword as our side of the battle was lit with faelight. The *shirak* screeched into the darkness at the light. Some perched along the back walls, craning their necks as they screamed while others circled the palace. We had their attention now, and they were not pleased with the intrusion.

Riven grabbed my hand. "I will be with Rheih." I pulled him into a tight embrace, feeling the warmth of the *diizra* he was keeping for me under his leather chest plate. I reveled in his scent, the warm birchwood that was the closest thing to home I knew mixed with parchment and ink. His hand caressed my back as we held each other, all our secrets told. At least if we died today, we would die as true to ourselves as we could be.

Riven cleared his throat, tears stinging his eyes. "If this is farewell—"

I pressed my lips to his. "No farewells. No last words." I stood on the tips of my toes and pressed my forehead against his. "I will find you when the smoke clears and we have won."

Riven's stare hardened as his eyes traced over every line of my face like a painter, committing it to memory by force. He pressed a kiss to my neck so no one else would hear his words but me.

"Go fulfill your promise, *diizra*." He pressed his hand to his chest, holding Brenna with all the gentleness he saved for me. "And then return so we can fulfill ours together." My throat tightened, too much to say anything back to him. Instead, I laced our fingers and pressed a kiss to his palm. Then Dynara opened a portal and Riven was gone.

The gates opened. I braced myself for even more soldiers to be let into the field, but it was clear these were not soldiers at all.

They were Halflings.

Hundreds of Halflings.

Damien was pushing them out of the city to tame our attack. The threat was clear. Use our full strength, and he would send down a hell storm of *waateyshirak* on the innocent Halflings we were trying to save. He'd just turned this into a rescue mission as well as a battle. I could almost feel his hand on my back, moving me like a pawn on a chessboard, delighting in the feel of my scars and the panicked heartbeat in my chest.

Syrra stepped beside me. "He believes he has us pinned."

"He underestimates us." I swallowed, knowing what had to be done. "We'll split into four units." I drained a skin of spelled water and watched as it broke into tiny droplets that clung around everyone's mouth and ears. The remaining droplets swirled through the air, searching for their keepers.

Syrra crossed her arms, considering the plan. "Two teams to pull Halflings out and two to fight?"

I shook my head. "We'll spare one to help them. Dynara can try to portal as many as she can. But the Halflings will have to fight for their own freedom today."

A deep horn sounded over the sea. Dynara opened a portal so we could see Myrrah through the veil of mist.

"Three dozen ships total." She shouted like we were leagues away instead of a few feet. "All armed and fully manned."

My stomach hardened. That was more than we assumed Damien had left. "Signal if you need help."

Crison grinned. "My flock can take a third on its own."

"And we have reinforcements." She wheeled backward so we could see the two dozen ships sailing behind her. Each one sailing with royal sails repainted in the colors of the Fractured Isles.

"They came to fight." Gerarda's face flushed. "There were enough of them left to come to fight." El squeezed her shoulder.

"Remember," I said to Myrrah. "Lead as many as you can into the channel and Feron will take care of the rest."

She tilted her head with a childish grin on her face. "After I try Nikolai's canons."

I reached through the portal and touched the white pin around Myrrah's neck. "Fight well today, dear friend."

Tears welled in her eyes. "And you, Keera. So we may never fight again."

Dynara closed the portal and I turned to Syrra and Elaran. "It's time."

Elaran nodded, dressed in all black like a royal soldier. She transformed into the pimply face of the Shield, and Gerarda pinned the forged fastener around her neck. Elaran studied her new body. "I was so angry when Hildegard told me I'd never be a member of the Arsenal. But"—she scratched her throat—"the uniform itches."

Gerarda and I gave each other a knowing look.

Syrra wrapped a thick cloak around her shoulders and pulled on the hood. In a crowd, she would look like a Mortal man preparing to fight. She pulled me into a tight embrace. "It is an honor to fight alongside you, Keera Waateyith'thir. And to do so clean of both our vices." She leaned back with tears in her eyes.

There was a hard determination in them that I didn't like. It was the same look Hildegard had given me when she was dragged in front of Damien's throne.

"The honor is mine, good friend." I nodded at the portal Dynara opened. "Take as many of them as you can."

Syrra nodded and stepped into the city of Koratha.

Dynara closed the portal and opened another for me, sweat already pooling at her brow. I gave her a concerned look, but she shook her head. "You have too much to worry about to fret over me."

I stepped through and stood beside Feron.

I assessed our ranks from his nest behind them. "Dynara, get your team ready and wait for Syrra's sign."

She nodded and disappeared. My stomach hardened trying to ignore the question if that would be the last time I saw my friend. The last time I saw any of them.

"What signal are we waiting for?" Feron mused, his voice calm and collected, as if the entire future of his people would not be decided today.

An ear-splitting shriek tore through the sky as one of the *shirak* stationed on the walls burst into shadowy pieces. "That," I answered Feron, pointing to Syrra's glowing sword.

I took out my spyglass. The Arsenal and the surviving pendants were stationed along the watch platform of the city wall. Their pendants pulsed as they tried to keep their control of the *shirak* in check.

It didn't work.

Five of the beasts opened their wings and propelled themselves into the air. The field of Halflings broke out into terrified screams.

I grabbed Feron's shoulder. "Channel them to one portal!"

He raised his hands and pulled a thick wall of stone from the earth. It split most of the Halflings from the soldiers as a second wall erupted, giving them only two directions to run.

Dynara opened portals on either side and sent the lucky Halflings into Myrelinth.

The unlucky ones were caught in the first attack. One of the *shirak* sucked in a small breath and blew a fiery spout of death onto the Halflings below.

Feron and I raised stone shields from the ground, protecting most but not all. Grief-stricken screams fused with the screams of terror as a second beast attacked.

"Gerarda, cover the Halflings in shadow," I commanded.

She lifted her hands, and black shadows flowed down the hill like rushing snowmelt. They joined and stretched, creating a dark fog that kept the Halflings from view. The *waateyshir* slowed its descent, confused and no longer able to see any movement except for the soldiers lining the city walls.

A portal appeared and Dynara stepped through. "Hurry!" she shouted at Gerarda.

Gerarda placed her palm over her face and chest and left. I held my breath, counting the seconds until I saw proof that they had survived the third fiery spout from the skies.

Nine. Ten. Eleven. A beam of pure light shot from the front lines of battle killing two *shirak* in its wake. I watched through my spyglass as a third dove for Gerarda. The Arsenal's pendants glowed bright once more as they took control of the beasts.

The *waateyshir* whistled as it plummeted toward the ground, filling its chest with enough air for a deadly attack. It spread its wings and Syrra leaped from the wall with her blood-bound blade raised above her head.

Her aim struck true. She pierced the beast's red center and it exploded into a blast of shadow. Feron raised his hand and Syrra somersaulted onto a ramp of stone.

A low horn blew as Gerarda launched another attack. I turned to the Order to see Damien's ships charging after Myrrah's as it sailed into the channel between the island and the city shores. Feron lowered the wall of stone he'd erected along the battlefield, clearing his line of vision.

Crison's flock of birds slowed the royal ships but not enough. Feron stood, his hands suspended in the air as he waited for the ships to sail over the right spot. His fists clenched. The ground shook as the white wall that surrounded Koratha was joined by its missing half. White stone erupted from the waters, splintering Damien's fleet to ruin.

Crison gasped for all of us to hear. "Holy shit, that worked."

"Thanks for the assist," Myrrah's voice sounded, and my chest loosened with relief.

Gwyn grabbed my arm as Gerarda felled another *waateyshir*. "It's time to send us in." She turned to Fyrel with their hands joined. My heart ached; they looked nothing like Brenna and me, but on the field of battle, it was like peering into a looking glass of what could have been.

I hugged Gwyn. "You are a warrior today." I placed my hand on Fyrel's shoulder. "You both are, and I am honored to fight alongside you."

Tears welled in Gwyn's eyes, but she said nothing. She only turned toward the city where Damien was waiting. Fyrel transformed into her bear form, roaring and pounding on her chest. Gwyn climbed on and I soared after them.

I landed beside Gerarda and lost myself in a blur of action. The Arsenal noticed my presence and focused all their strength on me. I flitted between my eagle form and my Fae form, fending attacks from every direction.

The *shirak* circled above me. The soldiers charged at full speed, their amber pupils bright and pulsing with no care how their movement caught the attention of the hungry beasts. Gerarda and Syrra used the distraction to their advantage. Gerarda ran, drawing the *shirak* away from the Halflings caught between the soldiers and our ranks. She exaggerated her movements, almost dancing to keep their attention as Syrra climbed the white wall.

I transformed, dodging a fiery blow and a stray sword. I shifted back and used my gusts to pull the air from every soldier's lungs around me. Three dozen men dropped to the ground.

Two more dropped from the wall. "Leave some for me, Keera," Elaran teased in my ear as she sent another sentry falling to his death.

I turned and saw a small group of soldiers approaching the portal Dynara had left open. Nikolai stepped through with a shaking sword in his hand.

"Dynara, close the portal!" I shouted, fending off three soldiers of my own. I blocked one swing and saw Nikolai dodge a death blow by a hair. "Someone help Nikolai!" I commanded into the water hanging from my lips.

Dynara appeared at the portal. Her hands glowed as she closed it with Nikolai still on the battlefield. I walked backward trying to make my way to Nik. I slashed my dual blades in all directions.

The gates of Koratha opened again. A flood of fresh soldiers charged through—each with a black eye and amber pupil. I lifted a thick wall of stone from the ground. It cracked along the bottom as I closed my fists. The whirling feeling inside my chest grew to the point of pain, needing release. I raised my arm and sent the strongest gust I could muster against the stone wall.

It teetered along the fracture. I clenched my teeth and kept my gusts pushing against the stone. My vision blurred from the strain as the wall fell and flattened the troops. Dust filled the air, obscuring my small victory.

My stomach sank as the dust settled. More soldiers poured out of Koratha, marching over the stone and their fallen brethren without any regard.

"Do you think I care how many walls you erect and flatten?" a voice called from above.

I recognized Damien's scowl. It lingered on the face of a pimply faced, broad-shouldered man. The Bow. The only Arsenal member Damien didn't give a pendant. If the silver bow fastener at his neck didn't mark him for who he was, the empty chest plate did.

"I have you outnumbered," Damien said through his Bow. "I have you out-armed. And now—"

The Bow's gaze shifted to something behind me. I turned. Nikolai was fighting four soldiers. More like prodding. He held two tiny daggers that looked even smaller compared to the soldier's swords.

One soldier lifted his arm, preparing to levy a heavy blow, and dropped his sword on his own head. The others straightened, turning their own weapons onto themselves. They dropped and their amber pupils faded.

The tether.

Whatever Damien had done, he wasn't ready to use it yet. My belly tensed as I stabbed my sword through a soldier's throat.

Fyrel charged toward Nikolai, swatting soldiers in every direction as she carried Syrra on her back. I transformed, soaring over the soldiers and landing on her white fur. There was a second flash of light.

I used my earth magic to trap a line of soldiers into dangling roots. Syrra jumped off, running for Nikolai to fight beside him.

The sentries along the wall no longer held bows but spears. Their points dripped in dark purple liquid. Poison. The Bow swung his arm and the first barrage came hurtling toward us. Fyrel turned, swatting the spears from the air like it was nothing. I gripped her fur, trying not to slide from her back.

"Fire at will," shouted the Bow down at his ranks.

Spear after spear whirled through the air. Each one aimed for Fyrel. She stood on her hind legs, shielding me and swatting bolts with both hands. She twisted, deflecting a spear to the field below.

I dangled from her back and watched as the spear hurtled toward Nikolai instead. "Nikolai!" I cried, letting go of Fyrel.

There was no time for magic. All I could do was watch as Syrra pushed her nephew to his knees. The spear pierced through her chest. Her last breath was barely a gasp as she crumpled to the ground, dead.

Nikolai screamed so violently the *shirak* above recoiled from the sound. He crawled along the ground and cradled Syrra's head in his lap.

"Raava," he whispered through the sobs. "Wake up. *Wake up!*"

He reached for Syrra's blade, left forgotten in a soldier's chest, as if that would set new life upon her lungs. But as soon as his hand touched the hilt he recoiled back in shock, his fingers burnt and blistered.

The golden sword had faded back to silver. Unclaimed once more.

Thick streams cut into my cheeks, but I couldn't let the beast above me go.

"Keera," Gerarda called, running toward two Shades who were holding a shield above their heads, ready for her to jump. I nodded and Gerarda ran. Sprinting like a mountain cat, she leaped onto the shield and was propelled into the sky. I waited until she reached peak height and threw my hands down, pushing her higher with my gusts. Gerarda let out a battle cry as a beam of pure light exploded upward directly into the *waateyshir*'s red center. It squealed as it died, fading into nothing as the others fled from Gerarda's magic.

She landed on top of a soldier and twisted his neck. I didn't wait to see the body fall. I ran to Syrra and Nikolai. Soldiers ran for us, but thick roots sprang from the earth and pulled them into early graves. I turned and saw Feron lift his faelight along the hill. He would hold the soldiers off long enough to get Nikolai to safety, but we had to be quick.

"Nik, you can't lay here," I urged.

He shook his head. "Heal her. Keera, heal her now."

"Nik." My lips trembled. "I can't."

I pointed to her sword because that was easier than looking at Syrra's vacant eyes.

"No. No." Nikolai shook his head with tears streaming down his face. "She died saving me."

"And there is no other death she would've wanted." I pressed my hand to Nik's cheek. "There is no greater honor to a warrior than giving your life protecting those you love."

"No, she wanted to live." Nikolai wiped his nose. "She wanted to see the world we would build together."

"No, she didn't." I pulled the spear out of her chest and folded her arms. "Syrra made her choice the day she sheared her hair. She knew she was never going to braid it into anyone else's. Maerhal's funeral was always going to be her last."

Nikolai's face fell. He caressed Syrra's smooth head, and he let out one last sob, finally seeing the truth of what his aunt had planned. To die for her people—to undo her biggest regret. She never wanted to be a survivor again.

A glowing thread of amber appeared beside Nikolai. It dissolved into a veil of mist as Dynara stepped through the portal.

Nikolai's shoulders drooped as he picked Syrra up under her legs and her back. He looked like he was cradling a babe in his arms. My heart tore. It was so unfair that Nikolai would bury the two mothers he had ever known, the two *ikwenira* who had held him just like that as a sleeping child. His son, his mother, and now his aunt. Nikolai had joined the rest of us and become the last of his bloodline.

My jaw flexed. I wouldn't let that bloodline die today.

He stepped through the portal to safety and Dynara closed it behind him. She held two small blades and gave me a hard look. She planned on staying. "You need as many as are able."

"Have a portal ready." There was a flash of light and I took flight above her head.

The Halflings who hadn't picked up fallen swords to fight had congregated along the edges of the battlefield. Only a small line of soldiers stood between them and our fighters. I let out a loud screech and hoped Dynara knew to track me through the skies. I tucked in my wings and dove for the soldiers. There was another flash of light, and I landed on the middle man's shoulders, perched like a bird, with my dagger through his neck.

I didn't kill the others with steel. Instead I cast a line of hot flame as tall as the white wall that surrounded the city and turned them to ash. Dynara was there in an instant. Her fingers still lit from her own portal as she opened another, four people wide.

"Run!" I shouted at the Halflings, ushering them through. I scooped up four children into my arms and handed them to anyone able-bodied enough to carry them.

There was a flash of red curls behind them as Gwyn tackled a soldier to the ground. Two others fell to the side, Elaran's arrows sticking out from their chests. They both pointed their weapons to the sky as a *waateyshir* plummeted toward us.

I tried to conjure water from the air, but it was too dry under the fiery canopy. I turned to Gwyn. "Create a storm!"

She gave me a sideways glance. "The smoke will just melt it away."

"I know."

Gwyn didn't need to be told again. She wiped her mouth, smearing blood across her face, and painted a rune into the air. When the amber light fused together into a gold spell, she pushed it toward the sky. As if from nothing, the spell transformed into gray clouds, growing wider and wider under the thick smoke. The snow had barely begun to fall when it liquified to water instead. That was all I needed.

I spread the water thin and waited for one of the *shirak* to fly beneath it. I took all my focus, but I wrapped the water around the beast mid-dive, trapping it in a liquid cage. Its shriek was muffled by the water, wings stretching, trying to find its way out. I fisted my hand and the orb turned to ice.

I looked to Gerarda but she was already running. The frozen orb dropped with the beast inside it, shattering on the ground as its shadow leaked out in all directions. Gerarda used her own shadow magic to blend into the darkness. The *waateyshir* didn't even know she was there until she punched her fist through its heart. Light erupted from its chest and the creature exploded into tiny pieces.

A chorus of deadly shrieks filled the sky. There were still over a dozen of the monsters left.

Gerarda kneeled to catch her breath. Her magic was almost spent.

"We've bested the other line." Elaran's voice rang out in my ear.

Dynara nodded without a word, disappearing through a portal to take the rest of the Halflings to safety. I tracked the beasts in the sky, waiting for one to attack.

The doors to Koratha opened once more. Tall catapults crawled out of the opening while thousands more soldiers marched at their feet.

"Did Damien sell everything except his throne?" Gerarda seethed. She held two short blades in her hands and snarled up at the first catapult.

The Arrow rode the machine like the crow's nest of a ship. His silver fastener gleamed in the light of the torches from the troop below. He raised his hand and the catapult sent a cascade of molten rock and purple flame through our ranks.

It was chaos. People lunged in every direction to avoid being hit. The Arrow sent his men running after us. The pendant along his chest shone bright and the lowest of the *waateyshirak* seemed to calm as they watched the chaos unfold.

Gwyn launched arrow after arrow. I used my gusts to send them farther into the ranks of our enemy, lighting their tips just before they hit. The earth shook, and Feron split the ground in two. The unprepared soldiers fell into the giant chasm and were crushed as Feron sealed it as quickly as he had created it. It killed a third of their men, but our magic wouldn't hold out for much longer.

Black cloaks led the second charge. The silver shield and dagger gleamed along their necks, but they didn't wear a glowing pendant. I gritted my teeth. Damien was still keeping one for himself even while his entire city died for him.

Dynara appeared behind the young Shield. The young man didn't stand a chance. She pounced on his back, his throat red with blood before he hit the ground. She spun her arm and jumped upward into another portal and fell from the sky on top of the Dagger.

I turned to Gerarda. "What have you been teaching her?"

She stabbed her blade through a distracted sellsword. "Efficiency."

The Dagger collapsed before Dynara could land her blow and they both tumbled to the ground. He reached for his sword but an arrow pierced his eye. He lay dead. Elaran nodded at me and lowered her bow.

Gwyn ran toward the catapult. Elaran used her arrows to clear a path as one of the *waateyshirak* dove toward us, but it wasn't quick enough.

Fyrel jumped over all of us. The soldiers froze in their boots as she swatted them into oblivion.

"Throw me!" Gerarda shouted at Fyrel.

The brumal bear turned its head and grabbed Gerarda between its claws, her tiny frame like a thorn caught in its foot. Fyrel snapped her wrist and launched Gerarda into the skies. The *waateyshirak* opened its beak, whistling as it sucked in a deadly breath. Gerarda's hand grabbed the bottom jaw and aimed her fist at the beast's red chest.

It roared as it exploded into nothing.

"Set those things on fire!" Gerarda shouted as I broke her landing on a soft gust.

I raised my hand, but Gwyn's voice echoed in my ear. "Let me try something first."

She stood at the bottom of the catapult. Her fingers glowed amber as she wrote a rune along the wooden shaft. The spell took hold and the catapult transformed. The wood groaned, growing taller than the palace to form a monstrous tree. The violet flames from the neighboring catapults set the leaves aflame as it grew so the entire canopy was a raging ball of magical flame.

Gwyn was a genius. In one spell she had created a weapon worth more than ten of my attacks. I kneeled, using my earth gift to keep the tree's roots from taking hold. "Gwyn, run!" I shouted and then I cast one immense gust at the trunk.

The tree teetered back then forward—unsure of which direction it wanted to fall. I gritted my teeth and kept a heavy wind against its trunk until my brow was covered in sweat. Finally, the tree fell, creaking like a funeral hymn as it landed through the wall.

It took most of the lookout with it, though the Bow had evaded death by an inch. His chest swelled as he looked down at the rubble and flattened bodies. Then he turned to me and his black eyes flashed with amber.

Damien snarled down at me. I stretched my arms wide, tempting him to jump from the wall like he had in our shared dream. It would save me killing Hildegard's successor.

Gerarda came to my side as the soldiers circled around us, trying to pin our fighters in. The Arrow appeared from the dust cloud at the base of the tree. Somehow unharmed.

His pendant glowed. He wanted us to be an easy target for the *shirak* and we had walked right into his trap. Exhaustion trampled through my body. If my own powers were weakening, then Gerarda and Gwyn were almost spent.

"How many more can you kill?"

Gerarda blocked a sword aimed for her neck. "Don't worry about me."

"How many?" I echoed as I gutted a soldier's belly.

Gerarda huffed a breath. "One. Maybe two."

I could almost hear Damien's laugh. This is what he had wanted—that we would expend our energy fighting the *shirak* and be left defenseless when his men came for our heads. Fyrel ran toward us in her brumal bear form. She swatted the soldiers out of the way, roaring in their faces until they fell back in fear and she stomped them into dust. Then she shifted back into her Fae form.

"I don't think I can hold that much longer," she wheezed, bent at the waist.

My heart throbbed against my chest, drowning out my thoughts. There were no other options. We had done everything we could, and we were failing.

Dynara opened a portal in front of six soldiers charging at her in a line. All six ran through it, plummeting from its opening in the sky before they realized what she'd done. She wiped her hands and closed the portal as the *shirak* snatched the men mid-fall. Blood splattered on my face as two beasts ripped one of the men in half.

Gwyn tackled two more soldiers, skewering them both through the middle. Fyrel swung at the second and missed as he fell to the ground with Gwyn's sword in his belly. "I've got you this time," Gwyn mused, pressing a soft kiss to Fyrel's lips. The girl's face broke into a wide smile despite her exhaustion. Even standing in a field full of dead Elverin and Mortals, Fyrel couldn't contain her excited giggle, but it turned into panic as two shadowy beasts plummeted toward us.

"Brace!" I shouted to Gerarda. She lifted her arms above her head without hesitation. I jumped, changing forms mid-leap, and wrapped my talons around her arm. I beat my wings as fast and hard as I could—trying to get Gerarda high enough to land one more attack before the beasts had a chance to use their fiery blast.

The *shirak* barely noticed us, cloaked in Gerarda's shadows, as I flew between them. The biggest opened its beak and started to whistle. One of Damien's soldiers used the chance to fling another round of flaming rock onto the field, pummeling his soldiers along with ours. I let Gerarda go and transformed midair, pulling a wall of rock from the ground.

An explosion of light burst behind me, illuminating just how many flaming rocks had made it past my shield and Feron's. My stomach clenched as the screams of heartbreak sounded from our ranks, drowning out the dying shrieks of the *shirak* Gerarda had vanquished.

I transformed back into my eagle form to land and found Gerarda collapsed and trying to stand on shaking legs.

Gwyn spelled two soldiers to attack their own men, taunting them with her laughter as Fyrel swung between them. I turned to help Gerarda but saw what Gwyn had not.

Dynara stood behind her, fighting a soldier who had followed her through a portal that was still open. A second man stepped through, and his spelled comrade swung for his head.

"No!" I shouted as Fyrel swiped the man's legs with her own. She smiled at me, proud and self-assured, as the spelled soldier's axe struck her head. I dove for the girl, trying to touch her skin before her body hit the ground.

But I was too late. Fyrel stared back at me, a ghost of a smile still on her face as her amber eyes faded and she rolled onto her back wearing an axe for a crown.

Gwyn let out a bloodcurdling scream. Her hands glowed as she pulled at her hair and spells drifted into the air like snow. One turned dark, growing and growing, until a swirling storm cracked with thunder. It tore down Damien's ranks, flinging the remaining catapults and the soldiers manning them against the city wall. Red splotches covered the white stone like raindrops on a cobble street.

The *waateyshirak* under Damien's control lined the wall like horses tied down to posts. They fought against the magic binding them, snapping and hungry as they watched the chaos down below.

But Gwyn didn't care. She didn't even notice. She ran for the soldier who had swung the axe and stabbed him in his black eye. She plucked it from his skull and crushed it with her boot. But that wasn't good enough. Her lips curled over her fangs as the rampage began. She slew soldier after soldier, claiming each of their eyes and turning them to dust.

Then she spotted the Arrow.

"Gwyn, no!" I chased after her with Dynara at my side. She portaled us closer to Gwyn, ready to fight the Arrow alongside her, but Gwyn was writing spells into the air. This time they didn't turn gold but black. She thrust her hands forward, and the spells latched onto the neck of the Arrow and the ten soldiers beside him. They grabbed their throats, the magic burning their flesh like roasting chains.

"Damien!" Gwyn screamed as she plunged her finger into the Shield's eye socket. She pulled the black eye out of his head, leaving the man to fall to his knees. Gwyn started tracing a rune along the eye. She chanted words even I didn't know, nose bleeding a waterfall of amber and gold blood.

"Gwyn, stop," I begged, but it was no use. I didn't think she could hear me at all. The rune sealed and turned black too. She held it up, squeezing it, and dozens of soldiers fell to their knees along the city wall. Each one with a black eye. The Arrow's pendant faded as he writhed in pain. I looked up and saw the new Blade bent over in agony too.

"You will carry the pain of every person you have ever hurt," Gwyn shouted at Damien. Even though he was somewhere in his palace, I knew he was writhing in pain too.

All the *waateyshirak* were in the sky now with no one using the pendants. They could smell the desperation and pain like sharks out for blood. Even though most of Damien's soldiers were dead, we were no match for the *waateyshirak*. We had nothing left to fight them. All our resources were spent. We needed Damien to tame them or every surviving Elverin and Mortal were going to become their feast.

Gwyn had to be stopped.

I clenched my jaw and called that whirling power inside my chest. A small gust formed at Gwyn's mouth, growing just enough to pull the air from her lungs. Her eyes widened in surprise and then narrowed with betrayal as she turned to me.

"I'm so sorry," I shouted, hot tears running down my face. Dynara caught Gwyn in her arms as she fell limp and pulled her through a portal. The soldiers stopped writhing in pain. Some clambered to their feet. The Arrow stood, pendant alight, and groaned as he used all his power to quell the *shirak* once more. The circle of beasts tightened and their snarls grew louder but none of them dove. I only hoped Damien's tenuous control could hold.

I picked up a dead soldier's waterskin and poured the contents out. My body ached as I used my magic to form a sphere and let it hover along the remaining city wall. "I speak directly to your king." My voice echoed through the debris and into the city. "Damien, you have proved your strength is too mighty. Let us claim our dead, and my people will surrender."

The Arrow's eye turned bright amber. "You think I will let you live after what you have done?" He scoffed. "You have destroyed my city. Killed hundreds of my people, thousands of my soldiers. Their blood is on your hands."

"Then kill me," I said in a calm, even tone. "Give us an hour to collect our dead, and I will walk out here willingly and unarmed."

Damien crossed his arms. "Why should I believe you?"

"What do you have to lose?" I shrugged. "We can fight until the city is nothing but rubble, or you can agree to the hour."

"It seems you get much more than I do in this arrangement." He lifted a brow. "Why give you the chance to flee?"

Hot towers of flame stood behind me and the sky cracked with lightning. "I have enough magic left to wipe this city to the ground, but even I cannot defeat the *waateyshirak* you have left. Accept my terms and your people shall not suffer anymore. Show us mercy, and I will show them mercy. Deny my request, and you will be a king of no one."

Concerned whispers started behind the city walls. Soon they grew into pleas of mercy that echoed out onto the battlefield.

Damien scowled, knowing he was left with no better option.

"One hour."

CHAPTER FORTY-SIX

I didn't spare a moment of that hour. I ran back and collected Fyrel's body myself. I tore a piece of tunic from one of our fallen soldiers and wrapped it around her head so Gwyn didn't have to see the gash the axe had left. I brushed her eyelids closed and let the girl rest in my arms as I made the long walk back to our tents.

My body was numb and my mind empty. I couldn't hear my thoughts over the screams and metal clanging echoing in my head. I put the young Shade on the small pyres Feron had conjured and Vrail grabbed my arm.

"Don't do this." Tears ran down her blood-caked face. "You don't have to do this."

Nikolai grabbed my other arm. "Why martyr yourself now? We're one people. The Elverin stand together, in death too if we must." His eyes were bloodshot from crying but they were determined.

I shook my head and wrapped them both in my arms. "No one else needs to die."

"You're giving us a few hours more at most," Nikolai scoffed.

I glanced between the two of them. "Then spend those hours together." I raised a brow. "I think you've both been waiting long enough."

Nikolai cleared his throat, but his eyes widened in shock when he saw the flush of Vrail's cheeks. He tugged on his hair and stood there awkward and wordless for the first time in his seven centuries. I cherished the laugh and turned to find Riven standing behind me.

"I heard" was all he said. It was all he needed to.

He knew me well enough to know that pleading would only be a waste of breath. A waste of time. I leaned against his chest and let the sound of his breathing calm me. I would need to be at peace to do what had to be done.

"I can come with you," Riven whispered against my hair. "My brother would not begrudge two deaths."

My blood cooled. Damien would draw it out and make one of us watch as he tortured the other. I didn't want to tempt him, not when he controlled a flock of *waateyshirak* that could scorch through the rest of my kin.

I shook my head and pressed a kiss to the tip of his nose. "No, you have a promise to carry out."

A tear cut down Riven's cheek, but he didn't take his hand off me to wipe it away. Instead, he pulled me tight against him and pressed a hard kiss to my mouth. A horn blew in the distance, and I knew I only had a half hour left. I wrapped my arms around Riven's neck and whispered a message I trusted only him with.

"Get Gerarda and Feron. Be ready to strike." My words shook against his ear. "You'll know when."

Riven took a deep breath and nodded. He knew I had my own promise to keep. And nothing was going to stop me from honoring that vow.

"I will follow you to whatever end, Keera Waateyith'thir."

My lips parted to give him that last farewell. All I had was a fool's hope that I could undo what another Faemother had done. Faelin herself had told me that I would not survive it. It would drain my gift completely and my life too.

Or many, many small ones.

I spotted Rheih's supplies. I assumed Faelin was referring to the other Fae when she'd said that, but Syrra had taught me that magic powers were only one kind of gift the Elverin could receive. I pulled out of Riven's embrace. I had an idea and I had to move fast.

"I don't think a bowl is going to save you." Rheih clucked her tongue as I rummaged through the shelves. I yanked the ingredients open, throwing the lids to the ground as I grabbed what I needed.

"If you don't stop, I'll be delivering his royal arse a corpse." Rheih swatted my head but I ducked.

I handed her a bowl. "The green paste. Now, and fast."

Rheih's eyes narrowed as I started pummeling cedar and birch leaves in my own bowl.

"How much do we need?"

"As much as you have."

Rheih whistled and Vrail and Nikolai appeared. I glanced around looking for Gwyn but didn't see her. Dynara must have left her lying among the injured somewhere quiet. I untied my leather vest, not caring that my entire torso was exposed to everyone within sight. Riven stared as I started slathering the thick paste along my arms.

"Go!" I shouted at him, nodding in the direction of Feron. I couldn't do everything.

Riven placed his palm over his chest and then his eyes, saluting me as a fellow warrior. And then he was gone.

Nikolai shoved a bowl into my hands. "I think it's best if you—"

"This isn't the time to be a prude." I shoved the bowl back. "Cover the scars along my sides."

Nikolai swallowed and balled the thick paste onto his palm. It was cool and damp. I spread it thin, trying to cover as many of my scars as possible. By the time we finished, it looked like I was wearing a green tunic.

Perfect.

I walked out of the tent. From the elevation of the hill, I could see the thousands of slain bodies Damien hadn't even tried to collect. It would take dozens of pyres to burn them all. Vrail sobbed quietly as I walked down the well-worn path the scouts had carved into the hill ferrying bodies back to the tent.

Elaran stood beside the trail and lifted her sword. "*Niinokwenar. Ganawiithir. Mayith'thir,*" she shouted.

Faemother. Protector. Savior.

The words echoed back, again and again, as the Shades lifted their swords for me to walk under. I kept my chin high though it trembled as I passed warriors with broken arms still lifting their swords in salute. We were all Shades until the very end. As I walked onto the battlefield, I saw Gerarda ducking behind one of the rocks Feron had pulled from the ground. She gave me a stiff nod and pumped her fist two times. Riven had given her my message. I squeezed my fist at my side in answer. I was too far away for Damien's scouts to see it, but Gerarda knew what it was.

Thank you.

In the distance an Elvish horn blew, low and forlorn as the sea slashed across their remaining ship. A smile tugged at my lips, happy to know that Myrrah would see tomorrow. My skin tightened as I saw Damien standing at the top of the white wall. I hadn't thought he would be daring enough to come himself. But while he would hide during the battle, he would always come to claim the victory. I fought the urge to fly up and stab him through with my dagger. But I needed to conserve what was left of my power. I had one last move to play, and if I did it right, Damien's death would come for him.

Five black guards stood behind him. The Bow and Arrow I recognized, but the other faces were new—some only just appointed to replace the ones Dynara killed. Their pristine cloaks and armor almost glistened in the torchlight. I stopped just out of range of Damien's archers. He smirked down at me.

"Citizens of Koratha," he shouted to the crowd that spilled out of the city and stood along the wall to watch my death. "May this day be known forevermore as the day your king vanquished the traitorous Fae of the west. Know that this death"—Damien raised a small dagger and pointed it down at me—"will only be the first. My might can no longer be questioned, and rest of the Fae will succumb to my army and Arsenal by the morrow." Damien's chest glowed; he was wearing one of the remaining pendants. His arm shook as he spoke, his temples damp. The pendant drained his energy.

"Keera has shown the vile nature of the Fae. They cannot help it, as my father knew. She convinced her people to go to war for her *pride*, knowing there was no chance she would prevail. Her hubris has cost her people their freedom, their dignity, and their lives." Damien's lip curled as he spoke, the calm mask he usually wore completely removed.

"But such selfishness is a mark of the Fae. Their lack of pedigree." Damien turned to face the crowd behind him. "Their selfishness and deceit have no place in a civilized society. It is why my father banished them from the kingdom. But I will not make my father's mistake. I will not rest until there are no Fae left to speak of." The pendant glowed brighter and one of the *shirak* circling above let out a bloodcurdling shriek.

Damien turned back, pointing the dagger at me once more. "Bring the gallows out to her."

Wooden wheels creaked against the pebbled ground as a dozen men pushed out a broken catapult. A thick beam was nailed horizontally across the center. It was hardly a gallows, but the noose would pull just as tight.

"I get no final words then?" I shouted up to Damien.

The crowd murmured uneasily.

"You have destroyed their city and killed their kin." Damien extended his arms out on either side of him. "No one cares what your final words are, Keera, protector of none."

I smiled. They didn't need to hear them.

"*Miithi'wiinar,*" I whispered.

Again.

And again.

And again.

At first I didn't feel anything except a tingle along my skin. But the tingle worsened until it felt like each scar was being recut by an icy blade.

"What is she doing?" Damien balked, walking backward toward the stairs. The Arsenal tightened around him, but everyone else went silent. My whispers grew to chants until I was groaning through the pain, but I didn't stop.

"Enough," Damien shouted, and his pendant pulsed. One of the *shirak* dove from its towering height. But then a beam of pure light burst from the ground behind me. The beast was obliterated into strands of shadow. I turned and saw Gerarda fall to her knees, reaching out for something on the ground to hold her steady. I needed to act now.

My flesh still burned as I lifted my arms and let the ground beneath my feet launch into the sky. I moved so swiftly the next *waateyshir* didn't notice until I used my gust to clear a hole through the smoke and thick rays of sunlight poured down on them. The shadowy beasts shrieked in terror, flapping their wings to move away from the light. Pieces of earth fell from the pillar as I pushed it to the point of breaking, trying to reach as high as it would take me. I soared past the smoke until cold mist pelted my face. Pain flooded my body. I had pushed myself to the brink of burnout. My skin sizzled against the cold air as the pillar beneath lurched and began to fall away.

I leaped off the rock, bloodstone dagger in hand. My arms flung backward as I traveled in the direction of the two suns and aimed my blade for the shadow seal that Faelin had made.

My breath hitched. Had I missed? Had I misunderstood? But then the tip of my blade scratched something hard, and I heard a rip. A wave crashed through me, a hundred times more powerful than anything I'd felt breaking the seals. My heart tore inside my chest, and I could feel my healing gift struggling to stitch it back together with every beat. I screamed as my magic was pushed past burnout and I lost control. My gusts swelled around me as lightning cracked through the sky. My breath hitched, and I knew it would be the last one I ever took.

It was a breath of victory.

The names on my arms began to burn. Each one turned hot and then cooled, somehow stoking my magic so it never completely failed. Name after name, scar after scar, new magic bore itself into me, tethering me to life by the thinnest thread. The shadow sun rained down molten sunlight. It poured like the fiery brimstone of Volcar, but it was not crimson fire, but white sunlight. Pure light magic that sizzled through the smoke, carving huge holes in Damien's shield of darkness.

I started to fall with it. A large piece caught the wing of one of the *waateyshirak* and it screeched in agony before it was consumed in pure light too. My eyes shut, unable to behold the sight. I kept them closed as I fell, seeing the flashes of light through my eyelids and feeling the shrieks of dying *waateyshirak* rumble my bones.

The cold air welcomed me as I passed through the smoke. Even though my magic was almost depleted, I transformed into my other form and let my wings catch my fall. The tower I had built crumbled to the ground leaving only a small portion of it standing.

I perched there, transforming back into my Fae self. Liquid sunlight continued to fall, mixing with the rain from the storm my outburst had created. Most of the *waateyshirak* were gone. A few had become nothing but specks in the smoking fumes of the Dead Wood. But they were a manageable number for the Elverin to hunt after I ran Damien through with my dagger.

The rain washed the rest of the paste from my skin and the soldiers gasped as they noticed my scars. I looked down. Each one had turned gold, their names etched into my flesh like a tapestry stitched with auric thread. Every name had blessed me with a tiny gift, just like the one I had blessed on Gerarda's shoulders. None were enough to break Faelin's magic on their own, but together they had saved my life. Or given me another.

I conjured some water to project my voice. Damien and his soldiers didn't need to know how close my magic had come to drying out.

"The *waateyshirak* are vanquished." I looked down at the soldiers. "Drop your swords now and no other need die."

There was a short pause and then a chorus of metal striking the ground. Damien scoffed in disbelief as half his army ran for the shore, leaving him behind to face his death.

I couldn't help the smirk crawling up my lips. "Damien has told you nothing but lies. The Elverin do not wish to harm you. Everyone shall be housed, fed, and cared for. Mortal and Halfling alike. If the king accepts his death, then no one else need die with him."

Damien lifted a frantic arm. "Seize her!"

But not even the Arsenal moved. Murmurs in the crowds turned to chants.

"Seize him!" they shouted. "Take the king!"

I grinned at Damien, but he didn't move. There was no scowl on his face. I wasn't sure if he was still breathing. I realized he wasn't in his mind at all. My gaze swept through the crowd, looking for what soldier Damien had taken over. The only way he would leave himself defenseless was if he thought he could strike first. The new Arsenal stayed in their positions, none clutching a weapon. I leaned forward looking for someone with one black eye in the crowd below, but I didn't see anything but sorrowful and shocked faces.

I heard the draw of a bow behind me. I turned, seeing too late that Damien had a soldier behind my back. I lurched to the side, but the arrow pierced my back, sticking me through the shoulder. I yelped in pain, falling to my knees as the man drew another arrow. But then his face went blank, and he looked down to see the sword that pierced through his chest.

Gerarda pulled out her weapon and stared down in awe. Not at the man that she had killed, but at the blade that now shone bright gold.

Faelin's sword.

Syrra's sword.

The Blade had claimed Gerarda.

She held up the golden blade and a bolt of lightning bellowed from the sky. The crowds of Koratha exploded into chaos. Soldiers fled for the beaches while Mortals ran for refuge, believing that the Elverin were about to sack the city. But the Halflings walked outside the gates in awe. They stared at the amber streaks along the white wall where so many of their kin had been hung and turned away. Laughter broke out as they crossed the field toward the torches Feron and the others had lit. Tears blurred my vision as I turned back to find Damien along the wall, but he was gone. I yanked the arrow from my shoulder and sighed.

A coward until the very end.

Gerarda wiped her blade on her trousers.

"Nice sword," I said, wrapping my arms around her.

She laughed. "Nice scars." Her fingers trailed over the gold of my bicep. We were the warriors who had lived, the ones with the responsibility to carry on.

I looked down at the golden blade. "I cannot think of anyone more worthy than you to carry it."

"I would have preferred if its last owner still wielded it." Gerarda cleared her throat. "Her sacrifice will not be forgotten." She turned back toward the tents where Elaran waited, injured and now safe.

"Go," I said. "Go find her." I knew how desperately she wanted to throw her arms around Elaran because it was all I wanted to do with Riven. But I still had a promise to fulfill.

Gerarda unlaced her chest plate and handed me her tunic. It fit snugly over my shoulders but was better than nothing. The fabric warmed against the heat of my scars. Her jaw pulsed four times. "Do you want help?"

"No. This I should do on my own." I nodded to the ships. "Make sure the city is defended and ships go out well stocked. I don't want them raiding the kingdom now that we've just won it back."

"It's no longer a kingdom." Gerarda's voice caught in her throat. "It's just our home."

"Go protect it," I whispered with pride. "I'll join you shortly."

She nodded and ran south to her love, and I ran north away from mine.

CHAPTER FORTY-SEVEN

It didn't take an eagle's eyesight to know where Damien had fled to. He had nowhere else to hide now that his people had turned on him. But his people didn't know of the cells below the city. It was a secret to most. That's why it was where he had spent most of the battle. The place where it had all started for me. The place of my nightmares, so even in victory, Damien had to remind me of the pain he'd caused.

The years Maerhal and I had spent locked down there. The weeks he had caged Nikolai inside the same cell as some kind of mental torture.

The tunnel to the black cells had been cleared. Thick wooden posts replaced the jagged rocks from the previous cave-in and protected against another. My mouth went dry as a hint of Elven wine wafted up from the lowest depths of the cavern, carried on a whistling breeze that reminded me of a faraway scream. My fists tightened around the blades I'd taken from dead men, and I listened for heartbeats waiting in the cells below. There was only one, faint in the distance, but it still sent a shiver down my spine.

This was likely one last trap Damien had set. I turned back to where the light from the upper level was just visible along the steep hill. I thought about waiting for the others. I shouldn't go alone. But I wanted to be the one to end it. And I wanted to do it on my own. Thirty years of grief had hardened my resolve. My magic coursed through my veins and tingled in every muscle. Whatever Damien had waiting for me down there, I could face and win.

We already had.

I pulled a faebead from the small pouch tied to my belt and crushed it with the toe of my boot. I followed the amber glow with my arms held in front of me, ready for a surprise attack from any twist or curve of the tunnel. But none of Damien's guards were lurking in the shadows. Instead, I found the room of black cells well-lit for the first time in my life. Giant torches flamed along the walls every few feet, filling the air with the stench of smoke. I didn't cough. Somehow the fire felt more like a cleanse, burning away the air Damien breathed before it reached my lungs.

He was sitting on his throne. I could only imagine his soldiers' faces when he ordered them to carry the gilded chair into the depths of the earth for their king. Did they know this would be his tomb? Maybe that's what Damien wanted. He sipped from a bulbous goblet decorated with rubies the size of my fist. Black currant and cherry filled the smoky air as he drank.

Damien's eyes narrowed. He gestured at the slab of marble beside him. There was a canister of wine and a matching goblet. "Join me for a last drink?"

I raised a brow. "Your last or mine?"

There was something smug in Damien's smile that set me on edge. He seemed too pleased with himself for a man determined to die on his father's chair.

"That depends." His good eye glinted over the goblet as he took another sip. "Though I suspect both."

I scoffed. "Your shadow army is destroyed. Your soldiers are dead or too wounded to fight. And the armada you purchased has fled."

Damien's mouth didn't even twitch. "Which is why I came here. A fitting place for the end of our game, I think." His jade eye looked at the ground. He had placed himself directly between the doors of my cell and Maerhal's. Bile crawled up my throat.

"How do you still not see what you've done? The people you've toyed with, the pain you've caused your own citizens? Are they truly nothing more to you than some pawns on a board to move and sacrifice at will?"

Damien drummed his fingers along his armrest. "Why should I care for the fear of those too meek to seek power when I was on the path to become a god?"

"You have fallen short." I glanced at the one gray hair above his left ear.

Damien scowled. "I should have attacked the Faeland years ago. The day my father found you in that Rift and took it as a sign of fortune rather than an omen of rebellion."

I smirked. None of the titles anyone had ever given me felt true. Not Blade, not savior or leader. But omen felt right. Haunting. Just like my face would haunt Damien into whatever world followed this. I let my hand fall to the white hilt of my dagger but didn't unsheathe it. Damien noticed and his lip twitched. Not in fear, but impatience.

I tilted my head. I had been dancing with Damien for too long and had witnessed too many people's last moments not to find the reaction odd. A man who spent his entire life searching for immortality would not be eager in death, even when he knew death was inescapable.

Damien still had one last secret.

I turned and scoured the room. I sent a gust of wind up the tunnel, letting the faelight that had followed me light the path, but no one was there. I stilled. No heartbeats other than Damien's or mine. We were alone. There was no ambush waiting for me.

"I'm glad to see you're learning." Damien's smirk was devilish.

I didn't waste time on questions. I used the thrashing power in my stomach to pull a thin strand of wine from Damien's carafe. It floated through the air like a snake, slithering toward his lips. He refused to open them, so I sent the wine up his nose. Damien jerked in his chair as the cool liquid made a sharp curve down his throat. But I didn't let it fall into his stomach. I wanted answers, and despite the ornate crown Damien had on his head, he was just like any other man. He would succumb to pain.

"It hurts, doesn't it?" I walked toward him as he writhed, and I placed a hand on the back of his chair. I leaned down close enough that my fangs could rip out his throat if needed. "It will only get worse as your lungs fill with fluid. Soon they'll be so heavy they'll begin to tear."

Thick tears streamed from Damien's bloodshot eye, but the black one was completely dry. He tried to breathe but his mouth only gurgled with wine-stained spit.

"If you don't tell me, the next flush will not be so gentle." I let go of the throne and stopped my magic. The wine fell in thick drops as Damien collapsed. He coughed up mouthfuls of bloody wine onto the ground and broke into a fit of laughter when he could finally taste air again.

"All the ways you could torture me, and you go for drowning?" He spat the rest of the wine at my boots. "Such magic is a waste on the likes of you."

My lip curled back in disgust. Even crumpled at my feet, Damien still hungered for the power to hurt people. I fought the urge to drown those fantasies from his mind forever. "Speak or I will show you how *inventive* I can be."

Damien wiped his mouth on his sleeve and leaned back on the throne, throwing his arm onto the seat. His damp skin was warmed by the glow of the torches.

I lifted my hand, fingers laced in flame. "Now."

"Magic is a powerful force." Damien's smug grin returned though his neck twinged in pain with each breath. "You have more than demonstrated how it can be used against your enemies, but you forget, Keera, that your enemy can use it against you."

The flames in my hand flared, turning almost white. "Do I look like someone patient enough for riddles and speeches?"

Damien lifted his chin. "Do you recall that blood oath you made?" His lip twitched upward. "Outside of Caerth. You smeared your amber blood across that pitiful Elf's face and swore no harm would come to him."

The blood drained from my face, leaving nothing but cold fear. "How do you know about that? Why would Nikolai—"

Damien raised the brow over his black eye. "He never said a word. Loyal to a fault."

He tapped his temple. Nikolai might not have said anything, but Damien didn't share a connection with his mind. He couldn't have plucked the memory from Nikolai's dreams. I had almost forgotten the oath entirely. Why would Nikolai worry himself with that memory while locked in a dungeon?

There was only one other person Damien could have learned that from.

Collin.

"But he wasn't there . . ." I thought aloud trying to piece together Damien's last puzzle. My breath hitched. Collin hadn't been there the night I made that oath, but he had been in the audience the night of Nikolai's feast celebrating the return of Maerhal. The night he told the Elverin of the oath I had made only days into our alliance to help me earn their trust.

I closed my hand and the flames sputtered out. "What does an old oath have to do with this? Is this truly what you want to spend your last words discussing?"

Damien shook his head like a disappointed tutor about to chastise a student. "I know that when you made that oath, you knew little of magic. You didn't know what you had promised. But how can you not see it now?"

I snarled, making sure my fangs were on full display. "I would never hurt Nikolai."

"Yes, you would."

I kicked him in the gut. Damien merely coughed and wiped his face again. Red blood smeared across his jaw and cheek. It was like an unmasking, his feral, predatory self finally on display with nothing to hide. The sight unnerved me.

"Explain or I will burn you until your skin blisters to ash, then heal you so I can do it again."

The briefest look of fear flashed across Damien's face before settling into cool resolve. He hoisted his other arm behind him so he was leaning against the throne, casual and unperturbed. Damien still thought he was in control. I gritted my teeth and started to pull the air from his lungs. He coughed and waved his hand.

"There was no time limit on your oath, Keera." He paused, making sure I had ceased my attack before continuing. "You made yourself vulnerable. For as long as you and Nikolai both live, you cannot do him harm. If you do, you die."

I laughed. "Most people don't have trouble not inflicting harm on their friends." I had bruised and nicked Nikolai many times in training practice. And I had definitely pained him emotionally more times than I liked to admit. None of those instances had triggered the oath. Damien was too confident. Feron had taught me enough of magic to know that the oath would only hold me to the spirit in which it was made. That night I wanted to convince Riven and Syrra that I wouldn't kill their friend. And Nikolai was nothing but safe around my blades.

"Yes, I'm aware of the sentimentality of lesser creatures." Damien started to pull at the cufflinks along his left sleeve. "It's what makes you so easy to manipulate."

He pulled back the fine black fabric of his sleeve. A burn circled his wrist. It was beautiful, delicate wisps of fine lines that would settle to an almost unnoticeable silver.

It matched the one around Nikolai's wrist.

"This is why you didn't kill him?" Rage radiated through me with so much force my voice shook.

Damien gave me a feline smirk. "I *couldn't* kill him. If he dies, I die. That's how tethers work."

I froze. Tethers were rivers that flowed in both directions.

"So when you kill me, you will be killing your precious Nikolai too," Damien said, reading the fear on my face. "And that blood oath you were so foolish to have made will claim your life for it. I may not have won our game, Keera, but neither have you."

My lips quivered as I threw my words at him like flaming arrows. "We have shattered your kingdom into pieces."

Damien's grin was dangerous. "And if you kill me, you won't live to see them fall."

"Did you think that would protect you?" I paced in front of him, needing somewhere to focus my energy so I could think. "Bind your life to Nikolai's, and we would let you live out the rest of your days in a cell instead of hanging you from the city wall?"

Damien jutted his chin at my exposed arms with a laugh. "You wear the truth on your flesh and still don't see it?" He shook his head. "You have been weighing the value of people's lives for your entire tenure as Blade. Deciding whose life was worth the risk and whose was not. Rudimentary and uncalibrated, but the math is written on your skin all the same."

"Make your point," I demanded through clenched teeth.

"I didn't tether my life to that dirty Elf as a chance to save myself, Keera. I know you too well for that." There was a glint in Damien's dark eye. His tongue ran across his bottom lip. Damien wanted this. He knew that one life, even one I cared about or would kill a thousand soldiers for, would not be enough for me to spare him.

It wasn't worth the risk.

"You have a debt to pay," he whispered. Damien knew the truth of it now; he knew how we had deceived him, but he also knew exactly what that night meant to me.

I had a vow to honor.

A promise.

Damien unbuttoned his collar to reveal the glowing light embedded into his chest. The pendant. Damien was using it to call back one of the remaining *shirak.* A loud screech shook the ground as the beast circled overhead. The skies had filled with smoke again, allowing it to fly freely. There was no time to get anyone else. There was no time to defend them before the beast attacked. My heart hammered in my chest. The fields were full of innocents collecting the dead. Many who would die if I didn't end this now. I could see Damien's heart beating behind the pendant—they were fused as one. Breaking it would kill him. And that would kill Nikolai.

My throat tightened. Had I not fought Riven and the others on trading the pendant because I knew that Nik's life was not worth hundreds? Had I not said that I would want any of them to make the right choice and let me die?

Damien had put me in the same position—balancing the value of people's lives until the very end. The job had always been mine. At least this time it would cost me my own.

I clasped the hilt of my dagger and pulled it out of its sheath. I couldn't save Nikolai. He wouldn't want me to, not if it meant dozens of deaths in an attack from the remaining *shirak*. But perhaps he could have a few more moments with Vrail. One last kiss, the farewell I had never gotten with Brenna.

Death didn't scare me. Hildegard and Brenna would be waiting. Syrra, too. And my promise would be fulfilled. I had worked through my regrets. I had overcome that darkness that had taken root in me. I would die happy knowing that Riven would have the chance to do the same. My only qualm was having to take Nikolai with me.

I waved my hand and two orbs of wind appeared, the size of a small faelight. I gently coaxed the smaller one to my lips and whispered a message for Vrail.

"Go to Nikolai. His time has come." With a second wave of my hand, I sent the ball whirling up the tunnel to find her. I only hoped Nikolai was close enough and she had enough time to reach him before I plunged my dagger through Damien's heart.

The second orb floated on my finger, as gentle as a kiss. I had whispered so many things to Riven in our short time together, shown him my love in ways words could never match. I had to trust that he would hold onto the truth of those memories as I said the things Riven needed to hear into the braided gust of wind.

"There is no one more worthy of my love than you, *rovaa*. I regret nothing, not a moment. Take care of Gwyn and Gerarda. May you find as much comfort with them as they gave me." I took a ragged breath and wiped my nose. "Braid your hair into mine and kiss me one more time before you light my pyre. And when you bury my *diizra,* bury Brenna's with it. Because my heart is yours, but hers was mine. Live long and well, Riventh Numenthira, I will wait for you."

My heart split in half as I waved my hand and my final words were sent to Riven. I was grateful that his powers were gone, so the world would not be launched into an endless night when he heard them. I lifted the dagger. The *shirak* shrieked outside, skating the walls of the tunnel. There was no time left. Damien wheezed over his throne, the pendant in his chest glowing brighter.

Blood oozed from his mouth. "Touching."

I didn't say a word. Those last words I had spoken to Riven were the truest I had ever said in my life. If I was going to die, I wanted to die with my love for him coating my lips and not a snide remark for a man I loathed.

A tear fell from my cheek and landed on Damien's forehead as he looked up at me. His mouth fell open and a pitiful puff of air escaped in shock as I rammed my bloodstone dagger through his chest. It shattered the pendant and pierced Damien's heart—the dagger he had made me use to claim Brenna's life. It was only fitting that it should be the one to end his and mine too. My only regret was that Nikolai would be caught in the bloodshed, but that was worth the end of Aemon's line.

The terror was over.

Damien fell to the ground first. He rasped for air, and each exhale splattered blood along his face and the ground. Something sharp pierced my leg and I crumpled. When I looked, nothing was there. The magic of my broken oath was invisible but deadly. It pierced my arm and my back arched in pain. Then it sliced through my chest just as I had with Damien and everything went still. Warm blood soaked through my leathers and covered my belly. I lay on the ground staring at Damien's face. The ring of amber in his black eye rippled like the small waves in a pond. I watched as they slowed, the life draining out of me too.

Blood pooled from Damien's lips, thick and hot against my face. He could barely move his mouth, but somehow he had the strength for one last word.

"Draw."

My laugh was nothing but my own blood. It spotted his face in amber, and I smiled knowing the last image I would see was Damien coated in the color of blood he hated. I hoped they didn't wipe it off before they presented his body to the city. The last of my magic whirled around the dungeon and blew out the torches. I closed my eyes, imagining that the shadows were one last embrace from Riven, and died.

CHAPTER FORTY-EIGHT

The pain lashed once more, and I screamed. When I opened my eyes, it was no longer dark in the room. Silver moonlight and warm daylight flooded the walls from the dozen faelights floating along the top of the tunnel.

I winced as Damien shrieked beside me. Gwyn pulled the dagger from his chest, and I felt the magic that had pierced my own heart recede. I lifted a limp hand. "Stop."

Gwyn ignored me. She flipped Damien onto his back and used her finger to trace a spell onto his chest. We gasped in unison as Damien's body began to heal and my own healing gift stitched my wounds together.

"You're only prolonging this," I muttered to Gwyn. I wanted to explain it all, to tell her that she was only giving Nikolai and the others false hope too, but I didn't yet have the strength.

Damien's eyes opened, and I saw the moment his vision focused enough to see Gwyn's amber eyes studying his wounds. Damien coughed out a laugh. "Always so unexpected."

Gwyn's top lip twitched. "I heard what you did. Keera is not going to die for you."

Her fingers glowed and she etched a rune into the glass of Damien's pendant. It shattered into pieces. Damien groaned in pain, but Gwyn's healing spell started lacing back the sinew and torn flesh.

I stared at the pendant on the ground. Damien was no longer a threat.

I flipped to my side and cursed my magic for working so slowly. I knew what Gwyn was going to do. Her eyes were feral. She blamed Damien for everything. Her years of torment, her loss of budding love. She was going to heal Damien completely so the oath that had almost taken my life would be in place once more. Then she would stab that blade back through his chest, killing Damien and Nikolai too.

"Gwyn, no!"

"Don't fret, Keera." Damien lifted his hand to Gwyn's soft cheek. "Gwyn doesn't have the heart to kill me."

Gwyn smirked. "You're right. I don't."

She glanced at me to see that I had fully healed too before tracing her finger along his chest. Damien's scream shook the walls but Gwyn didn't stop.

I gathered the strength to sit up and witnessed the horror of what Gwyn had done. Damien's chest caved open, revealing his beating heart like a bear had torn through his sternum. It would be more than enough to kill a man, but Damien wasn't dying. Whatever magic Gwyn had weaved was healing Damien just enough to keep him from bleeding out.

"Gwyn, what are you doing?" I asked, petrified.

She picked up the blood-soaked dagger and wiped it off on her trousers. "Getting retribution." Her fingers spelled something else along the blade and the bloodstone shattered onto her lap. I gasped like the wound had been inflicted on me. That blade had been my companion for more than thirty years, had stoked our own rebellion, and Gwyn had broken it without a moment's thought.

She grabbed the largest of the pieces and held it tight in her palm. I blinked in horror as amber and gold blood ran down her arm in thick streaks.

She held the fractured piece against Damien's heart. His scream was beyond human but he didn't die. Gwyn had used her magic to push the limits further than nature would ever allow.

I swallowed the dryness in my throat. It wasn't my magic Damien should have worried about.

Gwyn ran the jagged piece of blade along his heart. "Is this why you did it?" she whispered. "It's intoxicating holding someone's life in my hands, knowing I have the power to cause you as much pain as you caused me."

She cut again and Damien's shriek cracked halfway up his throat.

"Gwyn, that's enough—"

"Which organ of yours should I tear from your body?" Gwyn's voice was drained of all its joy and laughter. Damien glanced at me with wide, terrified eyes. I froze. I hadn't pictured torturing Damien before I killed him; all I had wanted to see was the smugness drain from his face as his blood pooled along my blade.

And I had.

But what Gwyn was doing was more than murder, and it would scar her in ways I couldn't even comprehend. I crawled across the tunnel and placed a hand on her shoulder. "Gwyn," I said, ignoring Damien's screams. "End this."

She caressed the back of my hand. For a moment she was the young girl in my room, lounging in the sand before the worst had happened.

"Very well." Gwyn traced her finger along his chest, and I thought she was healing him, but instead she coated her finger in blood. Then she brought it down the middle of her face and began to chant.

"*Moroq.*"

The same words Nikolai had told us about what Damien had done to him. The ritual that Aemon had used to bind Gwyn's foremother to him, and Damien had used to bind Nikolai to himself.

Gwyn was creating a tether.

I tried to stop her but I couldn't. I looked down at the back of my hand. Gwyn had not been caressing it at all but spinning a rune to hold me in place. All I could do was watch as the tether took hold around her wrist and then carved itself into Damien a few inches above the tether that bound him to Nikolai.

Gwyn stood over the false king. "How many nights did you spend tormenting me? The burns and bruises?" Gwyn scowled. "Sometimes the threats were worse. Your quick visits to my chambers just to show that you could hurt me anywhere, anytime. Nowhere was safe."

Gwyn stopped at his boots and crossed her arms. "It would take months to match the pain you inflicted on me." She huffed a laugh as Damien shuddered in anticipation of what was to come. "I wouldn't have though. Knowing you were dead would have been enough. Eventually. But then you had to make another tether. Claim another life as yours—as if witnessing mine and my mother's torment wasn't enough for you."

Gwyn stepped up along Damien's body with the fragmented piece of my blade still in her palm. Thick drops of amber blood fell onto his face and open mouth. Gwyn's lips tugged to the side as she bent down and whispered, "You sealed your fate, Damien. You wanted immortality, and I shall give it to you."

Her amber eyes flashed as she pushed the jagged piece of blade into Damien's heart. The veins in his neck bulged and his back arched against Gwyn's hand. She pushed him flat against the ground and drew another rune along his collarbone.

She stood as Damien's chest cavity stitched itself back together with a piece of my dagger inside his heart.

Gwyn wiped his blood on her sleeve and opened the trap door beside Damien. It was the same cell Maerhal had spent her life in. The same one Damien had kept her son in. Now it would be his prison too.

Stale air blew up from the depths. "You will not die," Gwyn said at the whimpering pile that Damien had become. "You will thirst but not drink. You will hunger but never eat. My magic will sustain you just enough to keep you alive. Each breath will cause you pain just as you pained so many. You will live in torment until the day I die." She held up her wrist where the new tether was marked. She kicked Damien in his chest and he fell back into the hole.

He landed with a loud *thump*, his whimpers echoing up the pit.

Gwyn giggled. "Or maybe Nikolai will die first and take you with him." She leaned over the hole. "Though we both plan to live a very, *very,* long time," she shouted down at him, and then slammed the door shut.

Gwyn stared at the latched door for a while before she turned around. Her face was changed. There was nothing left of the young girl I once knew. Her soft cheeks were sunken and hollow like those last few spells had fed on her and not just her magic.

She had done something she could never take back.

I stood and grabbed her arm. "Are you really going to leave him there forever?"

"And if I did?" Gwyn's jaw pulsed. "Has he not earned it?"

I swallowed. "My only concern is for you." I held up her newly branded wrist. "He held power over you for so long and when you're finally free of it, you—"

Gwyn gently pulled her hand free of my grip. "Keera, I love you. But I am old enough to make my own choices."

I let my hand fall and stood there unsure of how to respond.

A hint of a smile pulled at Gwyn's mouth. "But I appreciate your concern. If Damien spends a month or two writhing in pain, it will not scar me. He can wait for you to establish Elvish society once again."

"And then?"

Gwyn shrugged. "And then you can decide what to do with him. Hold a trial for him in front of the council. If they wish him dead, I will try to find a way to break his tethers." Her face turned serious. "But I shattered that blade for a reason, Keera. Your debt is paid. When Damien dies, it will not be you who ends him."

I opened my mouth, but Gwyn grabbed both of my hands.

"Promise me, Keera," Gwyn demanded, knowing the weight that word held for me. "We have more than earned a life beyond this. And there are still so many places that you need to show me. Set your blade down."

A tear rolled down my cheek. The whiplash of the past hour flooded my body and I swayed backward against the wall. My life wouldn't end in these godforsaken cells.

It wouldn't end at all.

I tightened my grip on Gwyn. I wasn't sure if I wanted to enter into a promise so soon after releasing myself from the first. But Gwyn was right, it was time for me—for her—to live. And that I had already promised to do.

I wrapped my arm around her neck. "I promise, Gwyn."

CHAPTER FORTY-NINE

I FOUND RIVEN AT THE EDGE of the battlefield. Hundreds of Elverin were laid out, some already wrapped in linen for burial and some merely covered by their bloodstained cloaks.

"It hurts to breathe," Uldrath whispered to Riven, who had his arm wrapped around the boy. His tiny hand held the limp wrist of his father, who was covered by a brown cloak.

Riven's eyes were misted, but he cleared his throat to answer him. "It will feel like that for a while. Your lungs need time to learn to breathe in air that your father has never touched."

Uldrath looked up at Riven, thin rivers dripping down his face. "But what if it stops and I forget him?"

Riven pulled out the *diizra* from his neck. "Your mother and you will make one of these for your father. And you'll carry it for a year. That's how long it will take for your lungs to adjust and for your sadness to lessen." Riven glanced at me, relief flooding his face, but he kept speaking. "Then you will plant his *diizra* back home, and Vrail will help you see him again."

Uldrath wiped his nose. "So he's not gone?"

"None of them is." Riven squeezed the boy and knelt to face him eye to eye. "Your father never wanted to leave you, Drath. But he fought today so you had a life larger than two small cities. And now you do because of him and all the others who fought too."

Uldrath's nose wrinkled. "I would have lived with him at home forever." He looked around at the burnt forest and the blood-soaked earth. "I don't like it here anyway." His lower lip trembled, and Riven pulled him into an embrace, holding him until his sobs tired.

There were no words to cure a pain like that.

It wasn't fair. It wasn't right. It just *was*.

The price of freedom was paid for in blood and grief. It tore at my heart to know that some as young as Uldrath would pay it too. Noemdra came and scooped up her son. Her tears had dried to flaky lines on her face.

Riven laced his fingers through mine but didn't say a word as we walked through the rows and rows of dead. Nikolai and Vrail stood at the end of the row closest to the tent. Their hands were tied together as they stared down at Syrra and Fyrel.

"Where's Gwyn?" I asked. I'd lost track of her when we returned.

Nikolai nodded in the direction of Rheih's tent. "She's helping the wounded. I don't think she can handle seeing this just yet."

I grasped Nikolai's shoulder, and he wrapped his arm around me. Finally, the reality of what we'd done came crashing down. There was so much to do, so much to rebuild, but it was ours to do it. But Syrra was gone. And Pirmiith. And Fyrel. And so many pieces of myself I didn't know if I was truly alive. Perhaps I had died on the battlefield when I tore into the second sun, only to wake up in an identical body made of grief. A sob burst through my chest and didn't stop. My knees gave out and Riven was there to catch me. He cradled me against his chest and just started walking.

He walked for what felt like hours and all the way I cried. Tears for everyone we had lost, everyone who was in pain. But for the first time I cried for myself. The weight of my promise no longer tugged at my shoulders, and despite the grief, I was lighter than I had ever been. Finally ready to leave my life as Blade behind and discover who Keera was.

Riven sat us down along the beach and I leaned against his chest, letting the rhythm of the waves count my breaths.

"Was it harder than you thought?" Riven whispered into my ear.

I turned my head to face him. "What part?"

"All of it." He wiped his eyes. "Killing Damien. I got your message and thought the worst."

I stilled. I wasn't going to keep what Gwyn had done a secret. I'd learned too well how fast a secret could spoil, but I didn't want to tell that story yet. It was too fresh, that pain too sharp to live through it again so quickly.

I cleared my throat. "I fulfilled my promise."

The words tasted only of the truth. I had pierced my dagger through Damien's heart just as I'd imagined a thousand times over. Just as he'd made me do to Brenna. I had never thought of what would come after. Now my entire body felt raw. Like I could break out into a fit of sobs or laughter at any moment. A rage bubbled low in my belly ready to boil at the slightest provocation.

Riven slipped the gold chain from his neck and handed the *diizra* to me. "Then this is yours again."

I clasped the pouch and let it dangle from my hand, not ready to put it on just yet.

"Did you mean it when you said you would follow me to whatever end?"

Riven's breathing stilled along my back. "Yes, that's as true now as it was then."

"And when we promised to do our best to *try*?" I pushed. "Did you mean that too?"

Riven lifted me off his chest and turned me around so I sat between his legs, folding my thighs over his. "*Diizra*, what do you mean to ask me?"

I took a deep breath. Somehow it felt like a betrayal to ask Riven something so big, so selfish. But I knew it was what I needed. What we *both* needed.

I lifted the *diizra*. "I want to do this right. I want a year." I cleared my throat. "I *need* a year. I never got the chance to mourn her, not truly, or really grieve what I've done. A year to let that settle without the threat of execution or war over my head—"

"You want to be alone." Riven's brow furrowed. "For a year?"

My shoulders fell. "Not entirely alone." I bit my lip, trying to find the words. "I just think I need time to discover who I am without the titles or the war room meetings . . . and I'm not going to find that if I trade one vice for another."

"Are you saying I'm bad for you?" Riven leaned back. "That I'm wine you cannot drink?"

"No, *rovaa*." I cupped his cheek. "But you could be. After so much darkness, I won't lie. I feel the need to bury myself in anything I can, anyone I can, to keep from feeling all this pain. But I don't want to do that." I brushed Brenna's *diizra* with my thumb. "I want to do what all Elverin before me have done. Spend the year healing and grieving and then come together ready and healed."

Riven leaned into my touch. "I will wait a century if you need it. We have the time."

I laughed and shook my head. "I don't think that will be necessary." I grabbed his hand. "You need time too, Riven. Your regrets still trail behind you."

His face fell. "That *will* take a century." His voice was full of spite.

"You see all my faults and failures yet you don't stack them up against my character. Why do you do that with your own?"

Riven swallowed. "It is not the same."

I tilted my head. "You told me that you saw me as a builder. But why can't you see that same skill in yourself?"

"Everything I've built has rotted away."

I turned back to the city we had freed. "You sparked the rebellion that did this. You imagined the future we now have."

Riven's mouth sat in a hard line.

I grazed my thumb along his bottom lip. "You told me of another dream. Maybe you should take the year to make it true."

Riven blinked. "What dream?"

"Vellinth," I answered. "You put too much faith in me. But that city is not my home, Riventh, it is yours. Take Darythir and all the Halflings that will join you and make it the home of your dreams."

Riven's mouth parted as if he could taste the laughter in the air. "Our dreams," he whispered. It was half hope, half question.

I leaned forward so my forehead pressed against his chin. "Build us a home, Riven, and I will join you in a year."

ONE YEAR LATER

EPILOGUE

THE SINGLE SUN SHONE down on us while the salty air wafted through my hair. It tickled my shoulders as I basked in the sunlight. It meant we were safe at least until the night came, but a *waateyshirak* hadn't been spotted near Koratha in months. Gerarda and her team had slain most of the surviving beasts, and I had quickly grown used to the peace.

I was glad to find that peace did not mean quiet. I sat for dinner each night with a rumbling belly and crawled into bed only dreaming of all the work I would do on the morrow. My hands had traded swords for hammers and axes. I forged homes by hand and with my gifts. Twelve short months and most of the cities had been repaired. At least well enough for the Elverin to start living in them again.

This was the last place on my list. The last home I wanted to make, not for me, but for all the Halflings who had grown up here too. I glanced at the crowd that had formed along the island.

Shades stood in groups, some had babes hung along their hips, while others stood in solemn couples ready to pay their respects to the ones we'd lost.

The Order was gone. It took weeks to clear the broken stone, and even though I could have patched the palace with my earth magic, I'd told the Elverin to clear it all away.

New beginnings shouldn't be haunted by ghosts.

But the ground remembers the roots even if the trees do not. I hadn't understood the depth of what Syrra had told me until after we'd won. Now I could only hope that she would be proud of what this island was to become. All those who had attended *Niikir'na* were not alive to pass those teachings on. And all of us who had lived at the Order wanted more than what we'd been given here.

I pulled the gold chain that had hung around my neck for the past year until the metal snapped. Nikolai stepped forward, a chain and *diizra* dangling from his palm too. He had decided there was no place else Syrra would rather be laid to rest. I grabbed his hand, and we walked over to where Myrrah was already waiting for us. She had worn her *diizra* for over a year.

She hadn't hesitated when I told her what I wanted to do. "Hildy would love it," she had whispered, holding her lover's ashes in her hands as I held Brenna's in mine.

Gerarda stood. Her hair was no longer short but flowed between her shoulder blades in the same half braid Syrra had worn. The golden blade was sheathed behind her back as always. I didn't know if it was the sword or the pride radiating from her cheeks, but she appeared taller somehow. Lighter, perhaps.

"It's time," Gerarda whispered, looking up at the sun that was about to hit midday.

Myrrah pulled her *diizra* from underneath her robe and handed it to Gerarda. Nikolai pressed his lips to his before placing the pouch in her other hand. I didn't give mine to her. Instead, I knelt along the grass and dug a hole with my bare hands. The damp earth clung to the callouses along my palms and caked under my nails, but I didn't care. I wanted the final resting place of the three women who had loved me, trained me, and befriended me to be warmed by my hand.

When the hole was deep enough, I placed all I had left of Brenna in the earth. A warmth spread through my limbs as I covered her *diizra,* finally laying her to rest. I had taken her with me across the entire continent. Myrrah had sailed me in circles as I searched for the perfect spot. The place that Brenna would have claimed as her own if she had lived. But nowhere was good enough. No view was pretty enough to settle in for eternity. So Brenna traveled all of Elverath only for me to bring her back to the only place she'd ever been. Yet I knew that was what she would've wanted. To rest easy upon the land she died on, standing as its protector, knowing it had been freed.

The wind whistled, and I swore it was the airy sound of Brenna's laugh. I patted the ground and three tears fell onto the soil as Nikolai did the same with Syrra's *diizra* to my left and Gerarda helped Myrrah bury Hildegard's to my right.

I stood and turned to the crowd behind me. Each person saved by the efforts of the Elverin we were laying to rest. Elaran broke from the group to help Myrrah take her place along the front of the crowd while Gerarda walked behind the small graves, her hands tucked behind her back. The two branches Syrra had carved into her shoulders were proudly on display. Tensing, she lifted her chin to look at me. "Are you ready?"

I nodded. Gerarda's harrowing voice drifted over the island, slow like a tide at first, but then as thrashing and commanding as the fiercest wave.

"Ish'kavra diiz'bithir ish'kavra."

From ash to flame to ash again.

A drum sounded in the distance and Gerarda's song warmed. She smiled as the final words left her lips, the ritual finally complete.

"El miinik dor zaagith dor miinik'awaa."

From seed to sprout to seed again.

I raised my arm over the ground and let myself be consumed by my magic. I had no thoughts, I had no intentions, I just let that warmth overwhelm me until the earth shook and golden light fell upon my cheeks. Thick roots burrowed into the ground underneath us in all directions.

Gargantuan trees sprouted from the island, each taller and larger than the Order that had once stood on the same ground. They were not Elder birch, nor willow like the Myram, but something altogether new. Fused at the base, they created a giant circle protected by a canopy of vines and flowers. Each trunk had a door, lit by faelights that illuminated the halls inside. They braided together, three distinct trees for three distinct warriors.

We had taken our prison and turned it into a home.

The crowd cheered as the three trees took their final shape. They rushed forward, eager to explore their new home, but I stayed rooted to the ground. Riven stood behind me. Even though he had kept to his word and given me space for the year, he did not rush me now. He only stood close enough for me to know he was there, but the choice was mine. I could feel the trepidation radiating off his skin. The year had healed us both in so many ways, but I knew Riven was still scared that I would not choose him at the end of it. The silly Halfling didn't realize this year had been exactly that. Me choosing him—us—so we could last a lifetime.

A year in the face of forever was nothing. And now we could begin again as we always should have been. Two whole people wanting to braid their lives together. No war or death to act as a catalyst. Just a simple choice. And I would always choose Riven.

I pushed off the ground and wiped my knees. I didn't turn to face him; instead I just walked backward, taking in the gigantic size of the tree in front of me until my back was pressed against his chest. Even then he didn't move. I lifted my arm and let my head rest in the crook of his neck as I played with his short hair. He'd shorn it completely to make enough braids for the funerals and had kept his hair only a few inches long. I turned my head to look at him and smiled when I saw he was already studying me.

His face was bright and his skin tanned from hours spent outside tending to the Halflings who split their time between Vellinth and the other cities. He buried his face in my hair, and I leaned against him, my body yearning for the touch I hadn't had for a year. It was a gentler touch, warmer too. As if both of us had learned to shine and now shone brighter as we stood together.

"I'm excited to go home, *rovaa,*" I whispered to Riven.

His hard face broke into unbridled joy. His thumb traced my bottom lip. "I'm excited to share it with you, *diizra.*"

Vrail appeared at my side and placed a hand along the trunk of the tree. "What should we call them?" she whispered. "Every tree needs a name."

"Baath'weywiin mithir," I answered.

I turned to the three figures who had appeared as soon as Vrail's hand touched the wood. Syrra and Hildegard nodded proudly, but I only had eyes for Brenna. She stood in the middle of them with a wide smile across her face and no scars along her eyes. Riven's hand tensed at my neck, and she bowed her head at him.

Riven bowed back, a tear falling from the corner of his eye and onto my cheek. Brenna laughed, twirling along the grass before breaking out into a full-speed run. I fought the urge to follow her and just settled in the moment, appreciating everything it had taken to get there. We would have as much time as we wanted for visits.

My throat caught, realizing the beauty of Vrail's gift meant that Riven and my family could meet the girl who had saved me so one day I could save them.

Vrail nodded, so engrossed in her own thoughts about the new tree that she hadn't noticed the three figures running through the meadow.

"I like that name," she said with a bobbing nod of approval. "The Promise Tree."

ACKNOWLEDGMENTS

KEERA'S STORY HAS COME TO AN END. Wow, that's the first time I'm writing those words down. I must admit, after so many words between us—me and Keera, me and you amazing readers—I'm at a loss for how to thank everyone who has touched this story over the past three years. This journey has taken so many twists I could never have predicted, both on the page and off. I'm not exaggerating when I say that it changed my life.

An Honored Vow was written during one of the most difficult years of my life so far. A year full of endless grief, heartache, fear, and an above-normal amount of depression (something Keera and I have in common). It was such a comfort to have these characters to return to, and I hope some of that comfort has coated the lines of this book and made it to some of you. Regardless, I cannot start off this list of acknowledgments without a huge thank you, *chi miigwetch*, to all the readers along the way. This series wouldn't have been such an easy place to get lost in without all of you. Seriously, y'all the best.

Thank you to Laura Schreiber for believing in this series from the very first book and putting it in the arms of so many more readers than I could have ever imagined. It wouldn't have been possible without your dedication, not just on this book but on the three that came before it. Keera and I both thank you.

I would like to extend my endless appreciation to the amazingly talented Kim Dingwall who brought Keera to life across four book covers. So many readers have found this story because of your masterful talent, and I can never thank you enough for realizing my character exactly as I imagined her. Actually, scratch that. *Better* than I imagined her.

And of course, thank you to Scooby Gang, who have brought so much laughter and light to this series. I'm so grateful that one single mystery led to so much chaos and fun. *Chi miigwetch* to all of you.

Hayley, thank you for your keen eye and edits across all four of these books and knowing my side characters almost better than me. Stefanie, thank you for all your help across the series and the first three years of my career. Thank you, Ardyce, for jumping into this series at its final curtain call and giving your best to Keera and the gang. Thank you, Jenny and Dan, and everyone else at Union who helped with getting this story onto the shelves and into readers' hands. I thank every single one of you.

To all the people who have held me up over the past year, I will continue to thank you in person just as I do here. Mom, thank you for the endless hours of phone calls and unwavering support through this series, but especially this book. Love you always.

To my dearest friend, Marissa, thank you for always answering my FaceTime calls and celebrating my little wins along the way. I can never tell you how much that means to me. I appreciate you so, so much.

To my sister, Emma; my brothers, Eric and Sag; my friends Emily and Abby; and my grandparents, Jo and Mike—thank you for all the laughs and distractions you gave me through this book. I needed them, just like I need you all. Dad, thank you for pretending you understand this ever-changing industry just so I had someone to talk things out with. Expect a phone call shortly. And to my therapist (you don't know I'm writing this so I'm going to call you Z), thank you for all our sessions. They not only helped me get through the writing of this story but to stick around long enough to see it through. I'm a better, healthier writer because of you. You should also be expecting a phone call shortly.

This may be unorthodox, but I'd like to acknowledge the younger version of myself. Specifically, the one who was contemplating a very dark choice in 2021, but who chose to write a story instead. This story. I'm so grateful that you made that choice and got to witness all the ways Keera changed you. Thank you for choosing to search for the light amid endless shadow, that strength has served me well this year. By the way, you're an author now. You did it.

And finally, *chi miigwetch* to my ancestors for blessing me with the gifts of storytelling so I could write this story in the first place. I *promise* I will always stay mindful and loving in how I use them.

About the Author

Melissa Blair (she/her/kwe) is an Anishinaabe-kwe of mixed ancestry living on Turtle Island and the author of the Halfling Saga. She splits her time between Treaty 9 in Northern Ontario and the unceded territory of the Algonquin Anishinabeg in Ottawa, Canada. She has a graduate degree in applied linguistics and discourse studies, loves movies, and hates spoons. Find her on TikTok at @melissa..blair.